Hot Maroc

Middle East Literature in Translation

Michael Beard and Adnan Haydar, *Series Editors*

For a full list of titles in this series, visit
https://press.syr.edu/supressbook-series
/middle-east-literature-in-translation/.

Hot Maroc

A Novel

YASSIN ADNAN

Translated from the Arabic by

ALEXANDER E. ELINSON

Syracuse University Press

The events of this novel are entirely fictional; its characters bear no relation to real life. Any resemblance to real persons or correspondence to actual events is due to a weakness of the writer's artifice.

This book was originally published in Arabic as *Hot Maroc* (Cairo: Dar al-'Ain Publishing, 2016).

Syracuse University Press
Syracuse, New York 13244-5290

First Edition 2021

21 22 23 24 25 26   6 5 4 3 2 1

∞ The paper used in this publication meets the minimum requirements of the American National Standard for Information Sciences—Permanence of Paper for Printed Library Materials, ANSI Z39.48-1992.

For a listing of books published and distributed by Syracuse University Press, visit https://press.syr.edu.

ISBN: 978-0-8156-1135-6 (paperback)   978-0-8156-5539-8 (e-book)

Library of Congress Cataloging-in-Publication Data
Names: 'Adnān, Yāsīn, author. | Elinson, Alexander E., translator.
Title: Hot Maroc : a novel / Yassin Adnan ; translated from the Arabic
    by Alexander E. Elinson.
Other titles: Hūt Mārūk. English
Description: First edition. | Syracuse : Syracuse University Press, 2021. |
    Series: Middle East literature in translation | Summary: "After
    becoming enamored with the internet and the thrill of anonymity he
    finds there, Rahhal Laâouina opens the Atlas Cubs Cyber Café, where
    his patrons include politicians, journalists, and hackers. However,
    Rahhal soon finds himself mired in the dark side of the online
    world—one of corruption, scandal, and deception. Adnan presents a
    narrative of contemporary Morocco—and the city of Marrakech—with
    an infectious blend of humor, satire, and biting social and political
    commentary"— Provided by publisher.
Identifiers: LCCN 2021003904 (print) | LCCN 2021003905 (ebook) |
    ISBN   9780815611356 (paperback) | ISBN 9780815655398 (ebook)
Classification: LCC PJ7910.D535 H8813 2021 (print) | LCC PJ7910.D535
    (ebook) | DDC 892.7/37—dc23
LC record available at https://lccn.loc.gov/2021003904
LC ebook record available at https://lccn.loc.gov/2021003905

Manufactured in the United States of America

"Years of treachery will befall the people when the
liar is deemed truthful and the truthful one is deemed
a liar; when the deceitful one is deemed faithful and
the faithful one is deemed deceitful; and when the
Ruwaybida makes pronouncements." It was then asked,
"Who is the Ruwaybida, O Messenger of God?" To
which he replied, "He is the worthless man who speaks
on behalf of the masses."

—*Hadith*

If what they see is good, they cast aspersions on it
And if what they see is evil, then everyone fights for it.
No one is safe from harm
And no one ignores a misdeed.

—Ibn Durayd al-Azdi

We only hide that which is truly meaningful and genuine.
That is why vile feelings are so powerful.

—Emil Cioran

Contents

Translator's Note

YASSIN ADNAN is a lover of language. A poet, literary critic, and cultural journalist, he is a writer who is highly attuned to the great richness of the Arab literary tradition, and the linguistic diversity of Arabic as it exists today in Morocco. One of the great challenges and joys of translating *Hot Maroc* was carrying this diversity over into English. Arabic is no different than other languages in that it is comprised of many registers that express and are determined by context and class—social, political, racial, educational, economic, and more. Arabic can be described as diglossic, or multiglossic. That is, Arabic has distinct varieties that are used under different conditions. The most basic division of labor in Arabic is between speaking and writing, and across the Arab world, in any given place, the spoken variety can be quite different from the written, and there are multiple levels of the spoken register. As for the written language, it is somewhat standard across the Arab world, but there is local variation, and different registers of the written language exist as well. In this translation, I have done my best to reflect the linguistic multiplicity that exists in Morocco today. As Adnan moves deftly between varieties of spoken and written Arabic, the reader is able to sense, to hear, the voices as we move through slums, university classrooms, upscale and working-class neighborhoods, political rallies, and all sorts of online worlds.

While my translation strives to remain as true to Adnan's Arabic as possible, I have also allowed myself some flexibility to reflect the rhythm and rhyme of poetry and song that is so essential to the novel, as well as the essence of vapid political droning and faux-intellectual speech and writing, the self-righteousness of ideological and uninformed religious arguments, and the colorful and artistic curses of Marrekechis young and old that would make a sailor blush!

Hot Maroc takes place in the 1990s and early 2000s, when the internet was just beginning to change life in Morocco, and worldwide. But of course, no time or place exists in a vacuum, and *Hot Maroc* is replete with references to the vast well of Moroccan literature, history, and culture—"high" and "low," written and oral, local, national, and global. Besides a few stealth glosses, I chose not to provide notes or a glossary. Not only do I think it is entirely unnecessary for understanding and enjoying the novel as it is, but it would distract the reader from the universal depiction of what makes people who they are, and how we interact with one another, in real life, and online. Those who need to know more about any given reference in the novel need only heed the snarky advice of the narrator: "So why did God create Google, you idiot? Why did God send Our Master Google, upon him peace, to the electronic illiterates among His servants? . . . At least type the name into Google and let it do its work."

In transliterating proper names, I have generally used the French spellings, since that is how names are spelled in Morocco (when using Latin characters). So, it is Jaouad instead of Jawad, Houcine instead of Hussain. Also, I think it is important to preserve the Moroccan-ness of the novel, and these spellings more closely reflect the sound of the names in Morocco by providing a visual cue to the Moroccan sound that tells us that they are similar to, yet distinguished from, their Egyptian, Lebanese, or Iraqi counterparts—all part of the Arab world, but speaking with different accents. I have transliterated names from the historical and literary tradition in a more scholarly way so as to give them the heft that they possess in Moroccan society (e.g., al-'Abbas Ahmad bin Muhammad bin al-Wannan al-Tuwati from Fes).

A few specific translation notes: Qur'an quotations are based on A. J. Arberry's translation. Bible quotations are from the King James Bible. The quoted verses from Labid's ode, "The tent marks in Minan are worn away," are from Michael Sells's *Desert Tracings: Six Classic Arabian Odes* (Middletown, CT: Wesleyan University Press, 1989); I have always found Sells's translation of pre-Islamic poetry quite wonderful, and as much as I tried, I could not match his closeness to the original, and poetic touch. Everything else is translated from the Arabic by me. I have translated the Emil Cioran quote in the novel's epigraph directly into English from the original French, not from the Arabic translation of the French. The original French reads: "N'est profond, n'est véritable que ce que l'on cache. D'où la force des sentiments vils." *De l'inconvénient d'être né* (Paris: Gallimard, 1973).

Alexander E. Elinson   Brooklyn, New York
                                        November 2020

Hot Maroc

*The Butterfly on Its Way
to the Slaughterhouse*

1

THE YOUNG POET, Wafiq Daraai, didn't imagine things would turn out so badly. At first, he spoke with a derision that made him seem smart enough for his adoring fans to laugh at his clever gibes. But the moment Rahhal grabbed his throat and throttled it, he understood that matters had taken a turn his fertile poetic imagination hadn't foreseen. He tried to set things right, to stop the game right there and beat an honorable retreat, but no! Rahhal had been seized by a sense of loftiness that plunged him into battle—a punch to the mouth, another to the temple, a roundhouse kick, and another one from the back; blows raining down here and there, but this was just a warm-up. Then came the moment of truth, when Wafiq found that Rahhal had grabbed his shirt collar to yank him down so his skinny knee could jab his face like a poisoned arrow—a hard knee like a sharpened rock breaking the surf slamming into it, like a knife piercing flesh and bone—resulting in a burst of red rivulets flowing from his mouth and nostrils.

Rahhal Laâouina—short, slight, with a rat-like face, and two narrow eyes—only resorted to violence when he felt suffocated and consumed by feelings of insignificance. All the way back to those distant childhood days, when it had occurred all of a sudden to Khaled Battout to pull him to the ground by his leg. Rahhal seized the moment when his perpetrator leaned over to execute his devious plan; he jerked Khaled's head down, then quickly lifted his knee, bringing it up to his face, causing the blood to flow.

Same technique, same precision, same lightning-quick way of turning his adversary's head a bit to the side, which allowed the knee to find just the right spot in the middle of the face. This was how Rahhal had always concluded his battles over the course of his twenty-five years. His decisive blow always came from the same source—the knee that was usually swiftly aimed at the face, specifically the face. Of course, Rahhal didn't always resort to hitting. But when he did, things had to be done decisively.

It was just like when Khaled Battout used to harass him in school, just because, with no clear reason. He wasn't a classmate or a neighbor who lived on the same street, nor was he competing for the attentions of one of the girls at school (since Rahhal quite naturally, innately perhaps, tried to remain as far as he could from girls). In fact, he wasn't known to have any friends in class, or even any companions. What happened was that Khaled was joking around once with his pals when Rahhal passed in front of them. Khaled stopped him with an affected charm and suddenly began to talk to him, imitating a monkey trainer in Djemaa Lfnaa Square, asking him to do the school principal's walk. Rahhal was flabbergasted and continued bewildered on his way with Khaled following behind, pointing his finger at him shouting, "Didn't I tell you?" while his friends exploded with laughter.

But what had he said to them to cause such laughter? What awful joke was it? Was he telling them about the monkey that wears a school frock, dressed up in a schoolboy uniform? About the monkey he shook hands with in Djemaa Lfnaa Square, where the monkey trainers have their performance area? No one came forward to explain it to him. Once, Rahhal was standing in front of the entranceway to the school cafeteria waiting for his portion of the delicious lentil meal (the likes of which he had never tasted at home, nor in the popular food shops scattered about the ramshackle neighborhood of Ain Itti outside the city walls) when Khaled stood towering over him. Behind him were four of the most beautiful girls in the school. His obesity didn't prevent him from performing an acrobatic leap. He did a pirouette in the air, then knelt on his right knee like a circus clown, leaning to one side as he gazed theatrically at his entourage before pointing at him:

"Didn't I tell you??? And he likes lentils, too . . ."

The girls exploded with laughter. Rahhal wished that the ground would split open and swallow him up. Once again he couldn't help but run away, putting as much distance as he could between himself and where he usually sat at the cafeteria door, rushing home, running as if expelled by his tribe. Oh damn, and the lentils? He forgot all about the hot, delicious lentil meal that the cook, Lalla Zubaida, would pour right onto the bread so he could take his portion and gulp it down on his way home. Rahhal did without the delicious lentils and spiced beans, renouncing the piece of tuna and cheese, and the thick strips of buffalo meat that he found difficult to chew. He gave all of that up and began to avoid the cafeteria altogether, no longer getting anywhere near its door until after he had scanned the area from afar with his two, rat-like eyes to make sure Khaled wasn't there.

2

WAFIQ DARAAI was a young, well-known poet. Stylish despite the simple way he dressed, his hair always carefully coiffed. Talented to a certain degree, yet seeing himself as a guiding star granted by God to the Arabs during their darkest, poetic night. His handsomeness gave him a certain amount of luck with the girls. That's why Rahhal attended his evening salon—not out of love for the poet, nor because he liked his poetry but rather because of the guaranteed feminine presence there was at all of his soirées. This is what Rahhal would try to surreptitiously enjoy from the distance he always strove to keep between himself and the world, specifically between himself and the fairer sex. Wafiq was a prose poet, and the posers who attended his soirées possessed neither poetic sensibility nor any appreciation of meter; rather, they attended mainly in order to get close to Wafiq. The emcee of the gathering being held at the House of Culture in the Riad El Arous neighborhood was a well-known local radio journalist. She introduced Wafiq as the "Rimbaud of his age." Wafiq, who seemed to place his trust in reckless flattery, dove right into reciting his poems in a way that his adoring fans found dazzlingly unique, whereas Rahhal found it pedantic, coquettish, and in fact, downright whorish. Rahhal is no literary critic, nor does he claim to be one, but he does hold a degree in classical literature, so he understands a thing or two about rhyme and metaphor. True, he found something of the *essence* of poetry in Wafiq's verse—metaphors that corresponded from one part of the poem to another, a few beautiful images here and there, contemplations that were not completely devoid of some intelligence—but when Wafiq started to perform in such a repulsive way that so pleased the young women, Rahhal pictured him writhing around like a prostitute doing a striptease. This was precisely why Rahhal always used to think of

Wafiq as a prostitute. Nonetheless, after the reading, all he could do was clap. Not as warmly and enthusiastically as the women did, but he clapped flatteringly; a cautious applause, like someone professing adherence to a faith not their own in order to avoid persecution. When the discussion started and the admirers' comments came one after the other, Rahhal was disgusted. All their observations were off the mark. Empty talk from silly girls who hadn't found anyone yet to explain to them that, although there was no law preventing them from falling head over heels in love with their handsome poet, they had no right to treat poetry so freely, so boldly. Rahhal, a specialist in Arabic poetry, didn't dare enter the discussion, whereas these gushing girls fawned disgustingly as this preening effeminate made no attempt to tone down their excessive flattery!

Deep down, Rahhal is a coward, and never before had he participated in a performance or attempted to speak at a gathering where there were more than three attendees. Nonetheless, he didn't even realize it when he found himself, for the first time in his life, raising his finger up to say something, with some hesitation, of course. A trembling finger, trying to rise up, then retreating and folding over onto itself before trembling back down. But the emcee noticed the hesitant finger and surprised him: "The gentleman in the back, please, please," then, in a joking aside to Wafiq, "so as not to limit the discussion to the young ladies."

The blood froze in Rahhal's veins. He was completely still, like a statue, as if he had turned into a scarecrow made of dried branches blown in by the wind.

"You, sir, in the back with the khaki jacket. You. You. Sir. Yes, you."

A woman in her fifties sitting next to him poked him. Ugh . . . What a fix! Who would have wanted to be in his shoes?

"Please stand up, good sir, so we can hear and see you clearly."

He thought to himself, *the whore hadn't asked the other participants before me to stand.* And now which foot should you stand on, Rahhal? His legs and his insides were shaking. His spirit may have been as well.

"I wanted . . . I wanted to say . . . to say . . ."

Wafiq cut him off with a despicable confidence:

"When in the presence of poetry, everything must be said. Go ahead, my friend . . ."

Rahhal almost collapsed back into his chair. He felt Wafiq smothering him even more, a choking feeling taking hold, grabbing onto him in front of the adoring fans, while he, like an idiot, didn't know what to say or how to say it. Then, the vicious thought flashed in his head, and spurred by his overwhelming feelings of defeat and insignificance and his crushed spirit, he said it. He let it fly:

"During the reading, I feel like you were faking a lot. You seemed to me like . . . like . . . like a pros . . . a pros . . ."

Then, with a boldness he didn't know he possessed, Rahhal threw the word in Wafiq's face, like a crazy fan tossing a firecracker onto the soccer pitch: "Like a prostitute. Just like a stripper."

Mutters of disapproval rose up around the room. It seemed that no one had been expecting such audacity from this meek creature whose knees were barely strong enough to hold him up. Wafiq alone seemed unfazed and not at all troubled by what Rahhal had said. He burst out laughing before commenting in a loud, yet pompous, voice:

"I apologize, especially to my dear ladies, but the gentleman is absolutely right in what he says. But the matter doesn't have to do *only* with the manner of delivery, as he thinks, nor specifically with the moment of recitation—despite the sanctity of this moment to me—but rather with the entire poetic process. You see, when you compose poetry, something immoral seeps into your soul and spreads throughout your entire being, your essence, something you can't get rid of, something stronger than feelings and deeper than ecstasy—a thing resembling passion, a total disintegration reaching one's very heart and soul. For this reason, I appreciate your observation, my friend, and congratulate you on your boldness."

Then, under a downpour of applause from his fans and at their insistence, when the emcee asked Wafiq to conclude by reading another poem, a gift of his poetic inspiration, he joked: "And now, my dear friends, the second act of the striptease. Where is my friend the striptease critic, so scrunched up in the back that I can barely see him? Lift your head up a little. The Disrobing Act, dedicated to you!"

The whole room exploded with laughter and everyone turned toward Rahhal, who couldn't bear the mocking looks all around him. He wished he could have disappeared. If only he were no more. If only his upraised finger hadn't volunteered him. No sooner did Wafiq start to read—everyone taken by the rise and fall of his gentle voice and by the acrobatic movements that added to his dramatic reading—did Rahhal make his way outside with uneasy, shaking steps, first jogging, then breaking into a run without paying attention to anything around him. He was sprinting as if fleeing from a terrible fright, a violent feeling of shame chasing him.

He didn't sleep at all that night. While he was accustomed to sleeping in his clothes—pajamas not yet having become part of his tribe's cultural heritage—this time he didn't even take off his khaki jacket. He tore off the old, white Bata shoes he had bought in the Sidi Mimoun flea market without untying the laces and threw himself on top of his blanketless mattress, spread out on the floor, no bed frame or anything. Because his pillow, stuffed with a mixture of wool and *halfah* grass, was somewhat rough, Rahhal preferred to hold onto it rather than place it under his head, and he remained tossing and turning in bed, defeated and broken. But, sometime well before sunrise, before the first light began to show, his soul retreated into dreamland. In the dream Rahhal went back to finish the scene *his* way. He stood in front of Wafiq at the end of the evening with everything he had wanted to say at that moment but hadn't. And no sooner did the arrogant poet attempt to press his faux-intellectual oeuvre than Rahhal grabbed him by the shirt collar . . . and the rest of the story you know.

Rahhal only destroyed his adversaries and opponents in his dreams. Ever since the age of ten, when Khaled Battout had tortured him for three straight years, unrelenting in his awful mockery until after Khaled got his elementary school certificate and began attending Mohammad bin Brahim Middle School, luckily, far from Abdelmoumen Middle School, where Rahhal would go a year afterward. Since those long-gone days, he had settled all of his accounts in his dreams. He would pay his adversaries back twofold, and always in the same way, with the same, quick blow from the knee. It's true that in reality, his knees would knock together as soon as he found himself in a difficult situation, and more than once he had shocked his classmates by fainting in class just because the teacher had surprised him by asking him to go up to the board. But of those same two knees, the ones that in real life knocked together in fear, the right one became all-powerful in his dreams.

3

RAHHAL DIDN'T UNDERSTAND why some people compared him to a monkey, or how others characterized him as a rat. These descriptions irritated him. Most of the time he understood them as insults, but he wasn't bothered by them. Deep down he was convinced that these absurd nicknames merely reflected the ignorance of the person they came from, and betrayed their inability to distinguish things. Rahhal saw himself as being closer to a squirrel than to any other animal. All this talk about monkeys, mice, and rats—even frogs, as he was once described by a dim-sighted neighbor—made no sense to the discerning eye that knows how to move effectively between human features and their animal counterparts. Mice, rats, and squirrels may be from the same order—Rodentia— but the squirrel has never been from the Muridae family. It is from a superior family. Then there's the tail. It's a fact that the mouse's tail is long and thin, whereas the squirrel boasts a thick, dense tail. But the biggest difference lies in the animal's morals, behavior, and lifestyle. Also, in its deep aspirations, in what unconsciously affects the corresponding person's conduct and his approach to work and life. For example, there's a type of squirrel that flies. Do rats fly?! Then there are other key differences, such as a strong sense of smell and a good memory. Never in their long, rodent history could rats dream of possessing a squirrel's memory. A squirrel couldn't possibly forget where it had once stored some nuts. Ever. Rahhal, then, was endowed with a squirrel's sense of smell, and a memory just as strong.

"You have the memory of an elephant, you tiny mouse." It was the high school history and geography teacher who addressed him in this way, but Rahhal immediately corrected the comparison in a low voice that only he could hear:

11

"Actually, it's the memory of a squirrel, sir."

It was for these reasons that Rahhal had always considered himself a squirrel, not a mouse. And for every person who passed in front of him, he could easily hit upon their corresponding animal. Once Rahhal got to know someone and absorbed the logic of their thinking and style of argumentation or their temperament for sarcasm, he could confirm his initial verdict. In those cases when he was wrong, he would readjust his choice of animal, more often than not from the same species he had leaned toward in the first place. In general, this isn't a science that's studied in universities. Rather it's a divine gift that has encouraged Rahhal since childhood to search the faces of his classmates and neighbors for the animals hidden within. Thus, in Rahhal's mind and in his imagination, humans could be traced back to their original animal states. Such is how things were in his special atlas of the world and its living creatures.

So, when Rahhal started to attend National Union of Students in Morocco (NUSM) meetings, which used to gather in the courtyard of the College of Humanities at Marrakech University, he didn't categorize the participants according to their party leanings as was usually done—this guy being from the Fundamental Democratic Way Movement and that one from the Vanguard Party; this girl from the Organization of Democratic Action and that one from the Socialist Union or the Party of Progress and Socialism. Not at all. Rahhal was never concerned with partisan alignment or ideological loyalty. Rather, he would always hone in on what was important. He would carefully study the person's look, their body shape, where the eyes were located in relation to the eyebrows, the size of the mouth, how round it was, how far the nose stuck out or how wide the nostrils were, the placement of the nose on the hard palate between the cheekbones. These were the details that most concerned Rahhal. After that came the core characteristics that most clearly connected the speaker to his or her concealed animal—the motions, the pauses, the looks, the smile, the posture, the way of speaking, the hand gestures, the knit eyebrows, the rhythm of breathing, not the mention the style and logic of how he or she speaks. Thus, Rahhal used to eagerly anticipate Comrade Ahmed the Hyena's speeches, whereas he grew bored with Atiqa the Cow's legalistic arguments.

Atiqa was from a village on the outskirts of Marrakech. Revolutionary by nature, charming, and extremely kind. Rahhal was envious of her comrades in the faction because of the considerable maternal tenderness she afforded them. Her strong, abundant body, the features of her radiant face whose kindness compensated for her lack of intelligence, the pureness of her wide eyes—all of that led Rahhal to think of Atiqa from the beginning as a cow. But what the brothers from the Islamist factions snickered about was that she would cook for the comrades in a secret burrow they rented in one of the lower-class neighborhoods adjacent to the college that they called "the Red House"; that she would drink with them, matching them cup for cup, and when they'd gotten drunk, they'd perform shameless acts on her, one after the other, well-pleased and well-pleasing, because the sexual communist principles they were steeped in compelled Atiqa to solve the biological problems of the comrades on the block with strong conviction and genuine revolutionary devotion. This tidbit of wisdom, which we could metaphorically call "militant fornication," reverberated in Rahhal's ears until it settled there and became a matter of fact, to the point where he was satisfied with the accuracy of his classification. For the cow is used in plowing and planting the earth, pulling and turning the millstone. And she doesn't keep her udders or her milk from the calf or from anyone else, just as she provides her meat and fat, even her skin as well, to whoever asks for it after her slaughter. What could possibly keep the comrades' cow from being loyal to her nature?

Even though Rahhal initially enjoyed picturing himself removing Atiqa's clothing piece by piece as she gave her speeches during the meetings—imagining himself having joined the queue of drunken comrades, having become one of them, drinking from their glass, eating from their plate, and with them, licking the same bowl—once he had finished "the deed" of mental ejaculation, washed away the ritual impurity, and begged God's forgiveness for what he had done by repeating His ninety-nine names, she would still be droning on so boringly that, after having satisfied his desire for her, she seemed like a languid, ruminating cow, chewing on whatever, paying no attention to whether it was clover or barley.

Ahmed the Hyena was more serious and dedicated to the principles of the National Union of Students in Morocco than those comrades who claimed to be Qâidis—"partisans of the base." But Rahhal didn't understand why Aziz the Greyhound insisted on quarreling with him by letting loose a torrent of fabricated procedural points every time he began to speak. Rahhal especially enjoyed Comrade Ahmed the Hyena's speeches, first and foremost because of the importance of the information he insisted on presenting every time. His speeches weren't merely stylistic or replete with slogans. Rather, they always gave you something new. Add to this the raw voice that entered hearts before minds, that lent support to his arguments—a wounded, musical voice that, when raised just a little bit, reached a level somewhere between a wail and a howl. Also, Rahhal was happy with Comrade Ahmed's speeches basically because of the way he always quoted great figures from the past, such as Karl Marx, Vladimir Lenin, Friedrich Engels, and Mao Tse Tung, not to mention the martyrs Mehdi Amel and Mehdi Ben Barka (all of this, according to Rahhal Laâouina's special theory, corresponded perfectly with the hyena's innate desire to dig up graves). On the other hand, Rahhal used to hate Aziz and was annoyed by his points of order. But beauty is in the eye of the beholder, and the greyhound in the eyes of its mother is a lynx. One time Rahhal overheard him talking with some of the new students in the college cafeteria about the importance of points of order, and how he preferred strict points of order over long, repetitive speeches.

In this, he was right. But who would dare say that to Atiqa the Cow?

According to Aziz, a point of order can destroy in a minute every part of a thesis the speaker has built up over the course of an hour. Or it can change the discussion's trajectory entirely. This is why Aziz preferred taking advantage of strict points of order rather than wasting time on full speeches. But Rahhal, the expert on animal natures, knows that the greyhound remains a greyhound no matter how big and round its head is. All the world's animals hunt for themselves, except for the greyhound dog, which has developed the habit of hunting for its owner. After the hunt has ended, the owner ends up with the better part for himself, while the greyhound is left with the inferior portion of the catch. That's what Aziz was like. At first, he used to thrash the party followers by endlessly demanding points of order in favor of the Progress and Socialism faction. But his father's death last summer prompted Aziz to begin a new round of struggles with a different view to the world after having felt the sting of loss and the bitterness of having lost a parent. He realized that the world was moving toward extinction, and that everyone in it would eventually pass to the other side. So, Aziz the Greyhound surprised everyone when he then registered his points of order on behalf of the students from the Justice and Charity movement, placing his innate skill in commenting and commentating at the disposal of the Islamist camp.

4

RAHHAL DIDN'T JOIN the discussion circles in the Faculty of
Humanities courtyard because he was looking for a struggle or out
of a love for politics; proof of this was the fact that he had spent
three years in school not getting anywhere close to these circles,
avoiding even the corridors that led to the courtyard where they
took place. However, when he found himself having been expelled
after failing the first-year exams in the Department of History and
Geography, he had no other option but to present his case to the
Student Dialogue Committee, which had inaugurated the season
with a vicious, combative battle to reinstate the expelled students.
Fortunately, Rahhal saw that Comrade Atiqa the Cow and Brother
Abdelghafour the Lizard were at the top of the list after having
joined the student struggle in recent years and failing, for the third
time in a row, to pass the second-year exams in French literature
(in Comrade Atiqa's case), and the third-year English literature
exam (in the case of Brother Abdelghafour). That these prominent
names—from each side of the political divide—were on the list of
expelled students forced the comrades from different brigades and
the brothers from multiple groups to walk hand in hand in order
to ensure the success of this fateful battle. Thus, they threatened to
organize a symbolic sit-in in front of the dean's office, and when the
administration didn't respond, they carried out their threat. They
also threatened to suspend their studies for an entire day in solidarity with the expelled students in order to make the other students
aware of the justice of this cause, which was part and parcel of the
Makhzen's systemic attack on the Moroccan people's sacred right
to education. But once again, the administration didn't respond,
so they carried out their threats. Finally, because the Cow and the
Lizard were essential elements, without which the meeting circles

would seem empty, and without whom any discussion was useless, the comrades climbed the mountain, followed by the brothers in solidarity, and a complete and open student strike was organized, which would continue until the expelled students were reinstated with no strings attached. That's how Rahhal returned to begin a new chapter in his university life.

▪ ▪ ▪

Rahhal's blind confidence in his squirrel memory is what had entangled him in his initial choice. He had thought that the Department of History and Geography was most appropriate for a person with a memory like his, that his ability to store information and then call it up would no doubt benefit him in this major. But after a succession of disappointments, he found that the geography of the African continent and the history of ancient Morocco were quite different from the hiding places for nuts that his counterpart, the squirrel, could easily find his way to whenever hunger gnawed away at his insides. In reality, Rahhal's memory was of the type that could store and recall news items and fresh information—the names of people and what they look like, sometimes the color of the suits he saw them in for the first time; worthless bits of information that people might share at this or that gathering, that they, themselves, would forget, but that he never would. It could be said that he had the memory of an informant rather than that of a historian or a geographer. That is why, when he returned to the college after the famous Battle for the Reinstatement of the Expelled Students, he decided to change departments once and for all and try his luck with grammar, rhetoric, prosody, poetry, belles lettres, and critical methods in the Department of Arabic Literature. Even though he was restarting his university career, Rahhal became less diligent now that he was splitting his time between attending lectures and going to meetings of the National Union of Students in Morocco. However, this time, he would do it the right way, by which I mean, very ordinarily. But this in itself was a dazzling success for Rahhal, who would obtain a degree in Arabic literature with a specialization in ancient poetry in only four years—years full of studying and accumulating knowledge, the culmination of which was a senior thesis on the history of the pre-Islamic era and its tribes based on the ancient Suspended Odes—the *Mu'allaqāt*—under the supervision of the esteemed Professor Bouchaib Makhloufi.

5

THE POLICY of filling the specialization gaps that successive Moroccan governments since the beginning of independence had continued to pursue was a good sign for Professor Makhloufi, who entered the teaching profession for the first time after only three years at the traditional Ben Youssef Madrasa School in Marrakech. That's because schools in the post-independence period were in need of those who could fill the gaps left behind by the mass emigration of French teachers and professors, followed by the firing of the Egyptian teachers in response to Gamal Abdel Nasser's alliance with Algeria during the Sand War, which the Moroccan army had plunged into against the Algerian military in 1963. That's why the teaching field became increasingly lenient and accepted people who sometimes didn't possess even the minimum qualifications to enter the profession.

Bouchaib, burly with a big, thick head that had managed to memorize the book of Allah (along with *The Alfiyya* by Ibn Malik, *The Mukhtasar* by Shaykh Khalil, and *The Matn* by Ibn 'Ashir in the Qur'anic school attached to the pure saint Sidi Zouine's tomb, which wasn't far from Marrakech), came to the Red City to complete his education in the Ben Youssef Madrasa. But right after obtaining his *brevet* middle school certificate, he found himself responding to the king's and the nation's call, going out to teach in the Ouarzazate region with an employment authorization number he was proud to share, whether it was appropriate or not. It was a clear statement and definitive proof that the independent state recognized Bouchaib and his favored position in it. And there in Ouarzazate, he—the Bedouin who traced his lineage to the Rehamna tribes—came into contact with his Amazighi Berber brothers, and saw teaching reading and writing to the sons of those villages as a part of the struggle that the king and the people had plunged headlong into against colonization and its divisive Berber Dahir law. In fact, following every prayer, he would lead the people in the village mosque (this was during a time when the teacher's role also extended, naturally, to that of faqih, or religious jurisprudent) and insist on reciting the Latif prayer that the nationalist movement had chanted in Fes against the colonialist decree: "We pray to you, O Kind One, asking for kindness with what fate has decreed. We pray that you don't divide us from our Berber brothers." These notions were not at all in the minds of the residents of the Amazigh village, but despite that, they continued to repeat all of these prayers behind Bouchaib, thanking God for the light of knowledge that this young faqih brought to the village (especially after Si Bouchaib started to pray for the people, deliver fatwas on matters of religion, and intercede in quarrels, despite the fact that the Makhzen only paid him for his teaching work). And because God does not withhold compensation for the best of deeds, Bouchaib found the calm and monotonous village life favorable for working at preparing for the baccalaureate diploma he had applied for as an at-large candidate, which he obtained on his very first try.

The "blessed" policy of filling the specialization gaps would make Bouchaib Makhloufi sign on to work at Ouarzazate High School as soon as it opened; in fact, he was one of the few teachers who held a baccalaureate degree in that region. And there he became one of the celebrities of the high school, despite the fact that the inspectors would complain of his lack of a clear teaching methodology, and of his enormous pedagogical weakness. So, while the "Sidi Zouine" mentality prevented Bouchaib from absorbing the modern educational methods that the ministry was adopting, the students, who came to the Ouarzazate boarding high school from all over— from the casbahs of Zagoura and the small villages of Tinghir and Kelaat M'gouna—found his lessons to be an extension of the mosque culture they had come from. Memorizing portions of Ibn Malik's *Alfiyya* didn't hurt them at all, nor did adding grammatical analysis to every word in the school textbooks from beginning to end; all of this increased Si Bouchaib's renown in the region and made his "educational" conquests known far and wide.

Si Bouchaib's marriage to Zohour, his cousin who lived in Rabat, compelled him to move there, where he taught for a few years in one of the high schools of the capital. And because the students of Rabat didn't care about Ibn Malik's *Alfiyya* or the grammar of Arabic case endings, Bouchaib felt an extreme frustration that, in the end, he would figure out how to rid himself of. He washed his hands of the sons of bitches who used to mock him and recoil from his ancient culture as they dangled names before him such as Marx and Lenin and other such bullshit *for which God has sent down no authority.* But what a blessing in disguise! Bouchaib took full advantage of this situation and enrolled in the Faculty of Humanities at Mohammed V University in Rabat to continue his education in the Department of Arabic Literature with a specialization in classical literature. While the University of Rabat was boiling over and leftist students were firing up crowds with slogans and organizing their ranks to embark upon a new Morocco that would rise up from the rubble of what they called "the Morocco of repression and vagrancy," Makhloufi was applying himself to his studies with venerable professors who continued to long for the goodness that existed in the small number of students who remained, despite the boiling over, who were assiduously devoting themselves to their lessons and diving deeply into polishing their knowledge of syntax, rhetoric, prosody, and ancient poetry. And because *if God knows of any good in your hearts, He will give you something better,* Bouchaib earned his diploma with an honorable mention and told his wife that there was no place for him in this city of atheists. Thus, he requested a transfer to Marrakech and returned to the Red City in the mid-1970s.

In 1978 they opened a modern university that carried the name of one of the seven great men of the city—the Maliki jurist Abu al-Fadl Ayyad bin Musa bin Ayyad from Ceuta, author of *Healing by Acquaintance of the Chosen One's Law* and *Arranging Perceptions and Lighting Directions to Know about the Famous Men of the Maliki School.* Yet again, the policy of filling the specialization gaps played a crucial role in Bouchaib joining the Faculty of Humanities in Marrakech. This was how an elite group from among the master's degree–holding professors was selected, and they were placed in the university to fill in the gaps that existed at that level. Thus, Bouchaib found himself teaching syntax, rhetoric, and prosody to first-year college students, and signing up to do his graduate thesis work on pre-Islamic poetry. From that day forward, he claimed to be immersed in preparing his thesis, and was consumed with teaching his students in the same, antiquated style that he had used when he taught the casbah students of the south in Ouarzazate.

6

RAHHAL DIDN'T HESITATE for a moment in choosing his supervising professor, because birds of a feather stick together. Also, the students knew that everyone who signed up to work with Professor Makhloufi on their senior thesis got a 17/20, regardless of the level of research or its quality. The important thing was to be disciplined, attend the regularly scheduled sessions that Makhloufi held with the students, follow his recommendations, and carefully honor his methodology. As for when it came time to defend the thesis, it was a mere formality for which Si Bouchaib would choose one of his colleagues from among the well-known "stopgap professors" so that things would go without a hitch.

"The important thing is to follow the research path step-by-step, seriously and with discipline."

During their first meeting, Makhloufi repeated this pronouncement for Rahhal and his associates who had registered to do their theses with him.

"First off, Professor Makhloufi" (he speaks of himself in the third person) "does not accept students who think they've crossed the river without getting wet, and are working on their final thesis as if it were their first book of criticism. We're not here to write books, but rather, to learn. Nothing makes Professor Makhloufi angrier than ostentation. A student is a student, and the university is a place for learning, not pedantry. Therefore, the professor strictly refuses to allow a single, misguided student to join his team. Those who adhere to materialistic and atheist schools of criticism are those who speak, whenever they deem it appropriate, about Marxism and structuralism, and who love to boast about their reading of Bakhtin, Barthes, and Lukács; who force the vocabulary of dialectics and class struggle into their research on the sources of ancient

Arabic poetry along with structuralism and intertextuality and other, similarly strange terminology. They are the ones who are the least capable of properly scanning the simplest shred of *tawil* meter. And most of them don't know the most basic rules of grammar. When analyzing a noun that has a definite article, they can't even distinguish between the assimilated *sun* letter that doubles the first letter of a word, and the non-assimilated *moon* letter that doesn't. But what makes the professor's blood boil more than anything else is when one of these cheesy poets infiltrates his group—these misguided hordes whom the atheist parties of the Left attract by publishing their weak, obscure thoughts in their literary papers. You'll see them walking around with clippings tucked under their arms, which they spread out in front of you to try to convince you that they, too, are poets just like Harith bin Hilliza al-Yashkuri. So, it certainly wouldn't make sense for the professor to ask one of them, for example, to memorize a portion of al-Yashkuri's ode, part of what he considers essential preparation for every serious student who wants to complete a thesis on this unique poem in which Harith defended his tribe's greatness with a magnificence unsullied by pomposity and a pride unadulterated by boorishness. But these days, after having lost their grasp of language, its secrets, and the meters and their patterns, poets no longer really possess anything other than vanity and pretentiousness!"

■　■　■

Amru bin Kulthoum's ode was not one Rahhal would have chosen on his own, nor one he really wanted to work on at all. For her part, it hadn't been Hassaniya Ben Mymoune's hope to be crammed next to him in the college library for long stretches at a time for an entire year. But what can you do? His finger always betrayed him in these sorts of situations. When he tries to put it up, it doesn't obey. The professor explained to the students that he wanted this year's research to focus on the role of the pre-Islamic ode in our understanding of the Arabian Peninsula's history before Islam: its kings and tribes, its wars and battles, its chronicles and momentous events. And of course, he didn't believe in individual work, nor in the brilliance of the student who will find the field wide open enough after obtaining his or her diploma for him or her to forge a path in critical and literary research. That's why each of the ten, jewel-like odes was to be distributed to teams made up of two to five students. Si Bouchaib began to assign the odes according to the names of who composed them:

"Who wants Imru' al-Qays? Who prefers Antara? What about Labid? Al-Nabigha? Zuhayr? Al-A'sha? Tarafa? . . ."

If Rahhal could have chosen, he would have picked Imru' al-Qays, but the professor uttered his name first, and it wasn't in the cards that Rahhal was in the running for the most distinguished among them. He had also hoped to work on Antara's ode. Let it be Antara, then, after losing the misguided king, Imru' al-Qays. But who would dare raise that trembling cowardly index finger? When Amru bin Kulthoum finally came up, there was practically no one left except for Mr. Rahhal Laâouina and his puny colleague, Hassaniya Ben Mymoune.

7

FROM THE GET-GO, Rahhal found it difficult to hone in on the animal Hassaniya was hiding underneath her loose jellaba and low-hanging hijab. Her small face gave the impression of some weakness and a natural inclination to compromise and surrender out of a lack of wit. Her narrow forehead reflected her shallowness and narrow outlook, and revealed her ignorance of anything beyond the surface. But the way her thin body disappeared inside her flowing garment, added to the subdued features of her face, made it utterly impossible for Rahhal to figure out Hassaniya's hidden animal. This made his task extremely difficult, for how can you interact in a natural way with someone whose animal counterpart you don't know at all?

Their first meeting in the university library was devoted to a preliminary reading of the ode, and adding the short vowels word by word—according to their supervising professor's guidance—as well as an explication of its difficult vocabulary, which required using the multivolume *Lisan al-Arab* by Ibn Manzur and the all-encompassing *Qamus al-muhit* by Fairouzabadi, both dictionaries available in their entirety in the library. Rahhal tried to steal a glance at Hassaniya's face to make out her features, but to no avail. The glance bounced back at him in vain, as if there was no face there at all. No characteristics, no outward traits, and no features. He couldn't even find her mouth. Hassaniya's very small, tightly closed lips, like the rest of her face, didn't reveal a thing. As if the redness of her lips and their edges had been erased by an eraser and her small mouth had become a disappointing extension of the yellow pall of her cheeks. O, your bad luck, Ibn Kulthoum and, O, the blackness of your night. Only the hazel color of her eyes preserved a glimmer of vitality and a flash of cunning intelligence on the otherwise pale, hidden face that was both deceiving and difficult to grasp.

As she lowered her gaze and buried her face in the open book between them, Hassaniya said:

"I suggest, Mr. Rahhal, that you go ahead and read the ode out loud. That way we can practice it a little bit before starting to put in all the short vowels."

What a mess! The wicked girl had surprised him. She had caught him off guard. Just as her features and characteristics seemed to have been erased from her face, his voice left him. As if it had fizzled away. He searched for it—between his lips, in his gullet, his throat, his chest, in the air stored up in his lungs—before he finally found an obscure, broken puffing that sounded more like a hiss:

"Actually, my dear friend . . . actually . . ."

Actually, what, you idiot? She didn't ask for your hand in marriage. All she asked you to do was to put your faith in God and read, which is what you two are supposed to be doing here together! Will you respond to her as the Prophet did to the archangel Gabriel when asked? "I do not know how to read." A heavenly message is it? And it will come down at this very moment from the heavens?! Read, you idiot! Read! You need to read the ode before moving on to some explanation that will open you two up to the poetically strange and obscure ways of saying things. Rahhal searched once again for the voice inside him, but he could only find a small, fragile, broken, whisper-like thread. A weak, trembling voice that seemed to belong to a boy who had not yet reached adolescence. He started at the beginning, stammering and stuttering:

> Ha girl . . . Ha gi . . . rl . . . Ha girl! Up with your bowl! Give
> us our dawn-draught
> And do not spa . . . re . . . And do not . . . spare the wines of
> El-Andarína

Then his voice gradually got louder and brighter as he continued reading the ode, with few mistakes, really, until he arrived at what the poet was saying:

When the ranks stand far from us, we thrust with
    lances
    And strike with swords when we overwhelm

At which point Hassaniya interrupted, correcting him:

"When *we* are overwhelmed . . . And strike with swords
    when *we* are overwhelmed."

She said it confidently, then added with a decisive tone: "If you don't mind, Rahhal, I'd like to continue reading."

■   ■   ■

Professor Makhloufi's research methodology was simple and clear. During the first meeting, he distributed the odes to small teams of students and asked them to work on reading, explaining, and voweling them. In the second meeting, he urged them to study the poems according to their poetic meter and the rules of prosody, and ordered each one of them to scan four verses; there are no two ways about it, according to Si Bouchaib, you can't work on an ode if you can't analyze its prosody. Then, in the third meeting, he asked the students to extract the names of tribes and famous persons, ranging from nobles to poets to warriors, and to take stock of the places mentioned in every ode, down to the mountains, streams, campsites, territories, and encampments, continuing work on these data by then explaining, analyzing, and arranging it all afterward. Everything in due time.

"Because Professor Makhloufi," continuing his speech on pedagogy, "is not the type of advisor who meets his students in the hallways to give them quick, rambling instructions during breaks, or while they are having a quick smoke between lectures. Advising," according to Professor Makhloufi, "is an essential, educational duty. Not something that we merely boast about and toss around like a slogan. Rather, it is something we translate into a set, weekly class, and organized meetings."

Bouchaib Makhloufi was a true elephant. An elephant in the truest meaning of the word; so much so that Rahhal didn't find the least bit of difficulty in capturing his animal essence during the very first lesson in rhetoric and prosody he attended in his first year in the Department of Arabic Literature. A fleshy mass with thick skin and two fat, swollen legs, as if the man had elephantiasis. His ample fat and flesh would prevent him from turning his head completely, even if a fire was burning in the back of his white jellaba. Thus, like an elephant, it was enough for him to watch only what was going on in front of him and to his sides. Then there was the milieu that Si Bouchaib preferred to live and work in, which, to a great extent, resembled elephant society, with its strict organizational structure that was essentially based on the respect the young show for their elders. According to the age hierarchy that elephants occupy in society, it is not possible to jump ahead. Thus, young elephants receive lessons daily and must learn the social rules and practice the collective norms along with the requisite display of respect to the elephants that are older than them. This order, perfectly respected in the distinguished society of elephants, is exactly what Makhloufi missed in our trivial human society, specifically in this college. That is why he insisted on handpicking his students so as to assiduously establish a pure, elephant-like society with them, with no room for obstinate dupes or phony posers.

Even when news of a ministerial memo circulated in the college, which would force stopgap professors to defend the theses they claimed to have been working on for more than a decade by giving them a year to complete them (otherwise they would be returned to the high schools they had been teaching at before), Makhloufi remained unfazed. Everyone talked about how his students were doing the research instead of him. According to reliable sources from the Union of Higher Education Teachers, he had chosen as his thesis title "History, Environment, and Ancient Arab Society in the Arabian Peninsula as Understood through the *Mu'allaqāt* Suspended Odes"—the same topic he had assigned to the students. But Makhloufi would remain steadfast in his plan and course of action, and nothing people said would move a single hair on his head. If some were surprised by the coolness of the man and his lack of annoyance about all of this innuendo, which prolonged his course and affected his academic reputation, Rahhal, who knew the extent of his professor's elephantization, didn't see anything in it that would cause any deep harm. For delayed mental growth in an elephant never causes any complications, nor does it place the slightest impediment before it as long as it remains among the rare animals that continues to learn for the duration of its life. From the cradle to the grave, as Makhloufi always says.

. . .

"What if we worked on Ibn Kulthoum and Ibn Hilliza at the same time, Professor?"

"What do you mean, my girl?"

"I am suggesting that my colleague and I work on the two odes as part of the same research project. This will allow us to better understand the period and delve more deeply into the tribal struggles that were happening during the time of the Lakhmid king, Amru bin Hind, and how they affected his gatherings and milieu."

"I love your enthusiasm, my girl, but you are the smallest group—there are only two of you—so how can I let you take on two of the most eloquent odes ever uttered by the Arabs, all by yourselves?"

But Hassaniya held firm to her suggestion, which hit a passionate chord deep in the professor's mind, and so it was agreed at the end of their first meeting with Makhloufi. It was the first of a series of meetings that he had begun to convene recently with the groups, each one separately, in order to study the students' research designs and define their general outlines before they moved on to the writing and editing stage. As for Rahhal, who was tongue-tied from shock, he didn't understand at all how this bedbug could allow herself to make such a decision in his name without bothering to consult with him beforehand.

Hassaniya didn't give Rahhal the chance to protest. She cut to the chase. In the school cafeteria, which he only visited for taking care of crucial matters or for meetings of the utmost importance. He had visited it, if we're aiming to be accurate, only twice. The first time to submit his dossier to the comrades in the National Union of Moroccan Students, which was following up with the case of the expelled students; the second with one of the brothers from the Islamic brigade to explain to him that there was nothing at all linking him to the leftist brigades, and that submitting his dossier to them didn't necessarily mean that he sympathized with their heretical ideas. Both times he had sat in the cafeteria, Rahhal had borne their financial burden—two coffees and a pot of tea during the first meeting, and orange juice during the second. Today he led Hassaniya there after having checked his pocket to be sure that he had enough for a drink at least. In any case, he wouldn't drink. He'd claim that he was abstaining from drinking because he was feeling extremely agitated. Neither coffee, nor tea, nor anything else. The important thing was that Hassaniya explain exactly what her position was. And so she did.

The story, as Hassaniya told it, was simple and convincing. She summed it up in a couple of sentences and the case was closed.

She had been walking around the used book market in Bab Doukkala when she discovered a dusty issue of an old Syrian magazine . . . or what remained of one, really; the first and last pages had been torn out, and it had no table of contents or cover. The issue contained a few literary articles, one of them being—oh, what a wondrous coincidence! —a study more than twenty pages long on the struggles between the Banu Bakr and the Taghlib tribes, their scandalous acts as well as their boast-worthy ones, based on the odes of Amru bin Kulthoum and Harith al-Yashkuri.

"More than twenty pages will be enough for us to work with, to which we'll add some stuffing, expand things here and there, include some poetic quotes, and we'll be done with this soap opera. Your friend wants to take advantage of students' efforts, so let him seize upon the efforts of an unknown Syrian researcher and be done with it. Is that so hard?"

She spoke with a clarity and severity that Rahhal didn't expect as he stood before this mysterious girl who surprised him day after day, his mouth hanging wide open.

8

RAHHAL'S RELATIONSHIP to dreams is somewhat strange. To him, the world of dreams remained like the Marhaba Cinema, where he would go regularly just to watch the first karate film, after which he'd sell his ticket during the intermission to one of the sentimental slouches outside, lovers of Indian cinema who idiotically followed its silly, romantic stories. To Rahhal, love was simply so many empty words. Luckily his dreams, just like his cinematic choices, remained locked in the number one genre of karate movies. Rahhal only dreams when there is a vengeful duel to be had, during which he retaliates against one of his adversaries and wrestles him to the ground after ramming his poison knee into his jaw; serious dreams that distinguish the dreamer and that allow him to boast of them when he's awake. Outside of the duels, kicks, punches, and sly knee strikes, the dreams—in their most peaceful sense—continued to contend with Rahhal's sleep until Hassaniya came into his life.

As for Rahhal Laâouina's virginity, it was firmly established, without a doubt. Until he got involved with the meetings of the National Union of Students in Morocco and got to know Comrade Atiqa, from only one angle, of course, he hadn't before dared to approach a girl. With Atiqa he felt somewhat weak. The many salacious stories the brothers first circulated about her made him wish that he could have joined the comrades in one of their soirées with her. If only he could sneak into the Red House one night and sit silently by himself in a far corner during their meeting. He didn't want food or drink, but no sooner would Atiqa take charge of the session, removing her pants and red or light blue or black panties (color not important) and open her legs with a militant generosity and a comrade-like ease, would he slip into the queue. Comrades are supposed to be democratic, for the masses, so it would be shameful for them to prevent one from the student masses, steadfast in gaining his portion of Atiqa's honey, from dipping his pen into the inkwell of her femininity. And because his dreams, which were always able to console him when one of those people vanquished or maltreated him, snubbed him and dashed his hopes at that exact moment, Rahhal decided to rely on himself. Thus, he came to wait impatiently for Atiqa's interventions. And no sooner did the comrade begin with the appropriately socialist and militant introductory words, would Rahhal doze off in his bed of waking dreams in the middle of the debate circle . . .

"Comrades. I extend a militant greeting to you from the National Union of Students in Morocco, a long-standing, democratic, mass, and independent organization . . . And when I say *independent*, comrades, I mean that it is independent from the Makhzen and its corrupt administration, as well as from the reform and conservative parties. Not from the steadfast masses of our people hailing from different quarters of this besieged nation that is being assailed by conquering reactionary, Zionist, and world imperialist forces."

Before Atiqa had even finished her preamble, Rahhal had removed all of her clothes and gotten started. He would attach himself to her breast like a nursing calf at its mother's teat to take its full, unreduced share of milk. And after having gotten his fill of sucking and biting, he would move down a bit to dig in below her navel and between her thighs searching for the honey jar, not dipping into it until having tasted her honey and giving her a taste of his. But Rahhal's problem was always with Atiqa's endless digressions that so annoyed him after having completed his liberating duty. In fact, he would be overtaken by a feeling of disgust for her afterward. He didn't know if this was a natural feeling that all people felt, or whether it was some unique repulsion that happened only to the rodent species when fate tested them with a cow.

. . .

With Hassaniya, it was different. Rahhal was unable to mentally remove her jellaba either in the cafeteria, where they went more than once at her invitation, or in the library reading room. Especially in the library. He would sit in front of her for hours, stealing glances that further aroused his curiosity. Searching for a way in and lying in wait for the charms and folds of her body to reveal themselves, but to no avail. Sometimes, all he wanted to know was what was underneath the jellaba. An intricately embroidered Moroccan caftan? A cheap chemise bought on the street? A tracksuit? A slinky nightgown in the modern style? He couldn't imagine her hair either. Was it long, combed into a ponytail and folded carefully underneath the head scarf? Or was it soft and smooth, parted in the middle and twisted into two braids like the village girls do? Or perhaps it was thick, extremely shiny hair that confounded Hassaniya, who didn't know how to keep it under control except by squeezing it into a small kerchief before wrapping her thick, dark scarf around it and leaving for school. But what if it was the sort of short, curly hair that no amount of brushing or arranging would tame?

Guessing wore Rahhal out. And when Hassaniya began to show up in his dreams from time to time, the questions became more intense and mysterious. At first, she came to him by way of pre-Islamic poetry, not from Ibn Kulthoum's ode, nor from al-Yashkuri's. Rather, she showed up in his dreams as a roaring flood from a verse of Imru' al-Qays. Like a horse, she began to bear down and rush off, to dart forward and retreat, and Rahhal would follow her with sleepy eyes, amazed, having never before seen a horse in his dreams. Hassaniya was prancing in his dream like a purebred pony:

> The flanks of an antelope, the legs of an ostrich
> The gallop of a wolf and the swift dash of a young fox.

The elegance of an antelope, the thin legs of an ostrich, the gait of a wolf, and the lithe body of a fox. What animal was embodied by this girl who has conquered your dream tonight in the form of a horse? Oh Rahhal, if only you had been bold enough to raise your finger straight up in the air when Makhloufi called out the name Imru' al-Qays. After all, what do the conflicts of Bakr and Taghlib have to do with you? Wouldn't it have been more useful to do your senior thesis on poetry that fuels dreams visited by horses? But then

Hassaniya would visit him less than a week later in another form, in a second dream. This time she appeared to roll in to the melodies of an Andalusian *mawwal* song, and she came in a gazelle's skin:

> A slender gazelle threw me her beauty
>> And the killing arrows came to heal.

The voice was in the background singing the verse and repeating it, while Hassaniya, in the form of a gazelle, pranced in front of him as Rahhal wondered, "Is this love? Ah, my Lord, is this love?"

He remembered Qays bin Mulawwah and his passionate love for Leila:

> I saw a gazelle grazing in the middle of a meadow
>> And I said to myself, "I see Leila appearing to us in full view."

Is it Hassaniya who now appears to you, Rahhal? And where? In a dream? In the form of a gazelle?

The next day, sitting next to him in the college library, he saw neither antelope nor gazelle. Her animal was hiding beneath her loose jellaba, her soul withdrawn from her face as she diligently copied out new paragraphs from the study in the magazine. Every once in a while, Hassaniya would stop to suggest that Rahhal open a quote here or add a poetic reference there, or even draw out a stupid digression to give Makhloufi the chance to make corrections and replay his nonstop record about the importance of getting directly to the essence, and the necessity of being careful about being redundant and avoiding digressions.

9

CLASS AFTER CLASS, meeting after meeting, Makhloufi would tout Rahhal and Hassaniya's work and boast about them to the rest of the research groups. It was clear that they were ably translating what he himself wanted to do in his thesis, and that they were providing a clear idea of the path that he would have loved to follow in order to complete his delayed research, but didn't know how. Following each meeting with them, the Elephant emerged happy and optimistic that his dream of overcoming the challenge of official inclusion in the college as a university professor was finally within his grasp. The professor was satisfied, and Hassaniya took responsibility for the task of copying, and even making insertions into the original article as she saw fit after Rahhal had entrusted her with full authority to add, remove, and alter; all of that freeing him up to attend rallies and the rest of the militant events and collective activities of the National Union of Students in Morocco. That's where he first got to know Wafiq Daraai. Of course, "getting to know" for Rahhal was always one-sided. But the precision with which he watches others and the exaggerated interest he has in people who catch his attention—everything they do, the way they speak and listen, and even how they withdraw from the circle for this or that reason, in addition to the way they draw on their cigarettes (in the case of those who smoke), and the brands of cigarettes they smoke, the extent of their loyalty to a specific kind—all of this deepens the friendship. Rahhal strives to know everything about his friends. Thus, he finds himself drowning in extensive, detailed reports that he has undertaken to compile for the benefit of his ambiguous friendships with them. But friendship doesn't always mean affection. Thus, for example, despite his great interest in Wafiq Daraai's personality, Rahhal felt pain in his presence.

No, not hatred or jealousy, but rather something resembling gastric distress. A mild gastric distress, but painful all the same, pressing on his bowels, especially when Wafiq would step up to the podium to recite his poetry during evening soirées.

"The strange thing is that for every occasion, he comes out with a new poem!"

"And what's wrong with that?" Hassaniya asks.

"What's wrong is the poetic fabrication and lack of seriousness. Empty words in front of a thicket of hands hungry to clap for poetry that doesn't pay the least bit of attention to the prosodic or rhetorical responsibility that a poet is supposed to be endowed with. And a poem every month! Do you find that normal?"

Rahhal couldn't understand how it was possible for a person to present a new poem for each evening meeting, one that was suitable for whatever the planned activity was. And the activities were ridiculously numerous: International Women's Day; World Human Rights Day; Earth Day; International Workers' Day; Detainees' Day; the Day of Remembrance of the Martyrdom of Saida Menebhi, Mehdi Ben Barka, Boubkar Edouraidi, and Moustafa Belhaouari. Evenings of song and poetry to close out weeks of solidarity with Palestine, Iraq, and all the vulnerable peoples of the world. And Wafiq always had a new poem that was just right for the occasion.

"Is this reasonable? Harith bin Hilliza worked on his ode for fifteen years. A decade and a half for one poem, and here we are still working on it today after so much time has passed. Amru bin Kulthoum only composed one poem during his lifetime—his ode—which he composed with sword and spear, with his flesh and blood, before putting it to meter and rhyme. Then along comes a so-called poet like Wafiq, who gives us a poem every month as if laying an egg? Poems resembling one another like factory-produced eggs! They display nothing more than mere claims rather than actual knowledge of language, rules of metaphor, attention to form, and imaginative imagery."

"You speak like Makhloufi," she cut him off. "Perhaps you've borrowed his logic and way of thinking . . ."

The observation stung. But deep down he found it difficult to reject. Ever since he was a child, Rahhal had felt severely deficient in forming his own ideas, even those having to do with the weather. He always waited for others to express an opinion, then he might comment on it. Usually he didn't. He would just adopt it in silence and leave it at that, considering it a sound opinion that required no further review. He had received most of the ideas that trace the lines of his personality this way. That easily. That spontaneously. And here he was today, satisfied with it in a way that was more like an article of faith, as if it had been sent down to him from Heaven. The field of debate and give and take had not been at Rahhal's disposal before this year with Hassaniya, specifically during the long hours they spent in the library. Before that, he satisfied himself by mulling things over, imagining himself in heated debates during which he would defend his convictions—other people's ideas that he liked and borrowed and came to consider personal convictions, that he believed in and loved to derive joy from, sometimes fighting desperately to defend. Often, he would find himself even more enthusiastic about them than those who had originated them. The most important thing to Rahhal was how involved he got, and how strongly enthusiastic he was, even if that involvement and enthusiasm was silent, unvoiced.

But Rahhal decided, despite all of that and quite suddenly, to emerge from his silence. He could no longer remain standing on the sidelines. Of course, it would be impossible to raise his finger inside the debate circle in order to participate in an intervention or even a point of order, for he was too much of a coward to risk that danger. And then, what would he say? It hadn't been established that he held a clear intellectual or political stance. He was merely a close observer. More to the point, during the meetings of the National Union of Students in Morocco, Rahhal hadn't found himself suddenly compelled to lean toward any of the many political or ideological currents. Besides checking on his animals and making sure that they didn't go against his initial classification of them, following any transformation that may have occurred to this or that animal, Rahhal silently enjoyed the finesse of the rhetorical dodges and debating strategies even if they were empty or fake—indeed, especially when they were empty or fake. He just enjoyed it. But as for actually intervening and having a narrow, entrenched position on this or that side, that is something he could never do. So, when he decided to come out onto the student scene, emerging from a certain passivity in order to exert a presence that had recently filled his being, he chose a way that wouldn't lose him a bit of self-denial, or that would go against his long-held destiny to live far from the spotlight.

Rahhal began to work calmly and in a very circumscribed way. But the important thing was that he had finally found an appropriate way to exercise a type of positive and active presence, rather than following negatively in silent agitation. He had been in need of an opening, and that was what Comrades Mourad and Moukhtar, two students who were withdrawn like him, provided. They didn't participate in the meetings, but Rahhal would learn that they were important figures in the Qaîdi faction. They held a special status. They were brilliant at attracting people to the factions, doing grassroots work, and completing some of the difficult tasks that secret work requires. In general, the comrades' place was ensured among the militants. Not even Atiqa hesitated to get close to them, despite their perpetual silence and choice to remain on the margins of the meetings, leaving leadership matters to the orators from their faction as well as of the allied and opposing factions. At first, it was natural for Rahhal and Comrades Mourad and Moukhtar to become close to one another—primal, even—because of their tendency toward the rodent species. Mourad was a desert gerbil, whereas Moukhtar was a rat, no doubt about it. But no sooner had Rahhal warned them about Wafiq Daraai, insinuating that there was a suspicious relationship connecting him to Fadel Serraj, one of the most notorious security officials in the city, than did the three rodents draw closer to one another. And to Comrades Mourad and Moukhtar, Rahhal became one of their secret foot soldiers who could not be ignored, for valuable information of this sort could only strengthen the two comrades' standing within the organization and assure their active role in fortifying it against infiltration. No matter that someone came afterward to explain to Comrade Atiqa (well-known for her special sympathy toward the suspected poet) how the aforementioned official was really Wafiq's maternal cousin, and that a long-standing quarrel between Wafiq's mother and her brother, which had resulted in the latter's usurpation of her share of the family inheritance, had practically severed ties between the two families since the beginning of the 1980s. But, none of these details were of any importance anymore. So, the comrades came to a decision and placed Wafiq Daraai's name on the list of suspicious elements, casting him out of the band of poets of the National Union of Students in Morocco. Apparently, the bitterness of isolation that Wafiq suffered during those years is what inspired most of the poems in his first poetic collection, *The Butterfly on Its Way to the Slaughterhouse.*

10

RAHHAL DIDN'T IMAGINE that the comrades' reaction would be
so harsh. The rejection Wafiq Daraai faced was unbearable. He
came less and less to the college and disappeared without a trace
from the debate circles. He started to avoid everyone. What Rahhal
hadn't anticipated was the harshness that Wafiq would face from a
silent faction of base partisans who don't normally make so much
as a peep during discussions; they only show up at the battles that
break out from time to time with the university guards or with the
Islamists armed with their clubs within the armed wing of the brigade, which is called, by way of misrepresentation, the Watchdog
Committee. This gang that had shouted such stirring slogans in the
courtyard whenever Wafiq finished one of his precious poems mis-
treated him now so completely that its members started to block
his way into the college and devoted all of their efforts to provoking him.

Rahhal is not the malicious sort who gloats over the misfor-
tunes of other living creatures. He remained deeply sympathetic to
Wafiq and his plight, and viewed the harassment he was facing as
excessive. But at the same time, he didn't deny feeling proud of his
friendship with Mourad and Moukhtar, especially now that Rahhal knew that his close associates, the Rat and the Gerbil, were the
effective movers of this gang. Neither Atiqa the Cow, nor Ahmed the
Hyena, nor any of the other known leaders and prominent speakers
of the brigade were able to control these militias and direct them as
Mourad and Moukhtar did.

However, what struck Rahhal far more than the pride he felt in
his friendship with the two venerable comrades, or the sympathy
he felt for the afflicted poet, was that colossal, magical power that
allowed a casual piece of information to shake a person's life so

much and destroy him so completely. He hadn't expected that this little nugget of information that Hassaniya had presented to him as an exhibit during her defense of one of her neighborhood's own sons, Wafiq Daraai, and of his right to compose poetry however he wanted, would have such an effect. However, the secret wasn't in the information. In fact, it wasn't a secret at all, since a good number of students who come from the Mouassine neighborhood knew about the relationship between Wafiq and his cousin Serraj. Rather, the magic was in placing this piece of information into the right hands at the right time.

. . .

Rahhal remained baffled for days, so taken with the power of his amazing accomplishment that even Hassaniya noticed his wandering mind and inattentiveness more than once. During their most recent meeting in the university library, she pounced on him:

"If you were going to come to library meetings like this, spaced out as if you've just smoked some hash, you might as well have stayed in the debate circles and not come here to distract me more than I already am. Fouad Wardi, one of the members of the Labid bin Rabi'a group, has declared all-out war on us, claiming that our research is plagiarized, that we're mocking Makhloufi, and that we're going to implicate him in an academic scandal, and you're not here! And just so you know, Wardi is threatening to reveal the source we've been plagiarizing any day now."

Rahhal had received a subtle hint to that effect from another colleague from the Al-A'sha group, but he had attributed it to the sort of loaded envy common in these types of situations. Let's be clear, these groups made up of four to five students, whose voices could always be heard in classrooms and lecture halls explaining, participating, or adding their own two cents, were working on a single ode and were still stumbling over the first part of the research project. Rahhal and Hassaniya, on the other hand, who had never distinguished themselves in any way and from whom not a peep had ever been heard in class for years, were working on two of the most difficult odes, and making such suspicious progress. Their work might not have caused any stir at all had it not been for the stupidity of Makhloufi, who had taken to boasting about them to their classmates during every meeting and seminar. So, it was quite natural that they be subjected to these nudges and winks. However, that a dangerous element such as Fouad Wardi, who enjoyed the protection of the Justice and Charity movement, was focusing on them in this way, that's what frightened Rahhal.

11

SOON AFTER Wafiq Daraai disappeared from the scene, Rahhal was hit with a bout of depression. He realized too late that he had lost someone who had meant a great deal to him. Rahhal was jealous of Wafiq for sure; sometimes he hated him, feeling at times that he couldn't bear his presence, but deep down, he really liked him. Wafiq was a very close friend. A one-sided friendship, yes, but it was a deep friendship that had become increasingly warm and attentive as a result of close, daily contact. Rahhal had found a special pleasure in watching everything Wafiq did. He had come to know his habits well, such as when he smoked and when he left the debate circle for the cafeteria. Just as he had memorized his schedule by heart: when he would arrive at the college and when he would leave, when he would stand on the edge of the crowd, generously doling out smiles to the girl comrades and victory signs to the guys, and when he would crouch in the middle of a circle focusing on the debate. So, when Wafiq disappeared, Rahhal was among the students most affected by the magnitude of this absence. And because nature fears a void, he had to find a suitable alternative.

Rahhal quickly became bored with the interventions of both the comrades and the brothers, finding them to be comprised primarily of a lot of fluff and repetition. Usually he would watch the circles' participants more than he would listen. He would watch everyone without exception: the one speaking and the one waiting to speak; the attentive listener and the absent-minded one; the one who believed in what the orator was saying as well as the one who was upset by him. Gradually, Rahhal began to feel especially drawn toward the Greyhound. Comrade—pardon me—Brother Aziz was not too charming a person, and he didn't possess the same charisma that Wafiq did, nor did he have the same power to excite others. In fact, it was quite the opposite. The guy was fragile, exhibiting signs of restlessness and a lack of self-confidence. Nevertheless, Rahhal found some amusement in watching him—the way the Greyhound stalked his prey, and the skill with which he pounced on a word while hunting for a valuable point of order, the glint in his eyes, then, the cautious way he would take a step into the circle (sometimes two), the imploring and insistent way he signals to the moderator his desire to be allowed to speak and then not responding to him when rejected, the way the circles' moderators from different factions were beaten down before him to the point where everyone came to know that Aziz's points of order were like pronouncements from God, not to be reckoned with. Whether he was beseeching and humble when asking the moderator to register a point of order, or lofty and preeningly arrogant as soon as he was granted the floor, Rahhal was fully entertained and didn't feel the weight of Wafiq's absence nearly as much.

Rahhal was also taken by the fact that, of the attendees of the National Union circles, Aziz the Greyhound's natural disposition made him the most capable of winning everyone's friendship—his vanguard comrades on the Left, his new brothers in the Justice and Charity movement, the enemy brothers in the Reform and Renewal Party, and the rest of the other brigades' militants. Even the other students acted more boldly with him than with the other militants. The militant's standing is secure among the venerable student organization, and of those militants, Aziz was closer than anyone else to the general student population and the one most at ease with other people. Rahhal's experience with animals allowed him to understand the secret of this affability that so distinguished Aziz's relations with everyone. The greyhound is an extremely friendly animal. Even birds of prey—like hawks, for example—are intimate and friendly with them during the hunt, so it was natural for Aziz to occupy this rank among the students. In fact, even Rahhal, who only talked to his two rodent friends, found himself getting close to Aziz, who was kind to him and went beyond mere greetings on more than one occasion.

It is for exactly this reason that Rahhal thought of Aziz. For if the greyhound hunts for the sake of others more than he does for himself, then why not try his luck with him? He might gain some booty from his prey. Also, it was his only chance to pay back in full the one who was working on Labid.

· · ·

Aziz the Greyhound didn't understand why an obscure lazy thinker like Rahhal Laâouina would invite him for a cup of coffee in the college cafeteria. But his kindness and humility forced him to graciously accept the invitation. Rahhal was terrified of the meeting. True, deep down he detested Aziz and considered him lacking in vigor, but the latter, despite his faults, remained a lively person, practicing his greyhound-ness out in the open and in public, not in secret, and his presence was always noticed. As for Rahhal, he was solitary and silent, so he found it immensely difficult to organize his thoughts in front of others. For this reason, he didn't know how or where to start.

"My esteemed brother. You know me well. Consider me a friend. Rest assured that I, with God's help, will be by your side. So, tell me, what exactly do you want?"

Rahhal didn't know how to respond to Aziz, who had begun to get annoyed by his hesitation. Rahhal was sipping his coffee bashfully, his eyes to the ground. Aziz stole a glance at his watch, irritated, as the time for the afternoon prayer was approaching. The brothers had decided to meet in the college mosque and then, together, descend upon the debate circle directly following the afternoon prayer to ridicule the comrades' decision to free the cafeteria from the grip of the college administration and charge some of their older militants who were recently released from prison with running it and organizing its business and advertising affairs. At that very moment they were presenting their own proposal that would define everything from the new prices—discounted, of course—for coffee, tea, and soda, to the suggested closing time, which would extend the cafeteria's activities to eight o'clock in the evening; in other words, two hours after the end of classes. Additionally, they were discussing the list of songs and records that would be allowed inside the university canteen, which included Fairouz, Marcel Khalife, Ahmad Kaabour, Alashekeen, Sheikh Imam, Said El Maghrebi, Khaled El Haber, Abu Arab, as well as bands that included the Iraqi Path, the Tunisian group the Search, and Colors from Marrakech. The Islamist students, in the event of their failure to destroy the project at its base, would try desperately during this afternoon's meeting to put forth a type of quota system by playing Islamic songs inside the cafeteria alongside the leftist choices. The battle was sure to be a defining one, and Aziz was preoccupied with it and the gravity of its ramifications, not having a lot of time to waste with a lazy squirrel.

"Aziz, my friend. I'll get right to the point."

The Squirrel startled him with a shaky, yet confident voice at the exact moment when Aziz was going to announce his displeasure by suggesting they postpone the meeting.

"Go right ahead, my esteemed friend . . ."

"You know how much I respect and admire you. I love your humility and consider you a brother, even though we've only exchanged words a few times. But you are well-loved, as you know."

"Please, you're too kind, my dear friend . . ."

"This is why I need to tell you what has come to my attention, because it's truly painful for me that a hateful person is taking aim at you."

Aziz began to get more annoyed. And as the Squirrel's voice gradually gained in confidence, the Greyhound started to collapse inside.

"Yes, my friend. May God allow us to hear what's best."

At this point, Rahhal would relate everything to him: How coincidence alone led him to the secret council of Qâidis speaking about suspicious elements that the Mukhabarat—the secret police—had planted inside the student body.

"And after having discovered Wafiq Daraai," added Rahhal, "they suspect another element in their ranks whose name they will announce soon, and they'll expel him from the faction after trying him publicly. But what concerns me about this is what I've heard from them specifically concerning your organization. They said that the Mukhabarat have succeeded in enlisting a student sympathetic to you named Fouad Wardi, and that the mission entrusted to this person is to cause a disturbance within your faction by spreading rumors accusing one of the Justice and Charity militants of being an agent for the Mukhabarat. It appears, and this is still according to Qâidi sources, that this Fouad Wardi has made up his mind about you and has apparently started—in a narrow and limited way—to spread a rumor that you're plotting against the Islamist faction. And there were those among the Qâidis who, at first, suggested warning you according to the code of militant morals that necessarily predominate among the different groups, but the majority supported the fundamental position of the Qâidis that sees the Makhzen and Islamic obscurantism as two sides of the same coin. Thus, they preferred to watch the conspiracy unfold as it was contrived against you, rather than warn you or your faction."

Aziz the Greyhound could no longer focus. The ground began to spin beneath him. The tea lost its taste in his mouth. Islamic songs began to churn around in his head along with those of Marcel Khalife and Sheikh Imam. He put his head in his hands to prevent it from collapsing onto the table, which made Rahhal feel more confident in himself.

"I didn't tell you this to upset you, my friend. But you're like a brother, Aziz, whom I love in God, and I'm not a mute devil who, after having learned all that I have about what's being plotted against you, could conceal it and remain silent. This is why I'm telling you, and I'm confident that you're smart enough to know how to eat the hateful snitch for lunch before he eats you for dinner."

Because, as the Prophet said, "God has mercy on those who, when they do something, do it perfectly," Rahhal didn't hesitate to inform Comrades Mourad and Moukhtar of what he had learned regarding the students of the Justice and Charity movement who had also revealed a suspicious student in their ranks named Fouad Wardi. Thus, no sooner did the Greyhound begin his campaign, running breathlessly from council to council warning everyone about Fouad Wardi and making known his diabolical plan, were there reliable reports from the comrades to confirm the news, considered by Aziz to be *a conquest from God and a clear victory*. Thus, *truth* has appeared *and falsehood has departed* after the notion triumphed inside the comrade's camp that secret police agents should be exposed, whoever they were, even if they were aimed against intellectual and political adversaries.

But Rahhal would be surprised that the system of punishments within the Islamic factions would remain less harsh than with their leftist counterparts. At least Wardi found someone among the brothers to defend him, citing the noble verse: *O believers, if an ungodly man comes to you with a tiding, make clear, lest you afflict a people unwittingly, and then repent of what you have done*. One of them demanded that he be banned from the advisory councils and sidelined at meeting circles, but without slandering him, citing the noble Hadith related by Ibn Maja: "Whoever covers up his Muslim brother's shame will have his own shame covered up by God on the Day of Judgment." Thus, Fouad Wardi was not slandered, nor was he chastised by the watchdog committees within the college, but he surely found himself living in an unfortunate situation, the source and reasons of which he did not know. And to be sure, his new misfortune, which hadn't crossed his mind or his imagination before, completely distracted him from continuing his thorough exploration and investigation into the case of Rahhal Laâouina and his colleague Hassaniya Ben Mymoune, and the source of their plagiarized research project.

12

RAHHAL WASN'T SEEKING GLORY, nor was he someone with great ambitions. The young man would have been kicked out of the college if not for the merciful fate that returned hope to his heart. He had switched departments and found in Arabic literature a warm embrace and solace from the dizzying vertigo of maps and dates. And here he is today, about to receive the degree he wants, just like everyone else, so that his father, Abdeslam—a man who hadn't experienced a proud moment in his entire, miserable life—could boast about him.

Rahhal always used to think that bad luck had been chasing his family and his tribe since time immemorial. There were so many tales of drought, livestock death, and continuous epidemics that had ravaged their countryside home in Abda since the colonial period that Abdeslam had lived through and narrated in excruciating detail. So many abuses by harsh and cruel caid rulers. Towns reduced to rubble with impunity during the Siba days when there was no central rule, their inhabitants being left to roam around homeless simply because one of the family's sons had behaved inappropriately in the caid's assembly, or because one of its daughters, one of the singing *cheikhat* of the day, got carried away with grief while singing about what was considered by the caid to be an allusion to him and a disparagement of his awesomeness. He remembers the story of Kherboucha the Zaydi (who was the most beautiful *cheikha* of the time, and the most famous one from Abda) and Caid Issa bin Omar, and how the colossal ruler assaulted this rebellious singer, who sang the famous song "I want unruly Siba, I don't want any rules," along with her tribe, the sons of Zayd. That's all Abdeslam was good at and where he shined: telling stories about plagues and famines, and artfully describing the caid's assaults and raids during those chaotic Siba days.

Rahhal felt that his father was twice as broken deep down inside as his body succumbed to ruin, and twice that with the shattered mien on his face. Up until now, he didn't know how this tall, thin, sickly man could live so satisfied and content, as if he were strutting around in utter bliss. From home to the mosque and from the mosque back home. Sometimes he would join the circles at the wall of the neighborhood clinic to watch the card and checker games in the evenings before returning happily home, as if he had just come back from a trip. Thus, Abdeslam moved about according to a small and limited itinerary, not waiting for anyone nor expecting anything new. He ate his bread and waited for death, calmly and tranquilly. As if life were something that didn't concern him. Had the man died already? Had he died before actually dying? Was he dead without realizing it? Was he caught up in the webs of ill fortune that had taken root in his mind? Sometimes, whenever his imagination ran away with him, Rahhal would compare his father to Makhloufi. But that didn't make any sense. It was like comparing apples to oranges; even though the two men came from poor, village roots, having both memorized the Qur'an during the last years of French colonial rule at the Sidi Zouine *zawiya*, in the same, ancient Qur'anic school. So why did Makhloufi struggle and challenge his fate and destine to find himself, in the end, a professor in the College of Humanities at Cadi Ayyad University? And why did Abdeslam, after having memorized the Qur'an, *The Mutuun*, and *The Mukhtasar* of Shaykh Khalil, return to the village to cultivate a plot of land that wrestled with the rain clouds for water and raise sheep who were always on the edge of death? And when the drought years followed, all he could do was flee to Marrakech to stuff his wife and son into a small room he rented in a slum dwelling in Ain Itti, not far from his new job at Bab El Khemis Cemetery, which extends along the bank of the Oued Issil River near Kamra. There, Abdeslam would crouch every day at the cemetery gate, which only opened for funerals in the 1940s, when it was donated by a pious woman as a religious endowment for Muslims and a burial place for their remains. When it got really hot, Abdeslam would seek shelter next to Boumehdi, the mute undertaker, in the shade where he would lean up against the large trunk of the Mastic tree stripped of its bark, the only available refuge in the middle of a desolate cemetery. Lofty palms here and there, short lotus trees, spiky plants, and some Indian fig trees. Boumehdi used to secretly tend a small field at the edge of the cemetery where he would plant pumpkins. When the pumpkins ripened, he would set up a stand by the cemetery wall so he could sell them to passersby. More than once he would go out to his stand and leave Abdeslam leaning against the trunk of the Mastic tree. He would ask him to watch over the cemetery and call him if the guard, who was always gone, suddenly appeared, or if a funeral procession went in unnoticed by the mute, even though he vigilantly watched the cemetery gate from where he stood in front of the pumpkin stand. Whether he was squatting in front of the cemetery gate or leaning up underneath the tree, Abdeslam would stand up whenever a visitor came along. He would calmly follow him to the gravesite, and as soon as the visitor went about praying over the dearly departed relative, shedding tears over his or her grave, Abdeslam would raise his rough voice in recitation:

> *Ya-Sin*
> *By the Wise Koran,*
> *thou art truly among the Envoys*
> *on a straight path;*
> *the sending down of the Almighty, the All-wise,*
> *that thou mayest warn a people whose fathers were never warned,*
>   *so they are heedless.*
> *The Word has been realized against most of them, yet they do not*
>   *believe.*
> *Surely We have put on their necks fetters up to the chin, so their*
>   *heads are raised;*
> *and We have put before them a barrier and behind them a barrier;*
>   *and We have covered them, so they do not see.*

Alike it is to them whether thou hast warned them or thou hast not
warned them, they do not believe.
Thou only warnest him who follows the Remembrance and who
fears the All-merciful in the Unseen; so give him the good
tidings of forgiveness and a generous wage.

It was precisely the wage that was of concern to Abdeslam, even though the wages in cemeteries were not as generous as they were in the verse. Thus, as soon as the visitor extended his or her hand holding what God had portioned out, he would moan the *khatam* prayer: "God, our Lord the Almighty, has spoken the truth." He would say it in a soft, warm voice, quite a bit different than the rough, jarring voice with which he usually recited the Qur'an. Then he'd go back to where he had been sitting at the cemetery gate or underneath the Mastic tree to wait for another customer. As for funerals, Abdeslam would avoid them because every cemetery Qur'an reciter would gather in front of the grave at the time of burial. Then, when one of the doyens of Qur'an reciters received the wage from the deceased's relatives after the mourners had withdrawn, it was rare that this "blessing" would be distributed between them equally. In general, Abdeslam felt like a stranger there. He felt like a stranger in Bab El Khemis Cemetery even after spending close to two decades there among the graves. For that reason, he has always avoided funerals and preferred individual visitors who would sit with their departed loved ones for a few minutes, after which he would accompany them with a handful of verses from Sura Ya-Sin, pledging its reward to their dead, more sound, and more beneficial.

■   ■   ■

Rahhal couldn't find any other explanation other than bad luck for all the defeats that had befallen his family and clan throughout the chaotic Siba era, the rule of the caids, and up to the present day. A sort of bad luck that relentlessly assaulted them. His uncle Ayad, for example, left for the city before Abdeslam, first to Safi, the capital of the Abda region, and then to the red city of Marrakech. He's the one who first gave his brother the idea of emigrating and who encouraged him to do so. Ayad came to Marrakech for the first time with a friend of his named Bachir, also a country boy, who came from a hamlet next to theirs. They worked together in construction while Ayad bragged constantly about his role in building the College of Humanities and the College of Law at Cadi Ayyad University, and also of his labors on the construction sites that built the convention center on Boulevard de France. None of these achievements meant a thing, really, for a friend the same age as him had steadily risen in the profession and quickly absorbed its secrets. He began to brilliantly decode architects' drawings and read their plans until, in the early 1990s, he became a building contractor, whereas Ayad remained a mere day laborer on his friend's construction sites.

Because Ayad was not completely satisfied with his lot, he would talk all the time in the village about how he was Bachir's right-hand man, and that the latter wouldn't propose a plan without consulting with him first. In fact, in village council meetings he would attribute every one of Bachir's successes to his own cleverness and skill. But luck is a son of a bitch. At work, Ayad persisted in entertaining himself during breaks on the worksites by telling stories to the rest of the workers about their first days in Marrakech; days when the boss, Bachir, couldn't afford to eat dinner. Sometimes he'd get carried away in telling the story and, in front of all of them, recount their first sexual adventures with the prostitutes of Marrakech, and how he and Bachir would sip glasses of spirits during these soirées until their nights turned into day and their miserable guests, who had sought refuge in the city nights from the drought of the surrounding villages, appeared even more young, beautiful, and attractive than the most noble of Marrakechi women.

Ayad's stories always made their way back to Bachir, who understood that his old friend didn't seem quite ready for the new situation, and that he was a master at dragging his reputation through the mud of memory. That's how the break happened between the two of them, and how Ayad found himself a construction worker on suspension. Now he stands every morning in Moukef waiting for someone who never comes. Someone who needs him to fix one of the ramshackle walls in Moukef's streets or one of the cracked ceilings of its homes, or someone to ask him to spread cement in a small, run-down room to conceal its holes and prolong its life if only for a short while longer. And when no one comes, he goes to Abdeslam's and steers him toward the walls of the clinic so they can watch the card and checkers players together. There's always a winner and a loser there, and the players alternate roles. It's only *their* clan that is destined to eternal loss. Thus, it seems that the Almighty, for wise reasons that remain unseen, has condemned the Laâouinas to play one role until God inherits the earth and everyone on it.

13

IN HIS FRESHMAN YEAR OF COLLEGE, Rahhal and his family moved from their slum in Ain Itti to the Moukef neighborhood in the Old City. It was like a dream come true for Abdeslam, who never expected such noblesse from his brother. But Ayad had now lost his job with Bachir. The house he had bought two decades before, located in the middle of a lower-class inn, had previously sheltered some traditional craftsmen before having been transformed by urban sprawl and the greed of its owner into a collective residence comprised of eleven shelters. This house—which consisted of three rooms, a kitchen, and a toilet—was more than Ayad needed, and this is why, in that large house, he began to feel dissatisfied. In fact, moving between construction sites and the embraces of prostitutes had resulted in Ayad neglecting to form a family to fill his life. Now, after having been fired from his job and finding himself held hostage to misery, loneliness, and boredom, he figured that the only way he could regain some of his balance was to fill the house with people—but not with a wife, for he was unable under the current circumstances to fulfill the demands of marriage. That's why he ended up bringing in Abdeslam and his family. Living in the middle of this hole would be a blessing for them, not at all like their miserable lives in the slums of Ain Itti, and he would be happy with them as they infused some vitality into his routine life. And that's how it went. Abdeslam and his family found themselves sharing Ayad's house with him in an alleyway that the authorities refused to provide lighting for, supposedly because of the informality of the construction, even though, according to its longtime residents, it had been standing there for more than a century. Not to mention that the same authorities had provided drinking water and a sanitation network in the 1970s, most likely because of electoral considerations.

The alley opened onto a wide plaza that was always jam-packed after having been transformed into a vegetable and fish market. On the right side of the plaza, Ayad used to line up beside a number of craftsmen and professionals with their simple tools at the well-known spot (or *moukef*, from which the neighborhood took its name) waiting for someone to hire them to complete a small, menial task that probably wouldn't take more than an hour or two, or a more important job that wouldn't take more than three days under the best of circumstances.

Ayad's house had been condemned by the Ministry of Housing. Because this designation wasn't followed by any serious steps that would allow the residents a new life, Ayad took the initiative to do some renovations to the house from the inside, secretly and without informing the authorities or requesting a permit, and now he has come to feel that he lives in a respectable house befitting his reputation as a construction worker, and not in a slum. Rahhal, for his part, quickly felt the difference. He who, during his difficult childhood, used to cross Oued Issil Bridge and go through Bab El Khemis toward Abdelmoumen Middle School adjacent to Moukef, who used to envy the kids from this neighborhood for their connection to Marrakech because they lived in the heart of the Red City. That day, he became one of them. He now lived in the heart of the medina, and from now on he could consider himself an insider and present himself to others as a real Marrakechi, from the venerable Moukef neighborhood.

In recent years, some of the alley's young people had begun to protest the woodshops that choked them and prevented their families from opening the windows to take in their share of Marrakech's warm sunlight during the bitterly cold winter. Similarly, they protested the bone-carving workers scattered all over their neighborhood, especially after reports were published informing them that this craft leaves behind dangerous environmental contamination. Some of them demanded that the tannery move out of Moukef, for the awful smells coming from the tanners' saddles made people's noses run, and the chemical materials used in tanning the leather began to sound alarms among environmental organizations of the city. All this while from time to time, some young folks set out to protest the vegetable sellers and fishmongers who had transformed their neighborhood into a garbage dump overflowing with waste. But Rahhal remained far from all of these battles, even after having become addicted to the National Union of Students in Morocco meetings. He wasn't a native of the neighborhood anyway, and he was bound to compare their new living conditions in Moukef to the crumbling life of Ain Itti, and he praised the Almighty for the transformation their life had undergone thanks to his uncle's generosity.

14

RAHHAL DIDN'T NOTICE the slight furrow of Hassaniya's brow at the top of her narrow forehead when he told her that he was a "kid from Moukef" during their first meeting in the university library. Generally, the features of Hassaniya's face were completely blank, making it difficult for anyone, no matter who, to read her thoughts. Despite that, Rahhal didn't take her affiliation with the neighborhood of Mouassine too seriously, since the three years during which he had repeated the first level in the Department of History and Geography had allowed him the pleasure of listening to Yahya El Mouassini's lectures on the history of Marrakech from the time of the Almoravids up until the beginning of the twentieth century. Dr. El Mouassini, one of the most distinguished professors in the college and the one who appeared most often on television, naturally focused on his rich and ancient neighborhood during his lectures. To him, Mouassine was one of Marrakech's most important and respectable neighborhoods. Wasn't it an extension of the Almoravid royal neighborhood where Kasr El Hajr (the Stone Palace) was? Wasn't it one of the most important neighborhoods of the sultan's city, which was built by the Almoravids before the Almohads proceeded to destroy Kasr El Hajr and move the princely emiral home to the Tamarrakecht Casbah, thus separating the casbah neighborhood, their new sultan's residence, from the Almoravid city, along with its neighborhoods, markets, and professional craftsmen with a no-man's-land—wide and bare—which they called Djemaa Lfnaa?

No, there wasn't anything in Hassaniya's accent, nor in her appearance or the way that she carried herself that would tell you she was one of those well-connected girls whose personal history might be deeply linked to this royal history. But what about her strange family name, Ben Mymoune? Shoot, how did he miss this detail?! During the Almohad period, the neighborhood was Jewish and was called Abou Abidan, and it had remained Jewish until the sixteenth century. However, Professor Yahya once told them that according to some historians, the name "Mouassine" could be traced to the old, isolated market that was set aside for a group of Jewish craftsmen who made knives, khanjar daggers, and different sorts of light weapons—specifically the sharp Moussa blade—so they named the Mouassine district after the blade sharpeners, according to the same word pattern as with the Sabbaghine district of cloth dyers, the Labbadine district of feltmakers, the Attarine district of spice shop owners, and other such names in the old markets of Marrakech.

Was her distant relative Ben Mymoune one of those blade sharpeners of Mouassine? Perhaps he would have lived secretly in the neighborhood, until the cellars' darkness shaved off the features of his face as well as those of his progeny. Did Ben Mymoune refuse to follow the order of the Saâdi sultan al-Ghalib bi-llah, who had ordered every Jew in Abou Abidan to move to the Mellah neighborhood that the sultan had had built to take in all the Jews who had previously lived in different neighborhoods around the city? Did he prefer living furtively in the new royal neighborhood close to the cemetery of his forefathers, sharpening the blades of Muslims, out of sight, watching as the mosque of the noble Saâdi rulers was being built over the cemetery and next to the asylum and famous Mouassine fountain? Perhaps, from his hiding place in one of the small, back streets of the new neighborhood, he followed the struggles of the pious with the religious scholars of the Merenid court after the mosque was built and prayers got under way and the sound of its muezzin began to drown out those of the rest of the city's muezzins. There's no doubt that the call to avoid prayer in a mosque that was originally a cemetery for the Jews was a source of secret joy in Ben Mymoune's soul.

Oh, Hassaniya. Was that it? Rahhal doesn't often need someone to verify a piece of information for him. It's usually enough for him for an idea to light a spark in his mind for him to fall in love with it until he comes to believe it, and it becomes clear as day. But nonetheless, origin stories, religious and doctrinal leanings, and intellectual and ideological ways of thinking are mere details, the importance of which are extremely limited to Rahhal. What concerned him most was exploring the depths of the animal lurking inside, and that was exactly the source of his bafflement and anxiety in his relationship with Hassaniya.

The fact was, Hassaniya's connection to Mouassine was something to be proud of. Even though she wasn't from Derb Chorfa Lkbir or Derb Chorfa Lsghir, but rather, from a sunken alley in the neighborhood, her standing remained secure. So, to a descendent of one of the poor tribes of Abda, who felt pride merely because his family was finally able to find a place to rest their feet inside a slummy residential commune in one of Moukef's inns, where his classmate, Hassaniya, lived, was exceptional. For it wasn't that far from Riad Si Aissa, the home of the caid of the tribes of Abda and Chiyadma and Ahmar, Aissa bin Omar, their utterly cruel governor. It was honorable enough for Hassaniya to be so close to this solid, well-heeled neighborhood.

For this very reason, Rahhal would strive to make Hassaniya happy and try to remain on her good side. No sooner did the news of Fouad being an agent for the Mukhabarat spread, which resulted in scandal in student circles, did Rahhal cheerfully bring her the news. But Hassaniya received it coldly and responded sternly, avoiding eye contact, as usual.

"You just found out? Poor you, always the last to know. I'm the one who never leaves the college library and I learned of the news a week ago, which is why I'm no longer worried about Fouad's threats. And it's also why I no longer bring it up with you. I've understood that God has hit him where it hurts and given him enough rope to hang himself. But for God's sake, you're the one who hops around morning and night from one demonic debate circle to the other. Over here are the Basistas, and over there are the Justicistas, and here is God knows who else. Hello? Did you just wake up? Did you finally hear the news?"

Rahhal had begun to get used to this tone from Hassaniya. He doesn't quite recall when his thin colleague had begun to speak so boldly, but it had become familiar to him. He had gradually come to accept it, with annoyance and irritation. With a type of silent resentment. But he didn't comment or protest. And for her part, Hassaniya didn't hesitate to criticize him, to further belittle him, or call his ideas and suggestions stupid, whether or not she had cause to do so. The strange thing is that he didn't respond. He was inexplicably dumbstruck before her. His squirrel was afflicted by a strange feeling of weakness in the presence of her hidden animal.

Rahhal wasn't so naïve as to tell Hassaniya the story of Fouad from its beginning and explain his involvement in what happened. In all likelihood, she wouldn't believe him anyway. So, he was compelled to remain silent, and let her rebuke him a little before they sat down to review the second to last chapter of the research study, having only two hours to go over it one last time before submitting it to Professor Makhloufi at the research seminar at five o'clock in the auditorium named after the Red City of Marrakech's poet, Mohammed Ben Brahim. Rahhal was waiting on pins and needles for this very seminar, only to prove himself to his dear colleagues in the Labid bin Rabi'a al-Amari group, especially their commander and flag bearer, Fouad Wardi (although he doubted that Fouad, after his resounding scandal, would dare even to show up).

15

FOUAD WARDI had only become aware of Rahhal's existence recently, when Makhloufi started to sing his praises along with those of his colleague. He peered for a long time into Rahhal's face and what caught his attention was the uneasy shyness tinged with displeasure that traced his features every time the professor praised his work. It wasn't a virtuous, modest embarrassment, but rather a frightened one that practically screamed, "Take me away." *Something isn't right here,* thought Fouad, who found this squirrel-like face familiar. One of those faces that had remained in the shadows without ever piquing his curiosity before. A familiar face in classes and lecture halls. Always there at the National Union of Students in Morocco meetings. But he had never before participated in a class or a discussion circle. So, when Makhloufi came to repeatedly praise the clear breakthrough that Rahhal and Hassaniya had made, Fouad asked that the professor allow him to peruse at least one chapter of their research project in order to get an idea about his classmates' methodology. Who knows? Perhaps Team Labid could benefit from their research methodology, design, and formatting style. And because of the trust the professor had in Fouad, he gave him a copy of the most recent chapter he had just finished reviewing, having only jotted down a couple of notes that called attention to two digressions that could be tempered without affecting the chapter's coherence. And because Fouad wasn't thickheaded like his professor, he noticed the Eastern wording of the paper and was convinced that Makhloufi was a complete ignoramus, and that the work in his hands had been completely plagiarized.

Rahhal, on the other hand, didn't wait for the research paper incident to get to know Fouad. For he had been following him since their first year in the Department of Arabic Literature. Fouad hadn't yet joined the Justice and Charity brigade, but he was a well-balanced student who held firmly to his Islamic grounding, which he would refer to whether it was called for or not. And the young professor of critical methodologies, Jalal El Rundi, known for his leftist tendencies, was extremely annoyed by Fouad's incoherent interventions, which sometimes aimed to firmly establish the strong foundation of structuralism in Islam, or to denounce the atheistic background of Marxism, even though the discussion was on methodologies, not doctrines. But Fouad's seriousness used to intercede on his behalf, even though Professor Jalal would sometimes rebuke this very seriousness, saying to him, "You're a young man, sir, so why do you speak with the sobriety of the professors at the Ibn Youssef Madrasa school for archaic education?"

However, Fouad's interventions in the National Union's circles had allowed him to gain a certain degree of respect ever since his first year. And even though he didn't devote himself assiduously to the circles, his rare interventions were powerful enough to make him an object of attraction for the Islamist brigades, from Justice and Charity, Reform and Renewal, and even some of the strict Salafi groups that had withdrawn from the Student Union and its circles (although they did continue to closely follow what was going on in the courtyard). In his third year, Fouad joined Justice and Charity without changing too many of his ways. Thus, his interventions during the circles remained limited and he continued to focus more on his lectures than anything else.

When Fouad chose to register to do his final thesis research with Professor Bouchaib Makhloufi, he didn't do so out of weakness or vulnerability. He isn't the type of student who aims to slap together a piece of research and receive a grade of 17/20 that Makhloufi wouldn't waver from so long as the student attends his boring colloquia, regardless of the seriousness of the research or its value. In reality, Fouad took refuge in Makhloufi, seeking protection in him from professors of methodologies and the modern novel, and the contemporary poetry of leftists from whom he learned during the years he had spent as a student of theirs how much they had diverted literature from its exalted function. Fouad knew that working with Jalal El Rundi and the likes of him would be difficult and might expose him to conflicts for which he was ready, even willing to face in the lecture hall, of course, but had no need for as long as it had to do with a thesis that he'd defend at the end of the year. And his grade might be crucial to guaranteeing a degree with distinction.

When Makhloufi proceeded to present the list of *Mu'allaqāt* poets at the beginning of the year, Fouad didn't choose his partners, nor did he think about how harmoniously his team would work together. His only concern was getting Labid bin Rabi'a, not because he liked his *Mu'allaqa*, but rather out of love for this venerable companion of the Prophet, who was considered among *those whose hearts are brought together*. It was enough that the Prophet, the best of the human race, had said about him:

The most truthful words uttered by a poet are those of Labid:

> Indeed, everything, except for God, is vain
> And every comfort is, inevitably, fleeting

Before the Prophet, may peace be upon him, added, "Except for the comfort of Heaven."

"Here I am, Labid, at your service," Fouad repeated to himself, then raised his finger high.

But three of the stupidest, most idiotic students all raised their fingers at the same time as well. It was clear that they had been lying in wait for Fouad. This poet of the Hawazin tribe didn't matter to them, nor did his *Mu'allaqa* that, as soon it was recited in the presence of the poet Nabigha he declared, "Go, for you are the greatest poet of all the Arabs." Nabigha al-Dhubyani's opinion didn't matter to them. In fact, they didn't know a thing about him. They had signed up with Makhloufi to guarantee a good grade on the thesis, and they had waited for Fouad to raise his finger so they could be in a group with him. *And God spared the believers of fighting.*

From the beginning, Fouad understood that there was precious little room for discussion with his partners. For they weren't literature people with whom he could delve into its finer points. They weren't people who held opinions that he could discuss or debate, nor were they those who followed student affairs enough that they would honor him as a militant and uphold his status as such. They were merely a gang of cheats who, in the rare moments when they honored the lesson with their presence, noticed Fouad's vitality and how much he knew, so they formed a group with him. That's how he found himself mixed up with them now.

From his first meeting with them, Fouad understood that it was up to him to produce the thesis on his own, for these fine men were completely useless. So, he decided to put his trust in God and begin his work, explaining to Makhloufi afterward his dilemma with the scoundrels that God had plagued him with. As soon as Makhloufi gave them the green light to start writing, Fouad holed himself up in his room for days, during which time he drafted three chapters in one go that discussed the biography of this venerable Companion of the Prophet, his horsemanship, high morals, and his beautiful devotion to Islam. And here, especially, Fouad focused on the famous story of him and the governor of Kufa, who sent for him one day and ordered him to recite some of his poetry during one of his council gatherings, at which point Labid responded resolutely, "I vowed not to recite any more poetry after God taught me what was in the Qur'anic chapters 'The Cow' and 'Al Umran.'" When Labid's response reached the ears of the Prophet of God's successor, Caliph 'Umar bin al-Khattab, he was pleased by it and ordered an additional five hundred dirhams to be added to the two thousand the poet was already receiving from the Muslim treasury.

But Fouad's shock with Makhloufi's response exceeded that of the governor of Kufa. For, after he presented his three chapters to the supervising professor, thinking that he would be pleased with his work and would praise his effort, Makhloufi surprised him with a look of indignation, which, luckily, he distributed in equal measure between Fouad and the other members of his gang.

"It seems, my boys, that a river other than the one we are plunging into has swept you off. The research framework is clear and defined. The topic we're working on is 'History, Environment, and Ancient Arab Society in the Arabian Peninsula as Understood through the *Mu'allaqāt* Suspended Odes.' When we say 'the *Mu'allaqāt* odes,' we are, quite naturally, talking about the very core of the Jahiliyya period that came before Islam. When I assigned you to work on Labid, I was thinking about his incomparable *Mu'allaqa*, 'The Campsites Were Effaced.' However, I don't see analysis of the *Mu'allaqa* in anything that you've written. In fact, you barely refer to it. The man lived for over a century, ninety years of which were during the Jahiliyya period, and he composed his *Mu'allaqa* during the Jahiliyya period, yet you talk about the governor of Kufa and 'Umar bin al-Khattab. How mixed up can you be? This is too much and totally inappropriate for students in their fourth year of undergraduate study. My boys, the man composed but one verse on Islam in which he said:

"The chaste man has no greater admonisher than himself.
Only a man's virtuous companion is fit for him.

"So forget everything you've written, may God set you right. Reread the *Mu'allaqa* and discuss it in the library as your colleagues have done. I hope your research takes its natural course just as it has with the rest of the students."

Fouad was flustered. He had chosen a venerable companion of the Prophet in order to work on his brilliant biography and his sweet, divine gifts, and here the professor was forcing him back to the pre-Islamic Jahiliyya period. Fouad was extremely frustrated. Therefore, he decided to wash his hands of the entire affair. As long as a seventeen was guaranteed with Makhloufi at the end of the year, let him teach the gang a lesson now and leave them to face their destiny. So, the joke was on them after Fouad explained to the ill-fortuned group that he, for his part, had tried, but his tireless efforts had gone unrewarded, so it was their turn this time to present their suggestion for the first chapter in the next meeting. He wished them luck and left them staring at one another, completely lost, as if they were being tossed about by the ocean's waves.

16

RAHHAL KNEW each and every member of the Labid gang since they were from his neighborhood: one is from Moukef, the other from Arset El Malak, and the third from Kechiche. They were known around the Old City for being huge Marrakech Kawkab FC fans. They accompanied the Red City's representative in the national championships for soccer wherever it went. They attended its matches for free, traveling on the team's dime to whip up its fans with the appropriate chants when the team was on the road. There were rumors that the college dean himself had gotten involved to recommend them to the professors of the department most obedient to the administration (and the dean's attention to them became even greater after he was elected as a member of the executive office of Kawkab FC). Makhloufi, as needs no clarification, was among the professors who were most obedient to the administration. It was enough that he considered his exaggerated bowing down before the dean as merely appropriate to his station. Sometimes he argued that implementing the dean's decisions and recommendations to the letter was an example of obeying those in authority that religious law requires. Thus, in this circus elephant, the administration found the best support to ease the affairs of these three musketeers. And who knows? Perhaps it was Makhloufi who gave them the idea to gain power over Fouad Wardi, whose potential he knew well when he had taught him eloquence, prosody, and syntax for two consecutive years.

The conspiracy was broad, then, and its threads were intertwined, but stupid Fouad, instead of turning the tables on everyone, or at least toying with them in a more intelligent manner and leaving the gang to stumble about as he had before, decided, after the first three chapters of research were rejected, to give in to

68

Makhloufi's direction. So he went back to the damned *Mu'allaqa* that had been frustrating him from the very first verse. And, when he started to enumerate the places mentioned in the ode, he was happy when Minan appeared in the first line:

> The tent marks in Minan are worn away, where she encamped
> and where she alighted, Ghawl and Rijam left to the wild.

But as soon as he went back to the sources, Fouad discovered that it was referring to another location in the realm of the Banu 'Amir tribe that had no connection to the Minan of Mecca where pilgrims throw seven stones at Jamrat al-Aqaba on the tenth day of Dhu al-Hujja. Someone like him who didn't like pre-Islamic poetry at all was like someone tilling ground that was rough, thorny, and hilly.

But why did he decide to focus on Hassaniya and I after tiring himself out digging around in these desolate river valleys? Why did he put Labid aside and begin to busy himself with Ibn Kulthoum and whoever stood with him?

Rahhal's sympathy toward Fouad turned to anger and a desire to take revenge. Luckily, the Greyhound was innately prepared to slip on any bar of soap placed in his path. Rahhal's scenario was solid. Thus, Fouad Wardi forgot all about Labid, Ibn Kulthoum, Harith bin Hilliza, and their *Mu'allaqāt*, as well as Makhloufi and his meetings that he stopped attending, devoting himself entirely to futilely defending himself against the charge of being an agent for the Mukhabarat.

As for Rahhal, all he had wanted was to produce a mediocre piece of research and receive a seventeen at the end of the year without Hassaniya pulling him into the spotlight. That's not what Rahhal was looking for. In fact, that's what he tends to avoid. He was already suffering from Makhloufi's repeated praises in front of the students that confused and made him ashamed of himself and of the world, so why did Fouad want to further his abuse by focusing more hubbub on him and his research paper? Rahhal didn't want anything from anyone. All he wanted was to finish the year with a degree (without distinction even) that would allow him the opportunity to pass the Ministry of Education examinations—elementary, intermediate, secondary—not important. The important thing was to make the miracle happen, pass some examination, and get a job with the state so he could get a public employee pension number, thus creating a single moment of joy in Abdeslam's life. He wanted to defy the ill fortune that fate had dealt him and his tribe and achieve something that might allow his father to take pride in him, at least for his own sake, after having isolated himself from people in recent days, visiting the village in Abda less frequently.

17

HASSANIYA WASN'T AT ALL WORRIED about what she was going to do after graduation. That's because Qatifa Jr., the son of Hajj Qatifa Sr., owner of the most well-known fabric shop in the Semmarine market, was only waiting for her to graduate from college so she could accept her job from him. Emad Qatifa had opened a private elementary school in the Massira neighborhood. A spacious, three-floor residence in a strategic location for which one of Qatifa Sr.'s important acquaintances had arranged a permit that allowed it to be transformed into an educational establishment. And because Hiyam, Emad's wife, had failed in running the school during its first year, his father advised him to take Hassaniya on as her assistant starting the following academic year.

Hassaniya possessed all the requirements for the job: she was calm, educated, serious, not too chatty, and she wore a veil. Moreover, she was their neighbor and had grown up in front of them, so it followed that her trustworthiness—and this was the most important thing here—was guaranteed. In addition to these considerations, Qatifa family traditions didn't allow that a man be hired to help Hiyam run the school, which would have left the wife to spend most of her day in the office with a male stranger. This would not do. Just as Hiyam's strong jealousy over Emad prevented him from bringing her a *female* assistant of the modern, flashy type, which would risk complicating things between them even more than they were. Therefore, Qatifa Jr. found the Hajj's suggestion reasonable. They were just waiting for Hassaniya to finish her studies so she could start working.

As much as Hassaniya would boast to Rahhal of her family's strong ties to the family of Hajj Qatifa, "the fabric man," the Squirrel didn't find it too difficult to figure things out and place the relationship into its correct frame: What could possibly connect a noble Marrakech family to her mother, Oum Hassaniya (other than living close together, of course); a widow living with her only daughter in a tiny house attached like a tick to their spacious home? Rahhal's burning imagination helped him out with all of the details, with no need for an omniscient narrator. He imagined Hassaniya's mother helping the Qatifa family with every task they needed help with: housework along with all the major household chores that usually preceded religious holidays and family events and preparing food for the Hajj's countless guests to his endless banquets. He pictured her washing and sorting through the wheat that would come fresh from their farm on the outskirts of Marrakech during the harvest seasons, splitting the red olives with a knife and crushing the green ones with a rock to remove the pit before placing them in airtight containers after adding water, salt, and slices of lemon to cure them during the olive harvest season. He could see her accompanying the women of the Qatifa family to the Mouassine baths to lather their bodies with homemade soap, scrubbing them with the loofah, then rinsing them with water, and applying the *ghassoul* clay mixed with rose water to their bodies to restore their vigor, and on their hair to remove the dandruff from their scalps. Not to mention the task of bringing hot water to them from the water basin located in the middle of thick clouds of steam deep inside the hammam.

Rahhal imagined all of this without uttering a word. He let Hassaniya say whatever she wanted. And despite that, he'd listen with some amusement. In fact, he gradually came to identify with her to the point where, when he would bump into Emad's older brother, Dr. Abdelmoula Qatifa, entering the School of Law, where he taught constitutional law, he would feel great pride as if it were *his* mother who scrubbed the bodies of Dr. Qatifa's mother and sisters in the hammam.

18

IT ISN'T POSSIBLE for a pelican to give birth to a squirrel after mating with mantis. This is a law of nature and, obviously, it operates according to a clear order. But, who ever said that the fates of human beings corresponded to nature's norms and are regulated by them? When Halima was blessed with Rahhal, a few years prior to Abdeslam fleeing to Marrakech to escape the years of drought that had afflicted both the green and the dry in the village, it was clear that divine intervention had decided to grant Abdeslam justice and rule in favor of providing some relief for him. That's because for a decade of marriage he had been wishing for a girl whose sunny smile would shine in his face each morning, or a son who would light fires of beautiful mischief in his routine life. Yet God brought nothing, and he was a man of faith. But Halima had little patience, and not much faith. Hence, she didn't need a medical review or tests to determine with total certainty that the defect was with Abdeslam, and she spread word throughout the village that this mule—her husband—was not at all able to have children like his peers. So, when Rahhal's embryo changed into a bone that began to acquire flesh day after day inside Halima's swelling belly, Abdeslam became the happiest person in the village. He wasn't that concerned with the winks of those malicious rumormongers, for he knew his wife well. She might yell in his face, insult him, and make fun of him in front of everyone, but she could never cheat on him. And generally speaking, his happiness with Halima's swelling belly was stronger than any sense of unease the winks and nudges might cause.

Halima held no illusions concerning her origins. She wasn't the granddaughter of Caid Si Eissa. Rather, she was from the village, from the same tribe; from a subtribe even more modest than the

Laâouina family. Nevertheless, she remained deeply convinced that her family had done her harm by agreeing to Abdeslam as a husband, he who wasn't deserving even of her fingernail.

> Oh woe is me and my shitty luck, I'm in such deep shit.
> Oh lord, what a man. Even if it were raining, I wouldn't let
>   him in.

Halima sang this tune nonstop to Abdeslam, in the village, then in Ain Itti, and even after their move to Moukef. She looked for any reason, no matter how small, to take possession of him and flog him with her vicious tongue. As for Rahhal, who continued to secretly sympathize with his father, he could never understand his mother's self-confidence, especially since he didn't find that this excessive self-confidence had any basis either in the historical past or the present reality.

Halima was a true pelican. Her mouth was wide and broad. As for her hyperthyroidism, the symptoms of which had presented themselves right after the wedding, it caused her thyroid gland to swell up in the shape of a tumor around the neck area, looking like the large crop that pelicans store things in underneath the beak. Also, because of her great big buttocks, Halima found it difficult to stand. And when she finally did manage to steady herself on her feet, she would waddle around ridiculously, just like a pelican.

Abdeslam, on the other hand, was a certified mantis. Tall and thin like a mantis. Calm, seemingly trustworthy. In Ain Itti and even after moving to Moukef, the neighbors would show him respect and refer to him as the faqih—the jurisprudent—even though the only knowledge of religious jurisprudence he possessed was the Qur'anic verses and chapters he had memorized and kept on hand for use in the cemetery. In any case, he was a faqih in the neighbors' eyes, and he clung stubbornly to his nickname. He could do no better than remain silent and kind, greeting children before adults with a "salaam alaikum," all in order to attain such a nickname and perpetuate the respect it bestowed on him. Rahhal sometimes thought that his father's insect was given its power over people through the same type of trickery that the praying mantis used with other nations, tribes, and languages. To the Greeks and the Germanic tribes, it is a "prophet," while the Arabs of the Arabian Peninsula call it "the prophet's mount." As for the Jews, they registered it in their name, calling it "the camel of the Jews." The Spanish consider it sacred, and their neighbors to the south—the people of Tangier, Tetouan, and Fes—call it "the pilgrim." As for the kids in the alleys of Marrakech, they treated it with reverence, bestowing upon it the name "my lord's she-camel."

The mantis's respect for farmers' crops, and its insatiable appetite for devouring all types of insects, prompted farmers to consider it the best guardian for their fields and farms. That's why they show it the same, mutual respect and raise their children from a young age not to interfere with them. They've given it names in every language that guarantee respect. Abdeslam, for his part, knew how to sell God's verses for a paltry price in the cemetery, and a little bit of respect in the neighborhood. Generally, he put his verses and chapters at the disposal of his neighbors for free. He'd recite verses for the sick or those stricken with epilepsy and say some prayers at the bedside of those about to die. And whenever an animal was slaughtered on the occasion of a birth, or a funeral came to the neighborhood, he'd join the reciters-for-hire in heated communal recitation of the Qur'an without asking for a fee.

Whenever Abdeslam is invited to an event or function at the neighbors' houses, he wears his clean, white jellaba. As for the cemetery, he goes there dressed in one of two jellabas: the dark marine-blue one or the olive-colored one; sometimes in his brown, short-sleeved *deraâ* when it was really hot. But what Rahhal never understood was why his father would wear the same old, faded grey jellaba whenever he wanted to travel to the village. Of course, the clean, white one was reserved for special occasions and functions, and would be unsuitable for going to the village. But what was wrong with the olive-colored one? And why not try, even just once in his life, embracing the family there while wearing his marine-blue jellaba? But it seemed that the mantis had its own, special way of doing things. This thin insect was used to changing its color to blend in with the environment where it lived, making it easier to hide from enemies, even though Abdeslam, in reality, had no enemies. This may have been due to his skill in avoiding all confrontations. All the reciters-for-hire who tried to create problems with him in the cemetery and who sometimes accused him of stealing customers from them, he would kiss their heads to apologize for things he hadn't done so as to assure them that anyone looking to pick a fight with Abdeslam was like someone looking for a white hair in a glass of milk. This is how Abdeslam became everyone's friend in the cemetery, from the gravediggers to the people who sold figs, dates, and vials of rosewater. Everyone's friend, in silence and from a distance.

Only at home would Abdeslam lose his deeply felt peace and harmony. Halima laid in wait for him. He would compel her to mistreat him, first through his silence, then out of his strong fear of her. Rahhal's respect for his father prevented him from discussing the subject with him directly so as to reassure him. In fact, Halima's threats were just chitchat and empty talk, and he shouldn't take them too seriously. Besides, she was a pelican, not a female mantis that could attack the male at any moment and bite its head off.

19

WHAT HAPPENED THAT DAY at the college surprised everyone.
The Battle of the Clinic was no different from all the other battles
the comrades had plunged headlong into over the last two months,
and no one imagined the security forces would respond with such
ferocity. The comrades in the Qâidi brigade had drafted a program
of escalating struggle without coordinating with anyone else and
began to implement it clause by clause. The other progressive factions continued to follow the recent battles without getting too
involved. The militants of these factions that followed the leftist
parties retreated and began to play an observer role after the Qâidis rejected the initiative of unified coordination that they had put
forth to build a new vision for the shared student struggle within
the National Union of Students in Morocco. The Qâidis' position
was absolute: They were against any initiative cooked up in the
headquarters of reformist parties allied with the regime. Also, this
suspect dish consisted of some political positions that contradicted
the NUSM plan of attack.

The Qâidi students didn't hold any position against the work
of unification, as was made clear by Comrades Ahmed the Hyena
and Atiqa the Cow during two extended discussion circles convened specifically to discuss the initiative. "The Qâidis," assured
the Hyena, "are the NUSM faction most intent on unity within the
student ranks. But what sort of unity do we want, comrades? What
unity do we want? Or, more to the point, what unity do they want
for us? To be united with dark, Islamist forces, as the nationalists
of the Organization for Popular Democratic Action demand? The
ones whose aged leadership betrayed the Left's principles by entering the Makhzen's fold, and who, today, call for mutual recogni-
tion among the different student elements while turning a blind eye

to the principles that severely limit the democratic nature and the progressive identity of our long-standing framework? With whom shall we unite, comrades? With the students of Justice and Charity? With foreign elements that, until recently, referred to NUSM as the Non-Believers' Union of Students in Morocco before deciding to infiltrate the organization in order to blow it up from within? And here they are having begun to reveal their fascist faces, just like when they attacked our comrades with knives in Dhahr Mehraz in Fes in what they so impudently called 'the Battle for the Liberation of Kabul.'

"Sticking to the work of unification to rebuild NUSM," the Hyena added, "remains a fundamental issue, but it should be based on the decisions made at the fifteenth national conference of our organization, and based on the nine orders of the Qâidi Democratic Program of 1979, and on our scientific Marxist conception that clarified, in detail, the working Qâidi unification processes inside the university, and in the presence of the steadfast and militant student bases. Therefore, it is up to our comrades in the reform brigades to first acquire legitimacy of the struggle, maintaining a daily presence in the public arena, and participating to widen the NUSM base with what will preserve the progressive, and aggressive, identity of the organization. Only then will it be possible for us to speak about unity based on a cohesive, militant grounding with the masses, not based on what is said in the salons of the leaders of these 'caviar' leftists."

For their part, the Islamists remained outside of the fray. The savage attacks on the Qâidis at the Universities of Fes and Oujda perpetrated by their brothers who were heavily armed with chains, swords, and cudgels, put them in a difficult position. And because their relationship with the comrades in Marrakech hadn't yet reached the same level of tension, they insisted on letting things calm down until the storm passed. Therefore, they avoided getting into any confrontations with the Qâidis after the Battle of the Cafeteria's Liberation, even though they felt ashamed after seeing that the cafeteria had been transformed into a red fortress—Sheikh

Imam, Said El Maghribi, collections of love songs, and other, strange collections that were not on the list passed around by the comrades during the famous meeting where the decision for liberation was made. But what annoyed the brothers even more was the backpedaling of the cafeteria's new administration, which consisted of two former Qâidi militants who had just been released from prison and who had enrolled in the university to strengthen the Qâidi militant reach there on the issue of the smoking ban, which had been enforced before. Thus, because of the accumulated clouds of smoke that turned the cafeteria into a smokers' den, the place became off-limits to the sisters and even to the other women students who found refuge in the cafés of the surrounding neighborhoods. Of course, the comrades weren't so concerned about the commercial angle of it, as much as they were happy seeing the space transformed into a private, closed club for Qâidis, leftists, and legions of smokers.

The decisions issued by the leadership of the Islamist factions that ordered its supporters to stand down and pursue caution until the investigation into the cases of assassination attempts on some of the Qâidi students in Fes and Oujda during the Islamic "conquests" there, all of this made coming to a settlement in the Battle of the Cafeteria in favor of the comrades a simple matter. This is what encouraged them to put together an ambitious, militant program, even though the students who came from far away had begun to leave the college for Essaouira, Kelaat Sraghna, and other cities and villages surrounding Marrakech in order to be close to their families while preparing for the upcoming exams. So, during a morning meeting in the cafeteria when Comrade Farid raised the issue of the lack of a health clinic in the dorms next to the College of Humanities and the firm intention of the dorm's militants to plunge into battle to demand their rights for a plan that provided for medical treatment inside the university residences, the humanities comrades were enthusiastic. They decided to kick-start a campaign the following day, which would begin with a morning meeting in the cafeteria and continue on to the dorms in solidarity with its residents, and in support of their militants in their rightful struggle.

20

WHERE WAS RAHHAL THAT DAY? Where was he?

Ah . . . He was in a meeting with his supervising professor. The final meeting where Bouchaib Makhloufi delivers his precious farewell address in which he thanks the students for their seriousness and diligence, and for their commitment to following his directions and suggestions before then granting them permission to print their theses, wishing them good luck with their written exams, and assuring everyone that when they reach the oral stage, with God's help, "Everything will work out for the best."

Rahhal has never believed in luck—or, rather, he has only believed in bad luck. He was confident that his bad luck was deeply rooted and hereditary, no way of getting around it. However, he also believes in the religious dictate known as "the parents' blessing." Could a person as humble as Abdeslam ever dream that a son like Rahhal would preserve his position as father, listen to him, and treat him with respect, even as he came out of Halima the Pelican's hot kitchen? So, it was "the parents' blessing," Abdeslam's blessing in particular, that caused Makhloufi to choose this particular day to deliver his farewell address to the pre-Islamic Jahili Battalion. Thus, the Squirrel found himself far from the battlefield that was littered with dozens who had been injured and maimed, and that resulted in fifteen detainees whose court cases were concluded that same week.

The absence of the student masses was clear from the beginning. The demonstration that started out from the courtyard of the College of Humanities included only hardened militants and some of their sincere supporters who had preferred to remain in school until the militant program was completed. Even knowing that, numerous times Atiqa had demanded the program be postponed until the beginning of the following semester, Comrades Moukhtar and Mourad—the Rat and the Gerbil—insisted on completing the program, even strengthening it with some cases they hadn't been aware of before, such as the case concerning the demand for a clinic that they had neglected to include in the full dossier of demands. And so, the demonstration left at lunchtime from the college's main hall toward the dining hall in the dorms.

The comrades expected elements of the university guards to get involved, and no doubt the watchdog committee took this into account in their response to this involvement. But they never imagined that, waiting there to meet them in the courtyard that separated the gate of the College of Humanities from the entrance to the dorms, they'd meet hordes of rapid deployment forces, who came from who knows where, no one knowing how they had managed to surround the place. This was a Makhzen-esque escalation that had not occurred to anyone, but it was difficult to step back, none of the comrades being able to sully his honor as an activist by calling on the demonstrators to retreat to the college, even if only to review the situation in light of the new data. Such a decision, wise as it might have been, would have stamped a mark of shame on the forehead of whoever dared making it. So, they began to compete, each shouting louder than the other, yelling out slogans louder and louder.

"I, comrade, don't intend to give up the popular mass struggle."

As more panic seeped into their hearts, their voices got louder.

"We'll never bow, we'll never bow. By the sound of the cannon, we'll never be cowed."

The blood was boiling in their veins. The comrades were confused. But they were shouting nonetheless. A mass hysteria possessed them.

"Kill them. Annihilate them. The people's children will replace them!"

The demonstration advanced cautiously toward the dorms. It moved forward in fits and starts in a somewhat confused fashion. It turned toward the dormitory gate. Then, as if a pack of wolves had been unleashed all at once from an invisible enclosure, the rapid deployment forces devastated the comrades' demonstration. They penetrated it from all sides and tore it to pieces. Those who were maimed and injured remained there screaming in the middle of the courtyard in the afternoon heat with no one to offer them even a drink of water. As for the arrests, they totaled fifteen students, but didn't include any of the brigade's hardcore members.

"The militant is the last one to be thrown in prison," the Islamists sneered, repeating this famous Qâidi statement as they discussed what had happened during their meeting in the canteen, now emptied of its leaders after news spread of the broad arrest campaign that would reach the Qâidis in the coming days. The cafeteria managers had completely disappeared. For they were new to such an era of freedom and didn't want to squander it. Thus, the Islamists temporarily seized total control of the situation inside the cafeteria. Once again, they banned smoking, as well as music, on account of the fact that the exam study period required the utmost peace and quiet. From their position deep inside the cafeteria, they began to analyze what had happened, confirming that not arresting the titular heads of the Qâidis was proof of their complicity with the regime.

Even though some of the students who were not true believers in the cause gave up the names of the brigade's leaders during the trial and confirmed the personal responsibility of some specific ones in calling for "demonstrating without a permit on a public street" that had brought them to court, the arrests didn't include any of these leaders. Things started to get more complicated when a rumor spread among the student ranks that Moukhtar the Rat was among the interrogators who received the arrested students at the secret police headquarters. It is said, and God knows best, that he was wearing a stylish suit with a necktie and shiny shoes, and that he was smoking a Marlboro during the interrogation, his bearing and features not betraying the fact that he had had another name and another life when he lived among them, there during the marathon NUSM meetings.

21

RAHHAL COULDN'T SLEEP ANYMORE. He tossed and turned in bed like a fish caught in a net. In general, Rahhal doesn't dream. Besides his battles, which had become fewer in recent years, and outside of the masquerade balls when Hassaniya would visit his dreams—sometimes in the form of an eagle, other times in a horse's skin or as a gazelle's specter—Rahhal didn't dream at all. But this time the dreams began to visit him daily, always right before the sleep, which only came at dawn now. They weren't really dreams; they were more like waking nightmares. Once, he imagined himself in the center of the demonstration yelling in the middle of the crowd, "I, comrade, don't intend to give up . . ." then the second line of the slogan got stuck in his throat as the masses faded away; whoever was in front of him and behind him abandoning him to face an enormous truncheon smashing down on his head, one blow after the other as he sinks like a tent peg until his head is flush with the ground. Rahhal exerts a fantastic effort to extricate himself but it's no use. He knows that he isn't sleeping. But despite that, he's unable to do anything. He feels thirsty. Should he get up to drink? He thinks about going to the toilet as his bladder is hurting him, but he can't and doesn't know why. He remains like that, pounded into the ground like a tent peg. He can't see anything. He can't hear anything. He's gasping for breath and feels his heart pounding. He opens his eyes but doesn't see a thing. If only the municipality had brought electricity to this wretched street, he would have turned on the light and conquered the nightmare's darkness. But there's no light. No light switch on the wall next to him. As for lighting a candle, that would require some effort, and he is feeling weak. His eyes are opened onto the emptiness. Dirt seeping into them along with worms and bugs. Rahhal screams without making a sound. As if he doesn't have a larynx.

Rahhal, Rahhal,
O he who lives inside us.
Rahhal, Rahhal,
The one with the beautiful name.

Sometimes he would dream that two members of the Mukhabarat were arresting him, making a beeline toward him among dozens of demonstrators. They would drag him roughly by his collar and lead him out of the demonstration to throw him into a large, beat-up van, like the ones sheep are driven to the markets in during the Eid al-Adha festivities. There he finds someone waiting for him who quickly ties his hands together and blindfolds him, then throws him on top of a pile of bound bodies inside the van. And whenever the door was opened for a new guest, he would hear the same, quick, skilled movement, then the human sack would be put down on top of him, or on top of the other sacks tossed next to him. The closed sacks were moving. Rolling around. Moaning. Whenever one of them tried to change position, it would mess up the arrangement and the groans would multiply. The van was there, parked not too far from the battlefield. Rahhal could hear screaming outside. The screams of the male students. The pleading of the female students. Their wailing. The sound of batons coming down on bodies. His brain nearly explodes. He tries to scream but he can't.

Rahhal opens his eyes and thinks about getting up from the bed. He needs to go to the kitchen to get something to drink. He's thirsty and his mouth is parched. Maybe he can stumble his way to the toilet to empty his bladder and get rid of the burning piss. But he doesn't get up. He feels a pleasant heat moistening the area between his thighs. A salty, painful heat. Damn, he did it in the bed. Still, he doesn't get up. He was awake. His eyes were wide open. "I'm a squirrel, not a fish that sleeps with its eyes open." Rahhal was no longer sure of anything. Was he a squirrel or fish? A fish caught in a net. He didn't know whether he was sleeping or awake or somewhere in between. He could no longer remember a thing and was no longer sure of anything. Many questions came to him one after the other: Questions about his mother and father; about his lineage; about Ain Itti and Moukef; about Makhloufi and Hassaniya; about Wafiq Daraai, Harith al-Yashkuri, and Amru bin Kulthoum; about the Cow, the Hyena, the Rat, the Gerbil, the Greyhound, the Lizard, and other animals he realized he hadn't observed enough during the discussion circles. He was responding to all the questions thoroughly, devotedly, and with squirrel-like accuracy. He spewed out information, details, facial expressions, jacket colors, cigarette brands, types of shoes. Like a faucet they had opened and that had broken in their hands, no one knowing anymore how to shut it off. He was going on and on, raving . . . Halima didn't know what to do with this cursed boy. As for Abdeslam, he would recite Qur'anic verses over Rahhal's head at dawn and only left him when he heard him snoring.

■　■　■

Halima didn't understand the secret of the strange state of serenity Rahhal enjoyed during the day, as if he hadn't been raving and babbling all night. "Was the boy cursed?" Halima asked Abdeslam without expecting an answer. Ayad wasn't going to get involved in their affairs. As for Abdeslam, he didn't ask. He had gotten used to not asking about anything that went on in this house. Only Halima asked and responded.

Rahhal, on the other hand, was struck with an intense feeling of happiness because he hadn't been among the demonstrators on the day of the Battle of the Clinic. At night he would be seized by nightmares and surrounded by dark scenarios that would show in excruciating detail what would have happened to him had he been among them; had he, too, fallen into the hands of the police along with those who were arrested, all of them unknown students no less obscure than he. Happy because everything that was happening to him these days was happening in bed, not in dark cellars. For this reason, whenever he woke up late (always after midday), he sat with Halima, Abdeslam, and Ayad around the lunch table looking content, with no hint of the wincing his face showed when he was raving.

"The boy has been cursed," surmised Halima as she rubbed her throat with her shoulder just as pelicans do. "The boy's cursed, no doubt about it." Then, glaring angrily at Abdeslam, "Woe is your son, you unfortunate fool. They've cast a spell on him, and you don't know what to say to me. One word. I told you. Cursed. Cursed!" But Abdeslam didn't say a thing. Ayad smiled, bowing his head in silence. For his part, Rahhal didn't speak to anyone. He ate in silence with a look of happy relief and a satisfied smile that Halima found strange and mysterious. No sooner would Rahhal get up from the lunch table than he would he lie down on his mattress, which was tossed right on the crumbling *zellij* tile, without a bedframe, and continue reviewing his lecture notes. At dusk, he'd go out for a stroll, which always took him to Djemaa Lfnaa. All roads in Marrakech lead to Djemaa Lfnaa, and every time he'd follow a different route.

During the journey, Rahhal knew how to bring himself some happiness. Sitting in the cafés of the square was an unattainable luxury for him. But he made a habit of buying sunflower seeds and took pleasure in cracking them the whole time he walked. This was his only pleasure. Sometimes he would resort to artful means to make himself happy with other small, concocted pleasures. On days when it was cold he would carry his only coat with him, old but thick nonetheless; a short, blue coat lined with cotton and with an attached hood in which Rahhal, because he was so slight, looked like a schoolboy. Sometimes he'd carry one of the two wool sweaters he owned. He had also bought them at Sidi Mimoun, the used-clothing market next to the Youssef Bin Tachfine Mausoleum. The first one made of gray cashmere wool, the second a cardigan decorated with a black-colored rose (Hassaniya always thought that it was for girls but wouldn't dare point that out). But Rahhal would only put on the coat or the sweater after the cold had stung him. His joy was in the pain, in relishing the pain. He would put up with the cold at first. He would shiver a little. Shuddering but striving to overcome it. He would continue walking quickly until reaching Djemaa Lfnaa, and there in the square he'd put on his warm clothing and delight in it. He takes pleasure in the warmth and is happy with the sweetness of walking around the performance circles and surrounding markets wearing something that warms his bones and protects him from the cold.

But today he doesn't need a jacket, because it's hot out. It's May. The month to prepare for exams. Rahhal is wearing a short-sleeved, khaki-colored summer shirt and gray jeans as he drags his feet along in rough, locally made leather sandals. He feels a lightness in his body as he struts, feeling all the happiness in the world flow through him. He is free, and that's enough. If nightmares afflicted him during those dark hours that he came to spend between sleep and wakefulness, then it's a punishment he deserved after having overdone it by attending the meetings of the National Union of Students in Morocco, forgetting that this country had laws. "May God strengthen the rulers," his mother would always say, and here he was, having thought that the grip holding the country together had loosened recently! Praise be to God, who allowed him to learn these lessons without spending years in jail like his poor colleagues, whose sentences added up to fifty years to be spent in the cold darkness. Even though they were there by accident. Just because they hadn't signed up to do their research with Makhloufi, which meant that Si Bouchaib hadn't invited them to his farewell address. Or perhaps it was because the scholarship money had been delayed and they didn't have enough to buy a ticket to travel to their villages and the neighboring cities, so they had spent an additional day or two in Marrakech waiting for the scholarship money to come in. So, it was a hardship followed by an ordeal. They might have joined the demonstration like they always do, as a sort of diversion. Maybe they were there by mistake. And now they had cases, trials, deliberations, lawyers, and mothers coming from distant villages to visit them laden with baskets and tears.

In Djemaa Lfnaa at night, life appears brilliant. Small suns illuminate the night of the square and make it more beautiful than all the mornings there ever were. Rahhal walks around the square filled with happiness. He doesn't go back home until after Ayad,

Abdeslam, and Halima have all gone to sleep. He goes into the kitchen. A pot of tea sits where it always is. Bread and olive oil. When it's hot, Rahhal loves to drink tea cold. He drinks the first glass with pleasure. The second, with bread and oil. He always wondered what Moroccans drank before they came to rely on *atay*—tea with mint—as their national beverage, and how people used to reset their mood before tea came into the country in the nineteenth century. Rahhal eats his dinner in the dark and slinks off to bed satisfied with his lot, not bothered by the nightmares that await him.

22

WITHOUT RAISING HER EYES up to his, in a voice that was quivering yet resolute, she said:

"I've thought it through, and I'm all for it. You can propose to me anytime."

Rahhal felt as if the earth was spinning around him. But Hassaniya would add in her trembling whisper, in the same, resolute tone:

"And by the way, my mom agrees, too. It's just up to you not to take too long." It's as if the young lady is proposing to you, Squirrel.

Rahhal and Hassaniya were engrossed in typing up their thesis. All the students type their theses in shops around the college in Daoudiate, where the typists are skilled, work quickly, and make few enough mistakes to make the revision process easy. All of them had practiced typing research papers for years on typewriters, when the process of making corrections wasn't as easy as it was now with computers. But Rahhal, terrified of getting arrested, looked for another shop far from the college neighborhood. And sure enough, he found a still-unmarried college graduate near the venerable saint Sidi Abdulaziz Tebaâ's tomb, whose father had opened a small shop for her off of the family home. And she would type one page for half the price they charged in Daoudiate, too. Rahhal found it to be a good deal and didn't find any difficulty in convincing Hassaniya. But as soon as they got started, they discovered that the girl had no experience. And other than the computer and photocopying machine she had in the store, the poor girl didn't possess anything other than her kindness, her confusion, and her completely open schedule. Because Hassaniya didn't hesitate, as usual, in laying responsibility on Rahhal, she left him to bear the consequences of his choice all by himself.

That's how Rahhal came to spend his days working diligently with Rabia in the shop dictating the research paper to her word by word, line by line. He would draw her attention to orthographical issues, such as when to put a *kasra* mark on the letter hamza in the word *that*, when the hamza should be written directly on the line, and when it should be written on top of the letter *y*; he'd explain to her the difference in how to write the hamza that comes at the end of a word, the hamza that appears in the middle of a word, and the regular hamza versus the hamza that elides. In fact, he came to dictate each word to her and to clarify unambiguously whether the letter *t* at the end of the word was a regular *t* or an end *t*. After the first few pages, Rabia shed her shyness and began to explain to Rahhal that she held an undergraduate degree in Islamic studies, not Arabic literature, and that in any case, she hadn't liked Arabic since she was a young girl.

"From the time I was in elementary school, Arabic and I have had nothing to do with one another, can you believe it?"

"Unbelievable," Rahhal muttered sarcastically to himself, as if she were proficient in French, or as if she had completed her university studies of *fiqh*, Hadith, and the roots of religion in Aramaic, or as if the Qur'an had come down in the Moroccan dialect, which was the only language she was good at.

But there was no room for discussion now. Rahhal was in a jam and he had to bear the responsibility for his choice. Rabia explained to him later on that it was her mom's idea. It was she who had suggested that her father open this shop in order to get the girl out of isolation, after having spent more than five years locked up inside the house. After graduating from college, she had been in a virtual prison. An only daughter with a religious father and three brothers. After graduation, they had come to treat her as a servant, with her rushing breathlessly back and forth between them, fulfilling their never-ending requests. Isolated from the world. She'd go out with her mother from time to time to run frivolous errands. But she didn't have a choice. She'd either accompany her mother on her sporadic visits with chatty relatives or remain a prisoner at home.

She answered all possible job ads, but God had forsaken her. She failed the exam for the School of Higher Education Professors. Her application was accepted at the Teachers' College, but once again, luck was against her in the exam. In general, Rahhal fully understood why. Her difficulties with improperly typing the end *t* and the regular *t* would have made her acceptance, particularly in the Teachers' College, a crime against future generations of students!

The senior thesis, titled "The Struggles of the Bakri and Taghlib Tribes: Their Infamous and Boast-Worthy Feats in the *Mu'allaqāt* of Amru bin Kulthoum and Harith bin Hilliza," was the first opportunity given to Rabia, who, since the shop's opening a few months prior, had only typed up complaints, administrative letters, and a few sales and rental contracts. She had basically been transformed, without her even realizing it, into a public scribe. But then this shy rat shows up one morning with a golden opportunity—a thesis project—and he starts desperately negotiating the price per page. He explained to her, for example, how the pages that contained poetic verses needed to be charged a lower price because of the lower word count, and he clarified to her how the first pages that had the title, the dedication, and acknowledgments thanking the supervising research professor are not calculated into the price in the shops surrounding the college, and so forth and so on . . . But Rabia didn't care about the price; she just wanted him to stay. First of all, so she could practice. She needed something to type in order to practice— a text longer than a rental contract. Also, because her mom made it clear to her that she wasn't going to get married unless she went out into the world for people to see her, and for her to see them. As for staying at home with nothing to do but fulfill the requests of those three boorish camels—her brothers—she'd be wasting her future and her life would end up slipping away.

That's how Rahhal found himself suffering along with her. They'd spend a full hour typing a short paragraph, and whenever someone came in for a photocopy, she'd excuse herself and attend to the customer's order as if Rahhal were a guest or a friend. Sometimes the customer would ask for an envelope or a postage stamp and she'd ask Rahhal to step in for her as if he were her co-worker in the shop. And whenever her mom or one of her brothers called her about some urgent matter that needed to be taken care of at home, she'd apologize to him and scamper away through the small back door that led directly from the store to the house and disappear for a while. Sometimes she'd be gone for half an hour or more, and when she came back, she'd bring him a cup of tea and a cookie, making it clear to him that they had called her to eat breakfast; the ten o'clock breakfast they insist on in Marrakech as if it were a confirmed supererogatory act.

At first, Rahhal was irritated by all of this, but gradually he started to sit in her spot and tried typing a few words. Even a few lines to save some time, or at least not to die of boredom. But gradually, he got used to it. In fact, he found that he typed better than Rabia, and faster, too. With fewer mistakes. Thus, the situation was reversed. She began to dictate to him and he'd type. Rabia was amazed by how fast he typed, considering he had never received any training in informatics or typing on the typewriter as she had. And when Hassaniya paid them a surprise visit one afternoon, she didn't understand a thing. Even though he tried to explain the truth of the matter to her, she didn't understand. Or rather, she didn't want to understand anything from him right then. In fact, she didn't want to hear from him at all. She came the following day, too. And when she visited him in the afternoon of the third day, she seized the opportunity when Rabia excused herself for a few minutes and left them alone in the shop in order to firmly inform him that she agreed, as did her mother. All he had to do was not delay.

. . .

Rahhal didn't recall broaching the subject of tying the knot with Hassaniya, or even alluding to it in passing. Had she become able to predict the future and read minds? The thought had never occurred to him either to keep it a secret or to announce it out loud. Sure, Hassaniya visited him in his dreams sometimes, and it was true that he had never in his life been close to a woman other than her, but despite its ambiguity, their relationship remained within a clearly defined frame. It was also true that he had begun to weaken in front of her recently, and that she had begun to lash out at him from time to time, not hesitating to scold him, even when he did nothing to deserve it, but this didn't explain it.

Was she jealous of Rabia? But what did Rabia have to do with it? Rahhal didn't dare ask any more questions. But he recalled Halima and the stinging criticisms that she flogged Abdeslam with, with or without reason:

"God, my lord, women are hitched to men. And me? You've decreed for me an ass and a good-for-nothing idiot. People speak to him and he just stands there with his mouth hanging wide open!"

Had Hassaniya noticed things he hadn't? One time, Makhloufi told them about Hind, the daughter of Nu'man bin al-Mundhir: "When they asked her about the baby she was carrying from Hujjaj bin Youssef, whom she hated, she answered them, saying:

Hind is nothing more than an Arab filly
   The descendant of horses ravished by a mule.
Who, if she gives birth to a colt, then good for her,
   And if she gives birth to a mule, it is he who brought the
      mule.

Rahhal used to love these verses. For Hind was just like him, tracing people back to their animal roots. But today the two verses began to reverberate inside his head as if it were his mom's poem: Halima, daughter of Wafi, son of Hajjoub. Is he the mule, son of the mule? Had he come to resemble the mantis this much even though they weren't of the same species, nor from the same animal family? Had things happened that he hadn't known about? And then here comes Hassaniya, coming onto the scene to take control of the situation while he like his dad, Abdeslam, seems like a deaf person at a wedding procession: "An ass and a good-for-nothing idiot. People speak to him and he stands there with his mouth hanging wide open."

"What's important is that things have become clear now," Hassaniya explained in a severe tone. "With or without a degree, I'll start working at the beginning of this coming September in Emad Qatifa's school in Massira, and I can guarantee you an opportunity to work with me there, Rahhal. But no one will prevent you from taking all of the possible examinations. If you can get into the School of Higher Education Professors, that would be great, and I would go with you wherever you're appointed. But if you pass the examination for primary school teachers, I won't leave my job to wander around hamlets, small towns, and remote villages with you. Get it?"

.   .   .

But Halima didn't understand. She didn't understand anything about it. The full package, nearly impossible for someone who came from such a long line of people with bad luck: an undistinguished, slight wife, but with a degree like her son. A mother-in-law prepared to welcome the groom into her home to live along with his wife. A job opportunity presented to her son beside his wife in Emad Qatifa's school in Massira. A motorbike that the school's owner would buy for them to ensure that they could commute easily between Mouassine in the Old City and Massira. What more could anyone want? Especially with an unlucky son like Rahhal, who hadn't managed to pass either the exams for School of Higher Education Professors or the exam for the regional educational center, not to mention the College for Primary School Teachers, to which he had shown some hesitation in applying, and they hadn't even accepted his application. For all of these reasons, from the beginning, Halima considered the whole idea of Hassaniya a golden opportunity that would save her son from the vortex of nothingness, even though she didn't understand why Hassaniya's mother had felt compelled to use all of these "satanic means," which ranged from magic spells to sorcery, in order to cause the Squirrel to fall into the marriage trap. If only she had come to her from the start. She would have sent him to her bound hand and foot on the back of a donkey! But this didn't deserve all of those incantations and machinations that caused Rahhal's eyelids to droop from sleeplessness that lasted for weeks. Had she mixed cattle dung with hyena brains for him? Or had she hired one of the jinns' servants for him from a faqih specializing in the magic of procurement? Did she get him with wax or with pepper? With salt or with frankincense? *Marrakechi women are truly incredible, with all sorts of magic running swifter than blood through their veins,* thought Halima, dazzled to her core about the women of the Red City, amazed with everything that was happening, but satisfied nonetheless with this lot that would open her life up to something new, that would deliver her from the monotony of the previous years.

According to her simple way of thinking, Halima had hoped that Rahhal would remain by her side in Marrakech, looking for any suitable job for himself rather than go as far away as possible as a teacher in some forsaken village in one of the oases of Zagoura or Errachidia or Tata, or in a hamlet hanging from the peaks of the Atlas Mountains that always promised cold and snow. His father, Abdeslam, the person they had in mind in the proverb about lethargy and lack of resourcefulness, left the land of his forefathers in the plains of Abda, no doubt at the behest of Halima, and fled to Marrakech, the City of the Seven Saints, so how could Rahhal, who had studied and actually understood things, leave Marrakech to waste the bloom of his youth holding on in the mountains or spat out like a pit in the deserts of the south?

"This is just me, and I'm only a woman who never went to school and doesn't understand anything. I wouldn't like it at all for you. Even if they ask for you and want you in the School for Teachers and shame you into it, my son, Rahhal, I wouldn't let you go there. Where would you go? Some shithole? Better for you to live with this little hedgehog you brought me without asking my advice than wandering around lost in deserts and wastelands."

■　■　■

A hedgehog . . . Did you say "a hedgehog"?

Oh, how could he have missed it? How did he not notice that this girl with the small ears and the head that almost couldn't be distinguished from the neck had the features of a hedgehog?

For months now, Rahhal had been chasing after Hassaniya's animal by looking at her face, in the way she spoke and her manner of silence, and the tone of what she said, in her walk and the way she sat, in everything she did; chasing her in books and dreams . . . all to no avail. Now, in this spontaneous outburst, Halima has drawn Hassaniya's animal out from its burrow with no effort at all, quite by accident.

You'll bury what years remain of your life in the embrace of a hedgehog, Rahhal. In the prickly embrace of an animal you didn't discover until after you set the date for the marriage contract to be signed. People are blessed with fresh, tender meat on the matrimonial bed, whereas you'll prepare your meat only to get pricked by quills, even though Rahhal had become a bit used to the quills of his slight hedgehog in the college library when she would prick him with or without reason with her injurious words. Just as he was familiar with her angry outbursts, during which she would continuously shoot her needles at him like arrows. You've become used to it, Squirrel. So who's to say that the ties of love that wind their way between you two on the matrimonial bed won't release your hedgehog from the burrow of her innate caution and that she won't voluntarily grant you her body and soul? At which time you'll pluck her rose as is your right, after you've shown that you can endure and tolerate the quills. You'll pass your hand over your hedgehog's small belly to find pleasure in the softness of her fur. The hedgehog's fur is soft, Rahhal, putting aside the quills. And he'll know how to convince Hassaniya that he isn't a dog or a fox—so she won't resort to unleashing her quills in his face—but rather that he's just a gentle, mild-mannered squirrel, nothing to be afraid of.

Oh, daughter of Wafi . . . Oh, Halima . . . Finally, you have solved the puzzle. Things had become clear now, and the Squirrel wouldn't lack the means to tame the Hedgehog.

23

THE AUTUMN WINDS blow over Marrakech's gardens, parks, and trees as September draws to an end. The entrance exam period has passed and Rahhal's and Hassaniya's friends who passed the exams have enrolled in training schools for primary and secondary school teachers, while those who flunked have gone back to throw themselves into the embrace of a deadly emptiness. Students went on with their university lives, embarking upon a new season of lectures, discussion circles, and endless cafeteria fights, whereas those who failed were deprived even of the routine of attending classes. Hung out to dry like clothes on the line, blowing in the wind, a sense of worthlessness gnawing away at them. As for Rahhal, he found himself face-to-face with what Hassaniya had suggested. He had no other option. And he couldn't have hoped for a better solution himself.

He stood ill at ease and submissive at the door of the principal's office, and after Hassaniya asked if he could enter, Emad Qatifa himself rushed forward to welcome him.

"Please . . . please . . . Mr. . . . Mr. . . . Rahhal, right?"

" . . . "

"Please, come in."

In a show of gratitude, Rahhal just nodded. He was nervous and flustered, unable to raise his eyes up to those of Emad, who seemed nice, while Hiyam, the actual principal of the school, remained sitting at her desk. She was totally indifferent. She didn't stir in her chair at all. She was silently watching the scene with an expression that moved between severity and detachment.

The meeting ended quickly, quicker than Rahhal expected, and without him having said a single word. He found himself in the courtyard of the house that had been turned into a school, having gotten the job right then and there, but not yet understanding exactly what his job was, or what exactly the position entailed. The school had a teaching staff whose names, along with the details of the subjects they taught, were posted on an educational chart hanging to the right of the principal's office, and Rahhal's picture was not among them. The school had a doorman, who stood at the gate washing Hiyam's car, watching over Hassaniya's motorbike and the teachers' bicycles, and selling single cigarettes to passers-by, so even this position was not available. What was left, then? It was clear that Rahhal would remain leaning up in the corner of the courtyard like a bench player on a soccer team. He would remain there until things became clear. Watching the students come and go, making himself available to everyone: Emad Qatifa, the owner of the whole thing; his wife, Hiyam, the principal of the school; and her vice principal and private secretary, Hassaniya Ben Mymoune.

·   ·   ·

When Emad Qatifa agreed to Hassaniya's suggestion of employing her husband along with her at the Atlas Cubs Private Elementary School, all he wanted was a guarantee that she'd take the job. There was a consensus inside the family council, headed personally by Qatifa Sr., that their neighbor's only daughter was qualified for this task because of her high moral fiber and university education, and that she was also more capable than a stranger to deal with Hiyam's mood swings. The condition that Hassaniya adroitly brought to the table in the form of a suggestion resulted in his de facto hiring, pending further clarification as to what he would do in the future. Thus, Rahhal received this opportunity without Emad or Hiyam having to worry themselves about the exact nature of his job. He found himself as an employee with no defined tasks. Besides his daily job driving the motorbike the school had given to Hassaniya, and outside of taking Hiyam's orders to the neighboring café and bringing back lunch sandwiches for himself and Hassaniya from the restaurants on Dakhla Avenue in Massira, Rahhal didn't really do anything of note. He would watch the students come and go, monitor this or that classroom whenever the instructor would go to the bathroom or head to the principal's office, and would waste the large part of his remaining time yawning in the school courtyard, lazy and resigned.

Hassaniya's boldness with Rahhal and the sharpness with which she occasionally addressed him emboldened Hiyam to do so as well, and then some. But as soon as she discovered that the man was not looking for respect, nor was he concerned with issues of dignity, she left him alone. For Hiyam absolutely loved petty disputes and stubbornly engaging in little skirmishes, and she had raised the fabrication of problems and picking of fights to an art form. But Rahhal was boring and weak. He wasn't the type who could keep up with her in that domain. And because Hiyam was a gracious winner, she despised him to her very core, not even giving him the time of day.

When Hassaniya spoke to her about his typing skills on the computer, Hiyam casually suggested that her husband open the building's locked garage for Rahhal, buy a computer and photocopying machine, and put them at his disposal. That's how he took on writing and copying all of the reports and private administrative documents in the school, as well as the teachers' documents and departmental exams, as long as the shop remained open to all. This would provide publicity for the shop and the school. With this arrangement, they found a real job for Rahhal to justify the salary he had been receiving for the past four months.

Emad, who welcomed the suggestion, also thought of negotiating a contract with Maroc Telecom that would allow him to open a *téléboutique* in the spacious garage. Thus, Rahhal found himself in front of a computer and photocopying machine with three telephones attached to the left-hand wall of the shop, open to the public.

∎ ∎ ∎

Minding the telephones won't require too much of you, Rahhal, besides exchanging the customers' bills for dirham coins, then emptying the bellies of these phones of the coins they held at the end of the day. Other than that, you'll have all the time you need to listen in on the lives of others from behind your rickety, wooden desk. "Hello, Naima?" "Hello,

Hajj?" "Hello, Hajja?" "Hello, my beautiful." "Hello, my love." "Hello."
"Hello." "You're hanging up on me, you whore?" "You remember what
you did!" Endless conversations. Provide the change to the customers and
enjoy yourself as you listen in on their conversations, on their lives. Pho-
tocopying is a mechanical procedure no less mindless than watching over
this or that classroom while waiting for a teacher to come back from the
bathroom. As for using the computer, typing on it and caressing the key-
board, there's no pleasure like it: clicking the t *with your index finger, the*
ring finger caressing the m, *the middle finger pressing firmly on the* n, *a*
light push on the b, *then running the pinky finger softly over the belly of*
the emphatic t. His fingers dancing and flying across the keyboard,
Rahhal follows what they do with his eyes fixed on the screen. He is
filled with a strange feeling of pride comparable only to the feeling
he got when he learned to drive his uncle Ayad's motorbike right
when they moved in to live with him in his house in Moukef. But
driving *here* is more enjoyable, and safer. Driving on a clear, white,
well-lit stretch. No jammed streets or bikes running red lights. No
buses polluting the air with their heavy black smoke or the roar of
their engines. No pedestrians walking outside of the crosswalks.
No honking car horns. Safe driving on a highway of light.

"Photocopy, please."

Sluggishly, Rahhal would get up. He'd turn on the photocopy
machine. Irritated, he'd take the document. He waits a bit for the
machine to warm up. Then: zzzzzz. He completes the task then
returns to the keyboard. But gradually he began to steal glances at
the documents. He'd look them over a bit as a way to kill time while
he waited for the machine to get going. But with time, he would
find that there was some enjoyment in making copies. This encoun-
ter with strangers, peeking into their lives through the documents
they would give to him was not devoid of pleasure, really. The task
wasn't as boring as he had first imagined it.

But let's set all of that aside.

Let's go back to our winged horse of light.

Rahhal's fingers became increasingly light and delicate during
their flights over the keyboard. He felt deeply grateful to Rabia. He

had benefitted more in the few weeks he spent at her side in her small shop in Sidi Abdelaziz than he had with Makhloufi, the other Arabic literature professors, and the discussion circles of the NUSM. How happy he was with his machine! He began to soar higher and higher, day after day. He finally found the letter *dhal* hidden among the numbers and figured out how to extract the *shadda* sign from its hiding place after his search for it over the last few days had completely exhausted him. The exclamation mark was still seemingly impossible, but he would not rest until he dragged it out of its hiding place, too. He would use the shift key and move all around the keyboard until he found it . . . Finally. Eureka! Eureka! He had accidently pressed on the number 1 and the shift key at the same time and there was the exclamation point, appearing before him slender and tall, standing there self-confidently on top of its small, solid base, raising its eyebrows and sticking its tongue out at him.

Way to go, Rahhal . . .

Drag the mouse by its light tail and continue your magnificent wanderings in and out of words and sentences. Align the paragraphs well. Type the title in large, prominent letters. Change the background color. Get rid of the extra spaces. Line up the margins and the blank spaces of the paragraphs. Use the spell-check while you type . . .

"One photocopy, please, my friend."

"Huh?"

"A photocopy of the card, if you wouldn't mind?"

She was tall and beautiful. Wearing a turquoise jellaba à la mode with macramé and silk threads. Her hair was jet black. Her eyes were dark. And her face was sad.

> Name: Nafissa Gitout
> Birthdate: 3/14/1971
> Profession: None
> Address: Douar Aït Mohammed, Commune (. . .) District of
> Sefrou
> This card is valid from 8/13/1989 to 8/12/1999

But what are you doing in Marrakech, Nafissa? Why did you come from Sefrou, the land of cedar and cherry trees? The land of cherries, the Cherry Festival, and the Beauty Queen of the Cherries Pageant? What is it that brought you here, you with the sad eyes? Work? What work, while you've listed "none" as your profession? What work, Nafissa? What's a beautiful girl like you doing in a city more than 250 miles from her hometown?

Rahhal was sure to survey the documents that were handed to him with piercing eyes before copying them. But some of the important information escaped his memory.

For example, Nafissa, the name of the hamlet and the region are included, but the commune is missing. Was she from an urban or rural commune? From Sefrou, the city, or from Bhalil? From Hermoumou or Bir Tam? He no longer remembers. That's why he made sure not to be so careless with such things in the future. Next time, he'd be sure to make an extra copy for himself—secretly, of course—which he would examine carefully and at his leisure after the customer has left.

Thus, a fabulous archive began to gather in the front of Rahhal's desk: identification cards, passports, residency certificates, marriage contracts, birth certificates and others for death, proxies for buying and others for selling, work certificates, small paper slips from teachers, educational inspectors' reports, exams from the instructors of the Atlas Cubs and the surrounding schools.

Rahhal would enjoy reading those documents, deconstructing their components and thinking deeply about what they contained. And the documents that interested him or excited him, or that made him feel at ease, he would choose them to practice on the computer. He'd place them to his left and move the mouse with his right hand. He'd open a new page in Word and start typing.

24

RAHHAL'S AND HASSANIYA'S wedding celebration wasn't a celebration at all. It was a day like any other and a night that held more misery than joy. A small banquet prepared by Hassaniya's mother, Oum Eid, in her house in Mouassine—beef with prunes, chicken with olives and lemon, and a tray of tea with the Ghorayba cookies with almonds and Gazelles' Horns that go along with it. That's it, nothing more. There were no drummers or *ghita* performers, no *daqayqia* band or *laâbat* troupe. Just Abdeslam; his brother, Ayad; and three of his fellow Qur'an reciters from the Bab El Khemis Cemetery, in addition to two notary witnesses. Hajj Qatifa Sr. was there for a few minutes. He greeted the groom's family, gave his blessings to the marriage, and personally supervised the completion of the marriage contract. He remained standing there until the two notaries heard his declaration of assent and the acceptance of two spouses, whereupon they certified it. He then paid them and left. Halima the Pelican ululated alone nonstop like a crazy woman. Sharp, continuous trills that went on for so long it seemed that they would never stop. She continued to trill and trill until she realized that everyone was staring at her, including the mother of the bride, so she swallowed her long tongue and sat watching this gloomy gathering, which looked more like a funeral than a wedding. The idea of a funeral would bear down even more on Hassaniya when Abdeslam and his friends suddenly raised their voices and recited:

Ya-Sin
By the Wise Koran,
thou art truly among the Envoys.

"Couldn't they have come up with something besides Sura Ya-Sin? Haven't they memorized anything else?" she whispered disapprovingly in Rahhal's ear.

"But it's the beautiful essence of the Qur'an. Everything has a heart, Hassaniya, and Sura Ya-Sin is the heart of the Qur'an, my dear . . ."

"Neither heart, nor kidney, nor spleen. It's my wedding night, so what's wrong with Sura Ta-Ha, for example? What's wrong with *the All-merciful; taught the Qur'an?* Man, let them recite *perish the hands* . . . if they want to, but Sura Ya-Sin?! This one's recited at funerals, at the graveside, and over the head of the dying, not at celebrations and weddings. Mark my words, though, this will be his last, Rahhal. If your father places so much as a foot inside this house after the scandal of tonight, my name isn't Hassaniya Ben Mymoune!"

The Sura Ya-Sin incident was enough to transform the quasi-wedding into a quasi-funeral. The two notaries took their leave and Oum Eid, who had noticed her one and only daughter's change in mood, began to put out the lights and gather up the tables. The bride left angrily for her small room to change her clothes and wipe the heavy makeup she wasn't accustomed to wearing from her face. Ayad understood that they should leave, so he led his brother and his two friends out. Halima was the last one to go. She took her time kissing Oum Eid. Loud kisses, one after the other. Ten on the left cheek and thirteen on the right. Oum Eid kissed her back even more loudly, resulting in what sounded like a popping sound (she was only doing air kisses).

. . .

"Get up, my boy, and go find your wife. Come on."

Oum Eid spoke to him with a wide, goading smile, in a tone not free of condemnation after she noticed that Rahhal remained withdrawn in the corner of the salon with his hands folded together like a schoolboy in class. *What's this idiot waiting for? The evening affair has broken up and his mother has gone on her way. Does he think I'm going to serve him couscous, or what?!*

"Get up, my dear, go ahead."

Flustered, the Squirrel got up. He took a hesitant step toward Hassaniya's bedroom, the only bedroom in the small house, next to the salon. Oum Eid's closet was smaller than a cell and narrower than a booth, with no door at all. But, on her own accord, she had chosen to make do with it as soon as Hassaniya got her high school degree and enrolled in the university. Thus, she had let her daughter, the university student, spread out in the room as she liked.

"Go in, my love, go in. Hassaniya's now your wife. According to the custom of God and His Prophet. Go in. Don't be shy."

The scenarios began to press up against one another in Rahhal's head as he stepped toward Hassaniya's room. Everything he had thought about, everything he had prepared, and what he had read in the book he had bought from one of the used-book sellers in Bab Doukkala on sex—the rules of marital intercourse, and the morals of intimate relations—everything bunched up in his head until his breathing became labored and erratic. He had drawn up a number of scenarios, carefully laid out his first steps, and memorized more than ten romantic lines he'd need to soften the mood. But everything collided in his head now and he didn't know where to begin.

"Knock, knock."

"Come in, Mother."

"No, it's Rahhal."

"Come in."

" . . . "

"I told you, come in. Come in, Rahhal . . ."

Hassaniya was scantily clad and reclining on her side on the bed. A bed made of cheap pine, but a bed all the same, not a mattress thrown on the room's bare floor, Squirrel. The two pillows looked soft, Rabat-style embroidery decorating their pure-white covers. Cheap embroidery done by machine, not by hand. The lower half of Hassaniya's body was wrapped in a blue, Mazafil blanket with a picture of a grinning lion on it. Hassaniya had undone the tie that she had wrapped her hair in during the party. Rahhal was seeing the Hedgehog's hair for the first time. Hair ironed hastily that revealed more imperfections than it concealed. Short, kind of frizzy, dry and brittle. It looked black, or brown. Rather, between black and dark brown. As for her light nightgown, which revealed her small, narrow shoulders and part of her skinny chest, he couldn't make out its color. It was dark, too. Almost the same color as her hair. The kind of nightgown that . . .

"Turn out the light, Rahhal."

He tried to be charming. It was his chance to set the mood and try out the methods of sexual diplomacy that the book's author had devoted an entire chapter to.

"Why should I turn out the light, Hassaniya? I want to inspect my land, to lay eyes on where I'll sow and plant my seed. To wander around my garden. To see the pomegranate ripen and the apple redden; to survey the patch of mint before I water it . . ."

"What mint? What shit are you talking about? Rahhaaaaal! I told you to turn out the light."

Her tone was sharp this time. And Rahhal, who had held out hope that there would be caresses and whispers, found himself jumping in fright and going back to turn out the light before taking a step into the darkness toward the bed. The battery that he had made such an effort to charge over the previous days was empty all of a sudden. Even the coitus prayer he had memorized fizzled away.

You are now in the Hedgehog's chamber, so be good and patient, and pray to the High and Mighty that you don't prick yourself on her quills, Squirrel.

"My Lord. May God allow this night to go well."

. . .

When Rahhal slipped in beside Hassaniya, he discovered that she had taken off her nightgown. She undid the bra, removed it from her small breasts, and leaned back gently. Even her breath left her. She was as still as a corpse. With a blind hand he touched the body lying next to him, which was like a stagnant pond, the water of which he found warm nonetheless. Rubbing the Hedgehog's belly along with her soft fur got him ready. He felt between his legs with the other hand. The sword was drawn and ready to thrust.

Still, he would have loved to say something tender before embracing Hassaniya and starting to touch, stroke, rub, and kiss, but he was afraid of receiving a disappointing response.

Better that you work in silence, Rahhal. He removed the necktie that was choking him, his summer shirt and pants, and finally his underwear. For the first time in his life he found himself naked before living flesh. Real, soft flesh, the likes of which he used to imagine during a wet dream, or when he was thinking about Atiqa the Cow's behind as he masturbated. He remembered the book. He secretly cursed Satan and remembered the book. The corpse-like body next to him was lifeless. Neither a sound nor a movement. He could take his time trying to recall what he had read. He remembered the third chapter, the most important chapter of the book—and its most enjoyable—where the author explained in excruciating detail the difference between the clitoris and the vagina. He clarified how the clitoris is a woman's essential sexual organ, not the vagina. A woman's clitoris becomes erect just like the penis; touching it, rubbing it, and caressing it brings the woman to orgasm and makes penetration easier. Rahhal pressed his left index finger below Hassaniya's belly. He searched for the patch of mint. He found it. He took his hedgehog by surprise and inserted his finger into her, then . . .

"Ay . . . ay . . ."

It seemed that he hadn't studied his moves well enough. Had he failed in finding the right spot? Or was it that the speed with which he had plunged his finger in had made his movement too rough, not at all gentle? In any case, he'd take another shot. He'd try to slip his finger in more delicately. Like in the book.

"Look, please. Doing it as if we're in some sort of a disgusting and bizarre porn flick, no way. Do what's required by the Sunna and as the Prophet has shown us and get your ass out of here!"

Look, Rahhal. You wanted to dissipate her fears by caressing her, and to arouse her until her little hedgehog secreted the moisture the author had discussed, thus making penetration easier. But she doesn't want it. He remembered the position as described in the

Sunna that was mentioned in his comprehensive book: he lifted her legs up to her shoulders and began to insert his little squirrel gently into her burrow. He was bewildered, scared of any angry reaction from her. But she returned to her stillness and, underneath him, played the part of the corpse.

"Heh . . . heh . . . heh . . . heh . . ."

It wasn't a scream or a moan. It wasn't the sound of a hedgehog, for this sounded more like a nursing baby screaming. It wasn't a scream of pain (women might scream at the top of their lungs when their hymen is torn). And it wasn't a moan (the moan is a sound Rahhal knew well. For Halima, who was always sick or pretending to be sick when she was feeling well, had made the moan something especially familiar to his ear). It was something else. The sound of a low cry. She repeated it four times then pushed him off of her. He had emptied himself for the first time into a real well, but without feeling a thing. Besides feeling warm, he didn't feel a thing. That trembling that would shake his very being during his wet dreams or when he ejaculated while masturbating wasn't there this time. Something was missing for him tonight. Is this what you had been wishing for, Rahhal? Where was the convulsion you read about in the book? The convulsion of sexual intercourse, which raises the one experiencing it up to the highest of heights for a few seconds. That climax that a person reaches in ecstasy before falling lightly, intoxicated, back to the ground while thanking God for the pleasure He has granted. Not a thing there. Just words in books. And what about the blood? Darkness enveloped the scene and the corpse was still. *I just want to look at it closely. I'll wipe away the blood and steal a glance just to find a bit of joy with myself.* But she didn't respond, nor did she seem ready to come out of her funereal stillness.

Ya-Sin; By the wise Qur'an.

Why Abdeslam? Couldn't you have found a chapter other than that one in your arsenal, Dad?

25

THERE'S NO DOUBT that Hajj Qatifa's prayers played a decisive role in the success of his son's business ventures. Emad's burro had come to a stop on the threshold of his high school degree. It was clear from his disgraceful grades that success wasn't guaranteed, even if he were to repeat the year. And even if he did cross this threshold, he would find an even greater difficulty registering for an appropriate university course. Therefore, on the advice of his oldest son, Dr. Abdelmoula, the Hajj got him a job at one of his shops in the Semmarine market. After a training period, which lasted a year and a half, Emad left the Old City for the new neighborhood of Massira (again arranged by his father), where hordes of mid-level employees had been heading since the end of the 1980s. He started out with a small shop selling fabric before opening a larger, two-story shop, where he sold office and home furniture and décor. Emad, who had failed in his studies, surprised everyone by using his natural business sense to gather a wide customer base from the segment of employees who were more concerned with being able to pay in installments and lines of credit than with brands and quality of materials. So, his business was brisk, and his operation expanded in a way that even surprised Hajj Qatifa. Within just four years, Emad had moved to a spacious building next to the Massira overpass, where he designated a department for fabric (the family business that could never be abandoned) and a second department for furnishings: bedrooms, leather couches, rugs, carpets, dining tables, dressers, and all sorts of lighting, ranging from enormous crystal chandeliers to red Chinese lanterns.

It used to make Emad happy whenever a person he knew entered his store—from family members and people from the old neighborhood in Mouassine who had moved to Massira, to friends from high school. He would welcome classmates, in particular, with exceptional warmth, and extend special lines of credit to them that one could otherwise only dream of. It was his way of rehabilitating his image in front of classmates who had done well, and who had witnessed his academic failure. After his old classmates had graduated from high school, they continued their training here or there for two or three years, four in the case of those who earned university degrees, then got petty positions that allowed them to purchase apartments in affordable housing units in Massira, according to the "buying at the cost of renting" formula, most of the time splitting the cost with their wives, who also worked. They now faced the challenge of furnishing these apartments, and Emad was at their service, of course. He generously suggested all sorts of ways of working with them. Happy to make them happy. He'd take a little of their savings and open up a comfortable payment plan for them. After some months, the classmates would bring their friends who were in the same situations, with the same needs. And always the same payment schedule for new customers, always the comfortable payment plan. This recipe was Emad's winning ticket. He became the king of furnishings in Massira and the surrounding neighborhoods. The king of installments, open to all payment-plan options. It was a successful formula, then. All of Emad's wholesome recipes in business were intuited in his heart, and he arrived at them generously and without prior planning. And then there was the matter of the "parental blessing," and the prayers of the Hajj and the Hajja, of course.

The school was something else. It wasn't so much a purely commercial project as it was a token of Emad's love for his wife. Hiyam was related to him on his mother's side. Her father, Hajj Maâti Blayghi, was an important merchant in the Semmarine market and a close friend of his father's. Her sweet smile had bewitched him, as did her large, dark eyes. Her distracted look seduced him even as a child. Her arrogant aversion to the children of the family hurt him and her fickleness scared him, but he got involved with her anyway, and the rest is history. He knew her difficult moods well and knew that loving her would be even more difficult, but his stupid heart didn't consult with him the day he fell into the pocket of her short-sleeved, rose-colored school frock. Hiyam was four years younger than Emad, but he continued to love her as she got older. He watched her breasts grow round, her backside fill out, and her body firm up. She had gotten taller, and she grew well into her own body. Her eyes were wide and her voice loud. Her laugh rang out, dripping honey, making it even more inviting. He would watch her in the neighborhood and at school. He would anticipate family gatherings during holidays so he could sit next to her at the table and try to brush up against her body, as innocent children do (with an innocence that became increasingly more wicked year after year; a pure, innocent wickedness; the wickedness of someone in love who has lost all volition). Despite that, Emad knew how to bury his love deep inside without saying a thing. He remained in love with Hiyam without words or letters or allusions. Just like that, in silence.

After Hiyam's graduation from the regional educational center as a middle school teacher of French, Emad proposed to her. His success in business brushed aside his embarrassment of failing to obtain the high school degree that Hiyam had pulled off with distinction. The bride would spend only one year as a teacher in one of the middle schools in the Marrakech suburbs. Then came the idea of opening a school that would allow the daughter of Hajj Maâti Blayghi, wife of Emad Qatifa (the business expert), to enter the door that most suited her training: an institute for private education, benefitting from the tax exemptions that the government had put in place to attract private investors and businessmen to invest in the education and training sectors.

The first year was somewhat difficult because of financial stumbling and numerous other problems. Hiyam found it difficult running the school and managing her relationships with the teachers at the same time. She didn't understand that it wasn't necessary to like them or to find them pleasant in order for them to work with her.

But when Hassaniya came along, the situation changed. Oum Eid's daughter knew how to make things right again and reset the work rhythm in the school. She interacted seriously with the teachers, was stern with the students, and most importantly, she knew how to satisfy Hiyam's vanity and gain her trust. Her mysterious, tiny husband secluded himself in the neighboring garage. It seemed that he enjoyed pretty decent foot traffic in the shop, especially at the end of the semester, when he'd be surrounded by students of Arabic literature, law, history, and Islamic studies with final theses that needed to be typed. The important thing was that he was there. He worked as a typist for the school, a public scribe for the citizens, and a thesis typist for the students. And let's not forget the driver's cap. Motorbike driver. Hassaniya's private driver between Mouassine and Massira.

As for Emad, he left the big house in Mouassine and bought a small villa in Massira. He settled in with his wife and plunged headlong into a happy routine. A successful business and a wife he truly loved. But love, like patience, has limits. Therefore, he would try to distract himself from her love a little bit and distract *her* with the Atlas Cubs School. He had a nice, social group befitting his position. Two lawyers, an engineer, a professor at the university, and the manager of a five-star hotel. The group would get together every Wednesday and Saturday evening at the piano bar of the hotel their friend managed on Boulevard de France. As for Friday, that was a sacred day. Those from the old neighborhood had to see Emad and his brothers in their white jellabas (sometimes in red tarbooshes, too) in the first rows of the Mouassine Mosque perform the Friday prayer next to Hajj Qatifa before they would head together to the big house, where a large dish of seven-vegetable couscous awaited them. The avidity Emad would devote to the Friday prayer in Mouassine was no less than the passion with which he approached the late-night soirées with his social group. Even the evenings he would pass with Hiyam at home, wandering around and flipping through the channels from American films to Arab series, weren't at all boring. Their beautiful calm and familiar routine—which Hiyam would sometimes ruin with her jealous fits—were no less enjoyable than spending late nights out. Every type of companionship has its special flavor. And Emad knew how to enjoy every available bit of free time he had. Thus, he became a permanent member of the Happy People's Club.

26

THE MILD STOMACHACHE that used to squeeze Rahhal's bowels in the presence of Wafiq Daraai at the college seized him whenever he caught sight of Hajj Qatifa's son parking his car in front of the shop. Emad was of medium build, wide-shouldered. His eyes shone with a clear friendliness. His smile was kind; a wide smile in the middle of his face that gave him a special charm. Emad's face was always clean-shaven, and his hair, combed in a naturally modern fashion, was always cut short. He usually had the top buttons of his shirts open in the summertime to allow his chest hair to stick out. His shoes were Italian. In the springtime he wore Lacoste jackets and his winter jackets looked like the ones movie stars wore. A gold quartz watch never leaves his right wrist. But Rahhal had never seen him before in a suit and tie. Emad made it a habit of raising his hand in greeting whenever he passed in front of Rahhal. He'd greet him with a perfunctory wave, his wide smile lighting up his pear-shaped face, then he'd saunter toward the door of the school. He wouldn't enter Rahhal's shop, nor would he stop in front of him, as if this shop had no place among his projects and enterprises. Emad wasn't interested in the *téléboutique*. Nor did he even get involved with the school's affairs. His visits became few and far between once he was satisfied that the project was standing on its own two feet and had begun to make its way. So, when he made an appearance at the Atlas Cubs School from time to time, it was to visit Hiyam.

As for what exactly Hassaniya's husband was doing in his den, this was the last thing on Emad's mind. Even though the contract with Maroc Telecom was in Emad Qatifa's name, Rahhal was the one who followed up with the agency on all of the accounts that had to do with the telephone calls' earnings and the percentage of the profit they were due. The sum total of earnings, including what the computer and photocopy machine brought in, would be reviewed by Hassaniya along with him. Rahhal wasn't working himself to death, though. For no matter what, he would get paid a monthly salary, regardless of whether the earnings went up or down. Despite that, it seemed that everyone was satisfied with his yield, including Hiyam.

It was difficult for Rahhal—and his shop—to remain outside of the visual range of Hiyam, who would not be so generous as to grant him even a small, fickle greeting. It seemed that she wore special glasses, and he was always just outside of their frames. At first, he was bent on anticipating the times she would come and go. He'd get up from his seat and prepare to put himself at her disposal. Who knows? Maybe she'd need him for something. But she wouldn't even look in his direction. She wouldn't see him. Even when she'd call him in to have him take care of some tasks—typing some administrative correspondence and pedagogical notes or making copies of a bunch of documents—she would speak to him coldly, without looking up. Did she look down on him? Perhaps. But despite that, Rahhal didn't feel any malice toward her. He would just think of Ali bin al-Jahm and recall his famous poetic verse:

Wild cows' eyes between Rusafa and the bridge
Rekindled my passion from where I know, and where I
know not.

But put Rusafa aside for now. We're not in Baghdad! We're in the Massira neighborhood of Marrakech. There's no Rusafa here. No Tigris River or bridge. Just the overpass spanning Dakhla Avenue. Why was it was built? None of the neighborhood's residents knew. An overpass with no rhyme or reason. As for the eyes that have slain you, Rahhal, they belong to a wild cow that roams among the cubs. A wild cow named Hiyam. It made you sad that Hajj Maâti Blayghi didn't choose the name Maha (which means "wild cow") for her. You were even more saddened because her stupid husband, who gathered up the cubs of Massira in a private school as a token

The Butterfly on Its Way to the Slaughterhouse | 115

of his love and passion for her, made no effort at all to figure out her animal, never treating her as a wild cow. Perhaps he had never even heard of Ibn al-Jahm and his verse, which would allow him to aim the proper poetic arrow at her.

Rahhal's affection for Comrade Atiqa's body in the days of the discussion circles in college, and the Rat and Gerbil twins clinging to her udder during the circles and in the cafeteria made him pay attention since then to how natural it was for the male members of the rodent class to cling so tightly to the female members of the cow family. The wild cow is a bovine. Wild bovines are not like milk cows, however much they may resemble them. Maybe she's a horse. A beautiful, white horse . . . "He has the flanks of a fawn, and legs like an ostrich" (as the prince of poets, Imru' al-Qays, once put it). She's a horse with the head of a fawn. The wild cow is a horse-fawn. The mare that was so exuberant in your dreams, Rahhal, the one that you thought was Hassaniya—the same crystal-white one, the same one with the well-proportioned body, and the tail that ended with a tuft of hair—it was Hiyam visiting your dreams before you had even met her, one time with you thinking she was a fawn and another time a horse. And here you were foolishly waiting for that taut, swelling body underneath Hassaniya's jellaba. How dim-witted you are!

At home, every Saturday night at around 10 p.m., Rahhal's weekly festivities would begin, as long as the first signs of the monthly bleeding didn't honor them with their presence and ruin everything. After turning out the light and removing his clothes in the dark, with the Hedgehog playing the role of a corpse underneath him, Rahhal would close his eyes and begin the Wild Cow chase. No sooner do his eyes meet the large, devastating eyes of the Wild Cow, even before passing his hand over her wonderful, attractive neck ("the sword precedes the censure," as they say), does he quickly empty his fluid into Hassaniya's well. Nonetheless, he tries to gaze for a bit longer into her dark eyes, drawing the gazelle to him and burying his face between her breasts, but the small hedgehog couldn't stand the weight of Rahhal's body on top of her, especially after having just finished his task and watering the mint patch. Thus, she brings out her quills and proceeds to prick him so he'll get up off of her. All of this happens in total silence. Rahhal doesn't even hear the faint "heh, heh" from Hassaniya anymore.

Oh, Ibn al-Jahm . . .

> Not everyone who drives the steeds has control over them
> And not everyone who causes something to happen can
> be said to have caused it.

"That was nice. Sleep tight, my darling," Rahhal would whisper submissively before turning off the light. Not the light that hurts Hassaniya's eyes when she's lying down underneath the pressure of the naked squirrel's body. Rather, it was another warm, intimate light that Rahhal would ignite for a brief moment while pursuing his wild cow, bolting around the hedgehog sanctuary.

. . .

While Rahhal came to accept Hiyam's fickle moods, putting up with her even when she yelled in his face for the most trivial reasons, Emad brought a lump to his throat.

They say that "smiling in the face of your brother is a form of charity." This idiot imagines that he's giving me charity with his smile. He thinks I feel happy when he passes in front of the shop, waving to me as if he's the crown prince. He plays the role of the compassionate boss and the humble chief. His game may have fooled the teachers of the school, who have come to tell tales of his generosity and mythic humility, but it won't fool me.

Rahhal cannot forget that he holds a degree, a diploma in Arabic language and literature from the School of Humanities and Social Sciences at Cadi Ayyad University in Marrakech. True, it was without distinction, and hadn't allowed him to get a position in the education field, but it was a degree nonetheless. An advanced degree recognized by the state. Emad, on the other hand, couldn't get into university in the first place to even dream of earning such a degree; he didn't even do well enough to get his high school diploma. *And today, because he's Qatifa's son, I'm an employee of his. He pays me, not because he's convinced of my potential, but rather, because I'm Hassaniya's husband and the one who drives the motorbike he bought for her so she could be here at the appointed time—half an hour before the students arrive for class—whereas his wife doesn't come in until after classes have started. And Hassaniya arranged everything.*

The stomachache squeezed Rahhal's bowels whenever Emad passed in front of him, or whenever he heard Hassaniya talking to her mom at home—with excessive enthusiasm—about his latest achievements. But whenever she had her period on Saturdays, and he found himself kept from the pleasure of chasing the Wild Cow around the hedgehog sanctuary, Rahhal would fall asleep defeated. And in his bloody dreams, the victim would be poor Emad. Always the same way. With the swift knee that easily and decisively finds its way to the face.

Once, Rahhal unexpectedly entered Hiyam's office. Emad had taken hold of her and wrapped his arms around her from behind. She was sitting at her desk with him embracing her saucily from behind. He was whispering in her ear and she was laughing. What was he saying to her? Was he kissing her long, bare neck? Was he licking it? Or perhaps he was tickling her ear with his lips and his breath. Was he biting her? Rahhal couldn't take it. He couldn't stand this situation. Without thinking, he lunged toward Emad with eyes shooting sparks, grabbed him firmly by the hair and threw him down next to the desk. Hiyam recoiled in her chair, terrified. As for her husband, after getting over the initial shock, he pulled himself together and lunged at Rahhal, intent on pushing him and knocking him down. But no go. Rahhal squared off firmly against him, surprised him with two punches to the stomach, and pulled him by his hair once again, but more strongly this time. Then he raised his knee quickly to ram it into his face, and the blood gushed up.

That happened a little bit before dawn.

The Squirrel Enters the Blue Box

27

THE KING IS DEAD, LONG LIVE THE KING!

Rahhal, like most people in the country, sensed the difference. People were breathing a new air in the street and on the bus, at home and around the neighborhood, in the markets and cafés, everywhere. True, the regime was one and the same, and even though the previous opposition government came to power in 1998, a year before Hassan II's death, it had been running the country's affairs with his full approval. "Change from inside the system, with continuity." This was the slogan of the time. The papers were talking about fierce opposition to the reformist initiatives launched by the new ministers on the part of the shadow government, and there were pockets of resistance to change. However, although the pace was somewhat slow, change was possible, and those dreaming of it were growing in number.

Hassan II died on a scorching hot Friday in July 1999. Moroccan television began to broadcast Qur'anic verses, and at first, Moroccans wondered why such a sudden righteousness and piety had struck the television broadcasters and programmers. The door was opened to many different interpretations, and rumors ran rampant. Agence France-Presse spoke of the king's probable death, according to sources close to the palace. But details remained blocked in France, while the people here remained in suspense until the Spanish press released a statement announcing the death of the Moroccan ruler.

The king is dead. But kings don't stay dead for more than a couple of hours. After that, they enter the history books and ascend to the level of myths. A king's death doesn't last more than a few hours. The king is dead, long live the king! That same day, loyalty was professed to the crown prince Mohammed, son of Hassan, in the throne room of the Royal Palace in Rabat. And the Government of Change, run by a previous opposition leader who had been sentenced to death during the Years of Lead, seemed intent that the transitional period pass smoothly, and that the young king take full advantage of the situation to fully put things on the road to reform.

The king is dead. Long live the king!

Many things have changed, Rahhal. Many things. The phone booths have disappeared and have been replaced by phone cards and mobile phones. Teenagers have even started to walk around with multi-ringtone mobile phones. Postage-stamp collectors have started to go extinct since email doesn't require an envelope, or a stamp, or even a mailman. Your Peugeot 103 motorbike that used to take you and Hassaniya to Massira has turned into a Fiat Uno. It's a used car, but the engine still pulses with determination, roars with power, and moves around with the perseverance of a worker bee. Hassaniya managed to get a driver's license and has now taken on the role of driver. When you stay late at work, you have to take the bus to Djemaa Lfnaa. Sometimes you slip in among some suspicious characters in the collective midnight taxis. And from the heart of the square, you turn toward the nearest alley that will take you to Mouassine.

Rahhal had started to work late more and more in recent years. The spiders of the cybercafe that he managed continued to weave electronic threads into webs with dedication and zeal until midnight, sometimes until after one in the morning when the weather in Marrakech was hot and the nights of the Red City made it tempting to stay up late.

The customers at the cybercafe were mostly young people. Teenagers. It happened that some middle-aged people would visit the café, too, but not with any regularity. The majority of the regulars were young boys and girls, students from the nearby high school. There were college students, too, and a few unemployed people as well.

Only if Hassaniya agrees. Our new life is here in Massira now and she needs to be convinced. The old, crumbling Mouassine house is no longer anything more than a place to sleep. A miserable place to sleep, that served as a refuge for a destitute widow to live alone with her daughter, but now it no longer suits us. Now it's just a place to sleep that's far away, that requires serious travel to get to. The Old City has become too confined for the people who have grown up and live there now, and life has truly come to be someplace else. In other places. Even those from well-connected, well-to-do Marrakech families have been leaving one after the other for new neighborhoods. Today they're living in Daoudiate, Massira, Azli, and Inara, even in the remote neighborhood of Mhamid, where its subdivisions and buildings spread like fungus next to the Marrakech Ménara Airport.

The king is dead, long live the king.

Oum Eid went off to meet her maker three years ago. She was glued to her television screen in the salon, following a new episode of a dubbed Mexican series, when God pulled His spirit from her frail body. Her tired soul flew silently and calmly with noble wings from her weak body without warning, and from that day on I've been trying to convince you, Hassaniya, that there's nothing compelling us to stay in Mouassine now that Oum Eid has left us.

Let's look for a small apartment in one of the buildings near the school. We'll furnish it using a comfortable installment plan from Qatifa's shop and settle down like everyone else does. The Old City is no longer fit for habitation, and traveling the distance between there and Massira has completely worn us out. Even Emad and Hiyam, whose families have lived in Mouassine for generations, have settled in a lovely, elegant villa in Massira. So why condemn us to this tortuous daily trip?

28

EMAD NEVER COULD HAVE IMAGINED how many punches and kicks he received during the Squirrel's blood-soaked dreams, otherwise he wouldn't have defended him so vehemently. When Hiyam suggested using the summer vacation of 1999 to add a third floor to the building in order to expand the infrastructure of the Atlas Cubs School by three new classrooms, she didn't let the opportunity pass to also suggest transforming the garage on the ground floor into an additional room. That way, the school would gain four new classrooms suitable for meeting the increased demand.

"And Rahhal?"

"What about Rahhal? Did I give birth to him and then forget about it?"

"No, Hiyam, you didn't give birth to him, or raise him. But he's been with us since the beginning. He's become one of us and I can't get rid of him without giving him some advance warning. Besides, my darling, he's Hassaniya's husband, and my father, the Hajj, is always asking about her and Rahhal, wishing them well every time their names come up. True, the *téléboutique* isn't doing as well as it was at first, but Rahhal is working hard at other things, and what he's taking in isn't too bad in any case."

Hiyam held firm to her position, and Emad held firm to his.

And the Squirrel wasn't there.

He was working as always, safe and sound, as if the shop where he worked was one of his father's estates. As if he had a legitimate work contract and employment number that guaranteed him a monthly salary and comfortable retirement after years of work. That's why he works in complete security. He eagerly types the students' papers, he listens to the telephone conversations of the *téléboutique* customers with an endless curiosity that is masked by his mild-mannered, neutral-looking face, and he builds up the photocopy archive in peace. At night he is careful about moving and turning over in bed so as not to annoy Hassaniya. And as he always has, he entertains himself every Saturday evening by chasing the wild cows around the hedgehog sanctuary, torturing Emad in his dreams whenever it was that time of the month and Hassaniya turned away from him. But Emad, who wasn't used to winning his battles with Hiyam, found a way out that would allow him to save face and satisfy his heart's delight, too.

What interested Hiyam was taking over the garage. So, he allowed her to close Rahhal's shop and turn it into a classroom, while he thought about the most appropriate way to better profit from Hassaniya's husband in the computer realm. No better way than by opening up a cybercafe. And just his luck, there was a commercial space available for rent on Dakhla Avenue not too far from the school. The shop was spacious, and suited Emad's ambitions, who had begun to seriously prepare for the cybercafe adventure. As for Rahhal, he had become absolutely sure during his daily travels across the blue screen, as he wandered morning and night from one internet site to another, that life had truly come to be in another place.

29

OH, RAHHAL . . .

What is this bliss?

Or were you dreaming of this luxury? And expecting all of this privilege?

It wasn't the screens all around the shop that made Rahhal so happy and filled his heart with pride, nor was it the new mission he devoted himself to when opening the doors of the night journey to sanctuaries of light and anchorages of blue flashes for the new customers. Rather, it was the clean, modern toilet the shop provided him. A well-lit toilet with light-blue paint occupying a strategic position directly in front of Rahhal's desk. The door of the shop between them was wide, its front window adorned at the top by a fancy, blue sign that carried the name chosen by Hiyam herself: "Atlas Cubs Cybercafe." The computers were arranged next to one another along the edges of the shop in a way that forced customers to surf with their faces fixed to the computer screens on the walls while Rahhal could spy on all the screens from his place behind the customers' backs; he was the only person with his back against the wall, so he could remain in command of the room and watch what was going on. And when he got tired of sneaking peeks at other people's screens, he would fix his gaze on the only open space that was right in front of him, facing his desk: the toilet. Thus, he purposely left the door of the toilet open so he could enjoy its marvelous cleanliness, and dreamy blue paint.

Rahhal thought about covering the toilet seat with a bag so that no one could use it; to keep even himself from using it. He would make this clean, blue space into a kitchen where he would prepare his delicious, easy-to-make tajines that Hassaniya would die for: a quarter kilo of chicken; two tomatoes; one onion; four potatoes; a clove of garlic; one spoonful of oil; a bit of salt, pepper, ginger, and paprika. He'd eat his fill of it, while Hassaniya would eat the rest, along with her fingers, so gluttonous was her appetite. The idea had occurred to him more than once, especially since the customers of the cybercafe rarely used the toilet because they were intent on taking advantage of their full hours and half-hours surfing and chatting. They didn't have time to waste on the toilet.

He was pressed by the idea more than once as he sat there distracted by the clean, blue paint in front of him, but he firmly rejected it. His toilet was too clean to mess up by cooking tajine, with all of its smells. Rahhal wasn't ready to sacrifice the most beautiful, romantic spot in his new shop just for tajines that he'd bring to the school to share with Hassaniya. But who knew? Perhaps Hassaniya would invite Hiyam to eat the tajines with them and he'd win her over, which would result in her giving the order that the Squirrel be appointed official cook (he still couldn't believe that he had been relieved of his role as driver).

Rahhal was also done with his daily round-trips from the Old City to Massira after Hassaniya had submitted to Hiyam's orders. For after she gave birth to twins, Hiyam was too busy with them for the Atlas Cubs. She started to come into the school later, and the work began to pile up for Hassaniya. Now Hassaniya was the first one to arrive and the last one to leave. She basically did everything. That's why Hiyam issued her strict orders that Hassaniya move to Massira. Emad was there to apply his soothing touch to this strict decision. He was the one who found the apartment in a building overlooking the Massira overpass, a five-minute walk for Hassaniya and Rahhal. And he was the one who took care of getting it furnished from A to Z, at his own expense. The Squirrel and his Hedgehog had to pay rent. But with the raise Emad had given Hassaniya in light of her new tasks, it became possible to carry the cost of renting a beautiful apartment with windows that opened onto two streets, and that also overlooked the Dakhla Avenue overpass (for which workers had dug a ditch to sink it underground, like a piece of décor that couldn't be justified, until they were surprised that every time it rained, the hole turned into a lake that blocked traffic).

When they left the Mouassine house, Rahhal realized for the first time that the small dwelling that was affixed like a tick to the Qatifa home had actually been a part of it. The dwelling didn't belong to Oum Eid. Rather, the widow had lived there with her daughter thanks to the Hajj and his charity. But what surprised Rahhal more was how depressed his Hedgehog became. He didn't understand why she was so sad. It was like when Abu Abdallah II left Alhambra Palace in Granada behind as he wept like a woman over a kingdom he couldn't defend like a man. But Hassaniya didn't shed a tear, for her eyes are stingy. She didn't cry and she didn't sob. Rather, her face went blank and took on an increasingly yellow pall, a strange absentmindedness taking hold of her.

For his part, Rahhal was happy with the new apartment and its modern bedroom and chic furnishings, even though what was more important to him was that he could now sleep in a place not too far from the shop. His true happiness was the shop: The Atlas Cubs Cybercafe. The other place where life had moved to.

30

THE NEW SHOP was really quite spacious. Spacious and clean. Its ceiling was noticeably high. As for the floor, it was made of beige, Spanish tile so smooth that when he stepped onto it for the first time, Rahhal felt as if he were gliding on ice.

Oh man, do you know what it means to find yourself in such a spacious shop with a high ceiling, a smooth floor, and a clean, well-lit toilet?

In Ain Itti, a toilet was a luxury that wasn't available to everyone. Most of the slum's residents did it in black plastic bags that were tossed into ditches that surrounded the neighborhood dug specifically for that purpose. As for basic needs such as peeing and performing ablutions, one could do that at home, letting the water make its way into the unsanitary canal system that ended in small streams running through the alleys toward the Oued Issil River. Rahhal and his family would relieve themselves in a narrow, secluded spot no larger than a square meter, with a small opening in the center that flowed into the ditches that cut through the alley. But when things got serious, everyone was afraid of clogging the hole, so the plastic bag was the only solution available to those who didn't want to venture to the edges of the neighborhood, where the residents of Ain Itti—even its girls and women—could take care of their needs in the open air, protected by divine providence and the barking of stray dogs.

Speaking of stray dogs . . .

There was nothing that helped Rahhal get rid of whatever waste there was inside his belly more than the barking. Without it, when he didn't hear barking in that neighboring wasteland, it was difficult. Ever since he was a child he had suffered from a strange difficulty in evacuating his bowels. It was only when the dogs barked, and because he was scared shitless of them, that it took God's omnipotence to soften what was in his belly enough for the disgusting paste to find the straight path out of his intestines. By the power of the All-hearing, All-knowing.

But, at Abdelmoumen Middle School, there were no dogs.

Oh, but there were.

Allal, the guard, did have two, huge black dogs. Two lazy dogs that didn't bark that much were always tied up next to his hut beside the sports fields. The guard would untie them after the students had left at six in the evening, and they would run around inside the school courtyard and on the playing fields. That way the guard could enjoy the good fortune of spending time with his children in the evening and throwing himself into the loving embrace of his wife at night, handing responsibility of guarding the school over to the two dogs.

But it was morning now, and the guard's residence was far from the toilets. The dogs were tied up and there was nothing to scare Rahhal as he crouched over the toilet, straining to rid his body of waste. He squeezed his stomach muscles. His thighs doubled up under his belly, and his breathing almost stopped from the pressure. He pushed and pushed, but to no avail. Rahhal would satisfy himself with one defecation session a day, preferring to take care of it at school rather than use the disgusting bags or do it in the open air, where the wind would slap his bare ass on cold days, threatened by the stray dogs, terrified by their barking. He was meticulous in setting aside that period of time in school for bowel movements; a carefully studied schedule that he maintained so as not to have to ask the same teacher for permission to go to the toilet two times in a week. Thus, he set his regular time on Mondays with the Islamic education teacher at 9:00 a.m. Tuesdays during Arabic hour. Wednesdays during Phys Ed. Thursdays he would ask permission from the math teacher. Fridays were no problem, since he'd fulfill his needs in the mosque's toilet before washing himself for the Friday prayer. Saturday he'd put it off until the last class of the week, Natural Sciences, two hours from 4:00 to 6:00

p.m. Sunday he'd do it in the cemetery when he'd visit his father, Abdeslam.

. . .

The difficulty Rahhal suffered in fulfilling his needs exposed him to punishment numerous times. He didn't pay attention to how much time he was taking while he squeezed his insides in the toilet. Once, he asked permission to go to the toilet at the beginning of class and didn't return until his classmates were preparing to leave, which resulted in a sharp rebuke from the Islamic education teacher. Things went on this way until one time when the math teacher burned his cheek with a nasty slap.

Rahhal was wounded, mentally broken. He'd crouch on the toilet pushing down on his colon and squeezing his stomach muscles as the resistant waste inside his large intestine refused to come out. He felt sorry for himself when he recalled the teacher's slap. He was squeezing hard, his hand on his cheek, when it occurred to him to pick up a piece of damp, red chalk that was laying in front of him. Shit, it smelled like piss. One of them had pissed on it. But it didn't matter. Rahhal held the nasty piece of chalk in his fingers and quickly wrote on the door in front of him: "Yacoubi the math teacher is an ass." Just as he was about to finish the sentence, he felt his legs shaking and his heart pounding. He imagined the teacher and the principal with his assistants yanking the door open and catching him in the act of writing "aaaaaaaassssss." His hand shook and his heart pounded, and still, he didn't know how he found the strength to finish the sentence as he squeezed his insides to empty them all in one shot.

From that day forward, he never went to the school bathroom without a piece of chalk, a colored felt-tipped marker, or a ballpoint pen in his pocket. No sooner would he squat than he would begin to write: "The principal's a moron." "Si Khalifa, the head guard, is a filthy hick." "Boushta El Doukkali jacks off." "Salima Chaoui is a whore who's screwing around with the gym teacher." He'd start with the students who hated him, then move to the teachers who punished him or who were harsh with him, then on to the administrators, just because they were administrators. And even when he wasn't angry with anyone, he'd amuse himself by incriminating one of his classmates, chosen at random, simply by shuffling the deck. Once, he insulted himself, perhaps to divert the blame. The important thing was to write an insult that would raise the adrenaline level in his blood and make his heart pound, then he'd push hard and liberate his bowels so he could go back to class without delay.

Rahhal didn't understand why these shit-memories imposed themselves on him here and now. He had gotten so used to the romantic, blue paint in the shop's bathroom. That's why he left the door slightly ajar, so the blue could ripple like waves in front of him, breaking up the oppressive beige color of the shop's walls and floor. The blue was clean and the toilet seat was shiny. Rahhal wouldn't hesitate to open the bathroom door whenever a customer closed it after using it.

He would slide his feet over the smooth tiles and brush the bathroom's wall with a soft, cottony gaze. But no sooner would he get a little bit distracted than his memory would bring him back to the toilets of his childhood.

▪ ▪ ▪

"Mourad Lamrini loves Nora the blonde in classroom #4 of second year."

Ay, yay, yay . . .

The sentence was etched into the door with a pair of compasses. Was it the cry of a confused lover? A desperate confession? Or the denunciation of an unfriendly spy?

At first, Rahhal thought that he was the only one who scribbled on the toilet's walls and door because of the difficulty he had defecating. But he soon discovered that it was a popular pastime practiced by nearly all the students. In fact, they graffitied in every way possible, using all types of available writing implements, including lipstick, in the case of the girls. Even those who found themselves without a pen would run their finger over the window glass, which was coated in dust, and sign their message. The scribblings in Abdelmoumen Middle School coated walls and tables, hiding themselves behind the moving panels of the blackboards, sometimes reaching the surface of teachers' desks like disgusting stains. But the toilet was enough for Rahhal, with his pressing need to scribble something just to empty his bowels as quickly as possible so he could go back to class.

"Mourad Lamrini loves Nora the blonde in classroom #4 of second year."

The sentence was still fresh, as if it had just been etched in.

Rahhal was also carrying a pair of compasses in his pocket. And because he hadn't prepared anything to scrawl that day, nor had he defined a purpose for his toilet sorties, he was preoccupied with the sentence in front of him. He didn't know Mourad or his beloved blonde, and he wasn't sure about what sort of love was being scribbled about. But he wasn't going to let the opportunity pass. He unsheathed his compass as he sat on the toilet while squeezing his stomach muscles and began to stab the corpse of love strung up in front of him:

"Mourad Lamrini is a dumb kid, and Nora the blonde is a whore fucked by all the students in classroom #4 of second year."

And that was that.

Rahhal quickly buttoned up his trousers and went back to class. He assumed that was the end of it.

But when he entered the same stall a little more than a week later (the last one in the row of boys' toilets), this time furious at the Islamic education teacher and bent on defeating him with a hateful sentence that hadn't yet formed in his head, he drew his pen to let his hand improvise the appropriate insult all by itself. While searching for the right spot among the accumulating scribblings on the door, he was surprised by a sentence, etched with scissors this time, below his last sentence:

"Mourad fucked your mother, you faggot . . . And Nora's too much for you and your stinky ho sister."

The smell in the bathroom was especially nasty that morning. It plugged up Rahhal's nose, but he'd tolerate it. He didn't even care about the resistant excrement. He forgot all about the Islamic education teacher. Now he had to find the right response for this lowlife who had insulted him and his mother, even being so audacious as to go after his sister! Of course, Rahhal was his parents' only child, no brothers or sisters. Nonetheless, insulting his sister so obscenely and accusing her of prostitution was something he could not remain silent about!

"Mourad, if you were a man you would've talked directly with your whore, not stayed and masturbated in the toilet while thinking about her . . . while your friends in rooms 4 and 5 fucked her to their hearts' delight from the front and behind. But *you* need someone to fuck you, you faggot!"

This time, relief came quickly. Rahhal liberated his bowels while he was in the middle of his fiery response to Mourad (or to the vicious slanderer who had implicated the student named Mourad Lamrini in this dirty battle).

31

MOURAD LAMRINI. Salima Chaoui. Najwa Benrahman. Wedad Tabayli. Ahmed Errounda. So many names, Rahhal, soaring in the skies of your memory from your days at Abdelmoumen Ibn Ali El Goumi Middle School and then Mohammed V High School in Bab Aghmat after that.

Names that were repeated, linked to obscene sexual insults in the bathrooms, or to chaste love poetry on blackboards and desks, or that, all by themselves, would light up the walls like small, hanging lanterns.

Ahmed Errounda was the high school's mythical Qays whose Layla everyone wondered about. Qays, the lover, whose love fire was so unbearable to Layla that her ghost began to float around the high school, oblivious to everyone, inscribing her confession on doors and walls in every possible language:

Ahmed Errounda . . . *Je t'aime.*

أحمد الروندة . . . كانحماق عليك

Ahmed Errounda . . . I love you.

Ahmed Errounda's lover couldn't pass by a wall without writing about her ardent passion on it, nor a blackboard without chiseling the secrets of her love into it.

Because all of the girl students—and the boys, as well—had become interested in knowing the identity of this destroyer of virgin hearts who was with them at school, people began to ask about him, which resulted in everyone discovering that this lover boy was closer to the legendary Antara bin Shaddad of the Abs tribe than he was to Qays bin Mulawwah. He was dark-skinned, broad-nosed, and muscle-bound, with coarse hair and a beautiful smile to boot.

Who was so unlucky as to fall in love with Antara? Where are you, Abla? Where are you? When will you alight in Jawa?

Abla remained out of sight in her lair. As for Antara, all the girls at school who started to watch him during recess took notice of his beautiful smile. And Errounda sat upon the high school's throne of stardom for weeks.

But after only three months of the Ahmed Errounda name and myth circulating about, the students of Mohammed V High School were surprised one morning by an announcement from the principal written in stern handwriting and clear script on the blackboard, making it known that the disciplinary committee of the school had decided to suspend Ahmed Errounda for two weeks after the guard had caught him behind the locker rooms absorbed in graffitiing his favorite sentence, "Ahmed Errounda . . . I love you," this time using spray paint of the sort used by tag artists.

.   .   .

Rahhal didn't love his name so much as to inscribe it on the walls, nor was he crazy enough to sign his idiotic bathroom scribblings. Quite simply, if he were to do that, he'd be found out pretty easily. He was the only Rahhal at Abdelmoumen Middle School. Even at Mohammed V High School in Bab Aghmat, no one had heard of any Rahhal other than him in the whole school.

Rahhal, Abdeslam? Rahhal?

Abdeslam, for example, was a reasonable name. Neither a masterpiece nor a timeless wonder, but it was a reasonable name. In other words, acceptable. It wouldn't draw anyone's attention. Why didn't you give me one of the Abd names? Abdelaziz, Abdelghafour, Abdelhaque, Abderrahim, Abderrahman, Abdessamiae, Abdelwudoud, Abdelhay. All of them names that bore a resemblance to other, normal names. But Rahhal?

Halima says that you gave me this name seeking a good omen from the pure saint Bouya Rahhal El Boudali. But Bouya Rahhal is buried in Zemrane and he hails from Tamedoult in the Akka river basin and you're from Abda. What brought you to him, Laâouina? You could have chosen one of the saints of Abda with a less stupid name and been done with it.

My uncle Ayad told me that when Bouya Rahhal was on his way to Tadla to visit Sidi Mohammed bin Daoud El Bouzeri and got to the Oum Rabia River, he found that the current had swept away the banks and the river had overflowed. Bouya Rahhal recited some words from Sufi *dhikrs* and the river parted in two, leaving a dry path down the middle through which he and his companions passed safely. There's no one greater or holier than you, Bouya Rahhal. But what does that have to do with me?

The picture that's in the salon—the old, torn picture that came with us from the countryside in Abda to Ain Itti and then to the salon of Uncle Ayad's house in Moukef—shows a strange image of Bouya Rahhal riding on the back of a lion in a prison cell. Those who know the story say that it is one of the miracles of this saint, who is buried in Zemrane. When the Black sultan wanted to do away with him by putting him into a prison cell with a lion, this lion didn't eat him. And when the sultan came to check on the situation, he was shocked to find Sheikh Rahhal El Boudali riding on the back of the lion with the king of the jungle wagging its tail underneath him like a cat.

But you're a mantis, Abdeslam, and your wife is a pelican, so what do you have to do with saints whose miracles transform lions into cats?

Rahhal wasn't so happy with his name as to display it on doors and walls. In fact, he still found it difficult to say in public. But at the university, specifically at the demonstrations of the National Union of Students in Morocco, he would dress the wound of his name with the bandage of militancy. There, he discovered another Rahhal who had performed his own modern miracles; who allowed him to come to terms just a little bit with his name.

The throngs were advancing loudly toward the dean's office during the Battle for the Reinstatement of Expelled Students. The only way Rahhal had of getting back into the university was by participating in the battle. Slogans had been chanted one after the other since morning when all of a sudden, one rose up that made the Squirrel's heart skip a beat:

Ask Rahhal . . . Ask Zeroual
Revolution done right now!

Ask Rahhal? Rahhal who? And about what? Of course, it couldn't be Bouya Rahhal El Boudali.

No, it had to be another Rahhal that the Squirrel would become better acquainted with on the day of the great celebration: the victory celebration of the steadfast and fighting student masses in the Battle for the Reinstatement of Expelled Students. It was on that day that Rahhal first met Wafiq Daraai, who recited his ode titled "They Won't Expel You from the Air." Strange and bizarre words that bore no relationship whatsoever to poetry as Rahhal knew and understood it, but nonetheless, Wafiq won the admiration of both the comrades and brothers and elicited their applause. However, the icing on the cake came at the end of the evening. A musical singing group came up onstage. The group consisted of young men and boys from the Old City who were all wearing black, as if in mourning, with Palestinian kaffiyehs draped over their shoulders. They began to sing:

Pull the trigger
We shall liberate Jaffa, Nablus, and the rest of the country.

Rahhal didn't want to liberate Israeli-occupied Nablus, or Spanish-occupied Ceuta for that matter. All he wanted was to sign up with the Department of Arabic Literature after his epic fail in History and with all of its classes and Geography with all of its maps.

The last song was the surprise of the event. This time they sang for his own country:

My country
You aren't a barren woman, nor a widow cut off from it.
Oh Mother, beautiful, beloved,
Even if they sell you
On the franc or dollar market,
Even if they dress you

In shame and ripped rags,
The blood of the free will still flow and flow
With the name Rahhal, Rahhal, Rahhal.
Rahhal, Rahhal,
O by the life that flows inside us.
Rahhal, Rahhal,
O what a beautiful name you have.

The comrades knew the song by heart as if it were the national anthem. They sang it with an almost Sufi-like devotion, as if in a trance. Everyone repeated the chorus enthusiastically: "Rahhal, Rahhal, O by the life that flows inside us. Rahhal, Rahhal, O what a beautiful name you have."

This name that you didn't like before, you stupid squirrel? Look at how wise Abdeslam was. He gave you a name for the future, the value of which you wouldn't comprehend until this crucial moment in your life as you taste victory for the first time and celebrate your triumphant return to the university's warm embrace.

The Squirrel would later learn that it had to do with the martyr Rahhal Jbiha, one of the most prominent militants of the Marxist 23rd of March organization. He was arrested in 1974 and spent more than a year in the awful secret Derb Moulay Cherif Prison, where he and his comrades were subjected to all manner of torture before being brought before the court in January 1977 to be handed harsh sentences. Rahhal got thirty-two years. He and his comrades conducted a number of hunger strikes, calling for improved conditions inside the prison, one of which lasted for forty-five days. That's the strike during which Saïda Mnebhi died. On October 13, 1979, Rahhal died in an attempt to escape the noose of imprisonment.

Rahhal, Rahhal, O what a beautiful name you have.

A beautiful name in the song. Difficult in real life. Quite cumbersome, in fact. The Squirrel began to feel some pride at having such a symbolic name. At the same time, he felt the weight of responsibility.

It was difficult for such an undistinguished squirrel to bear the burden of such a heavy name.

Oh, Abdeslam. What was wrong with Abderrahman or Abdelghafour or even Abdennabi? Why, Mantis, did you have to burden me with a weight I cannot bear?

32

THE KING IS DEAD. Long live the king.

Long live the multi-ringtone mobile phone. Long live modern technology. Long live blue screens.

When the poor population gets a mobile phone and surfs the kingdoms of electrons, they forget all about their misery. The world becomes as small as a village. It becomes available to people in the cybercafes that have begun to spread like fungus, all at democratic prices. Not too expensive for the poor. Two dirhams for a light, passing visit. Three dirhams for half an hour. Five for a full hour. For the loyal customer, the second hour costs four dirhams, and so on. A few dirhams and a few words of every foreign language is enough for the virtual people of God to surf the multilingual pavilions of blondes. That's for the guys. As for the girls, a bit of Arabic is enough to make flashing red hearts leap from the Atlantic Ocean to the Persian Gulf.

Long live technology.

As for Rahhal, he was at the heart of it. In the right place at the right time.

He opened a Hotmail account, not to email anyone, but rather, just to have an account with Hotmail. He set another one up on Maktoub, not to use to chat with Arabs online, but rather, because it just made sense for him to have an account on Maktoub. The third one on Yahoo, similarly because it was Yahoo. The fourth? He still hadn't decided.

All of the cybercafe's customers were new to the scene. Most of them were still at the discovery stage, which is why whenever a new person came to the shop, he would stand in front of Rahhal to request a computer and a helping hand. This one wanted to open a Hotmail account, that one a Yahoo account, and Rahhal stayed up late opening online accounts for them here and there; a new service that seemed magical to those heading to the cybercafe for the first time. Therefore, he set a price for it of thirty dirhams. The account was free, but Rahhal made thirty dirhams for every account he opened and the customers found that to be perfectly reasonable. You couldn't get an online account that did the same thing as a post office box that held letters for the customers in the Massira Post Office for nothing, right? And Rahhal's mailbox was better because you didn't have to pay more than the registration fee on the first day for it to remain open for you forever.

Customers came and went, taking turns at the computers and dragging mouses over the desktops. But a small family gradually began to form around Rahhal. Salim was a high school senior dazzled by the new, virtual world. He had two email accounts so far, one with Hotmail and the other with Yahoo. Sometimes he'd come in with his father and sometimes with his sister, Lamia. Always searching for information on the web, and every day needing to print out his search results, which he knew how to flaunt in front of his classmates.

Samira and Fadoua would come in together, sit together, and leave together. Specializing in chat rooms, they became a single online persona. They loved to chat with young guys in Arabic, French, and English. Username: Marrakech Star.

"Two in one. Shampoo and conditioner," Qamar Eddine Assuyuti would tease them whenever he glimpsed them entering the cybercafe. Qamar Eddine was the son of Shihab Eddine Assuyuti, the most notorious Islamic education teacher in Massira High School, and the one whom the students joked about the most.

"Which one of us is shampoo, and which one is conditioner?" Fadoua would ask in a conspiratorial voice.

"To be honest, I'm still working that out. When I decide that you're the shampoo, I'll let you know."

Qamar Eddine knew all about Marrakech Star, especially since Fadoua and Samira ran to him for help with all of their messages that were in English. He'd explain anything that was unclear in the emails they received from all over, and correct their replies so they could travel across the internet with fewer mistakes.

Qamar Eddine's English was good. So was his French. But he liked to say over and over, whether anyone asked him or not, that, regretfully, his Arabic wasn't so good. There never seemed to be any regret on Qamar Eddine's face when he repeated this confession. In fact, he practically shone with a hidden pride. Did he say it to spite his father, Mr. Shihab Eddine? An Arabic teacher who moved to Islamic education not out of an abundance of religiosity, but rather out of laziness and a desire to wash his hands of grammar lessons. Islamic education wasn't a core subject for science or humanities students. Two hours per week for everyone. A number of students considered that class a break that they'd spend on the sports fields, in front of the school, or at Rahhal's place in the case of those who could pay the price of skating along the screen's ice and surfing the light's waves, especially since Mr. Assuyuti didn't take regular attendance.

Qamar Eddine didn't really hate his father, but he hated talking about him. He preferred hanging out with friends who didn't go to Massira High School, and thus didn't know a thing about Mr. Shihab Eddine and had never heard the jokes or funny stories about him. Fadoua and Samira were an exception. Even though they were in Mr. Assuyuti's class, their relationship to Qamar Eddine was born in the cybercafe, and had nothing at all to do with school. Not to mention the fact that he was a handsome young man who was brilliant with languages. So, his friendship was a real win for both members of Marrakech Star.

Qamar Eddine was always available in the shop to the point where Rahhal came to leave him in charge of the cybercafe whenever he had to step out to deal with some emergency situation or go to the school to take care of one of Hiyam's ever-urgent requests. Qamar Eddine began to enjoy Marrakech Star's electronic adventures and conquests, which stretched from East to West. This one was serious, that one was chaste, and this other one's intentions were noble. This one wanted to visit Marrakech because of her eyes and asked about the best hotels and airlines. This other one suggested that she come to London, in which case he would take care of the airline ticket, and he would welcome her in his apartment, where she would stay with him as his dear, honored guest for a week or a full month if her precious time allowed it. Yet another one suggested with frightful humility that she do the Umrah pilgrimage to Mecca.

But no sooner did the Nigerian Amelia's sun rise in the cybercafe than did Marrakech Star's fade. Fadoua noticed that Qamar Eddine lost his focus whenever the black Nigerian sun appeared. Sometimes Amelia would come alone. Other times she would be accompanied by her friend Flora. Then Yacabou would join later. It might have been a strategy to keep Rahhal from forbidding the three of them to sit at one computer, since the shop's rule was well-known: No more than two people sitting at each computer.

No one knew the nature of Yacabou's relationship with Amelia and Flora. Was he their brother? A relative? Or perhaps he was the lover of one of the young women? With Africanos, it was always hard to tell. At any rate, they were all lucky because apartment and building owners didn't ask them for their documents. Even if they were Muslims from Mali or Senegal, they wouldn't be scrutinized the way Moroccans are. Young locals find it difficult to live with their girlfriends without a marriage certificate, but with the Africanos, no one asks. That's how they live together, five to ten of them in a small, two-bedroom apartment with a kitchen and a bathroom. Generally, Qamar Eddine wasn't too concerned with these details, since he wasn't actually smitten by Amelia. She just made him happy. The way she looked and her smile cheered him up, that's all. That and because he found sitting with her a pleasant opportunity to chat in English, which she was fluent in. But there was a more important reason . . . a tad sensitive. Better not to get too much into it in front of the others, especially Fadoua and Samira.

Qamar Eddine wanted to get out of his country by any means necessary. He was sick of Shihab Eddine and the boring life he lived at home. He was sick of the college that he only went to rarely now. He was even sick of the damned cybercafe that, it seemed, he had become addicted to. He was sick of Rahhal's snooping—every time he turned around, he found the rat looking at his screen. He was sick of the history teachers who would come en masse to the cybercafe to talk. They didn't have set hours, but when they honored the place with their presence, they came as a group as if going to the mosque. Each one occupied a computer and rather than riding the waves and surfing, they'd chat as if they were in the teachers' lounge. They'd tell stories about how much worse things had been in the Hassan II era and about how much better things had become under the young king; that there were more freedoms, that there was a new vitality and initiatives for change. Qamar Eddine wasn't interested in his father's colleagues' stories. He couldn't see any change at all. And who said he wanted to know how life was under Hassan II? He was young then. And today he felt that he had grown up. He didn't want to go backward. He had no time to waste on this sort of talk. Qamar Eddine wanted another life. The kind of life he saw in the movies. The kind he saw on television. The kind of life that God's chosen people were living up north. Qamar Eddine wanted to escape. Emigration is a sacred right. He didn't understand why he should have to stay in a place that was strangling him, with creatures he didn't like. He didn't understand why he wasn't entitled to cast this whole, irritating world from his days and nights—from his life, his future—and just take off.

33

"OF COURSE I'M CHRISTIAN. Why do you ask?" responded Amelia.

"Just a normal question. But could we speak outside?"

She left Flora alone at the computer. She excused herself using a local Nigerian dialect, of which Qamar Eddine could only catch Yacabou's name, which was repeated three times. Once outside, he invited her to Café Milano, across the street from the cybercafe. He discovered that Amelia smoked. As soon as Asmae, the waitress, put the cup of coffee down in front of her, she took out a pack of Marquise. She lit a cigarette and offered the pack to Qamar Eddine.

"Thanks, but I don't smoke . . . I won't take too much of your time, but I want to know about Christianity from you. What I mean is that I want to know more. I've read about the Trinity and holy unity, about Lord Jesus' divine and human natures, about the difference between Orthodox and Catholic Christianity, and between Protestants and Anglicans. I've also read the Sermon of the Mount dozens of times and I've memorized parts of it in Arabic, French, and English. Do you want proof? How about this one? 'Ye have heard that it hath been said, an eye for an eye, and a tooth for a tooth. But I say unto you, that ye resist not evil, but whosoever shall smite thee on thy right cheek, turn to him the other also. And if any man wants . . . if any man wants . . . ' Wait, I forgot. But there's another bit that goes: 'Ye have heard that it hath been said: Thou shalt love thy neighbor, and hate thine enemy. But I say unto you: Love your enemies, bless them that curse you, do good to them that hate you, and pray for them which despitefully use you, and persecute you. That ye may be the children of your Father which is in heaven, for he maketh his sun to rise on the evil and on the good, and sendeth rain on the just and on the unjust.' There's also 'seek and ye shall find,' which I've memorized by heart. Listen . . .'"

"No, you listen, Qamar . . ."

"Abdelmessih—Servant of the Messiah. My new name is Abdelmessih. You're the first person I'm telling, so let's keep it between you and me."

"Listen, Abdelmessih. There seems to have been some sort of misunderstanding. When I told you I was Christian, I was speaking in general terms about my family's religion. But believe me, I'm not Christian in the way you think. I don't go to church, I don't read the Holy Book, and I haven't memorized the Sermon of the Mount. In other words, Christian in name only. Take it from me quite simply. Please, let's go back to the cybercafe. Flora's waiting for me."

Qamar Eddine was at a loss for words. His discovery of Christianity had come by accident. It had started by surfing porn sites. But because the rat in the shop was burning a hole in his back with his hungry, probing eyes day and night, he switched over to surfing emigration sites. After that he started to jump around, freestyling all over cyberspace. Then, hop. Another unencumbered jump and he found himself crossing, without prior planning, to the other shore to follow Jesus the Messiah:

"Master, I will follow thee whithersoever thou goest." And Jesus saith unto him, "The foxes have holes, and the birds of the air have nests, but the son of man hath not where to lay his head."

What you say is true, Master. "The son of man hath not where to lay his head."

Qamar Eddine was taken aback as he received Amelia's cold response. He was in the most pressing need for someone to support him during this critical time of his electronic search for the truth. Amelia was his Black angel, *his father who art in* the cyber. His mother. His sister. No difference. He had discovered the tolerance of saints in her smile. But she had disappointed and hurt him badly. Can you imagine? She doesn't read the Holy Book and she hasn't memorized the Sermon of the Mount!

Amelia was dumbfounded. Ever since they had started coming to the cybercafe, Flora and Yacabou had brought it to her attention that Qamar Eddine had attached himself to her, or at least that he was noticeably interested in her. From that day on, she watched him. She liked how handsome he was. She liked his witticisms, his cheerfulness and cleverness, his good English, and the kind way he spoke to everyone. Why not? A delectable young man deserved her attention. Amelia was prepared for anything with Qamar Eddine, from a torrid love affair to a passing fling. And that afternoon, when he invited her to the café, she went with him happily and enthusiastically. And then the fool forces her into a heavy conversation about the Trinity and the Sermon of the Mount?! Amelia knew about Qamar Eddine's fantasy of emigrating, but she hadn't imagined that his madness would drive him to consider Christianity as a way to leave the country. She was a Christian from a long line of Christians. If priority were given to followers of the Lord Messiah, she would have gone straight to Europe from Lagos, with honor and dignity, without having to take this long detour across the desert only to find herself and her companions stuck in Morocco. They hadn't been lucky enough to slip into Spain, nor could they return to their country and face family and friends with their failure, after having squandered the family's money on such a long, difficult journey.

34

QAMAR EDDINE seems to take pleasure in being everyone's friend in the cybercafe. He moves among the computers like an electronic butterfly. Sometimes he's with Salim, helping him do his homework, and other times he's with Fadoua and Samira, explaining a message in English that has just appeared in Marrakech Star's account. Sometimes he takes Rahhal's place when he's out, and sometimes he exchanges whispers with Yacabou after having lately discovered that the Nigerian guy was more religious than his two companions.

Abu Qatada was the complete opposite of Qamar Eddine, aka Abdelmessih.

He didn't talk to anyone. He entered the cybercafe with his right foot forward while reciting the two verses of refuge. While it is true that saying *salaam alaikum*—may peace be upon you—is a duty for all Muslims, Abu Qatada found it difficult to raise his voice in greeting whenever he entered the cybercafe and found the two half-naked girls with that pimp, mistakenly and falsely named Qamar Eddine, "the moon of faith," sitting between them.

"What kind of moon of faith is that? More like moon of shit! Moon of misfortune, not moon of faith. May God curse the day he was born."

As for the African group, Abu Qatada was careful to leave sufficient space between himself and where they sat. Sure, "there's no difference between Arabs and non-Arabs, nor between white people and black, save for in religious devotion," as the prophetic Hadith says, but the black faces of the Africanos don't betray any modesty or radiate devotion. Not because they were Black, God forbid! Our lord, Bilal, the muezzin of our Prophet—upon Him the purest of peace and prayers—was an Ethiopian slave. Islam was so generous with him that the beloved chosen Prophet described him as a man of paradise, saying, "What an excellent man Bilal is. He is the lord of muezzins. And muezzins will have the longest necks on the Day of Judgment." Abu Qatada noticed that Yacabou's neck *was* as long and thin as a giraffe's. But his dark face could not radiate the light of Islam any less, he and his two ugly slave girls, who practically never left his side. They looked like two ugly black goats. *May evil befall him* and *them*, Abu Qatada thought, then asked for God's forgiveness.

His name was Mahjoub Didi. He was an employee at the Regional Agency for Water and Electricity. Married with two children. What annoyed him more than anything else was when a dull-witted colleague at work would sing "Didi, didi, didi, didi waah." Because he was so boorish, his colleagues avoided singing the famous Cheb Khaled song in front of him, but they'd wink knowingly about it at one another when he wasn't around. As for "Abu Qatada," it was a nickname chosen for him by one of the brothers—may God bless him for it—at a sweet-smelling *dhikr* session. And from that day on, his name at divine assemblies and on enlightened websites was Abu Qatada, after the glorious companion of the Prophet, Abu Qatada al-Ansari al-Khazraji, may God be pleased with him and give him satisfaction.

35

"BIG BROTHER IS WATCHING YOU!"

Qamar Eddine would repeat this sentence in English from time to time, mocking Rahhal.

"Sorry, sorry, I meant to say, 'Little Brother is watching you!'"

The cybercafe would shake with laughter.

It had to be admitted that Rahhal's English was just above nil. As for his knowledge of English literature, it wasn't much more than what Amelia knew about the Islamic theological teachings of Imam Malik. In any case, Rahhal was a product of the Department of Arabic Literature with a specialization in ancient poetry: pre-Islamic epic odes, poetry from the Umayyad and Abbasid periods, as well as from al-Andalus and Morocco. He didn't even read novels in Arabic, a language he's very good at, so how could he read them in other languages? And because no one ever explained to him that the reference was to George Orwell's famous novel, *1984*, in which Big Brother watches over everyone, he continued to wonder deep down why Qamar Eddine was boasting about his two brothers—the big one and the little one—in the cybercafe when he only had one sister, who was pursuing her graduate studies in Rabat.

"Little Brother is watching you!"

Qamar Eddine's prodding didn't irritate the Squirrel at all. Qamar Eddine was protesting the way Rahhal treated customers' screens in the shop as private property, fixing his mouse eyes on them as he pleased. That annoyed Qamar Eddine to no end during the first stage of his virtual life, when he was still addicted to porn sites. To this day he hates it when people snoop around his blessed sites. That's why he began to avoid illustrated pages that included pictures of churches, icons, and ecclesiastical drawings. Mostly, he would take texts and paste them onto a blank page and then read them in Word at his leisure. And when he was done, he'd toss the file into the trash bin and log out.

But in Rahhal Laâouina's kingdom, there was no place for trash bins. As soon as the last customer would leave after midnight, Rahhal would take a few minutes, sometimes more than an hour, to examine the computers. He would inspect each and every one. He would scrape around inside and tear the cover off of the secrets of those who have hidden themselves in the digital shadows. A number of them left their accounts open. Same with members of the online forums. For example, Brother Abu Qatada often minimized the screen and left after hearing the call to the evening prayer, leaving the forum page open with the discussion between brothers continuing along: one time about the need to kill and sacrifice the self should an occupier come to a Muslim land. Another time about using the fraudulent electoral system as a means to gain control and win government posts. This time the discussion was heated, and always about elections. The brothers in God strongly objected to the candidates' heretical self-promotion, and likewise to the notion that all members of society have an equal vote, no matter their degree of learning or religious devotion. As for Abdelmessih's Holy Scriptures, Rahhal would retrieve them from the trash bin and transfer the Arabic ones to his personal computer so he could go over them leisurely the following day.

This amounts to extra work that Rahhal does before closing up, except that he's the one who opened up the accounts for all the club members in the first place. His prodigious squirrel memory stores everyone's login names, real and made-up, and remembers all the passwords. Veils are lifted and the secrets behind them revealed. That's how Rahhal Laâouina knows everything about the flocks of his happy, cybernetic kingdom. Even the Nigerian community in the Atlas Cubs Cybercafe had their secrets revealed to him after they transferred their activities to the electronic realm. Amelia and Flora are gay, but they prostitute themselves to men right now as they wait for the emerging and promising women's market in Marrakech to open up. And Yacabou works for them as an escort, a personal guard, and an intermediary. As for his relationship with Flora, it's a cover, silly Qamar Eddine. It's just a cover.

Yeah, Rahhal. You see them moving in front of you like puppets. None of them knows that they're in your pocket. Their real and made-up names. Their interior and exterior lives. Their dreams and their delusions. Their ruses and their wild, made-up tales. Their innocent virtual friendships and their illicit electronic adventures. Everything is in your pocket, Rahhal, but you've got to be smart about it. Be extremely careful that these secrets remain hidden. Keep them to yourself, you scrawny squirrel. Otherwise, if, for example, Abu Qatada found out that Qamar Eddine had lost his way so much and deviated enough from his path and his religion for his name to become Abdelmessih, and that the two Nigerian girls were ladies of the night, he'd call for jihad right then and there; a crushing war would erupt in the cybercafe. So Rahhal enjoyed spying on the members of his new family with just enough care to give each one of them a feeling of total safety. Besides, they were at home and in the embrace of their happy family here in the virtual jungles of the Atlas Cubs Cybercafe.

36

OVER HERE THERE'S HOT MAROC, and over there is everything else. Hot Maroc. Hot Morocco. That's how the site got its name.

An online news site that provides hourly coverage. You'll find all the country's news there. Fresh ripe news. Politics. Money and business. Sports. Art. Travel. Religion and religious pronouncements. Regional and local news. Protests and demonstrations. General freedoms. Crime. Behind the scenes of politics and society. Opinion articles. Videos. Hot talks. Full scoops. And culture news, too.

Rahhal came to start his day with news from Hot Maroc. The first thing he'd do after opening the shop and turning on the computers was open his amazing online news site that brought him back to the public sphere—he who hadn't purchased a newspaper in his life. Ever since leaving the discussion circles of the National Union of Students in Morocco in college, he had been completely cut off. All he knew now was the Hedgehog and her quills; the Pelican and the Mantis and their lazy, daily routine in his uncle Ayad's house, where the trio from Abda would eat their food and wait for death to come; Hiyam and her ridiculous and urgent errands (once, he was even sent rushing to the women's hammam because she had forgotten her mobile phone there); and this de facto family in the cybercafe that fully embraced him, and that he fully embraced, counting every breath he took as he counted theirs.

Hot Maroc was a free ticket that returned Rahhal to his country. Just like an emigrant who has been abroad for years, completely cut off from what was going on back home, and then here they are, finally coming back—without having to bear the cost of travel—to drown in its affairs and sorrows.

Breaking.

Scoop.

Exclusive.

There's always some breaking news item published on the first page. Breaking news items coming one after another. Hot like fresh bread right out of the oven. Alive like a fish just reeled in. And Rahhal was addicted to the fresh bread and fish of the news site. So addicted that he'd go back at the top of every hour to see if another breaking news item had appeared.

But Hot Maroc was more than just a news site to Rahhal. It was a space for him to express himself and defame others. His new toilet stall. At first, he couldn't believe his eyes when he realized that the comments section was open to all. Underneath each article or news item there was a space for comments. It was amazing! You can write whatever you want, Rahhal, without the smells clogging up your nose. Comment as you please, sitting relaxed at your desk, not crouching with your legs bent under your belly, twisting your guts on the toilet. Now you can interact with what you read from your place here in Massira in the Atlas Cubs Cybercafe. You can freely express your opinion in total secrecy without anyone asking about what your name is or who you are. Check out the list of commenters. There are full names. There are first names: Karim, Khalid, Mouna, Saeed. People sign off according to cities or regions: Samira from Marrakech. Farid from Meknes. The Casaoui. A Guy from Sefrou. The Sahraoui. A Free Amazighi Berber. Girl from the North. Just write your name and email address and comment to your heart's delight.

Rahhal almost went crazy as he read his first comment, which posted just minutes after he had sent it. It was on an opinion piece about elections and democracy in Morocco and the Arab world, written by the well-known Moroccan thinker Issam Louzi. The article attempted to explain how "we can reconcile elections and democracy in the Arab world despite the fact that, in principle, it is not possible to reconcile the part with the whole, or the ends with the means. True, it is not possible for the democratic process to function without free and fair elections," added the article's author, "except that elections and ballot boxes do not necessarily lead to democracy. How is it that . . . ?"

The article was long and the analysis was painful to read. Rahhal wouldn't waste his time reading it in its entirety. But his comment was ready. Where are you, Abu Qatada? Where are you? He recalled the heated discussion that had ignited in Abu Qatada's electronic tent a few days before around the issue of legitimacy in elections. He borrowed Mahjoub Didi's name as a nom de guerre, as well as his email, and opened fire.

"What democracy, what elections, and what nonsense are you talking about, you secular jackass? Elections that give everyone an equal voice? Believer and sinner alike? The chaste veiled woman and the ostentatious whore? The learned and the ignorant? *Say: 'Are they equal—those who know and those who know not?'* And don't elections lead to polytheism next to the Lord of Heaven and Earth? Legitimacy is to God alone. Authority is to God alone. *Or have they associates who have laid down for them as religion that for which God gave not leave? But for the Word of Decision, it had been decided between them. For the evildoers there awaits a painful chastisement.*"

May your religion be victorious, Abu Qatada.

Rahhal wasn't expecting so many likes. More than fifty likes so far, while the original article hadn't gotten more than seven. Readers liked your comment, Squirrel. True, Rahhal didn't actually agree with Abu Qatada. And he wouldn't go so far as to accuse democracy and elections of blasphemy in such a repugnant manner, but the reading public's embrace of his comment filled him with enthusiasm and pride. He had to look for another topic to dip Abu Qatada's pail into. And God is the one who bestows success.

37

WHAT?! IBN AL-WANNAN?

The news hit him like a bolt of lightning.

It was one of those cold, December mornings, and the shop was still empty. Rahhal was wrapped up in his khaki jacket, but was still shivering. He needed the breath of the internet surfers around him to warm him up a bit. Waiting for the arrival of the Nigerian diving team that had recently started to come early to the cyber-cafe for reasons Big Brother hadn't yet figured out, Rahhal began his usual electronic journey around Hot Maroc and the news item shook him to his core.

It wasn't just a brief news story, but rather, a long, expansive article published on the home page. It talked about Wafiq Daraai's trajectory and his exceptional experience, his two new poetry collections, which had been published one after the other by two well-known publishing houses in Beirut and Cairo this year, and it explained what the judging committee had taken into consideration when they chose him to receive the Ibn al-Wannan Prize, which the Association of Moroccan Poets grants every year to the Moroccan poet with the strongest output and greatest prominence.

Rahhal didn't have a chance to finish reading the article, because the pain prevented him from doing so. The abdominal pain had returned to tear away at his insides. A strong, sudden pain that neither cumin, ginger, nor chamomile could do anything about.

Wafiq Daraai?

Ever since he disappeared in college after the comrades had discovered his collaboration with the Mukhabarat and viciously kicked him out of their fold, you haven't heard a word about him, Rahhal. But had you forgotten about him? Well here he is now, reappearing on the scene having won the Ibn al-Wannan Prize. Ibn al-Wannan,

Rahhal? Abu al-'Abbas Ahmad bin Muhammad bin al-Wannan al-Tuwati from Fes. Ibn al-Wannan, whom we studied in our second year, spending an entire semester analyzing his epic poem (known as "The Shamaqmaqiyya" after his nickname, Abu Shamaqmaq) with Professor Abdelmaqsud Taheri in Moroccan Literature class. I challenge you, Wafiq, to produce one line of that poem for me. My God, are you kidding? Wafiq was a French literature student. What does he have to do with Ibn al-Wannan? I'll cut off both my arms if he's read the poem or even heard of it, and I challenge him to recite a single line from this poem that's in the *rajaz* meter, rhymes in the letter *q*, and consists of 275 verses.

Ah, Professor Abdelmaqsud . . .

> My refinement is adorned by my knowledge, so you will not
> see
> Anyone whose poetry is as perfectly formed as by me.
> If I compose praise poetry, my praise heals
> As if by pure, liquid honey.
> If I compose satirical poetry, my satire is like
> Something that sticks in the throat, making it hard to
> breathe.

We couldn't do any worse, Abu Shamaqmaq! A prize in your name is now granted to cheesy poets. But it's not your fault. I will seek vengeance immediately, on your behalf.

The news was still hot, the article fresh, and there was no comment below. Therefore, Rahhal, it's up to you to open things up.

Name: A Former Qaîdi Basista Student
Comment Title: The Poetics of Denunciation

I read with interest your article about the prince of cheesy poets, aka Wafiq Daraai, who was awarded the Ibn al-Wannan Prize this year, and I was surprised that the article's author neglected a key element in his biography—that being his collaboration with the Mukhabarat, not a trace of which appears in his poetry. The militants of the College of Humanities at Cadi Ayyad

University in Marrakech know their poetic counterfeiter—what I mean to say is, their poet, whose poems glitter—essentially as a Mukhabarati element who served as a mole within the ranks of the National Union of Students in Morocco. So why completely ignore this extremely important part of the man's life story? The poet is a product of his environment, and someone with his history of cooperating with the Mukhabarat by denouncing noble militants and writing police reports on them couldn't possibly keep hidden this part of himself when he goes to write a poem. That's why we implore the critics, may God grant them the best reward, to pay heed in their next study to this side of our poet's personality and compose a study for us on "The Poetics of Denunciation in the Poetry of Wafiq Daraai." May God have mercy on Ibn al-Wannan once again, with you having killed him a second time by granting a prize that carries his name to such a cowardly spy.

Rahhal's stomach cramps gradually began to subside without need for a prescription or any other treatment. He felt better now. But he wouldn't stop there. He still had more in his bag of tricks:

Name: A Guy from Mouassine
Comment Title: Pride and Glory

As someone from Mouassine, all I can do is express my pride and joy at having come across this happy piece of news. Imagine, someone from my neighborhood winning the most prestigious poetry prize in the country. I'm practically flying, I'm so happy. So, allow me to present my warmest congratulations to Police Commissioner Serraj and to the entire Daraai family in Mouassine on this achievement. Who would have known that Wafiq, who, when we were kids we used to call Girly Wafiqa, whose underpants we would so often steal at the neighborhood hammam so we could play with his ass when we were younger, would become such a great poet? Therefore, I apologize, Wafiqa—I mean Wafiq—for everything that happened in the hammam so long ago, and please rest assured that I feel deep remorse, as do all the other neighborhood kids. We've forgotten all about that and ask God for forgiveness. Today we're so proud of you and delight in your gift. May God grant you success and we hope for even more brilliance for you.

But Professor Abdelmaqsud Taheri would have an opposing opinion. Rahhal didn't know for sure whether Professor Abdel-maqsud, who taught him Moroccan literature in his last year before retiring, had passed away or was still alive and kicking. But what was certain was that the man was nowhere near the internet. What Rahhal *did* know was what this name meant to an entire genera-tion of Arabic literature students in Marrakech as well as all those who majored in Moroccan literature and graduated from different Moroccan universities after all having studied his magisterial book, *Maghrebi Poetry from the Period of the Idrissid State to that of the Alaouis.*

Name: Abdelmaqsud Taheri
Comment Title: Poetic Food for the Soul or Poetic Fodder?

In the name of God, the Compassionate, the Merciful, and prayers and peace upon the last of the prophets and messengers. First of all, I absolutely disassociate myself from the two com-ments posted above. It isn't important to me whether the afore-mentioned poet has any connection to the Mukhabarat or with any other secret or known state apparatus. And I don't like to get into discussions about asses. Whether the poet is one of the stallions of poetry or merely an effete lacking any honor or mas-culinity, this triviality is of no concern to the scholarly critic or academic researcher. What concerns me, may God allow you all to prosper, is the poetry itself. Is what the poet—the so-called Wafiq Daraai—writes poetry, or is it poetic fodder? Is it metered, rhymed speech that nourishes the heart and soul, or is it merely food for asses? This is the question I grudgingly put to the dubi-ous committee that has allowed the prestigious Ibn al-Wannan Prize to sink so low. In fact, I direct my question to Wafiq Daraai himself, along with the so-called poets like him. Is there anything in your mad ravings and your intellectual metaphors and blind talk about "The Butterfly's Slaughterhouse" and "Birds That Bark about Dissonant Foam" or "Protocols of Geometrical Poverty" and "Mummies That Copulate within View of the Void" with which we will liberate Palestine and return the Arab community to its former honor and greatness? No! A thousand nos! And have you studied the Moroccan poetry of today, the pools of which you would want to slip into, and whose patios you'd want to relax on? Do you know who Ibn al-Wannan was, Wafiq Daraai? Are you familiar with the artistic genius of his time, the glory of his age, Abu 'Abbas Ahmed bin Muhammad bin al-Wannan from Fes, also known as Abu Shamaqmaq? Do you know the man for whom the prize you won today is named? I have no response, simply because I'm going to guess that you have no response. So, take joy in your poetic fodder after you've cast poetry out into the kingdom of shit that you have established on top the ruins of the Arabic ode. There is no power nor strength save for in God.

It would be unseemly to leave Professor Abdelmaqsud Taheri's questions hanging out there unanswered. Therefore, Atiqa entered the fray with her own. Rahhal was surprised that Atiqa's name popped into his head right then. He smiled when he remembered how nice she was to Wafiq so long ago. Perhaps you've finally changed your position, you revolutionary cow. This time the butterfly was the entry point—*The Butterfly on Its Way to the Slaughterhouse* was the title of this bastard's first poetry collection. "Would you allow this rotten sentence to serve as a title for a poetic collection, our esteemed Professor Abdelmaqsud?"

Atiqa's noble stance concerning the title, along with her judicious critical sense, her beloved interactive spirit, and the vitality with which she responded to Professor Abdelmaqsud Taheri, all of it greatly pleased Rahhal, so he rewarded the girl by allowing her free rein to go on at length:

"With what skin will your butterfly go to the slaughterhouse, you so-called versifier? Skinning something requires you to scrape and separate the skin from the flesh, but what will you skin from a butterfly that possesses only its wings? Wings that are too thin to flay, you wannabe poet. Because they are made of such delicate material, they'd quickly disintegrate with just a small rub between two fingernails. If you had just the smallest amount of sense, you would lead your poor butterfly into a small incinerator, not a slaughterhouse. It's as if you'd never heard of how much butterflies are drawn to the light. As if you can't distinguish between a butterfly and a bat. But what to do when the latest poets like you stitch together idiotic sentences willy-nilly and call the revolting product 'poetry' or a 'prose poem.' To hell with poetry if it's those rocks that you wrap in cellophane and throw at the world and people who, like morons, are satisfied with their foolishness. To hell with poets like you and your kind."

After that, the faucet was opened up all the way. All the comments flowed just as Big Brother had composed them: insulting the latest loathsome poets who compose this type of rotten, foundling ode called "the prose poem"; abusing Wafiq Daraai and his benefactor, Commissioner Serraj; condemning the role of the Mukhabarat security apparatus in the country's political and cultural life; condemning sexual deviancy and shedding light on the Islamic legal position concerning homosexuality. It was Brother Abu Qatada, may God reward him, who took it upon himself to deal with this last subject in detail, stating clearly that homosexuality was considered the most reprehensible of acts and the greatest of sins that shook the throne of the Merciful, and that the legal punishment for this act in this world was death, and in the next world, everlasting torture in the fires of hell. Abu Bakr from Hadramout related on the authority of Imam Ja'far bin Muhammad al-Sadiq that he, the Prophet of God, prayers on him and his family, said: "He who has sexual intercourse with a young boy arrives in a state of ritual impurity on the Day of Judgment that the water of this world will not be able to wash away, and God will be angry with him. He will curse him and prepare hell and a terrible fate for him." Then he said, "When a man mounts another man, the throne shakes because of it, and if the man is taken from behind, God imprisons him on the bridge to hell until he finishes settling the accounts of the rest of creation. After that, he is ordered to hell and then tortured at each of its levels until he is cast into the lowest one, out of which he will never emerge."

38

BUT WHAT ABOUT WAFIQ DARAAI? Where was he during all of this? What had God done with him?

The Squirrel would have given his life for just a glimpse of Wafiq's face as he opened Hot Maroc with this coursing torrent of electronic sewage. He was dying to know what his old friend's response would be. Hot Maroc was the first to publish a news item that the newspapers would only publish the following day. That's why it was without a doubt that Wafiq, as well as his dark-eyed houris and fawning entourage, along with the whole tribe of poets, had all stumbled across the news on Moroccans' number-one news source, their shaded electronic oasis. And Rahhal was an expert in welcoming everyone with his poisoned comments. Wafiq might now have regretted the day he first knocked on poetry's door, and the moment the judging committee decided on this year's Ibn al-Wannan Prize. But why doesn't he respond? *Wafiq, I knew you in the discussion circles of the National Union of Students in Morocco as an eloquent orator, an intelligent discussant, and a dominant and wise debater, so why don't you respond? Why don't you dip your bucket in? Or is it that the sewage has surrounded you from all sides so that you no longer know which buckets to throw in, and into which troughs? But who said that I would wait for your response? Just a moment, Wafiq. A moment, please, and you'll see something from me that hadn't yet crossed your mind.*

The Squirrel hurried over to Qamar Eddine. He asked him to step in for him and deal with Abu Qatada, whose computer had suddenly stopped responding. Most likely it wouldn't need anything other than to be restarted, but the idiot still didn't know how to restart the computer, even after having been glued to the screen for hours. Generally, he was satisfied opening his jihad websites and drinking from their never-ending springs. He passionately followed discussions on the blessed forums and seldom tasked himself with the burden of contributing even a short comment.

Qamar Eddine pulled himself up. He grumbled to Mahjoub that it would be best if he stood up and made some room for him to sit down. Abu Qatada grudgingly got up from where he was sitting. Qamar Eddine's rebuke confused him. This wicked one had taken him quite unawares. But now he was in urgent need of his services. Thus, he'd allow the opportunity to pick a fight with him pass while in this difficult situation. He cast a glance around the room. All eyes were on their screens. Thank God. It didn't seem that they had noticed what had happened between him and this faggot. Even Rahhal, who usually counted every breath of the Prophet Muhammad's nation, was engrossed, enthusiastically writing something, panting like a hunting dog lurking over its prey:

Name: Wafiq Daraai

Comment Title: Oppression at the Hands of Kin is the Harshest Torture

Friends, I never imagined that they would aim all of these arrows at my chest on such a momentous day, when I was expecting you all to celebrate the prize that my brothers in the Association of Moroccan Poets have honored me with. It pains me greatly that some friends would go back and rifle through old notebooks. I don't want to discuss everything that has been said. But, for God's sake, isn't it the right of every person to make mistakes in his youth? Is it a crime for someone to be close to the security apparatus? Is that enough to accuse him of collaboration with the Mukhabarat? We are sons of today, brothers. Even if we suspect that a person made a mistake in the past, did not our generous Prophet say that "Islam effaces misdeeds done before." I am truly saddened on a day I thought I would be the happiest being on the face of the earth. Unbelievably sad.

Rahhal carefully reviewed this comment. He added some spices, such as "aiming arrows" and "for God's sake" and "rifling through old notebooks," just as he made certain to deliberately quote a noble, prophetic Hadith. One. Two. Three. Then he unleashed the comment. A minute. Two minutes, and it appeared on the screen in prominent, lit-up letters. But where did this Karima Laroussi come from? Which passing cloud did she pour down from this morning? In a quick, sympathetic response to Wafiq's comment, in her follow-up titled "Enemies of Success," Karima showed her displeasure with these unavenged comments, which came out of spite from hateful people who were taking turns at punishing our delicate poet for his success with their crude talk (as if being crowned a winner was a crime, and excelling at something was wrong) before, at the end of her comment, congratulating our "unrivaled" poet and asking that he continue his "impressive" creative path despite "the schemes of the schemers."

Despite "the schemes of the schemers"?

Come here, you whore, you've just met your match!

It wasn't just Karima who was on Rahhal's mind now, but rather a fear that other nice posts would follow. Therefore, he decided on a quick, crushing response—stern and resolute—to this lovesick girl in order to shut down any possibility that the discussion take a turn toward the position she had demarcated.

Name: An Old Lover

Comment Title: Overwhelming Passion

Good evening, Karima. You'll know who is addressing you just by reading this comment. I'm the person who loved you truly and devotedly for five years before you turned on me and betrayed me for that asshole, Wafiq Daraai. How sad I was when I learned from your friend Safaa' how quickly he threw you to the dogs after having gotten what he wanted from you. But I was more saddened to see that you are still in love with him and that you desperately defend him, despite what he did to you. It is true that love is blind and that passion is overwhelming.

Good, Rahhal. That's how you rein in that stampede of boys and girls enamored with Wafiq Daraai's poetry. Now you have to apply yourself in order to definitively respond to your friend. His supplicating comment, "treating those close to you unfairly," has begun to gain him some sympathy. You need to intervene, Squirrel. Your prey is right in front of you, so aim your electronic knee at his face.

Name: Son of the People
Comment Title: Aren't You Ashamed?

The audacity, my friend. So brazenly you say that Islam effaces previous misdeeds, as if you were a Buddhist or a Magi whose Islam only just found its home a few days ago. Aren't you ashamed? We knew you as a Qaîdi *basista* at school and your published writings exposed your hateful secularism all too clearly, so how can you dare speak the words of the Prophet and use his noble speech in your filthy response and shaky defense? May God curse he who has no shame. Go to the Mukhabarat, or the Sikhs, or even to the Sabeans. We don't care about you at all. Your ass? Do what you want with it. Just don't shove the readers of this distinguished forum up it. What matters to me, honored sir, is that it's the people's money that will find its way wrongly into your pocket. A full ten million centimes that you'll bag unjustly and under false pretenses for your stupid poems. *God has sent down no* inspiration *for them.* In fact, you wouldn't have known how to get them published in the first place without your dubious connections. Of course, the whole matter wouldn't have moved a hair on our heads if your corrupting and corrupted friends at your infernal Association of Moroccan Poets had paid you from their own pockets. But the check will be paid by the minister of culture from taxpayers' pockets and, God forbid, the money of orphans and widows and the poor will be squandered. Do you understand now what it is that so annoys us, you third-rate versifier? It's the people's money that concerns us, not teenagers fondling your ass in hammams or how close you are to Commissioner So-and-So or Colonel What's-His-Name. So, we inform you right now—and the invitation, by the way, is meant for all those esteemed readers of the honorable Hot Maroc news site—that we will stage a sit-in in front of the National Theater next Saturday to prevent this farce. We will not allow you to steal our money and suck our blood. You'll see on Saturday.

Sunday morning the Squirrel burst into tears when he read the news. Was he so proud of his victory that it made him cry? Or perhaps it was his good-heartedness that got the better of him, and sympathy for his old friend that overwhelmed him? Above all else, the news was more powerful than a person as fragile as Rahhal could handle:

"It is lucky that the Minister of Culture missed the Ibn Wannan Award ceremony held at the National Theater in Rabat yesterday evening, on account of a government emergency. Otherwise, the minister's position would have been difficult had he attended a celebration from which the award-winning poet Wafiq Daraai was unexpectedly absent. The organizers at the Association of Moroccan Poets were surprised that he had shut off his phone and cut off all communication with them two days before the ceremony. Therefore, the Marrakechi poet Samia Belghithi, a member of the administrative office of the Association of Moroccan Poets, stood in for the award-winning poet and received the award plaque from the director of the Department of Culture on his behalf. This ceremony caused some mayhem to break out when a group of around twenty attendees took it upon themselves to shout out slogans critical of cultural and political corruption, as well as prose poetry and the wasting of public money. The police needed to be called in to forcibly drive them out of the theater. It is worth mentioning that the Association of Moroccan Poets has issued a statement condemning Wafiq Daraai's irresponsible behavior, an embarrassment to Moroccan poets."

39

"HAS HIS HEARING GOTTEN THIS BAD? Or does he intend to make me yell out his name like a crazy woman as if he isn't here?"

Abdeslam has known his wife has had difficulty moving since she was young. That's why she would always issue her commands to him and Rahhal from her spot in the kitchen. Chastened, they would come together to where she was sitting. Today Abdeslam had secluded himself in the dark room that Rahhal had occupied when he was a university student, leaving Halima to bark in the courtyard while he sat in calm isolation, turning a deaf ear to her.

The strange thing was that Ayad was next to her most of the time. They would drink an afternoon glass of light, minted tea and chat. But as soon as she needed something, even something so small as a spoon, she would call Abdeslam to bring it from the kitchen. And Abdeslam would pull the hood of his jellaba up over his head, cutting off all communication.

"Ignoring me, I see? Have you lost your hearing? Yeah, go, Laâouina, I want you deafer than you are now. You know I'm sick, you son of a bitch, and you leave me here to yell and shout!"

But when were you ever well, Pelican? Halima is a professional invalid. She talks about nothing but illnesses and diseases and folk cures and herbal remedies that, over time, she has become an expert in. There is no lack of sicknesses in the world anyway. They have different symptoms and various ways of treating them, along with drugs and cures prescribed by doctors for relief to come, with God's permission. But all her life, Halima has remained loyal to two rare illnesses, no more. Boutabek is a purebred disease that only afflicts the Abda and Chiadma tribes, as if the Almighty Creator had distinguished them from ordinary mortals. There was a single specialist who treated this rare illness, Fattouma Bint Masoud Zenboub.

Whenever the disease struck Halima hard, traveling to the village was the only way for her to regain her health. Fattouma would rub castor oil under her armpits. She'd massage the area well, then wash the armpits with soap and water. After that, she'd rub them with hot argan oil, then begin to suck on the dampened area underneath her arms and spit into a pan as she muttered an incantation under her breath that seemed to be the secret of her wisdom. The treatment would last for two nights, and on the third day Halima could return to Marrakech healthy and cured as if nothing had been wrong. The second illness was called Boumezoui—an obscure disease that was widespread among the Abda and Chiadma tribes. But it seems that the doctors of Marrakech who came one after another to treat Halima in the large Antaki Hospital in Bab Khemis for the past thirty years were at a loss. Of course, the swelling of the belly accompanied by pain in the area below it, in addition to continuing rumbling coming from it, and sharp pain that quickly moved to the right side of the lower belly, all of these are symptoms of irritable bowel. But the headache that almost split Halima's head in two and the fever that would rise from her lower back, likewise the strange choking feeling she had, all of these were additional symptoms that continued to baffle the doctors and cause them to mix up their prescriptions. As for Halima, whenever her neighbor asked her how she was doing with her illness, she would sigh bitterly before responding: "My dear, thank God. It is He who grants healing. Anyone who says there's a doctor other than God, praise Him, is lying."

For three decades, Halima has repeated the same sentence, word for word and sigh for sigh. Rahhal was surprised that the Pelican didn't get bored of this, as if it were dialogue in a play that the director categorically refused to make even the simplest change to.

When a neighbor would approach her during the last days of Ramadan saying, "Thanks to God, Ramadan passed well and it's almost over now. Blessed are those who have fasted," Halima lets out a sharp, deep sigh and hisses like a viper: "Ah, my dear, it's life that passes. Ramadan, what of it? Ramadan comes and Ramadan goes."

"How're you doing with the heat?" Neighbors always include that question in their morning greetings during the hot Marrakech summers, and Halima has come up with a theatrical response for it that delights everyone who is tempted to play along. She puts her hand below her cheek then begins to move her head in a circular motion before opening her hands as if she's about to sing, employing her famous and indispensable sigh for the benefit of whomever she's talking to: "Oh, my dear. We are weak before our Lord, praise Him. When the cold comes, he defeats us, and when the heat comes, he destroys us. May You be praised, O Great One."

Even though Rahhal had effectively memorized all of Halima's stock phrases, he remained taken by how amazing she was in executing them. He was surprised by the sudden humility and the artificial misery, along with her feigned piety, religiosity, and full repentance before the power of the Creator Judge, as if the pious woman who spoke was not the same one who, before, had fumed with rage, spat in Abdeslam's face, and cursed his family and tribe from his first forefather to his most recent one, whose right eye had been put out by God at a young age so he could only see through his left; who, despite that, had put that remaining bleary eye into the service of His Excellency, the caid, by watching over the movements of the freedom fighters of the tribe and the neighboring villages in the colonial days, transmitting news of them first and foremost to His Excellency.

May God have mercy on the past, on the Grandpa Laâouina days. Laâouina Sr. was a member of the caid's court, and whomever the caid was satisfied with, the Lord favored. The good times lasted until the 1970s. Abda was drowning in plenty before the consecutive years of drought shattered the village, forcing its young people, and some older ones, too, to migrate to the surrounding cities. Longing for the harvest nights of old continued to eat away at Abdeslam's heart, filling his spirit and his very being. He hears Halima screaming and her endless demands, but whenever he soars toward the village of his youth and remembers the kindness of his mother, Yamina, and the mischief of his brother, Ayad, returning him to the sweet and simple days there before the drought, he becomes completely detached. Halima's calls and insults no longer reach him. They've come to knock on a wall made of cold, thick glass that he has surrounded himself with over the last few years, and he has come to enjoy the sight of her drawn-out screams smashing into the invisible barrier before falling to the floor in front of him, as if he weren't there.

Halima says she's sick. What sickness? She's healthier than a tyrant. What's ailing her is a severe lack of oxygen. People breathe slowly and take their full fair share of oxygen, whereas she doesn't allow it to reach her lungs. She walks heavily but she pants. As if when she breathes, her nostrils are like a constricted bellows blowing on a cold fire. She gasps rather than breathes. She doesn't even know how to derive benefit from her theatrical sighs, her only chance to exhale slowly from her mouth while her heart and bowels can rest a little.

Halima says she's sick, but the sick one is Abdeslam. Ever since Rahhal left home and the Hedgehog banned him from setting foot in her den in Mouassine, Abdeslam has been sick. At first, he tried to rile the Pelican up. He began explaining to her that it was their right—no, their duty—to visit the groom in his home to make sure everything was all right. But Halima used the excuse that Rahhal was newly married and that their home was small, not to mention the fact that he wasn't alone there. His wife still lived under her mother's wing. Moreover, what would they do at their place anyway? Abdeslam knew that Halima, like him, burned with longing to visit her son but she was afraid of the Hedgehog and was avoiding her mother. She says that Marrakechi women are witches, and that only God who created them could stand them. Abdeslam remained a stranger in his brother, Ayad's house. Even when she prepared her exquisite tea right before the afternoon call to prayer, she would call Ayad in, forgetting all about Abdeslam unless she needed something in the kitchen. Then she'd start yelling:

"Abdeslam! Hey, Abdeslam. Go to hell, Laâouina. I'd like you to be even deafer than that!"

Halima says she's sick. But if the Pelican has taken sickness on as a profession, your hobbies, Mantis, are obliviousness and silence. Even a small transistor radio was too much for your family in the Ain Itti days. Rahhal won't forgive you for this, in particular. During the time they had for singing at the end of class, his classmates at Antaki Elementary School in Bab Khemis used to sing the songs that would crash down on the national radio waves in the morning. They used to sing them enthusiastically together in class, sometimes under the supervision of the teachers. But Rahhal was unable to keep up because Abdeslam didn't see the importance of providing a radio for the family. A silly little radio. And despite that, you used to insist on dragging a fat horned sheep on the Eid of the Sacrifice into the slums of Ain Itti. As soon as the sheep slipped out from between your hands, the young unemployed guys who would always be leaning up against the wall would volunteer to chase and grab it, then help you drag it home. You used to feel proud with what looked like a procession. The sacrificial animal is definitely a tradition, but it's just a tradition. Even Abu Bakr and 'Umar, and they are who they are, didn't adhere to it. So, did you have to insist on it every year when you couldn't even find enough money to buy your only son the proper clothes for school? A white, black-headed ram with horns, fat, expensive, no limp or redness in the eyes. A sheep exactly according to Sunna, the Prophet's example, sure. But you never thought about a measly battery-powered radio, Abdeslam?

That's why, when God graced his electronic spiders with YouTube, Rahhal found himself like someone who had reclaimed an old life. Not only did he have to make the best of his time now, but he had to make up for lost time, too.

All the songs that had slipped away from his early childhood began to come back to him: "O You with the Power and Might"; "I Love You, and Hope to Forget My Soul Should I Forget You"; "O Marrakech, O Rose among the Palm Trees"; "Hassan's Voice Calls Out with Your Tongue, O Sahara"; "The Springs of Laâyoune, in My

Eyes So Fine, the Red Waterwheel Is Mine"; "The Crescent Moon Is Gone"; "O Emissary of Love, Where Have You Gone?"

Then there was that song the teacher taught us in third grade on March 21, on the occasion of the first day of spring. It was about spring and its title was . . . it was . . ."Atlas Spring" by the Amanna Trio. Rahhal, do you remember that song?

> The fluttering bird sings a ghazal to the hills and they blow
> a kiss
> To a butterfly floating around the trees, the moon's smile
> they miss.
> The waterwheels brush the face of the fields, and perfume
> bathes the plains in its mist.

Then there were those other songs. They weren't by the Amanna Trio. No, the voice wasn't Moroccan. It was a tender voice as if it were a dream. Ah, what was it, Rahhal? "The Heart Got Hung Up." That was the title exactly: "The Heart Got Hung Up." He typed the title into YouTube, revved up the search engine, and a clip of the propagandist Abu Hattak al-Matiri exploded in his face. The sheikh started yelling at the beginning of the clip: "By God, anything other than God that the heart gets hung up on is agony." No, Mr. Sheikh. It wasn't "The Heart Got Hung Up" exactly. Rather, it was *my* heart. *My* heart. "My Heart Got Hung Up." You've got it. That's it. Oh boy, Rahhal:

> My heart got hung up on an Arab girl, luxurious in her
> silken garments, bangles, and jewels.
> She has eyes that, if she were to look at a monk who fasts
> and prays to God,
> He'd lose himself in love as if he had never fasted for a day
> or prayed even once, like a fool.

He listened to it on YouTube sung by Talal Maddah, then by Tariq 'Abd al-Hakim. But when he tried Hiyam Younes, his heart fluttered, his temperature rose, and the blood pulsed through his veins. This is the voice that had held onto your senses, holding firm to your emotions ever since childhood, Squirrel. It was as soon as he entered Bab Khemis, on his way to Antaki Elementary School, coming from Ain Itti, that his ears had picked it up like a radio receiver, swept in on the warm waves of the radio. One radio heard by everyone. "This is Rabat. Moroccan radio broadcast. And here are this morning's songs." He'd walk slowly in front of the metalworker and saddlemaker shops. All of them on the same wavelength. And Hiyam Younes, whose name he didn't know at the time, rang out in her girlish voice, and he fell in love with her, his heart getting hung up on her as if she were the child in the song's lyrics, wishing that Abdeslam would buy them a small battery-powered radio so he could enjoy the morning songs. Oh Hiyam . . .

> She has Hijazi eyes and Najdi insides, Iraqi limbs and a
>   Roman behind,
> Tihaman body and Absan lips, Khuzan teeth and Durran face.

And her name was Hiyam. Listen, Emad. Listen. Her name was Hiyam. And her name became Hiyam. As if we had been promised each other since the beginning of time. Just listen, Hiyam, daughter of Hajj Maâti. Here's the rest of the song:

> I played chess with her and my knights came one after the
>   other, quickly mixing with the king.
> Each game won was worth a kiss, and kissing her cheeks
>   was like kissing the new moon.
> So, I gave her ninety-nine kisses, eager, and yet another one,
>   too.

On YouTube, Rahhal finally found that small radio that Abdeslam hadn't bought for him. And he discovered how deep his love was for Hiyam. His heart had been hung up on her since his days in Bab Khemis and at Antaki Elementary. As for his soul, it has been in love with her for eternity.

Oh Hiyam, if I were a poet I'd write poems about you and collect them in a book called *The Wild Cow's Pasture*. I'd write ghazal poetry for you more beautiful than the love poems of Qays and more creative than what was in that song. But poetry has become scarce and "the poets are gone," (as the great Antara once said) and I'm not so much of a fraud to compose just any words about you. Tonight, I will not let you escape. I will hunt you in the Hedgehog's pen and when I have your neck in my hands, and your smooth cheek within my reach, I'll kiss it all over, but I'll have to hurry of course, before the Hedgehog, who has no patience whatsoever for bedroom games, starts shooting her arrows at me.

40

EXACTLY TEN DAYS after the wedding, Rahhal and Hassaniya returned home from school late because of transit congestion (they hadn't yet gotten the moped) and they found him there. There was a tray of tea and a plate of *ghorayba* cookies. And, to the surprise of her daughter, because the widow took so much pleasure in the retired construction worker's stories, she insisted he stay for dinner. Ayad didn't need too much persuading to sit back down in front of the television. He ate dinner with them, enjoyed another cup of strong, sweetened tea, and didn't leave until Hassaniya turned off the television. This wasn't his only visit.

After the widow passed away and Rahhal and Hassaniya moved to Massira, Ayad's visits continued. Rahhal was busy composing one of his fiery Son of the People comments when a smiling Ayad knocked on the shop door with a handful of keys. As if he was expecting the Squirrel to lift his head and notice his wrinkled forehead, his close-together eyes and his rat-like features, and be cheered by the visit. Usually, the customers in the cybercafe don't annoy Rahhal. One of them will calmly slink off toward an open machine in the hopes that the Squirrel won't come out of the state of absorption he has fallen into all of a sudden. And Rahhal doesn't start to keep track of the time until the moment he notices that the customer is there. This works in the customers' favor, especially the high school students; free time that can sometimes exceed fifteen minutes, an unspoken arrangement that gave Son of the People as well as Abu Qatada the calm they needed to write their sulfurous comments.

But Ayad, how could he make *him* wait?

The Squirrel understood that his uncle's visits were being handed down to him as God's law, no way to refuse or delay them.

Therefore, he asked Qamar Eddine to watch over the shop while he stepped out for a few minutes and went with Ayad to Café Milano. Qamar Eddine, who practically lived at the cybercafe and didn't leave until it closed, was happy to take on these tasks. In return for watching over the cybercafe when he was gone, as well as lending a helping hand to customers whenever one of those electronic donkeys was stopped at a roadblock from time to time, Rahhal gave him a voucher worth ten to twenty hours, depending on the amount of work Qamar Eddine did for the shop's customers. (Each regular now had a five- to ten-hour card. They would pay a special price in advance for the card, as determined by Rahhal: three dirhams for those with five- and ten-hour cards, two and a half dirhams for those with twenty-hour cards).

The strange thing was that Asmae would always ask Rahhal what he wanted to drink. As for Ayad, she no longer asked him. She treated him as she would a friend, bringing him a pot of strong tea with wormwood leaves, and putting an extra chunk of sugar down in front of him. Even the waitress in Café Milano has come to know how sweet you like your tea, Ayad. Rahhal would quickly sip his tea or coffee then go back to inspect his marvelous electronic creations, leading them in their quixotic battles against the world. Ayad preferred to wait in the café.

Waiting for what, you rat?

Lunchtime if it was a morning visit, and dinnertime if it was an evening visit. And because the will of God is unavoidable, Rahhal was obliged to bring him home, but not before torturing him by making him wait. So Rahhal aimed to dawdle as much as would annoy his uncle, and he'd make him wait for hours. But the floor of the café could shake underneath Ayad's feet and the ground on Dakhla Avenue could swallow up the building, and Ayad still would not budge. Rahhal's lunch was always cold leftovers. He made tajines before going to sleep. He prepared the lunch tajine at night, then went to sleep after having drunk some tea and eaten something light, like a boiled egg smashed into olive oil with a bit of salt added to it, or a piece of La Vache Qui Rit cheese and two slices of mortadella. As for Hassaniya, it was impossible for her to fall asleep without her digging deep into the next day's tajine.

When Oum Eid was alive and well, Rahhal didn't have to worry at all about food. They would walk into the house and find that the widow had taken care of it. But as soon as she died, the Squirrel discovered the bitter truth. The Hedgehog, who ate like a hippopotamus, didn't know how to boil an egg. He even had to make tea himself if he wanted to enjoy some. That's how he humbly donned the apron.

■ ■ ■

The annoying thing about Ayad was that he involved himself in things that were none of his business. He'd go with Rahhal up to the apartment for lunch and then insist on waiting for Hassaniya. "My dear uncle, keep your gallantry to yourself. We don't wait for one another to eat lunch. Whenever one of us finds the time, we go to the apartment and eat whatever God has apportioned for us. We work and don't see one another until nighttime." And then there was the holy custom called the afternoon nap—only devils don't nap! Even though the Squirrel had eschewed this ritual, Ayad would never miss it. So Rahhal would leave the apartment and Ayad would stay behind, snoring in the living room like a fat angel. At first, he used to let Hassaniya stumble in on him lying there, but, after she explained that she'd turn the world upside down the next time she walked into her apartment to the rhythm of anyone snoring, he started to invite his uncle for a second pot of tea with Asmae at Café Milano.

Ayad always insisted on involving himself in things that didn't concern him. He was the only one bold enough to once ask Hassaniya about having children. One morning, Rahhal was surprised to see him so he took him to Asmae and the café and left him sipping tea to wait for him. When they walked into the apartment for lunch, they found Hassaniya had come in before them that afternoon. Rahhal got the table ready and the three of them hovered over the tajine. Hassaniya seemed annoyed with Ayad's intrusion. But she made a habit of hiding her annoyance with silence. Exaggerated silence. Ayad made annoying sounds when he chewed, like bubblegum bubbles popping, which got on Hassaniya's nerves. And as if he wanted to get on her nerves even more, he sprang a question on her:

"So? What are you two waiting for, Hassaniya? You still don't want to bring us a baby boy or girl to brighten our world?"

Hassaniya was shocked by the question. The food stuck in her throat. She drank a cup of water. She took two gulps and glared at Rahhal, as if he had suggested his uncle ask the question. Perhaps she wanted *him* to answer.

Rahhal mumbled confusedly:

"That's up to God, Uncle."

"But as God Almighty says, 'Make it happen, my servant, and I will help you,' trust in God Almighty."

"Sure, trust in God Almighty," Hassaniya snarled before getting up angrily from the table. She disappeared for a few minutes then glared at the two rats with a hateful smile on her face and said to Ayad: "Say 'hi' to your brother and his wife, and good luck to you and Abdeslam finding *that* verse in the Qur'an." Then she slammed the door behind her and left.

Rahhal had never broached this subject with Hassaniya. He didn't know whether she had thought about having children before Ayad had asked her. But at least he was happy this way. Any unforeseen event that might destroy his current life was beyond him. Pregnancy, labor, delivery, the children's hospital, and a pile of flesh screaming in the house day and night. Milk, nursing, changing diapers. Never. Rahhal couldn't bear an upheaval like that. He was happy with his daily routine, familiar with it. He didn't need anything unpredictable to turn his life upside down. Then, picture, Rahhal, that you had children. Would you give mankind a wonder of a little angel with a sweet smile? Would your baby be like the child in the Dalaa and Pampers ads? No doubt you'll give birth to a rat that looks like you. An indistinguishable squirrel with rat-like eyes running and howling behind you. And when he playfully climbs up onto you you'll put him on your back and try to play with him, maybe tickling him, and he'll scrunch up his face in front of yours and scream. You'll find yourself in front of a small, disgusting-looking rat. You'll hate him, Rahhal, and you'll hate yourself even more. Rahhal avoids looking in the mirror because his rat-like face confuses him and makes him tense. So why, Ayad, would you want a repulsive reflection of that same face made of flesh and blood?

Even a girl would be nothing but a hedgehog like her mother. A hedgehog that would disrupt your life even more. No, never. I don't want children, Ayad. We have no need for them. And no doubt, Hassaniya feels the same way I do. One squirrel in the house is enough for her, and one hedgehog is enough for me. And if it was Halima who set you on us, assure her that pelicans are like the red-necked ostrich and the emperor eagle; they've gone extinct in this country.

"Uncle, I've got to get back to work. But before I do, may I invite you to a glass of tea at Asmae's?"

41

ASMAE WASN'T EXTREMELY GOOD-LOOKING, but her natural flirtatiousness, neither put on nor coquettish, pulled at the Squirrel's heartstrings. Her good body pained him and he couldn't look at her for too long. Broad-chested with breasts running amok like two young foals that practically tore through her tight T-shirt, and a respectable behind that she framed well in her skintight jeans. The clothes were a work requirement, nothing more, and at her core, the girl was a good, friendly, village girl. No doubt her father had emigrated from one of the surrounding drought-stricken villages just as Abdeslam, Ayad, and so many others had done. And because the majority of those who came from the barren villages failed to educate their children and prepare them well, it was only natural that Asmae found herself working as a café waitress.

But Asmae didn't want to stay at Café Milano. Rather, she wanted to leave the café and travel to Milano. The real Milano in Italy, not the crowded and noisy Milano of Massira, where the air is fouled by clouds of smoke that fill it as if there were an impromptu competition going on between the customers over who could burn out his chest with the greatest number of cigarettes. One of the customers talked to Asmae about a work opportunity there in the hotel services field.

"Work no different from what you do here, but in a more pleasant setting. And in Milano. The real Milano."

"And Italian?"

"In the job I'm putting you up for, language doesn't matter too much to them. What you'll need, what's necessary for the job, you'll master in twenty-four hours. You just need to be friendly, serious, tireless, and as hardworking as you are here with this undeserving riffraff." His name was Younes, but they called him Talios. He lived on the first floor of the building across the street from the café, directly above the Atlas Cubs Cybercafe. A handsome young man in his thirties, always traveling back and forth between Italy and Morocco. He would order more than one drink for himself each time he sat there, and he only smoked Marlboros. Unlike others who carefully hid their pack before pulling out a practically lit cigarette, Talios would generously offer his cigarettes to others. He wouldn't stay away from the café for too long. Two or three months, then he'd return. And every time he'd come with a new car. Some people whispered that he worked in smuggling. Hashish and stolen cars. But none of this mattered to Asmae. He could be trusted, as long as he came and went, dignified and honored while passing through the customs and border police barriers, and came to the café covering his drinks as well as those who sat with him and leaving a respectable tip on top of that. As for what people say, it never ends. Most of them speak out of envy. "These Moroccans are so jealous. At least Talios has something to be envious of. But, I still haven't done anything to be jealous of. And I won't let them rob me of my dreams. Of a light flashing in the distance; a flicker of hope, however dim it may seem. I need to stick with him. I won't tell anyone about it. But I won't let the opportunity slip away."

Younes gave her the email address of the manager who she'd be working for. He explained to her that he was Moroccan—from Khouribga—and that she could write to him in Arabic. All that was needed was a copy of her national ID card and five attractive photos that showed off her lithe body.

"The pictures are the important thing. You need to appear pretty in them. Cheerful, smiling, and happy. You need to look happy in the pictures. This is absolutely essential. In Italy, no one employs someone who's sad. Go to a professional photographer. And it would be best if he took the pictures in a park or a luxurious salon, not in his studio. A few extra doses of seduction wouldn't hurt a bit. The photographer will help you. They know how to take pictures these days."

"But how do I send him all of these things?"

Younes pointed to the cybercafe in front of her.

"They have a scanner at the cybercafe. And the email address I gave you will be more than enough. Just bring your ID card and the photos to the guy who works there, explain to him what you need, and he'll take care of sending them."

The Squirrel used to feel crushed every time this lioness stood in front of him in the café. He'd be thinking about tea and find himself ordering coffee. When he'd be wishing for strong coffee he would be so shaken up he'd order orange juice. He didn't understand why he was so rattled by Asmae. He wasn't in love with her, nor did he even desire her, but her body destroyed him. Your weakness before a certain type of cow is a proven fact, so what's with you and lionesses, Squirrel? But, the question really was, what has brought this young lioness to your lair?

When Rahhal saw Asmae's pictures, he was completely stunned. They defied description. It was more than he could take. A body that was compact and elegant all at the same time. Flowing without hanging loosely. Strong and firm, yet graceful and smooth. In the pictures she wore a red shirt that was cut extremely low in the front, showing off as much as possible without putting everything on full display. As was usually the case with Asmae, the shirt was tight enough to show off her torso's charms, and short enough to reveal her beautiful belly button and light a fire in him. This was the first time she had come through the cybercafe door, so she seemed a bit confused as she explained what she wanted to Rahhal. He explained to her that it would be best that he open a Hotmail account for her from which he could send the ID card and pictures, and that's what he did. The order was for just five photos, but Rahhal scanned all the pictures the Lioness had in her possession. More than ten photos. Five of them in a beautiful Moroccan salon, perhaps a hotel lobby. The others in the park. Rahhal sent five of them—the pictures in the salon because they were the most erotic and exciting—and left them in front of him floating like bubbles of light on top of the computer desk, while he buried the rest of the photos in the archive.

As soon as Asmae stepped out of the shop, Rahhal began to monitor her email. But in vain. Every time Ayad came and was forced to wait for the Squirrel in his corner at Café Milano like a fixed deposit, when lunchtime would come and he would run into Asmae, she'd ask him if there was any news. Always the same, no answer. Even Talios disappeared. They had arrested him at the Port of Algeciras, his car loaded with three kilos of hashish that he had hidden inside a double hollowed-out cavity he had devilishly constructed inside the car's frame. At least that's what they said at the café.

42

DESPITE ABU QATADA'S REPUTATION with the brothers and sisters who considered this man—who, in God, didn't fear the reproach of any reproacher—their living waking conscience (always enthusiastic to condemn the errors of secularists, the lies of democrats, and the trifles of liberals and those who follow them with similar offenses toward the Day of Judgment), Son of the People was a special case. There was no way to compare him to any other crafter of comments. He became the unrivaled star of Hot Maroc. Let's take "likes," for example. The most important columnists at Hot Maroc would write their exhaustive articles on an issue of public interest that the whole country would be drawn to, and one of them might get two hundred likes after a week of discussion. As for Rahhal, a quick comment on a stupid daily news item that might take him two minutes to write as Ayad stood over him waiting would net him likes from far and wide. He'd gulp his tea, park his uncle at the café, and come back to find the like machine in full swing. Sometimes he'll get five hundred likes in three days. Was it success granted by God? Or some sort of acceptance? The important thing was that Son of the People had become the unrivaled star of the site. He had readers for whom his comments replaced the original article, and female admirers who couldn't stand his being away.

"Whoever starts out well, advances." You spoke the truth, Ibn 'Ataallah. You are correct, Iskandari. Son of the People made a royal entrance onto the electronic battleground from his very first comment. Like a bench player put into the final match in the last breaths of the second overtime period, then scoring the winning goal. Son of the People didn't do anything more than compose a very simple comment on the Ibn Wannan Prize awarded this year to the poet Wafiq Daraai for the world to be turned on its head. The minister backed out of attending. The award-winning poet boycotted the ceremony. The committee that awarded him the prize issued a statement denigrating him. And a small group of internet vagabonds gathered on one side of the National Theater in the capital and proceeded to shout out slogans. The police broke the ribs of six of them and arrested three others. One item from the MAP News Agency said that the three who were arrested had tried to derail the peaceful demonstration by interrupting with shouts calling for bringing down the regime.

Rahhal had every right to be proud of Son of the People, and he favored him over the others. For he, like Rahhal, was a master of the knockout punch. He had the same lightning-quick knee that the Squirrel often used to smash his adversaries' faces in his dreams. Son of the People, quite simply, cuts to the chase. He hates trickery and beating around the bush. His matériel is always at the ready: charges of treason; accusations of conspiring with the Mukhabarat agents; going after his adversary's honor as well as that of his mother, his wife, his daughters, and his aunts, and presenting embarrassing facts about him. Son of the People always made sure that a bit of the information he presented was true in order to guarantee the trust of the readers, especially those who intimately knew the targeted person. After that, level as many false charges as you can! Son of the People is particularly keen on preserving the readers' trust, even though they don't really read. Most of them just peer down from the balcony of the title at the picture accompanying the subject and then begin to look for Son of the People's response. After, say, twenty comments in which they discuss the article's subject, they agree or disagree with the author; they attack or defend the person who produced the article. Then Son of the People fires off a shot and the comments follow one after the other. Forty. Fifty. One hundred. Two hundred. Most of them don't return to the original article to discuss it. Rather, they move around in Son of the People's universe. They recall *his* words. They interact with *him*. Sometimes, they might disagree with him, but with him and his comment, not with the article and its subject.

After the national team was disqualified from the Africa Cup, a topic that didn't concern Rahhal in any way whatsoever, voices were raised demanding a comment from Son of the People. The team came home after the first round with tails of defeat between their legs, and the news was published on the front page of Hot Maroc. "The Lions Leave the Africa Cup in the First Round," with a subtitle that really grabbed Rahhal: "The Atlas Lions Are No Good at Roaring in African Jungles." Rahhal didn't even read the article. It was all the same to him whether the team was eliminated or won the cup. It didn't matter to him at all. It was only out of habit that he found himself scrolling through the comments. And there was Khadija from Nador, writing what seemed to be a passionate cry for help: "Why haven't we read your comment on this disaster, Son of the People? Can't you taste the disgrace? Is it okay with you that teams from countries crushed by civil wars and mangled by famines beat us?"

What exactly do you want, you bitch? Your loser team was eliminated from the Africa Cup, so what am I supposed to do about it? Why are you yelling at me? Do you think I'm the king of the world? He almost hit the down button and went to the next page, but the following comment sang the same tune: "Well said, my dear sister. I don't understand how Son of the People can keep from making any remark on this subject in particular. We all know how patriotic he is. Our only fear is that he is sick or something bad has happened to him. But anyway, absence has its reasons. May he have a good reason for not commenting." A reader from Guerçif wrote a comment with a subject heading that simply said: "Son of the People, May God Cure You, My Friend."

No, Rahhal. You need to get in there right away to staunch the flow of idiotic comments. True, there's nothing that connects you to the topic, but what can you do? The call of duty, brother. The call of conscience. Just perform a quick, routine maneuver. They've become addicted to your acrobatic somersaults, so don't deprive them. Khadija from Nador, for example, won't be able to sleep tonight unless she gets her fix. Anyway, you don't need to know the rules of soccer, nor do you have to have watched games you don't follow at all. You won't have to conduct a full-scale investigation into the topic. The story is very simple. You can just exaggerate everything the way you always do, and your readers, my boy, *die* for your exaggerations.

Name: Son of the People
Comment Title: And They Ask You about Lions?

I am not sick, my friends. But I have refrained from commenting in order to avoid any sort of a clash with you. There are comments from people who imagine themselves FIFA-accredited sports analysts. Others see themselves as theorists putting forth long-term plans for improving the caliber of Moroccan soccer. And all of them talk about the Atlas Lions without batting an eye. Lions went extinct in the Atlas Mountains a long time ago, so all we can do now is pity them. Now there are just monkeys hopping around there. Like the monkeys that played in the Africa championship. Effeminate monkeys with gold chains that seem more concerned with their hairdos than in scoring the winning goal. Most of them are émigrés from France and the Netherlands who don't even know the national anthem. This team, my friends, doesn't concern me and I don't expect a thing from it. I'm not an idiot who would futilely demand that the Atlas Monkeys roar.

Fadoua and Samira stood over Rahhal, seeking his help creating a profile for Marrakech Star on Facebook. He hadn't yet opened himself up to this new electronic continent. For now, he turned them over to Qamar Eddine until he could practice how to do it later on. Experience taught him that the contagion spread through the ether as fast as fire through straw. Today Fadoua and Samira, tomorrow Salim, the day after that, the Africanos. The electronic legions would flock to join Facebook like a herd of lost souls who believed that a new religion had appeared on the scene, and they rushed to embrace it. He needed to prepare for this starting now.

He opened an account for himself on the new social network, practicing the technique of developing profiles, trying out its different icons, then setting the appropriate rate.

"But I'm busy now. Go see Qamar Eddine."

As soon as the two girls hovered around the Christian-without-news-from-our-Lord-Jesus, Rahhal found himself inserting himself between them. It seemed he had changed his mind. He needed to learn how to subscribe right away, and it was an opportunity to get the password that would be given to Marrakech Star in order to light up the Facebook sky.

Qamar Eddine didn't spend more than twenty minutes on it, but it was enough to assure Rahhal of his new electronic goose that laid the golden egg. Also, enough to notice the fearsome coup Son of the People had started to lead when he returned to Hot Maroc. Seventy likes in less than half an hour, and twenty-five comments. "And that's just the beginning, and on, and on," as the song goes. They came in the form of self-criticism. They apologized to Son of the People and praised his wisdom and the extent of his vision before swearing not to insult the Lions anymore. Everyone started to talk about the Atlas Monkeys and to repeat the word *monkey* so nonchalantly that a stray commenter demanded that the readers of Hot Maroc show some athletic spirit, making it clear that "defeat is like victory, and elimination is like winning. You need to accept both of them comfortably," before including at the end of his comment wishes for every success for the Atlas Monkeys in the upcoming international qualifying matches.

43

RAHHAL OPENED UP HIS HOTMAIL ACCOUNT. He made some space by deleting some of the spam messages that had accumulated in his inbox. He realized that he barely checked his email, having spent so much time wandering around in other people's email. But what would he need email for, anyway? To send messages to Halima and Abdeslam? Or to check what was going on in the villages of Abda?

Today he opened his Hotmail just to make sure that his account was still active, because he'd need it to set up a Facebook profile. The Facebook walls attracted Rahhal more than any of the other features the site provided. He didn't want to set up photo albums, or participate in closed-group discussions, and he wasn't interested in lists of friends. The only thing he was drawn to was the writing wall, and scribbling on it as he pleased. A simple wall he could scratch a word into and then leave. Scribbling with total freedom, and signing it with his new Facebook name: 24/7 Samir.

But the wall on Facebook goes on forever. It has no limit. Not like the walls at school or in the toilet stall. Write, Rahhal, write. Write whatever comes to mind. But how to reach the readers? This isn't Hot Maroc, which provides your virtual creations, Abu Qatada and Son of the People, a place to sit, a throne of stardom. This is a louder, more boisterous space. A raging sea that dizzies those who sail on it, and you, Squirrel, have neither paddles nor sails.

For 24/7 Samir's profile picture, he chose a verse from Muhyi al-Din Ibn 'Arabi—"I believe in the religion of love wherever my mounts might head / for love is my religion, my creed"—written in ornate Arabic calligraphy. He was intent on presenting himself as a poet born in 1981. And it was in that guise that he sent a few friend requests to some random profiles. But the response wasn't what he expected. He began to write some dreamy phrases and sayings on his wall, but in vain:

Don't worry about someone who loves you in the beginning. Rather, worry about who loves you to the end.

Loneliness is painful, but it is better than being with those who only remember you when they are alone or in need.

Tears don't change reality, but they soothe the heart.

Man only makes life when life makes a man out of him.

You can't pluck the scent of a flower, even if you crush it underfoot.

A young student whose profile had seduced him, both by her gaiety and by the naturalness of the photos she posted, whom he had asked to add to his list of friends, responded arrogantly to him: "Excuse me, Mr. Mustapha Lutfi Manfalouti. Don't get me wrong, but let's be honest, romance and I don't mix."

The Squirrel regretted presenting himself to these wretches as a sensitive poet. Do you see, Wafiq? Do you see, you idiot? You dress up as a star and no one even cares about poetry and poets. Girls these days aren't romantics, you moron.

But what's all this about Wafiq, Rahhal? What does he have to do with it? Forget the man for a bit, my friend. You're the one who chose 24/7 Samir and "I believe in the religion of love" and talk of loneliness, tears, and the scent of flowers. Wafiq Daraai has nothing to do with this, so don't obsess over him. Keep 24/7 Samir, this profile isn't all bad. You might need it someday. As for now, you can storm through this calm Facebook environment as much as you like. Just get the Lioness out of your burrow, Squirrel; send her out into the wide-open electronic terrain and you will see something wonderful!

Rahhal jumped up from where he was sitting. He stood at the shop door, scanning the tables of Café Milano. Asmae was there carrying a tray full of orders: three coffees (one espresso and a pair of cafés au lait), a pot of tea, an orange juice, and three croissants. She moved like a wounded lion that had been thrown into an absurd circus by her rotten luck. And instead of roaming around in wide open pastures surrounded by forest, she found herself compelled to move between tables of animal trainers, clowns, and acrobats here in this stupid café that looked like a third-rate circus.

Asmae no longer asked Rahhal about what happened to the email. She wasn't expecting a response from anyone, especially after Talios disappeared. She seemed to have given up. But Rahhal didn't tell her about two emails. The first one came asking about Younes right after he disappeared and before news spread in Café Milano of his arrest. The second one came two months later, asking the Lioness to send her cell phone number as soon as she could so they could call her from Milano to begin making travel arrangements and prepare the necessary papers after finally receiving approval for her application. Rahhal wasn't comfortable with these two vague emails, especially since they came without a signature. He was similarly uncomfortable with this mysterious job that Asmae would get in Italy that didn't require her to learn Italian. Just the alluring photos that accentuated her charms and revealed her assets. *No, Asmae, I won't leave you by yourself to meet your doom.* This is why Rahhal closed the subject after unilaterally deciding to refuse the job offer.

The Lioness is coming, you bastards.

You packs of wolves and foxes.

The Lioness is coming, so clear the way.

He chose the name "Hiyam" for her. Just like that. Because of his infatuation with Hiyam, or maybe in spite of it. Her name was Hiyam, and that's all. No last name or nickname. A student at Cadi Ayyad University. City: Marrakech. Personal data needed to be included in the account. Date of birth: February 14, 1990. Gender: Female. Relationship status: *C'est compliqué.* That's what Rahhal chose, keeping in line with some of the other mined profiles. What does it mean for your relationship status to be complicated? Are you involved with someone or not? Do you have a boyfriend, a husband, a fiancé, or not? And what does "complicated" mean, anyway? Are we to understand that you have a bird in hand but you're prepared to hide it for the sake of the eyes of the first eagle that lands at the top of the tree? But whatever. Rahhal would use this expression that so tortured him in order to torture others. Hiyam was an open-minded university student, ready to make the acquaintance of men and women alike, and her relationship status was complicated. What else? That was enough.

Rahhal chose her profile picture carefully. A racy photo that looked more like an attractive Italian actress than a waitress at Café Milano. He collected the four other photos in an album he opened for her fans. He wrote one sentence on the wall. He chose it from among the romantic Manfaloutian 24/7 Samir quotes: "Tears don't change reality, but they soothe the heart."

He set the Lioness loose and after the first few minutes, he was surprised by how many were caught. Friend requests poured in so fast he could hardly believe it. And the comments poured in, too:

Really, Hiyam, very wise. "Tears don't change reality, but they soothe the heart." You said it perfectly. Good for you, may God bless you. I feel that you're hiding the beautiful soul of a poet inside you.

Every tear has its ending, and at the end of every tear is a smile ☺.

O cruel world, don't shed tears on a smooth cheek.

Do not blame me for shedding tears
At the time of departure, tears are a weapon that helps.

Hiyam, I hope you mean tears of joy. Didn't the poet Hafiz Ibrahim once say:

I thanked your beauty for my tears
for tears are the measure of emotion.

Sons of bitches, they've all become poets. Everybody is lecturing on the secrets of tears. They're citing the wellsprings of poetry and explaining measures of emotion. Hiyam was happy to dole out likes.

She made likes lightly and elegantly, and accepted friend requests and such . . . until 24/7 Samir sent a request and she accepted it. But he didn't comment on tears and what soothes the heart. It seems that he was still wounded by the response of that braggart who described him as Manfaloutian, overly poetic.

44

IT HAPPENED JUST LIKE IN THE MOVIES. Movies that Rahhal didn't know about because, outside of the few karate films he had watched in his childhood, he stopped going to the movies long ago. And television movies were outside of his orbit because there wasn't any electricity, either during the Ain Itti days or in their hovel in Moukef. After he got married and settled down in Mouassine, Oum Eid always spent her evenings in front of the television screen following her never-ending Mexican and Brazilian soap operas, then the Turkish ones after that. And even after Oum Eid passed away, the happy couple moved to Massira and found that, among the things he had provided for them when he furnished the apartment, Emad Qatifa had included a high-end, name-brand television with a powerful satellite dish that, unlike the others, got channels from everywhere, East and West. But Rahhal would come home late from the cybercafe thinking only of tomorrow's tajine that the Hedgehog would eat her dinner out of, before she would go to sleep.

That's why he didn't understand that what happened to him happens a lot in movies the same way, with the exact same scenario. He had finished his quick scan of the computers, extinguishing their electronic flames, shutting off the lights, and locking the cybercafe. He jammed his hands into the pockets of his khaki jacket and headed home. "All of your coats and jackets are khaki, man, as if you were enlisted in the auxiliary forces," commented an exasperated Hassaniya once. But this coat in particular gave Rahhal a feeling of warmth and security. He was walking with his head down and his back bent so he didn't notice them until they were on either side of him. They were big and tall, boorish and strong, wearing dark coats. One of them had a thick moustache and the other one's face was spotted with old pimples. When he looked up he found himself pressed between them like a pickle in a sandwich.

"Come with us. No speaking, no yelling. We're the police."

"T . . . t . . . t . . ."

"We said, no speaking. Until we get there. Then you'll understand everything."

But he wasn't speaking. He didn't want to speak. His teeth were chattering. Rahhal didn't feel like he was walking as he went with them to the car. Rather, he was suspended in the air between them. They were walking and dragging him between them like a wounded sheep.

In the car, the one with the thick moustache was putting a blindfold over his eyes when the other one nudged him and said:

"Hand me your phone right now."

"What phone?" the terrified squirrel asked in a weak, dry voice that sounded more like a hiss.

"Don't play dumb with me, give me your cell phone, you rat."

"But I don't own a phone. I don't need one. It seems that there's been some sort of mix-up. There's been some sort of mistake. And, besides, I really don't own a phone. Why would I need a cell phone? We only have one, and it's at home with Hassaniya. All she uses it for is to respond to Hiyam. She basically bought it for Hiyam. I don't need it. Who would call me? Who would need to call me? No doubt you're looking for someone else. This is a mistake."

These words swirled around in Rahhal's mind without reaching his throat. His voice was completely lost inside his chest. After that, even the hissing sound he was making let him down, and he found himself unable to speak. But his companions weren't in a hurry. The car was tearing up the road. Outside he could hear the roar of engines. The din of car horns. *Toot. Toot. Toot.* However, gradually, the chaos gave way to calm. They must have been on the outskirts of the city now. After about half an hour, the car stopped. A dog barked somewhere nearby. The sound of a large door creaking open could be heard. The car went in. Then poof! The car door opened. The car door was yanked open and the Squirrel was dragged through winding hallways. Going up. Some stumbling steps. Twisting to the left. Going down four steps. A bend to the right. A quick step. Three knocks. A deep voice came from behind the door: "Enter." So they entered.

"Welcome. First, take the blindfold off. Welcome, Rahhal. Please, sit down."

It was a young man, about thirty years old. He welcomed him with a familiar smile as if they were friends. He understood from the respect the one with the moustache and the pockmarked face guy showed in his presence that they worked for him.

"I'm truly sorry. There wasn't another way to invite you here. We didn't mean to frighten you. But we are in the utmost need of you and your help. And the nature of our work requires that we remain secretive. That's why we brought you here this way, at this time. Again, I'm sorry . . ."

The Squirrel began to call up some semblance of composure. He fidgeted in his chair. He straightened his neck a bit. Then the question smacked him right in the face, no room for beating around the bush.

"Tell me, Rahhal. Who is Abu Qatada?"

"But how . . . ?" mumbled Rahhal, his voice still weak and hesitant.

"It's a simple question, my friend. You have a person in the cybercafe whose nickname is Abu Qatada. Who is he?

"Ah, Abu Qatada. Of course I know him."

This time Rahhal said it without the slightest bit of confusion. Yes, he pronounced the words in a weak, shaky voice, but bright and confident at the same time.

"So, you know him?"

"Of course, of course. He's one of the cybercafe customers. His real name is Mahjoub Didi. An employee at the Regional Water and Electricity Agency. Married. Father of two. Lives in the building that faces Nour Mosque. And in fact, he belongs to the Islamist Justice and Charity movement."

The officer was unable to hold back a slight smile that flashed across his face. He raised his eyes to the two asses standing at the door and shot them a sharp look that could be interpreted in more than one way. Then he turned back to Rahhal.

"Bravo, Rahhal. Excellent. I salute you for your help. But we know Mahjoub Didi well. And because we know him, we really doubt that he, himself, is Abu Qatada."

"I swear to you that he's Abu Qatada. The man is at the cyber-cafe every day. Every day he's in front of me. Right in front of me. I know him well. I can assure you . . ."

"Okay. Alright. Let's forget about Abu Qatada for now. We'll get back to him in a moment. But tell me, there's another person among the cybercafe's clientele who concerns us, even more dangerous than Abu Qatada, and I hope the information you'll provide on him will be just as accurate as your information on Mahjoub Didi."

This is it, Abdelmessih. They've figured you out. You decided to become a Christian without Jesus' permission. Just like that. A passing whim. As if the country had gone astray, without a Makhzen or rule of law. Don't you hear what the minister of Islamic affairs repeats day and night about the spiritual security of citizens? Don't you read Hot Maroc? Authorities and other outright rectifiers target evangelicals and Shiite Moroccans these days. We're Maliki Sunni Muslims, you idiot. Didn't you read Ibn 'Ashir's Manzuma? *Didn't your father, the esteemed Mr. Shihab Eddine Assuyuti, teach you the famous verse of Ibn 'Ashir's poetry: "According to the 'Ashari pact and the law of Malik / and the Sufi path of al-Junaid al-Salik"? This is the creed of all Moroccans, my friend. The Sunni creed. The creed of God's unity and de-anthropomorphic nature that common sense dictates. The creed of Abu al-Hasan al-'Ashari. We're on the path of Abu al-Qasim al-Junaid, the bringer of charity. According to his way, things are made whole, deeds follow the straight path, and people's behavior is made right. As for the theological school, it's Maliki. So, what's with you and Christianity? Don't count on me to cover up for you today, Abdelmessih.*

"Go ahead, sir. I'm at your service."

"Tell me, Rahhal, who is Son of the People?"

What? Son of the People? Rahhal felt the ground spinning beneath his feet; the ground spinning and the sky collapsing on top of it as he shrank in his chair.

"Son of the People, Rahhal. Don't disappoint me. You've been good and cooperative up until now. But I've begun to miss your voice. Notice that I'm still awaiting your answer."

If only it were a nightmare. A suffocating, terrifying nightmare, but in your sleep and not here between these dark-colored walls. If only the earth would split open and swallow you up, Squirrel. If only an earthquake would strike Marrakech at this very moment.

But at that very moment, the door opened. A short, slight person entered. He was about forty. Wearing a high-end, dark gray suit and a light mauve shirt with a dark mauve tie. It looked as if they had been displayed that way on the mannequin in one of the shops and he had bought them together so as not to tire himself out choosing the colors and making sure they went together. He was carrying a pack of Marlboros in his hand. He entered with quick, confident steps. They all stood out of respect for him, including the officer.

"You morons, what have you done to the man? Didn't I tell you to be gentle with him? You especially, Hakim. I told you specifically. Didn't I say that he's an old friend?"

Without waiting for a response, he turned toward Rahhal, extending his arms theatrically and somewhat exaggeratedly as if to embrace him, before stopping midway. Rahhal's eyes were fixed on the mouse-like face, whose original features hadn't been lost to the accumulated fat.

"Wait. Comrade Moukhtar?"

"Which Moukhtar, or Mahjoub? How dare you? You're talking to Commissioner Ayadi. So speak politely to the commissioner." The one with the thick moustache jabbed him roughly.

The commissioner didn't comment on the roughness of the guy with the moustache. Perhaps it pleased him that one of them had given the Squirrel's ear a little tweak to make him better appreciate the gravity of the situation.

"How are you, Rahhal? You married a student who was with you at the university, and now you manage a cybercafe in Massira. Very good. But did they explain to you why I called you in?"

The officer interrupted: "Commissioner, we asked him about Abu Qatada and he tried to pin it on Mahjoub Didi from the Justice and Charity movement. Can you believe it?"

"Ha, ha, ha!"

The laughter came from the heart this time. A loud laugh that made the commissioner's eyes water. He took a moment to wipe them with a tissue as he continued to laugh, before continuing:

"Wicked, Rahhal. Wicked as usual. Did you forget the day at school when you claimed that Wafiq Daraai worked for the Mukhabarat? You blew the poor guy away. You slaughtered him. Ha! Ever since that day, I've known you weren't so simple."

All of a sudden, the Rat's face went back to its former sternness. He glared at the guy with the moustache and the one with the pockmarked face then yelled at them:

"You two! What are you waiting for?"

They exchanged glances, then rushed out with confused steps until the one with the pockmarked face stumbled and almost fell over. Rahhal smiled to himself when he saw the ass stumble. *And you say, "Don't play dumb with me, give me your cell phone, you rat." Who's the dumb one now? Me? Or you who can't tell the difference between a rat and a squirrel. The Rat, you ass, is the one yelling in your face right now making you practically fall over. I'm a squirrel, and I don't have a cell phone.*

"Listen, Rahhal. I don't have time to waste with you. You can play around with the others like this fine young man," he said pointing to Officer Hakim who was leaning up against the wall and following the conversation, "but not with me, understand? I even know what you ate last night."

∎ ∎ ∎

The Squirrel was baffled as he listened to his former comrade. Odd! The Rat knew everything about Abu Qatada, Son of the People, and the others. And he wasn't angry at Rahhal. In fact, quite the opposite. He seemed pleased with him, with his fiery comments, sly tricks, and acrobatic flips in Hot Maroc.

"Today we just need to change our style. We'll move from the amateur realm to the professional. Do you understand, Rahhal? You'll remain as you are. But the maneuvers will become tighter. By the way, there's a girl who regularly comments on Hot Maroc. Her screen name is Hidhami. Do you know her?"

"How could I not know her? I've mopped the floor with her many times. Son of the People, in particular, always makes an example of her. The last time . . ."

"Idiot!" The Rat agitatedly cut him off before lighting a cigarette and trying to restore his calm tone. "This is why we called you in, Rahhal. This is exactly why we called you in. You're a student of Arabic literature, so you must know the famous verse:

> If Hidhami says something, believe her
> Because what Hidhami says is the truth.

"Of course I know it," he mumbled in a trembling voice like a schoolboy giving the wrong answer about something he had memorized.

"'I know it, *Commissioner*,'" Hakim interrupted. He said the sentence calmly and sternly as he pressed down on each letter. He was directing what he was saying to Rahhal. The message was received, and increased Rahhal's confusion as he squirmed in his chair. Then his weak voice emerged, trembling even more:

"Of course I know it, Commissioner."

"It's good that you know it, but what you must also know is that Hidhami has no use for discussions. She has no time to waste bickering with Sons of the People or sons of bitches. She's there to say her piece and leave. What people like you need to do is believe her. Believe her first, then place her directives in their ears like an earring. Then, building on that, they can act freely. After that, you can take your pants off for Hot Maroc if you'd like. You can shit all over everyone, including your mother and father, for all I care."

"There's also Naim Marzouk, Commissioner."

For the first time, Officer Hakim cut the commissioner off. He did it gently. Commissioner Ayadi nodded his head, acknowledging the value of the observation.

"Ah, this is important. It's good you reminded me, Hakim."

Then he shifted his gaze to the Squirrel, looking for clarification.

"Come now, what's with you and Naim Marzouk?"

"Nothing at all. I have no connection to him, Commissioner. I follow everything he writes. I follow him as I would any brilliant columnist. Sometimes I disagree with him. That's all there is to it."

"That's not all there is, Rahhal. Son of the People treats Naim unfairly quite a bit. He's impudent with him whether or not there's a call to do so. It's true that he's an arrogant writer, a bit vain, and sometimes he exaggerates. But he is gifted, and a lot of people like his style. The most important thing is that he is inspired. Do you know what I mean? This man is inspired. So, from now on you're to consider him as a prophet who's been sent. Is what prophets say open for discussion? True, it might need some explanation and elucidation, sometimes a bit of clarification and justification. That's a role Son of the People might become proficient at later. Get this straight, too, especially now that Marzouk's adversaries have begun to multiply lately. Understood?"

"Understood, Commissioner," Rahhal muttered in a low voice.

"So, as long as you understand, Office Hakim will explain what you need to do."

"You haven't left me anything to add, Commissioner. Rahhal is an intelligent person and no doubt he has understood what is being asked of him. All that remains is for me to emphasize the need to keep up the same daily pace of work. But as the commissioner said, you have now moved from practicing a hobby to working at a profession. You will receive information regularly about some people. I know that you will use it well. Your salary will reach you by WafaCash every month. A text message will arrive on your mobile phone with the transfer number. This phone is my gift to you. For the salary, the commissioner has been generous with you. Perhaps because you're an old friend, he has decided to pay you ten thousand dirhams per month. The important thing is that our work and correspondence remain top secret. Understood?"

Did he respond that he understood? Really, he hadn't heard a thing. It was like he was sleepwalking. He remembered that the Rat shook his hand warmly. Officer Hakim accompanied him to the door. There, the one with the thick moustache received him, and the one with the pockmarked face put the blindfold on again. The road didn't feel so long this time. It was as if he wasn't there. As if he hadn't woken up yet from a dream that seemed more like a nightmare. Suddenly, the two asses threw him out of the car without stopping as if he were a bag of garbage, after which the car took off as fast as lightning. Rahhal rubbed his eyes. There was no one at all passing by on Dakhla Avenue. No life there. Just two cats exchanging meows in front of Café Milano.

He remembered his hedgehog. *My God, what will I say to her? Not about Commissioner Ayadi and Officer Hakim and the one with the thick moustache and the guy with the pockmarked face, for this is a secret we've already buried. Rather, what will I say about the tajine. What will I say to her who cannot sleep without digging a deep trench in the next day's tajine?*

As soon as Rahhal turned the key, Hassaniya jumped up from where she was. She had been in the salon squatting with her head in, waiting for him to return home. Her dry, stringy hair was piled up scarily on her head. Like real hedgehog quills. However, it was her face that seemed strange to Rahhal after it had taken on a yellowy goose-poop colored pallor that was yellower than mustard. Hassaniya hadn't changed her clothes yet. She hadn't yet put on her baggy orange pajamas that made her look like a circus clown.

"Where were you, Rahhal?"

Her voice barely left her throat. He could barely hear her.

"At the police station."

"The police?"

"I was coming from the cybercafe when a police car stopped me. There was an ID check. I didn't have my identification card so they took me to the station to confirm my identity."

Hassaniya looked at him quizzically.

She was wondering with her eyes, the features of her face, with all the strength she had. Her thoughts shouted, "And then?" but her voice failed her.

"At the station I came across an officer from Massira who comes to the cybercafe from time to time. He recognized me and intervened on my behalf so they released me on his word. That's it."

Target practice would start now.

He was expecting the Hedgehog to start bombarding him, and he waited calmly for it. As the poet Mutanabbi says, "Every man has a fate he expects," and Rahhal was expecting the Hedgehog's quills. But Hassaniya threw herself down on the couch in the middle of the salon that faced the door, and whispered in a low voice:

"Why don't you take your ID card with you, Rahhal? Please, take your card with you from now on."

Her voice was broken, mixed with a pleading tone. He didn't believe it, nor did he trust her sincerity.

"Did you eat dinner?" Confused, he surprised her with the question, a feeling of guilt for lying weighing heavily on him.

"No."

"Can I make you something?"

"No, no. It's three in the morning. We should go to sleep."

But they didn't sleep. Rahhal was replaying the strange events of the night from the beginning. From the time when the two stubborn mules surrounded him as he left the cybercafe. Comrade Moukhtar. Commissioner Ayadi. "If Hidhami says something." The "inspiration" that hits Naim Marzouk while the readers are sleeping. As for Hassaniya, she tossed and turned, somewhat out of character, considering she usually starts to snore the moment her head hits the pillow.

Your hedgehog is scared, Squirrel. More scared than you would have thought. Or maybe she has started to fall in love with you and worry about you without you having noticed.

45

LIFE ISN'T JUST ABOUT MONEY. Rahhal didn't even know what to do with it. Proof of that was in how perplexed he was with his new salary. He didn't know what to do with it or how to spend it. Rahhal worked for Emad Qatifa at the cybercafe for 2,500 dirhams a month. Hassaniya ran the Atlas Cubs School by herself and worked like crazy, morning and night, for a salary of just under 5,000 dirhams. The apartment's rent was 2,000 dirhams. What remained was just enough for them to live on. They were happy with their lives. At least they had no complaints. Or rather, they didn't talk about it so that one could complain to the other. Or, more to the point, they didn't discuss anything at all; this, or anything else. Otherwise the Hedgehog would discover what was going on inside the Squirrel's head, and the Squirrel would know what the Hedgehog was hiding underneath her prickly hide. But 10,000 dirhams all at once. What are you going to do with it, Rahhal? Respectable pay for an employee at the eleventh salary step. And for what? For stupid online stories that you entertain yourself with at work.

Commenting was your hobby, Rahhal, and here it has become your occupation. A strange occupation befitting the son of Abdeslam Laâouina and Halima Zanboub. A mother whose hobby is pretending to be sick, and whose occupation is illness. And a father whose hobby is silence, and whose occupation is accompanying the dead to their graves. My new occupation is the same as my hobby: dancing on virtual tightropes, fabricating lies, fattening up rumors, poking others with electronic needles. Just like that. Silently. From a distance. But ten thousand dirhams all at once! My lord, that's a lot . . .

Of course, Hassaniya needs to remain far from it. But he would have to find some places to spend the new salary. At first, Rahhal thought about setting aside a small monthly stipend for

Abdelmessih. That way he could employ him secretly without Emad Qatifa knowing anything about it. But this was risky and he feared the consequences. So, he made do by explaining to Qamar Eddine that he would need him to help out more in the cybercafe. In exchange, he'd give him carte blanche to use the internet for free whenever he wanted.

"You're a friend now, Qamar Eddine. I won't treat you the way I treat the others," Rahhal added with surprising munificence.

Qamar Eddine didn't believe his ears at first. The last thing he would have expected from Rahhal was something so generous. He was extremely moved. He warmly hugged the Squirrel, who realized that no one had ever hugged him in his life. Neither the Pelican, nor the Mantis. Not even the Hedgehog had ever embraced him, in bed or out. Even when he mounts her as he hunts wild cows in the hedgehog pen, her hands remain at her side. Only today, when Qamar Eddine squeezed his thin body between his arms, did he realize this. You've missed out on so much tenderness, Squirrel. Goddamn you, Hassaniya. Qamar Eddine didn't understand right then why the Squirrel burst out crying.

The next morning, Rahhal let Qamar Eddine know that he would be out starting at three in the afternoon, so he'd have to take his place in the cybercafe. He'd take charge of everything for him starting with reception, typing services, scanning, and other things, and ending with the cashbox. "But the most important thing is to deal with the clients respectfully. All of them without exception, including Mahjoub Didi, got it, Qamar Eddine?"

Rahhal's family visit was almost like a break-in. He slinked in after having realized at the door that he still had his old key. Halima did not know how to show her joy at seeing the Squirrel. She fidgeted in her chair and moved her hands welcomingly. She looked like a pelican that didn't know how to use its wings on dry land, or how to jump with its tangled feet. Ayad was lying prostrate close to her like a sluggish lazy donkey. Rahhal kissed his mother's head, extended his hand to greet his uncle, and asked about Abdeslam.

"He's lying down in your room. I yelled for him until I was blue in the face. I wanted him to come drink a bit of tea, but I swear, he didn't respond. I don't know what's wrong with him, why he's playing dead."

Then she shouted, "Abdeslam! Hey, Abdeslam!"

But, this time, the Mantis responded. He seemed happy that Rahhal was visiting. The Squirrel kissed his father's hand, then sat down. The Pelican began to transmit the latest news as Rahhal, Abdeslam, and Ayad sipped their tea. The house's situation is improved a lot, really. Ayad repainted it. Electricity has finally honored it after some young activists from the neighborhood staged a demonstration in front of the Regional Water and Electricity Agency, then in front of the municipal government building. It was no longer acceptable that alleys in the heart of the kingdom's tourism capital remain deprived of electricity, waiting for a promised restructuring that they'd been waving in front of them since the 1970s. Now the house had television. Movies and television series that the Pelican would follow, and headline news broadcasts that Abdeslam and Ayad would diligently watch, only falling behind when it was time for the evening prayer and they'd go with everyone else to pray at the mosque.

"Okay, I'll celebrate electricity coming to the street with a refrigerator. You'll have to make space for it right away because it will be here within a month."

They also needed a refrigerator so that they could drink cold water like everyone else, especially when it gets really hot in Marrakech, Rahhal thought. The old, earthenware pitcher was sitting at the entrance to the kitchen. The pitcher that Rahhal used to drink from in the Moukef days. Not the exact same one, mind you. Every spring, the Pelican brought a new pitcher, a pitcher decorated with tar. But all pitchers look the same in the end. Now, Abdeslam had the right to drink cold water like other people. Like people who lived in cities, who had children who earned money. Strange, Halima didn't ask how, or from where. She seemed happy, enthusiastic—so enthusiastic that she began to swear with the utmost faith that the inventor of the refrigerator would never enter hell, even if he were a Jew! Since he had refreshed everyone, God would cool *him* on Judgment Day. That evening, Halima devoted her entire broadcast to a discussion of refrigerators, their brands, their models, and their prices. Every additional piece of information she presented demonstrated her complete ignorance on the matter. But, at the end of all of it, she whispered an essential piece of advice to Rahhal. It wasn't about how much room it would take up, or its energy capacity, nor was it about the need to pay attention to how much electricity it consumes. Rather, it was about eggs. The plastic compartment for eggs on the refrigerator door must be covered.

46

MANY THINGS started to reveal themselves to the Squirrel now. It turned out that the blindfold the two asses had put on him as they dragged him to meet Commissioner Rat was nothing compared to the basket he'd had over his head all of these years. Years spent commenting every day in Hot Maroc, you idiot, and you didn't know which way the wind was blowing. You were like an untied cow roaming around. Fuck you! You were so happy with your brilliant expositions and acrobatic somersaults, your responses to this one and winks from that one's channel. You're like a deaf person at a wedding party, clueless. You should be ashamed of yourself; you were like a deranged prostitute opening her legs for free.

Abu Sharr Guevari, the far leftist who you would always avoid and keep Son of the People away from after you sensing the intensity and lash of his tongue, he too was in on the game. Did you read the comment he left this morning right after Hidhami's directive?

Naim Marzouk's column seemed heavy this morning as he brought it down on the back of the well-known businessman Redouane Bidaoui. Redouane had apparently stood there with his mouth gaping wide open at an international colloquium organized by the Mediterranean Union of Contractors in Paris where he invited Morocco to synthesize economic life in the kingdom and do away with the rent-seeking economy, which struck deeply at the national economy and inflicted serious yearly losses on the national budget. He emphasized that fighting the rent-seeking economy as well as the bribery and corruption that are intrinsically linked to it required a bold political will that hasn't existed up until now. Bidaoui also demanded that the field be opened up to national discussions in order to work in a clear environment that would allow healthy competition and equal opportunities. Naim's response came long and broad. He discussed Bidaoui's addiction to top-shelf whiskeys and invited him to pay attention to his health because addiction greatly affects physical health and mental capacities. Just as he implored him—while on the topic of morals and morality—to set aside some of his precious time for his dear daughter, Salma, who had become a cocaine addict. Then, that the bouncers at the Negresco Night Club were complaining about the problems she caused for them with her constant fighting in the club and her vulgar words that pierced their ears when she would insult her male and female friends, along with the workers there. What was strange was that the same gang she would walk into the club with at the beginning of the night would be her enemies by the end of it. Thus, it wouldn't be a bad idea to take the virtuous young lady to a psychologist to balance her out a little bit and improve her behavior and the way she talked in order to preserve what remained of the family's reputation. That is, if the Bidaoui family had any reputation left at all. Hidhami's word came very brief. Bold and perfectly aimed: "A whore lectures about honor."

Rahhal had just started to turn the subject upside down, looking for an angle, a way in that would elevate him in the eyes of the Rat and whatever wolves and jackals stood behind him. But just as he was feeling his way, searching for the end of the thread, Abu Sharr Guevari appeared ahead of him with a solid comment:

"Moroccans are a free and militant people. And the masses absolutely refuse to receive lessons from the rotten bourgeoisie. We tossed colonialism out the door, and refuse to let it come back in through the window. If the bourgeoisie, who are known for their blind allegiance to Western capitalism and their loyalty to world imperialism, long for the days of colonialism, free Moroccans and their revolutionary vanguard of workers, peasants, and students refuse to go back to the time of colonial dictates. We refuse to allow Paris to dictate our political economy. And we say 'treason' to those traitors who ally themselves with the colonizer of yesterday against their country and their people. Long live the working class!"

Long live the working class, Abu Sharr.

Down with whiskey and cocaine.

Naim Marzouk returned to the topic with two additional columns, which he devoted entirely to criticizing Redouane Bidaoui. He insulted him with pure hatred. As if the man had killed his father. Basically, Naim Marzouk is a professional hustler, but one had to admit his skill and dedication. Even Rahhal, who had been annoyed with his arrogance before, was fond of and sympathetic to him at the same time now. That is to say, it is understandable when someone excels in insulting a person who directly offends you or to return the favor of a stubborn opponent who harasses you in more than one way, and wounds you on more than one occasion. But Naim Marzouk insults people he doesn't know and has no relationship to. In fact, deep down, he might even respect them. But instructions are instructions. That's exactly why Rahhal sympathized with him and valued the difficulty of his mission. He insults according to instructions, yet he insults from the heart, giving it his all. Is there anything more sincere than that? To dive headfirst into insulting people you have no relationship with, just because you are required to perform your duty as fully as possible? And whenever it occurred to Marzouk how noble these people he insulted were, he threw himself against them and insulted them even more artistically in order to convince himself first and foremost that they were not as he thought. They were not as noble as he thought they were. And no sooner does he finish his column and read it does he become completely convinced of its contents, and its extraordinary prejudice is transformed into solid hatred for his enemies. How could you not sympathize with and love someone like Naim? A person so dedicated to his work. Who hates from the heart. In fact, he prospered by programming his heart to hate.

But wouldn't it be better to reserve your sympathy for yourself, Squirrel? You're just a stupid member of the chorus that stands behind Naim Marzouk, yet they give you ten thousand dirhams a month, the pay of an employee at the eleventh salary step. How much do you think they pay Naim Marzouk? Feel sorry for yourself, you moron. At the end of the day, you're just a racing rabbit.

One of the racing rabbits that run around in every direction to keep the Chameleon out in front.

Ah, I forgot to tell you that Naim Marzouk is a chameleon. He is as determined as a chameleon. He doesn't leave one tree trunk without first grabbing onto another. He moves from one newspaper to another and always knows when to leave and how. His exits are always loud, and he always leaves with dirty laundry that he knows how to sell. He begins by publishing it as an article series in the competing newspaper, which he has usually secretly made an arrangement with beforehand, prior to leaving for its competitor. Didn't the Arabs say long ago: "More determined than a chameleon: It doesn't leave one trunk until it has grabbed onto another"? He is introverted like a chameleon. Some weeks ago, they published a profile of him on the *Atlas Magazine* website making clear how shy a person he really is. He lives alone, doesn't stay out late, doesn't go to restaurants or bars, and doesn't have any friends. In other words, just like you, Mr. Chameleonic Squirrel. There is a resemblance between the two of you. Now do you understand why they chose you to be a racing rabbit for him? The way he surprises his enemies as he aims his unanticipated arrows at them strongly resembles the way the chameleon surprises its prey. Just as the chameleon moves with the sun, facing it wherever it moves, so too does Marzouk follow the coin, moving around and around. And Marzouk changes the color of his skin, just as the chameleon does. Finally, Marzouk is a predator, just like the chameleon, which doesn't hesitate to eat anything it can fit into its mouth, from insects to lizards to rodents. And just as the chameleon doesn't move around to capture its prey, Marzouk does not exert too much of an effort to acquire his material. All his information comes to him sufficient and adequate. He just re-forms it, refines expressions, adds his well-known spices, and the dish is ready to carry Chef Naim's signature.

■   ■   ■

But, it appears this time that the Chameleon has managed to place his feet on one tree trunk while leaving his long tail wrapped around the branch of another. He held onto two intertwined branches of two enormous trees laden with fruit, at the same time. The daily *Future* newspaper, which had appeared recently in Rabat, announced it would publish Naim Marzouk's famous column. Of course, that's not possible. The contract with Hot Maroc says . . .

"There's no contract or anything of the sort! We came to an agreement with Hot Maroc and that's all there is to it. Not all Moroccans are online. There are countless people who swat flies for hours in cafés. They order a café au lait for five dirhams and nurse it for five full hours. A dirham per hour. And because the café owners buy newspapers and make them available for free to this segment of the population, we are of the opinion that reading about how you see them would cheer them up. Generally, they are in cafés in abundance, chatting and frittering away their time. It wouldn't be a bad idea to get them reading. And we'll do it. Because they, unlike what the so-called intellectuals and end-of-times philosophers think, are not averse to reading. They just need something that will spark their interest. And you, Naim, know how to write that thing. So, write for them. They have the time to read; their commentary will flow freely. They also love to open fire at anything that moves. And they absolutely adore insults. So, insult whomever. The more you insult, the more they'll love you. And every time you denounce the corruption of all these opportunist elites who waggle before them, these people who just sit in the café will feel a kind of self-satisfaction. Doing nothing wrong, doing nothing at all. At least they're without blemishes. They just sit in the café drinking cafés au lait, smoking, coughing, blowing their noses, farting, going to the toilet every once in a while, returning to their cold coffee, smoking, coughing, and talking about the corruption that's running rampant in the country and that touches everyone. They'll be happy with you because you'll distract them, Naim, and you'll give them back some self-esteem. That's why we came to an agreement with the folks at Hot Maroc. You won't lose a thing. We'll republish the same article in paper form, and you'll receive adequate compensation for it. Do you still have objections?"

Neither Naim nor anyone else knew which blimp brought Ibrahim Tanoufi into journalism's hangar. The competing newspapers say "the roof leaks," that Tanoufi just fell in. But Naim Marzouk knows more than anyone else that the house's roof is made of iron. It never leaks. Nothing in this country happens by accident. There was some sort of wisdom behind the appointment of Tanoufi—former soccer player and owner of the Tanoufi Patisserie Shops—as head of the most important national newspaper. A newspaper independent of the state, the government, the parties, the unions, the organizations, the workers, and the moneyed lobbying groups. Practically independent even of the people and society at large. Still, despite its independence, or perhaps because of this independence, it received commercial advertising backing from the most important economic organizations and the largest companies in the country. The *Future* had also become one of the strongest sources of scoops and fresh news. Always winning the breaking news, and its sources were always reliable. It became an ideal platform from which Naim Marzouk could launch his missiles at anyone who moved or took any initiative without permission, because it was clear to everyone that the country was well under control.

Flouting the current journalistic custom of publishing daily columns on the last page of the paper or at the bottom of the first page, the *Future* began to publish Naim Marzouk's columns in the middle of the first page, accompanied by a cropped photo of him wearing a T-shirt and a cocked cap. As if he were from the people and of the people. And it appeared that Tanoufi's editorial policy was a success. The paper sold like none before. Even Rahhal started to buy it regularly after Hidhami wrote a comment on a report published by Hot Maroc about the successes of the new pulpit ("I'm amazed that there are people who start their day without having read the *Future*"). After the fights started to break out in Café Milano over Marzouk's column because all the tables wanted the newspaper at the same time so they could read it, specifically because of his column—because the café couldn't buy a copy for every table—Asmae came upon a solution that wasn't half bad; every morning when she bought the newspapers, she'd pass by the photocopy shop and make at least ten copies of Marzouk's column. Then she could relax. That's how she came to distribute a copy of the column to the café customers with their orders, then step out the door to breathe in some fresh air. Asmae couldn't stand the disgusting smell of smoke inside anymore. She couldn't stand a great many things now that hadn't bothered her at all before. Her mood had soured and her strength was always sapped.

It appears that your health has begun to betray you, Lioness.

47

DESPITE THE FACT that Hiyam hadn't set foot in the cybercafe since it opened, her orders and prohibitions have flowed freely to everyone over the years. She stood over Rahhal on opening day and ordered him to type up what amounted to the domestic law for the shop and insist that all customers respect its clauses. An abridged domestic law made up of four points she wrote herself:

> No more than two people sitting at one computer.
> No smoking.
> No outside food.
> No speaking loudly.

Hiyam's Law remained in effect for everyone with few, rare exceptions. Sometimes Rahhal would overlook the Africanos and let them crowd the three of them in front of a computer. Same thing when the teachers from Massira High School would come and sit around the machines and websites and start to chat as if they were still in the teachers' lounge at school enjoying themselves at break time. But their visits were few and far between. So, the sanctity of the shop remained protected. That is, until Yazid showed up at the Atlas Cubs Cybercafe.

What was it that made Yazid get up from his regular seat in Café Milano and consider joining the electronic caravan? There must be some secret behind it. Because Yazid had disappeared from the neighborhood and the café for an entire year, with him saying that he had been in Canada. In Café Milano, they say that the "Canada" that kept Yazid away from the café, the neighborhood, and the city was none other than Boulmharez Prison. The reasons for his arrest remained unknown. But whatever the case may be, upon his return, Yazid decided to broaden his horizons a little bit, so he added the cybercafe to his vital area of operations.

Everyone in the cybercafe interacted carefully with Yazid. His presence was annoying, his fake charm silly, and his sexual innuendos were shameless. Not to mention the fact that he talked loudly, as if he were in his own living room.

From day one, Rahhal understood that things would be difficult with this dog who, Rahhal discovered with very little effort, tended toward the family of barkers.

Yazid swaggered in wearing a flowing white *deraiya* and small babouche slippers that just barely covered the bridge of his feet, with his heel hanging out the back. Thus, he tottered back and forth like a ridiculous peacock. Under his arm he was carrying a photocopy of Naim Marzouk's article, apparently taken from Café Milano. He held his café au lait in his hand and after a loud theatrical "helloooo" that was meant to get everyone's attention, he threw himself into a chair in front of the only available computer and got to work in a loud voice. He moved through the cybernetic waves and proceeded to live broadcast all of his electronic stops and starts.

"Let's have a look at this Hot Maroc's soup to see whether it's still hot or if it has cooled down. Have a look. Let's see . . . and this shit Facebook, how do we deal with it? Come on, man. How does one go about cramming himself in with these Facebook bandits? Please, come here."

His broadcast was constant as he enjoyed himself while sipping his cup of coffee. Rahhal had gotten used to customers walking in with a bottle of water or soda. But coffee? This was the first time it had happened. Someone as careless as Yazid could easily spill his coffee on the keyboard. So annoying. Also, Rahhal didn't want this sort of behavior to repeat itself in the shop. Perhaps he had to clarify things from the get go with this guy.

"Uh, my friend . . . my friend . . . please . . . it's not allowed."

"What's not allowed?"

"The coffee."

"Coffee isn't allowed?"

"That's right, not allowed. Coffee isn't allowed," Rahhal said sternly after mustering up all the courage he possessed.

"But you named it a cybercafe, you fucking moron . . . café . . . coffee . . . Can't you read, or what? It says *café*, meaning coffee. If it were called a cyberbar, I would've brought beer and wine here to your ass, and then you'd try and tell me it's forbidden, too?"

The Squirrel was stunned. He began to shrink in his chair into almost nothing. *My Lord, you've sent a new Khaled Battout to torment me.* It appears that peaceful days in the cybercafe are under threat with this scoundrel. The important thing was that Rahhal was tongue-tied. His natural, deep-rooted cowardliness overcame him. But he couldn't believe what happened next.

Yazid opened up his email. Rahhal discovered that the man had a Hotmail account. Perhaps he had opened it in Canada, since he had never availed himself of the Atlas Cubs' services. Then, very spontaneously, as he was scrolling through his mail, he took a cigarette out of its pack and lit it. He inhaled deeply and took a sip of coffee as he remained transfixed on the screen.

"Uh, excuse me, my friend. Please . . ." Rahhal implored.

"Now what?" Yazid asked impatiently.

"Please, read what's written on the sign: 'No smoking.' This isn't my rule. I just work here. This is a rule imposed by the shop's owners."

"No, don't worry about it. No one here, damn his mother, will dare light a cigarette."

"But haven't you just lit one?"

"No, calm down," Yazid assured him. "I won't let anyone else smoke in this cybercafe . . . Just mind your business."

Yazid quietly presented the fait accompli, without fuss. He drank his coffee and smoked his cigarette, promising Rahhal that he would personally oversee the strict adherence to the domestic law of the shop, and he would prevent any potential transgressions by others. He meant only the others . . . As for him, not to be taken into account, of course.

They say, "This cub is from that lion," and it appears that this saying applies to the dog family, too. Yazid is the son of Moulay Ahmed Malkha, enemy of the kids at the Nour Mosque. He would besiege them in the mosque and not hesitate to bark at every one of them who messed up the washing up area or pushed one another when they were lined up. Even though the parents complained repeatedly to the imam and the muezzin about how rough he was and how badly he treated their children, Moulay Ahmed didn't listen to their complaints. God's house is sacrosanct, and he was there to preserve the house's sanctity from these little devils and their fooling around. But deep down inside he despised the little ones because they never hid their laughter during the group recitation of the Hizb chapters after the sunset prayer. They were laughing at him. Moulay Ahmed hadn't memorized the Qur'an either in a *msid* or *kuttab* school. But his arrogance prevented him from reaching into the Qur'an cabinet to take a Qur'an out and read along with the rest of the group. Instead, he would take advantage of the raised voices during the group recitation and follow along with the group of readers and those who had memorized it, moving his lips before raising his voice at the end of the verses, following his intuition. Generally, after "the All-hearing" comes "the All-knowing." But sometimes he goes astray with "the All-knowing" while the group recites, "He is the All-hearing, the All-seeing." There was no referee and no linesman to monitor the process and point out his offside by waving a flag under his nose. Just these mean children who didn't hesitate to laugh in his face. These little devils. These heathens. Unbelievers will be chastised . . . painfully. In the Qur'an, chastisement is usually painful. But, no sooner did Moulay Ahmed start reciting the verse, powerfully and confidently, did he realize at the end that this verse escaped him, replacing *painful* with *terrible*. "And the unbelievers—for them awaits a terrible chastisement." The adults continued their collective recitation with great serenity while the little thugs sneered. They made fun of Moulay Ahmed's confusion. They made fun of him as he repeatedly went astray. "Thy Lord wrongs not His servants." This time, his intuition was right. Thy Lord wrongs not His servants, the Almighty God has spoken the truth. As soon as those praying finished reciting the Hizb chapters and the Imam was done with his prayer, Moulay Ahmed had started a new chapter in his hunt for these "sons of bitches" who don't give any regard to the sanctity of God's house.

Before God accepted his repentance and guided him to the path of prosperity, Moulay Ahmed had been a die-hard soldier in Marrakech's bars. He had tried every bar and gotten drunk at every table, and was banned from entering all of them, so he gave up drinking because he had to, not out of any sense of nobility. Nonetheless, his repentance was sincere, thanks to God. The reason he was banned from entering the bars was that Moulay Ahmed Malkha made it a habit of sitting with a group of people and taking charge of whatever table he was sitting at. In fact, he would deal with new customers generously and invite them to join his table, adding another table if necessary. By the time the evening was practically over, he collected what each person owed for the drinks, claiming that he would settle the tab. And sure enough, the customers left and Moulay Ahmed remained behind with dozens of empty beer and wine bottles in front of him. When the waiter came to settle up, the honorable sir would claim that he didn't have a dime and that, quite simply, the waiter could call the police.

There is a Moroccan law that prohibits the sale of wine to Muslim Moroccans. A law put in place by the French colonial authorities during the Protectorate period to prevent the locals from intruding on the bars and mixing with the colonists inside. But this old, racist, colonial-era law was deemed acceptable by the conservative current in the country and remains in effect, even while Morocco produces forty million liters of wine each year, 85 percent of which is consumed locally. This is exactly the little loophole that Moulay Ahmed knew how to squeeze through. Because no one was going to call the police in the end—to avoid prison time, having to pay a fine, and the revocation of the liquor license—so Moulay Ahmed found himself thrown out in front of the bar with bruised ribs and a face covered in blood. He used to hit one bar multiple times. One time he'd come in a traditional jellaba, another time in a long overcoat, and yet another in a chic suit and tie. One time he'd be wearing a cap, another time a tarboosh, and yet another time with the hood of his jellaba up. They'd see him one day with a beard, then with a thick moustache and no beard, then clean-shaven, and so it went. Moulay Ahmed Malkha did this for years until all of his different looks were discovered and he was banned from all the bars of Marrakech, without exception.

This cub is from that lion. Yazid is his father's son. All there is to do is deal with what God has ordained for you, Rahhal. For we do not ask You to reverse Your judgment, God, just to act gently with it.

48

WE MUSTN'T FALSELY ACCUSE PEOPLE. It wasn't Yazid who put Rahhal in such a bad mood that it affected his performance. It has to be admitted that, since the beginning, the Squirrel has felt the weight of the responsibility. Before, he used to comment on Hot Maroc anonymously. No one knew him. Or at least, he didn't sense that there was anyone who knew him or was observing him. Today he has been enlisted to write and comment. There is always someone waiting for his comment. That someone will evaluate him for sure, and he'll either be satisfied or he'll find him weaker than expected. For exactly this reason, writing a short comment became more difficult than pulling a tooth.

Nevertheless, you need to work, Squirrel. You need to return to your old productive ways. Even though no one is calling attention to your poor performance, and even though your salary comes to you no matter what, you still need to prove that you're worth it. Don't disappoint Commissioner Rat.

Rahhal continued to work hard. He cleverly utilized the information that came to him from Officer Hakim, and the number of likes that his comments racked up assured him that Son of the People and Abu Qatada hadn't lost their star power yet. Nevertheless, opening up Hot Maroc no longer brought him the joy it once did. Now it was work, and is there any rational person who goes to work happy and cheerful? Moroccans go to work in spite of themselves. Forced to go, not out of any sense of heroism. The majority of them don't work at all. Rather, they just watch the clock. Rahhal came to approach Hot Maroc with the same, defeated mood that all Moroccans generally have when they go to work. Nevertheless, he would write his astute comments that racked up more likes than any other member of Maestro Naim Marzouk's chorus, including his strongest competitor, Abu Sharr Guevari.

Whenever the Squirrel felt suffocated inside Hot Maroc—and he felt that way a lot—he would search for diversions on Facebook. Rahhal stumbled across many people there. Wafiq Daraai. Issam Louzi, the well-known writer. Jalal Erroundi, the methodology professor at the university. Fouad Wardi, the Labid guy from his college days. Aziz the Greyhound. Even Atiqa the Cow, who had gotten even fatter. She presented herself on Facebook as a militant feminist and a teacher at one of Azilal's high schools.

Who else? Khaled Battout? It's him. In the flesh. Still short and fat. Rahhal noticed that his old adversary appeared broken in the photos. He hadn't posted more than three photos, in which he looked extremely ragged. Even the nature around him was ragged. Little emaciated olive trees in an empty field, thirsty pine trees, prickly plants, and he's smiling for the camera like a dolt. Battout captioned his profile photo: "With my friends in the field next to the post office." They were drinking tea with naïve joy as they all looked directly into the camera. It looks like your friend works as a postman in a miserable village. Even his posts contained no small amount of misery: "He whose zeal remains in his belly won't derive any value from it." Oh, Battout, it's as if you never left Antaki Elementary. To this day you're still repeating those proverbs the principal would write on the blackboard and ask the teachers to explain to us at the end of class. Rahhal thought about sending Khaled Battout a friend request to show some interest in him for a bit, but the man was too much of an idiot for anyone to be interested in. It wasn't in Rahhal's nature to open fire on an ambulance, or to aim his virtual punch, what would be the final blow, at a real-life defeated adversary. So, Rahhal just left Battout's depressing page feeling sorry for him. He was truly amazed at how his deep-rooted hatred for his old antagonist had transformed into conflicting feelings that swung between Schadenfreude and pity.

Mahjoub Didi was there, too. Mahjoub—who, at first, ferociously resisted the idea of joining this suspicious spy site—he had even circulated a global petition demanding that people stay off of it. Here he was now with his full name and his real picture.

But how did you come to change your view, Abu Qatada?

Mahjoub explained to him that the call to boycott came immediately following an insult to our Prophet, upon Him the purest of prayers and blessings, after they noticed the Facebook administrators colluding with those who let fly insults against the Lord of creation when they allowed them the space to move freely inside this suspect social site. But the weak response that was due to the flickering faith of Facebook Muslims caused the Islamist boycott campaign to fail. Therefore, some of the brothers suggested changing tactics, by "organizing a group return to Facebook, where we're currently trying," Mahjoub added, "to destroy the Zionist Judeo-Christian design of this satanic siege from within. This will come from three strong groups formed by the brothers, may God reward them with the best of rewards: the Muhammad the Prophet Is the Greatest Leader of All Time group; the Islamic Awakening group; and the We Will Pray in Jerusalem for Palestine group. Hundreds if not thousands join these blessed groups every day, Rahhal, and you must set up a Facebook profile for yourself as soon as possible and join us to strengthen the Merciful's soldiers in the holy Facebook war, which looks like it will last a while. *But God will perfect His light, though the unbelievers be averse."*

Rahhal did not join any of Abu Qatada's mujahideen groups. In general, he had no desire to pray in Jerusalem. He had never even set foot in the neighborhood Nour Mosque. Not out of unbelief, or apostasy, God forbid, but rather because he was busy in the cybercafe and it would be difficult to leave his work every prayer time and go join the ranks of Mahjoub Didi, Moulay Ahmed Malkha, and Mr. Shihab Eddine. That's why you won't be able to depend on me with this Jerusalem thing, Abu Qatada.

But forget about Jerusalem now, and go to Marseilles, Rahhal.

Yes, I did say Marseilles.

To Marseilles, then, Squirrel.

It appears they have a Mediterranean poetry festival there. And they've invited Wafiq Daraai, as if poets had gone extinct in the Land of Egypt, Mesopotamia, the Levant, and other founts of authentic Arabic poetry. This vain little poet son of a bitch! What's he doing there?

24/7 Samir had made his way onto Wafiq's list of friends a while ago. He sent a friend request with a long, polite message telling him that he was one of his faithful readers, that he had been following his astonishing experiment since his first collection, *The Butterfly on Its Way to the Slaughterhouse*, that he was truly proud of his gift, his dazzling experiment, and he would be honored if the great poet would humble himself to accept his friend request. Wafiq answered with a brief, polished message and accepted his request immediately. From that day on, 24/7 Samir just sat there. He kept an eye on all the poet's electronic deeds. He didn't contribute a comment or a like. He just watched until Wafiq stunned him by posting a series of delightful photos. From where? From Marseilles . . .

Wafiq's adoring fans filled the wide-open space with comments expressing how happy they were with their beloved poet's presence at such a major event as the Echoes of the Mediterranean Festival. The likes were flying through the air. If Facebook had a "trill" button, it would have been deafening. The atmosphere on the poet's wall was festive. And Wafiq made sure to like every comment posted under his album. Comments on the album. Others on the pictures. On each and every picture. But 24/7 Samir preferred to comment on the album: "Is this poetry's function, Wafiq Daraai? You in whom we took such pride? Is this poetry's function? Muslim Children of the Islamic community are dying in Palestine and Iraq and you're living here cheerful as can be? The poet who was the conscience of this community and its ringing voice is getting drunk with the French at a festival attended by Israelis and smiling like a moron for the camera, indifferent to the blood of pure, noble children that flows in more than one Arab and Islamic country? I'm shocked, Wafiq, my friend. It seems that you have shaken my faith in poetry and poets."

The shot was resounding. Its echoes reverberated on Wafiq Daraai's wall. One of Wafiq's adoring fans tried to defend him.

"Hey, slow down. No need to exaggerate. This is an international poetry festival. It is an honor for Morocco that our young writer is participating in this literary event, so please, don't exaggerate."

"What exaggeration are you talking about, miss? Because I truly don't understand. I'm talking about the civilizational, moral, and edifying role of the poet. That's all. If that role doesn't concern you, well, I respect your viewpoint. But it concerns *me*. When I looked closely at the pictures and found our beloved poet, Wafiq Daraai, slurping down wine in restaurants and parties with Jews in France as is clear in more than one picture in the album, I said to myself that maybe it was our duty to warn him that his religion forbids alcohol, and while it is his right, we must call him out as a poet entrusted with our emotions and the essence of our community, whose children are daily exposed to massacres by those with whom he gets drunk in the pictures. I want to call your attention to the fact that the Almighty is quite decisive on this point in His noble book when He says: 'Never will the Jews be satisfied with thee, neither the Christians, not till thou followest their religion.' The Almighty God has spoken the truth. If, my esteemed friend, you have found in my words any offense toward our friend Wafiq, well, I apologize."

"No . . . no need to apologize, 24/7 Samir." Okay, here's another madman falling from the sky. There's no picture of him, and his screen name is Ibn Jala. But the game will definitely get more interesting after he joins it. "No need to apologize, because you have articulated what is on many people's minds. So, don't apologize for your concern for your community. Personally, I used to respect this poet and love his experiment. But after today, after his true nature has been revealed, I declare for all to see that his friendship no longer honors me. I will end it now. And I call on everyone who is honorable to follow my lead so that these striving, plundering litterateurs who run panting after festivals in the West understand that we are sons of a proud, free community that will not accept injustice and the words of all those who don't heed its sanctity, and all who have forsaken it and betrayed its trust."

What was strange was that more than one virtual friend of Wafiq Daraai clicked "like" on what 24/7 Samir and his comrade said. Five people responded immediately to Ibn Jala's call to remove Wafiq Daraai from their list of friends. But 24/7 Samir remained fixed there, waiting to see what was going to unfold. And Wafiq did not disappoint. After only an hour, the poet opened Facebook. He was just coming back from another soirée. He added a picture of himself reading some poetry with a beautiful Frenchwoman next to him. She might have been the translator. He was looking happily at her while she read his poetry in French. The audience looked huge. It looked like they were reading in a public plaza. Next to the audience sitting there listening, there were young people walking around the plaza where the poetry had made them stop for a moment. The space is truly enchanting, Wafiq. He added another picture of intellectuals eating dinner in a fancy restaurant. There were wine bottles scattered on the table and the glasses were full. While the two new pictures picked up likes, 24/7 Samir was thinking about a new comment with which to break the poet's back. But as soon as the comment ripened in his mind and he was about to spit it out like a poison dart underneath the album, he discovered that it wasn't even there anymore. No album, no picture, nobody liking anymore.

Wafiq, who had come from his poetic reading overflowing with self-satisfaction, and a bit tipsy, wanted to have his friends and adoring fans share in the atmosphere with the new pictures he started to post to a flood of likes. But then the poisonous comments destroyed his mood. The coup led by 24/7 Samir took him by surprise, so he took down the whole album. Perhaps he's left the hotel now, he who had been ready to go to sleep, and went looking for a new bar where he could soothe his spirit.

Oh, Wafiq. So fragile, my old comrade. If I knew who this degenerate was who called for removing you from the list of friends, I'd seek vengeance for you. But don't worry, I blocked him, and I recommend that you do the same. And, in all honesty, I'm proud of you and the path you've chosen, Wafiq. If only you didn't sometimes go too far in provoking your friends' feelings with these sorts of damaging pictures. It's July, my friend. The hell of the Red City is raging and the heat in Marrakech is unbearable. And here you post provocative pictures taken in fancy restaurants with you eating fish and sipping beer and white wine with blondes in a spectacular atmosphere, you embracing them quite naturally and them embracing you unreservedly while I'm here in this heat with Yazid suffocating me with his heavy presence! May God forgive you, Wafiq. May God forgive you, my friend.

■ ■ ■

But wait . . . wait . . . I don't believe my eyes. Who?

Emad Qatifa himself?

Rahhal didn't meet Emad on an electronic street corner, or run into him in one of those virtual cafés by accident. Rather, the son of Hajj Qatifa walked right into the Lioness' den. He knocked very politely and amiably at the door, then, like a stupid beast of prey, entered Hiyam's den all on his own.

> Name: Emad Qatifa
> City: Marrakech
> Occupation: Businessman
> Relationship Status: Married

So, what do you want, Emad?

Qatifa explained to her that he had a particular weakness for the name Hiyam. "I have a history with this name that perhaps I'll tell you about later if we're given the chance to get to know one another better. As for why I'm sending you this friend request, Hiyam, well, it's because I'm quite taken by you. A girl of your beauty and charms who still manages to preserve her morals, who is interested in poetry and literature. Don't think that I'm quick to judge you or that I'm just flattering you with these words. Never, for I've been following your profile for a while. The truth is that whenever you post a new update, I find myself learning something. I say to myself, *This is a young woman who is cultured and open-minded beyond her years.* That's why I've sent you this friend request, affectionately and innocently. I'm really glad you were kind enough to accept. As long as we're in the same city, it would make me very happy if we got to know one another better. My dear Hiyam, I assure you that you won't regret it."

I won't regret it?! Regret what, you idiot?! Of course I won't regret it, Qatifa. My response to you will arrive shortly.

"Thank you, Mr. Emad, for your polite message. Regrettably, it isn't clear from your profile which college you graduated from or what your major was. This is vital to me. I make sure always to inform myself of the interests and areas of learning of my Facebook friends in order to optimize the benefits. So, it is important to me that in your next message you give me an idea of your field of specialization. I'd be happy to get to know you within the framework of a respectable friendship on the internet, but don't look for more than that. In all frankness, even though I'm a very open-minded girl, I would not allow myself to meet a married man and drink coffee with him, for example. I would feel as if I were betraying his wife. Even if he found that sort of betrayal acceptable, I would not. But again, I'm very happy to be innocent Facebook friends with you. I await your next message to tell me more about Hiyam. What is it that draws you to my name? Is it because you love Hiyam Younes?"

But the response came as a disappointment to Hiyam. Emad Qatifa admitted in his message that he didn't know Hiyam Younes. He didn't know who she was at all. It was the first time he had heard this name in his life. So why did God create Google, you idiot? Why did God send Our Master Google, upon him peace, to the electronic illiterates among His servants? Is it not where we take refuge when a beautiful, honorable girl asks us something to which we don't have an answer? At least type the name into Google and let it do its work, then we'll respond. It won't do for you to say to her stupidly that you don't know. And on top of that, you ask *her* about Hiyam Younes?

You've disappointed me, Emad. I thought your cultural knowledge would be better after all the riches you've accumulated. But the donkey that wasn't blessed enough to get his baccalaureate despite all the private

lessons, extra sessions, and tutoring can't become a genius overnight.
You've really disappointed me, Qatifa, so allow me to teach you a short les-
son, with your permission, of course.

"My dear Mr. Emad. You didn't answer my question about your academic specialization, even though I insisted on this very point in my message to you. This can only be explained in one of two ways. Either you didn't read my message and didn't deal with it respectfully, which causes me great pain. Because I demand the same amount of respect from my Facebook friends as I show them. When you don't respond to a person's questions, you are essentially demonstrating your low regard for them. Or, you have no academic standing at all. In that case, allow me to be clear with you. How will I personally benefit from being friends with you? Me, a lover of knowledge and literary and intellectual discussion. As for Hiyam Younes, whom you don't know, allow me to recommend a few links of her most beautiful songs, available on YouTube as you will see. You could have exerted the smallest effort and Googled her yourself, but it seems that you are the type of person who prefers things to be simple. Well, I'm not a simple woman. Even being friends with me on Facebook, my friend, Emad, is not as simple as you think. Good day. Hiyam."

You hit him hard, Squirrel. You mopped the floor with him. He won't get close to the Lioness' den anymore. He'll regret the day he ever thought of writing to Hiyam. He'll regret the day he thought of setting up a profile on Facebook. He'll . . .

No, it can't be. It's him. Emad Qatifa . . .

"Ms. Hiyam. I read your email and now I'm sad. I need your cell phone number immediately, Hiyam. I need to talk to you. There are many things I need to explain to you so that you don't misunderstand me. I need to talk to you tonight. I'm begging you."

49

FINALLY, gentle winds of change started to blow over Hot Maroc. The policies of the pulpit and the basic rules didn't change, but on the editorial level, noticeable transformations occurred after the news site sent for a new editor in chief—a young, effeminate man who used to oversee the Culture and Arts page of the *Midpoint*, where he had carried out a true cultural revolution. Even though he was of the type that Rahhal, a graduate of the Arabic Literature Department, might swear had never finished a single book in his entire life, the man carried out his blessed revolution.

The first victim of Anouar Mimi's—known simply as Mimi—revolution was the Arabic language itself. There can be no culture, no thought, no literature, no artistic creation without language. That's why it was natural to start the revolution there. Because it seemed that, since Mimi had hated Arabic syntax class in elementary school, he began with grammar first and began to make an example of it. What was beautiful was that Mimi was the pleasant sort of man who knew how to transform his faults into things to be proud of. You'd find him sipping beer with actresses who had graduated from the bars of Casablanca rather than the Higher Institute of Dramatic Arts in Rabat, and he had still achieved some fame. You'd find him with them mocking journalists who still used phrases like *wheresoever, similarly, hence,* and *in accordance with.* He considered his new language—which had no place for formal connecting words, no need to think about the proper way to write certain letters, or to be meticulous about word derivation and its function, or to pay attention to plurals and their rules—contemporary language, the language closest to the people. Mimi was comfortable in this regard. That's why Morocco, specifically in the Arabic press because its Francophone newspapers didn't allow anyone to mess around with Molière, might be the only country in the world where it is possible to practice written journalism with no need to know the basic grammar of the language you're writing in. Because in the end, no one cares.

Then came the role of culture, which Mimi curtailed in favor of writers' disputes and battles over travels, prizes, and whatever else had to do with contentious "literary" issues. News of the stars. Actors and actresses. Singers, especially the active type that turn the noria waterwheel of Casablanca's cabarets, where Mimi regularly spent his nights. This is the way his news came:

The handsome actor Wassim Taghi was seen comin' out of a popular bath in Derb Ghallef at eleven, day before yesterday. He was wearing a dark purple jellaba embroidered with wide macramé trim and big braids. He was wearing yellow babouches made of pure leather. Hope you had a nice bath. And nice jellaba and babouches, sir!

The only thing to report in Derb Sultan these days is the disgraceful state the well-known television writer appears to be in. He just recently [spelling corrected] published a novel and poetry collection at the same time with a prestigious Casaoui publishing house. He comes home every night in the middle of the night, stumbling drunk through the alley. May God forgive him and that's all.

The rising songstress Salwa Khafaji was seen at a cooool to-do in a hotel lobby in Ifrane with a well-known movie director whose name we won't mention so as not to make his wife, the beloved dark-skinned actress, angry with us. But, don't let your imagination wander. Maybe it was just an innocent [spelling corrected] trip to enjoy Ifrane's alluring nature far from the clamer [sic] of the studios and the suffocating atmosphere of home.

Inside a well-known mall in Casablanca, one of the stars of the series *Zeitouna Garden* was seen arguing with a salesgirl in a jewelry shop. The aforementioned actress did not bare [sic] in mind the mall's sanctity, nor that of the television screen that esteemed viewers see her on. Our sources that followed the fight up close [correcting the spelling, for she pronounced it, and he wrote it as "up clothes." You idiot!] confirm that the famous actress poured out a flood of humiliating sexual insults before throwing herself at the lady's hair and pulling it out. May God destroy you all, you two-bit actresses.

Those who know about the Behind the Scenes section of the newspaper say that in fact, there was no argument, no mall, nothing of the sort. Just that the series met with notable success, but not according to the number of viewers or from the media splash. And because Mimi, who was constantly hopping from café to café and from bar to bar, did not have enough of an ass to sit on—either in terms of language or literary tools—to take five minutes to write an article of three hundred words on a series, unlike his colleagues, who still believed that being a journalist meant debating a subject with clear arguments and a modicum of analysis, Mimi preferred to approach the subject in his own way.

Because the four stars of *Zeitouna Garden* were graduates of the Higher Institute for the Dramatic Arts, they were beyond Mimi's reach. Therefore, he sent his hounds off that way. And the plan really worked. The actresses, each and every one of them, called the editor in chief of the *Midpoint*, who praised their abilities and lauded their skills as actresses before transferring them to Mimi. Every one of them confirmed that the news, which was republished by a number of newspapers and sites—after the necessary corrections had been made—had tarnished their reputations. It would have been better for them to have revealed the identity of the woman involved in the argument if it really did happen, "Rather than punishing us just because one person was a badly behaving *méchante*. Let the misbehaving one bear responsibility for her behavior and be done with it." But Mimi, who affirmed the truth of what happened, having witnessed it quite by accident, preferred to keep the name of the one involved a secret so as not to tarnish her artistic career while she was still young and just starting out. Noting that this was just an opportunity to get to know them. "Consider," he said to each one of them, "that the *Midpoint* belongs to you. All of your news and activities will make their way into our Arts section, which will publish them with great pleasure."

Mimi had used the same ploy countless times, and he always managed to end up with the cell phone number of his victims, without their friendship preventing him from setting a trap for them some day in the future. His effeminate mannerisms and goo-goo eyes put them at ease when they met for a drink or dinner. But as soon as a tidbit of interesting news or an incendiary rumor fell, quite by accident, into his hands, he struck without mercy. He didn't let the tiniest ephemeral bit of news slip through his fingers, even if the one involved had just bought him drinks the previous night. That is how the effeminate Mimi became such a feared journalist. He was invited to all the kingdom's festivals, without exception. Artists, journalists, and critics discussed movies, plays, and art shows, while he tracked the gossip of the organizers and stories of tensions and internal quarrels, looking for organizers' transgressions during the opening ceremonies, gathering information about conflicts and side squabbles, furtively snapping pictures of actresses as they danced and actors as they got drunk during the closing ceremonies to publish them afterward in the *Midpoint*, accompanied by his nasty comments. One time Mimi published a picture of the head of a film festival hugging a young, beautiful woman. He included a nasty comment before discovering that she was his daughter.

■ ■ ■

As soon as Mimi set down his saddle bags at Hot Maroc, his editorial touch became clear. With the exception of Marzouk, over whom he had no control, Mimi demanded that all of the journalists and editors be very brief. People don't like it when journalists go on and on. People don't come to Hot Maroc for our theories and ideas and deep political analyses. "Whoever wants sociology or anthropology or bullshitology, let God have them pull it out of their ass," he boasted in front of his team. Hilarious. No one has time for this empty talk these days. People just want the news. Even if it's unreliable. If the news is unconfirmed, we'll republish it the following day in a new form so it will be confirmed. We'll whisper it in a café into the ear of another colleague from another pulpit to republish it his way. That's how it will be confirmed. What's the problem? The important thing is that we understand our role and our mission at Hot Maroc. We're here to give news to the people. News, news, news. Not philosophy. People like to read the news in a minute, two at the most, then they make their way to the comments to see how the street is interacting with what's going on. And because what concerns people is exactly this street interaction, *we* need to be close to the street and its language. That's why they brought you here, Mimi, my darling. Your cultural revolution at the *Midpoint*, specifically in the linguistic realm, has proven effective, especially in a country so attached to its illiteracy. And also because you know how to find news, and how to create it when there is none.

Mimi came to political news using the same style he had used in the Behind the Scenes pages and in writing about artists' scandals, benefiting from the climate of freedom to deride that was prevalent in the country. And then, in the end, because politics isn't about ideas or theories or principles. Politics is news and what goes on behind the scenes, and this is exactly what Hot Maroc did. Priority goes to the news item. And a news item that isn't able to propel the readers into commenting on it isn't a news item.

Despite that, we need to concede to Mimi that a point of positive transformation occurred during his flourishing tenure, which was the relatively new acceptance of opposing voices. Previously, there was no forum where a known opponent or a serious commentator could speak on any subject. For those, the way was absolutely blocked. Only the shadow fighters, such as Son of the People, Abu Sharr Guevari, and the like could wriggle in there, along with hordes of jokers, wanderers, beggars, parrots, angry Smurfs, web assholes, virtual bandits, and children of the electronic street, all of whom had nothing to lose. As for those with clear points of view and words that were heavy as lead, there was no place for them at Hot Maroc. But an important relaxing of the rules would occur in the Mimi era that made the site more democratic. Mimi himself had nothing to do with what happened, though.

Amine Rifaai had written an inflammatory article on corruption, which everyone, in principle, rejected, but which everyone accepted as if it were an inevitable destiny. It was an angry article, coming as it did from the wretched consciousness of a militant who had withdrawn from party work early and left union work immediately after retiring to take up action within the dynamic civil society fight against corruption. The article might have enjoyed some leeway because it was written with fervor by a sincere citizen who had never claimed to be revolutionary or radical. But the article's use of sensitive and detailed information to bolster his claims pushed some to discipline Rifaai in order to make an example of him. Once again, the tasks were distributed among the conductor, Naim Marzouk, and his well-known choir. They knocked the daylights out of him. All the sins that the man may have committed, or was suspected of having committed as he plowed his way through the Ministry of Justice, were compiled in a nasty article by Naim Marzouk, every sentence of which was like a bullet that could kill a camel. Then the comments came raining down like arrows. Son of the People reminded Rifaai of the years he had spent as an employee in the Appeals Court of Marrakech and how he had stunk up the place by lobbying some dishonorable lawyers, which resulted in his disciplinary transfer to Errachidia. Githa from Errachidia admitted that she was a neighbor of the fine gentleman and spoke of the adultery of his wife—who would receive her lover, a well-known date merchant in Errachidia—as soon as her husband would go to work. Some do-gooders intended to inform him of the wife's betrayal right then. But after learning of his own corruption and his bad reputation in the court, they repeated what the Almighty said, "Corrupt women for corrupt men, and corrupt men for corrupt women," and they asked God for forgiveness. As for Abu Sharr Guevari, he reminded him of the suspicious moves he had made with his former comrades in the party to assure his youngest son his current post as a university professor. Nabila the Injured sobbed hot tears on the electronic wall before announcing her decision to definitively leave union work after the shock of hearing about Rifaai, whom she had considered an example and a role model, before Hot Maroc thankfully revealed his true ugly face to her.

Amine Rifaai was thunderstruck as this treacherous bullet hit him. But despite that, he restored the truth in a counter statement. He mentioned his spotless work history and his activism, which was well-known to the public and his loved ones. And he explained that his transfer from Marrakech to Errachidia was arbitrary, following a vicious sectorial strike that his union had led. Just as he defended the morals of his wife, who gave their children the best of upbringings before the Creator of the Heavens took her to be beside Him in the bloom of her youth, and how he became responsible for raising the children himself until they all graduated and became important state functionaries, the envy of all. As for his youngest son, the critic and well-known literary scholar, his books, papers, and published studies sufficed to defend his academic worth. Finally, Rifaai clarified that all he possessed was his apartment that he lives in now and the car that he sold just a few months prior, since he didn't need to move around so much after he retired and left union work. The statement wasn't published on Hot Maroc or in the *Future*. The poor guy carried it in his pocket for more than two weeks as he wandered around cafés and forums to deliver it orally to whichever friends and comrades cared to hear it, until he suffered a stroke. Rifaai finally went to receive God's forgiveness, having reached about sixty-five years of age.

From that day on, Mimi began to let the injured and the wronged exercise their right to moan on Hot Maroc, the number one news site of Moroccans. And those who asked him to be more tolerant with the right of reply and statements of truth, and to publish excerpts of corrigenda, also warned Mimi that he needed to be manlier. So, he grew a ridiculous little moustache and took out the earring that used to adorn his left ear. And to the astonishment of the gang at the pub, Mimi assured them that he was seriously thinking about getting married.

50

IT WAS PROBABLY A MISTAKE that Rahhal hadn't put things right between Abu Qatada and Abdelmessih. Every time he went out to take care of something, or just to visit Halima and Abdeslam in Moukef, he sang the same tune. To start, he advised Qamar Eddine to avoid any contact with Yazid, and to not fall into his harassment snare. And he told him to take care of Abu Qatada as best as he could.

"Your brother, Mahjoub Didi, is an ass on the computer. He'd drown in an inch of water. So, if you leave him to wallow around, Qamar Eddine, you'll make things more difficult for him *and* you'll waste the shop's time that he'll spend waiting for me to connect him again with his brothers in God. So treat him as you would any other customer, don't make trouble."

Abdelmessih always used to intervene to help Abu Qatada, even the last time, when he didn't know what to do with the computer Didi was using and couldn't restart it. So he generously gave him his own favorite computer. He didn't know that this noble gesture was the mistake of a lifetime.

Abu Qatada couldn't betray his brother in God, Mr. Shihab Eddine Assuyuti. They prayed together in the Nour Mosque, and they shared an affection and compassion for one another. How could he become aware of such a grave secret and not inform his brother? It would be a great betrayal. That's why he told him exactly what he had seen.

"Your son, Mr. Shihab Eddine, was deep in conversation with Girgis the Copt, and it was as if, God forbid, they were of the same sect. Qamar Eddine called him 'Brother Girgis' and the Egyptian responded with 'Brother Abdelmessih.' Then the enemy of God wrote him a verse that seems to have come from their book that they call 'holy,' but we know how corrupt and full of contradictions it is. 'For as we have many members in one body, and all members have not the same office. So we, being many, are one body in Christ, and every one members one of another.' Then, my esteemed professor, the muezzin called, his voice of truth rising up, so I wrote down the odious verse and came to tell you the unmistakable truth. While I was running here, I repeated the prayer that Aicha, may God be satisfied with her, said about the Prophet: 'O God, O Stirrer of Hearts, make my heart steadfast in your religion. O God, O Stirrer of Hearts, make my heart steadfast in your religion.'"

Mr. Shihab Eddine didn't wait for the second call to prayer. In fact, he doubted that he was still in a state of ritual purity. He left the mosque at once and headed straight for the cybercafe. Rahhal had just come back and Abdelmessih was giving him the balance sheet when Mr. Shihab Eddine entered in a state no one had ever seen him in before. He was panting as if he had just been running. Panting and shaking. Abdelmessih didn't understand what was going on until Mr. Shihab Eddine lunged at him with all of his strength. He threw him to the ground and began to hit him. He wanted to punch him but didn't know how. He tried to bite him, but failed. He pulled his hair. He dragged him with both of his hands. He shook his head and beat it on the ground as he howled like an injured wolf with the blood coursing through his veins like a madman. Then he raised his right hand up high and slapped him across the cheek, yelling:

"A Christian, you apostate! You were registered at the university but didn't go, so we said to ourselves, 'He's a young man with a different view of life and the future,' and we left you alone. You stopped going to the mosque, so we said to ourselves, 'He's just a bit deluded. He'll return to the right path,' and we let you be. You took up in this infested hole and we said to ourselves, 'Let him open himself up to the world,' and we didn't chase after and watch over you. And the result? A Christian all at once?! Just like that, you miserable wretch?! What will people say about me? A butcher and he eats turnips for dinner! If you were a fag with fuckers playing with your ass, we'd pray for your protection. If you doubted the existence of the Creator we'd say that even God's prophet, Abraham, had doubts and sought answers (after which his heart was satisfied), and we'd pray for your guidance. But a Christian, you lowlife! A Nazarene, as if the Lord of Strength hadn't chosen his last prophet for this community and from it?!"

Not many people understood exactly what happened that night.

An ambulance took Mr. Shihab Eddine to the hospital in a state of severe nervous breakdown. Qamar Eddine spent the night in the cybercafe. He couldn't face his mother after this dark, evil deed had been revealed. As for Mahjoub Didi, he didn't come into the cyber-cafe for more than a month. Was he afraid of Qamar Eddine or Rah-hal Laâouina? When he finally did come back one afternoon, he didn't speak with anyone, and no one spoke with him.

51

RAHHAL DIDN'T BELIEVE HIS EYES AT FIRST. The friend request came with no attached message. It was a friend request. But from who? From His Highness Prince Fares himself? Do you believe that, Rahhal? Do you believe your eyes? The prince is sending a friend request to the Lioness. Was it in Rahhal's power to hesitate or refuse? To explain to His Highness that Hiyam wasn't Hiyam? It was more complicated than the prince imagined. But Rahhal would accept the request. He couldn't do anything other than accept. He accepted the princely request and his head was spinning. He accepted the request while thinking about Commissioner Rat and about the internet foxes, about its snakes and its scorpions, and about all those who count the electronic breaths of all creatures. What will he say to them and how will he respond if they catch him playing around now? And with who? With a prince. You're playing around with a prince, you vile rat! You're nothing but a rat with a squirrel's tail. It's him, His Highness Prince Fares exactly as we see him on television. He was wearing a black smoking jacket fit for a prince, and he was smiling, just as he does on the news during national holidays, at formal dedications, and in pictures.

The next day, Rahhal went to scroll through his email and was shocked. There was a message from the prince. An extremely polite message confirming how much His Highness liked Ms. Hiyam's profile, and expressing his pride in her high literary taste. Then he asked her, "Are all Marrakechi women like this?" He closed the message with a happy face. A Facebookian happy face quite common in these sorts of correspondences, but with a princely touch. Even on Facebook, princes don't smile as we do. They have silky smiles. Velvety smiles that invite a special type of acceptance. But if the prince found out that the one who received his message and who was reading over his innocent conversation with Hiyam was Rahhal Laâouina, son of Halima the Pelican and Abdeslam the Mantis, what would be your fate, you miserable wretch?

Are all Marrakechi women like this?

The prince is from Rabat. Born and lives there, in the capital. Perhaps he doesn't know Marrakechi women that well. As for me, I don't know Marrakechi women or women from anywhere else, for that matter, so how will I respond to him now, Hiyam?

Would the Cinderella story repeat itself?

Confused, Rahhal didn't know how to respond. He left Qamar Eddine in charge of the shop and went to Café Milano. He ordered a black coffee and sat. Asmae unenthusiastically placed the coffee down in front of him. Even when he asked about her health like his uncle Ayad always did, she didn't answer. She heard and moved her head as if she was going to say something, but she didn't utter a word. She dragged herself off and stood staring outside. As if she weren't the girl he once knew. She looked exhausted, depleted, moving listlessly between the tables. Larbi, the café's owner, was also sitting at the door. Rahhal looked closely at him for the first time and noticed a hint of Cinderella's wicked stepmother. But at Café Milano, there was no sign of the birds and the kind mice that helped Cinderella with her chores. Asmae had been on her feet since 7:00 a.m. She works until 10:00 p.m. There are no birds there, Asmae. No witch and no slipper. The prince asks whether all Marrakechi women are like you, and I don't know how to respond.

Rahhal couldn't sleep that night as he lay awake thinking about how to respond to the prince.

"Your Highness, the prince. Your lofty message made me very happy. I consider Your Highness' presence with us on Facebook a sign of your humility. So, Your Highness, please accept my sincere thanks for your generous attention and also for your love for the residents of Marrakech, as well as for all of the Facebook-ists of the tourism capital of your happy kingdom. Know that all Marrakechis like myself thank you profusely for the efforts you exert to exalt this community and allow it to flourish. May you remain a great asset to us. *Salaam alaikum*. May peace and God's blessing be upon you."

Rahhal sent his response and breathed a sigh of relief. As if someone had removed a huge weight from his chest. And now, my friend, you need to review this entire film. Hiyam is a ticking time-bomb that will explode in your face, you reckless fool. You need to get rid of her right away. Kill her. Block her way and crush her with Hassaniya's car or have her commit suicide. But she can't remain there. This isn't Emad Qatifa, Rahhal. This is His Highness Prince Fares. Do you understand what that means? His Highness Prince Fares. He was still examining the matter from various angles when another hot coal, even hotter than the previous one, landed in his inbox:

"What if you left me your phone number, Hiyam, my friend? I am visiting Marrakech soon and perhaps I'll call you ☺ . . ." (With the princely smile, of course).

Goddamn you, Squirrel. Didn't I tell you to be done with her? Why didn't you do it? You broke it, now fix it! What will you send him now? Your cell phone number? Your hedgehog's number? What are you going to say to him, for God's sake? This is a prince, you lowlife. Now you're messing around with princes? Who are you, you rat, to screw around and deceive princes?

Rahhal closed Facebook and left. The following day, he didn't go in to the cybercafe. Not because he didn't want to, but rather because he couldn't. His temperature rose unexpectedly and fever stilled his bones. Qamar Eddine came to him at the apartment, got the keys, and went back to open the shop. Rahhal stayed in bed for three full days. On the fourth day, Hassaniya compelled him to go to work.

"You don't have to give in to illness. The fever is gone, so don't exaggerate, Rahhal," Hassaniya said. He was hesitant but for the big question mark that appeared on his phone. It was Officer Hakim. A lone question mark with no accompanying comment. Rahhal tried to interpret it: Where are you? What's up with you? Why have you disappeared? Maybe it was all of these questions at once. Rahhal went back to the shop. He pulled himself together and went back. He reclaimed his chair at the head of the table. He opened up Hot Maroc. There, he found the news on the home page: a young Moroccan man who worked at a bank in the city of Kenitra had been arrested for impersonating Prince Fares. The court considered the young employee to have committed "despicable acts," while the defense deemed the charges against his client illegal since there were no laws on the books governing internet use in Morocco. As for the union of journalists, it published a release saying that Facebook shouldn't be taken so seriously, whereas more than one rights group and youth organization sided with the young employee. Rahhal didn't have time to condemn or pardon him. He logged into Facebook. He entered Hiyam's den. He went straight to the inbox. The message was still there. "What if you left me your phone number, Hiyam, my friend? I am visiting Marrakech soon and perhaps I'll call you ☺ . . ." He tried to click from the letter to the prince's profile, but it wasn't there. The prince had disappeared. The princely pictures with the smoking jacket were gone. The smile was gone. *Ah, if only I weren't so busy, and Officer Hakim weren't waiting for something new from me, I'd travel to Kenitra to protest in front of the courthouse against you, you thoughtless fool. Against you and the union of journalists and the rights groups and youth organizations, and against the stupid lawyer who's defending you. You've given me an ulcer, you bastard, and still, they stand with you. Sir, a prince is a prince, above me and above you, and he may excuse you from your bullshit. But what about me? What did I do to you? You almost killed me, goddamn you!*

52

MAY GOD BLESS YOU, MARRAKECH STAR.

Fadoua and Samira were intent on organizing a visit to Mr. Shihab Eddine Assuyuti at the clinic. Salim and his sister went with them. Rahhal declined. But what the two girls didn't expect was for Yacabou to join them. The Nigerian with the long neck that looked like a giraffe's neck insisted on accompanying the delegation to the clinic where Professor Assuyuti was. His insistence seemed strange at first, especially since the delegation was essentially made up of Professor Assuyuti's former students. It wasn't possible to say no to Yacabou, though. Besides, it would just be a quick, five-minute visit to see the patient and make sure the professor was doing well, then they'd return to the cybercafe.

But with Yacabou, the visit lasted a full two hours. And the squadron only left the clinic after finishing off all the juices that visitors had piled up next to Mr. Shihab Eddine's bed during the two days he had been there.

It all began with Fadoua's passing comment confirming that she didn't believe what she had heard about Qamar Eddine, especially since it had come from Mahjoub Didi.

"Sir, everyone in the cybercafe knows that Mahjoub hates Qamar Eddine, even though your son never hesitates to help him out whenever he hits an electronic pothole. But Mahjoub's heart is filled with hatred. He hates everyone in the cybercafe, especially Qamar Eddine. That's why I fear that his denunciation is false and has no basis in truth."

This is where Yacabou entered the fray. His French is broken but his ideas are clear, and his argument made Professor Assuyuti sit up in his bed.

"*Non*, Monsieur Assuyuti. There is a basis for what Mahjoub said. Your son, Qamar Eddine, is obsessed with emigrating and wants to leave the country any way he can. Due to his naïveté, he thought that claiming to be a Christian might work to his advantage and give him a better chance of emigrating to Europe. He's asked me about this many times. That's why it's very possible that he has used a made-up Christian name to make contact with some people he thinks might be able to help him with this. Lately he has started to talk about Georgia. I don't know who turned him on to this place. Maybe because a number of Copts from Egypt have started to emigrate there. But this doesn't mean that Qamar Eddine has become a Christian. Never. Not possible.

"First of all, in order for your son to become a Christian, sir, he'd need to be baptized. The Messiah himself was baptized. John, the son of Zechariah, dunked him three times in the Jordan River. I know that Qamar Eddine's body has not been submerged by a priest or sprinkled with water by a minister either in the name of the Son, the Father, or the Holy Spirit. And before a baptism happens, the church chooses two Christian fathers who will agree to adopt him as a son, after which he'll carry their family name until a new name is chosen for him later. Nothing like this has happened with Qamar Eddine. You are his only father before God, the angels, the saints, the mosque, the church, and the whole world. As for the name Abdelmessih that Mahjoub was talking about, it's just one of the many screen names we all choose from online. Your son is confused, sir, but he isn't a Christian. In order to become a Christian, he needs to go through the ritual confession. Your son has not confessed to anything, neither to a priest nor to anyone else. There has been no confession. Just a false denunciation from Mahjoub Didi, and unfortunately you believed it without question. But don't worry, Mr. Assuyuti. Fadoua, Samira, and I will come back to visit you tomorrow. Qamar Eddine will come with us. And you will embrace each other in front of us. Tomorrow morning, Monsieur Shihab Eddine."

Professor Assuyuti bowed his head in silence. A thick cloud that had been blocking him from the world and its people began to clear. He didn't know how to respond to this thin Africano with the long neck. He wished that he had the strength to pull him to his chest. To hug him first before embracing his son the next day. Assuyuti seemed bewildered, yet happy to his core. His happiness was confused and he didn't know how to express it. All he could do was open a carton of juice and pour it for them, and each time he did so he said, "Please, my children, have some juice."

53

WHEN YAZID'S PHONE RANG, all movement stopped in the cyber-cafe. Everyone was drawn into his stories. Generally, he spoke casually, as if he were in his bedroom, speaking loudly, sometimes shouting. And he lied a lot. The lies came as easily to him as breathing.

"Buddy, I'm in Rabat right now . . . Yes, if I swear . . . in Rabat. In Rabat . . . Just yesterday I told you I was going to Rabat . . . I have something I need to take care of, then I'm going to Casa. Saturday, *inshallah,* God willing, I'll return to Marrakech . . . Be cool . . . Okay . . . Bye."

The conversation itself was enjoyable. An enjoyable break that didn't annoy the café's customers anymore. But the most powerful moment was Yazid's comment after he hung up. He always had a final word that he'd save for the end. An insult he'd hold onto for the whole conversation, that he'd save for the very end. He always used obscenities when he hurled insults, after the conversation has ended, of course. Even when he didn't insult, he would surprise the customers with some short comment that would nullify everything he had promised the person he had just been speaking with. Then he'd go back to surfing the blue electronic waves, immediately live broadcasting what was happening in front of him on Facebook or commenting on what breaking news was published on Hot Maroc. Sometimes, when he was in a good mood and his cell phone was charged up, he'd surprise his cyber family with amazing performances. He would sometimes hide his number so it wouldn't be visible to the person he was speaking with, then dial some random number. He'd deepen his voice and prepare his supply of nastiness and stock of insults, then he'd proceed to ruin the day of the stranger whose number had chanced to fall into Yazid's hands. Sometimes he'd put the call on speakerphone and the café's customers would hold their breaths as they listened to the confused reactions of the baffled person who didn't know where this rubbish was tumbling down from. Other times Yazid would have them follow only his side of the spectacular performance inside the improvised comedy and let them guess at what the other person was saying:

"Hello?"

" . . . "

"Naji?"

" . . . "

"This isn't Naji? Why? What's *your* name?"

" . . . "

"You can't answer a question with a question. How rude is that? Now tell me, what's your name? Abdelkrim?"

" . . . "

"What do you mean it's not Abdelkrim? Are you related to Khadija Naji?"

" . . . "

"Yeah . . . Khadija Naji is your aunt. Meaning Abdelkrim is your cousin."

" . . . "

"And your aunt's husband, do you know him? Did you know that he used to sell bras in the Lakriaa market in Derb Sultan? The loser didn't even earn enough for dinner. I have no idea how he was able to open a shop on Anfa Avenue and buy a house and car."

" . . . "

"Get out of here, you stinky Doukkali hick. That was when you still sucked your thumb and didn't know how to wipe your own ass. Get out of here, you're an embarrassment to your entire family!"

" . . . "

"You're from Casa? You must be kidding! Okay, tell me, how many generations in Casa?"

" . . . "

"Come, Mr. Casaoui. Do you like the Widad team or Rajae?"

" . . . "

"The red jerseys of Widad?! What an idiot!"

"..."

"Who's with you? Figure out who's with you. Actually, tell me, do you like Real Madrid or Barcelona?"

"..."

"Real?! I knew you knew nothing about soccer. Okay, let's go, Mr. Real. You have five seconds. The name of Real Madrid's left defender . . . five, four, three, two, one . . . Stop. Nothing?! Get out of here. Go on, my boy. Talking to you is a waste of time."

"..."

"It's none of your business who I am. You should be honored I called you."

"..."

"Now you wanna talk shit, you son of a bitch? Why don't you go kill yourself, you stupid fuck?"

Rahhal didn't understand how Yazid came up with all of this information or where he got it from. And what preoccupied him the most was that he didn't know where reality ended and fabrication began. Also, did Yazid know these people at all, or was the play pure, blind improvisation? The strange thing was that they remained patient, not hanging up on him. But frankly, Squirrel, would you end the call if you were in their shoes? Rahhal would sit stunned while Yazid gave his performances. As for the Atlas Cubs clientele, they understood that their friend was a lost cause and had gotten used to his stupid antics. For his part, Yazid felt free to do whatever without caring about anyone. It was only the three Africanos who would, under no circumstances, interact with him or sit next to him.

"No, sir, give them your computer and keep them away from me. I always say that these Senegalese should never sit next to me," he shouted in Rahhal's face.

All Africanos are Senegalese as far as Yazid is concerned, and besides, it's not just he who thought like that. In general, Moroccans considered all Black Africans to be Senegalese unless given proof to the contrary. Maybe because of the regular annual pilgrimages of

Senegalese Muslim adherents of the Tijani Sufi path to their lodge in Fes that had been going on for centuries, Moroccans had gotten used to seeing Senegalese Africans more than other sub-Saharans.

"The important thing is to give me some space!" Yazid would fume.

Everyone in the cybercafe was embarrassed, but they ignored the situation. Yacabou suppressed his anger and gave Rahhal a chance to find another spot for them. Most of the time, Qamar Eddine would give up his spot and go sit next to Yazid. The two girls prayed that Yacabou would let it go, and convinced him to do so. But Rahhal caught Yacabou looking hatefully at Yazid. The long-necked Nigerian's stares were fiery, blazing with pure hatred.

If they were to find Yazid's body one day drenched in blood in the middle of Dakhla Avenue, it would be certain that Yacabou was behind it. No question. Even after everything was smoothed over and the three Africanos took their seats far from him, Yazid didn't stop broadcasting. As if he were justifying it. But utilizing his natural rudeness as he addressed everyone and no one in a loud voice, as if he were an imam delivering a sermon from the pulpit, but without a staff to lean on, and without feeling the need to stop:

"Don't get me wrong. I'm not racist or arrogant. God forbid! But, my friends, I can't stand the smell of this dung beetle. The smell of his armpits makes me dizzy. What can I do?"

Then he turns toward Qamar Eddine, smiling wickedly and insincerely:

"Hey, Qamar Eddine. Tell me, what's the name of the poet who said, 'Don't buy a slave unless he comes with a stick'?"

That's all your memory has retained from what you learned as a child, you imbecile? His name was Abu Tayyeb Mutanabbi, you worthless piece of shit. And you should have asked me, not Qamar Eddine, thought Rahhal.

Yazid didn't know that Rahhal had a degree in Arabic literature, anyway. But everyone knew Mutanabbi's famous poem. Anyone who went to public school in the 1970s and 1980s and into the mid-1990s knew the poem and had memorized its stinging verses. All Moroccan schoolchildren with black skin were burned by the poem, and their classmates would constantly torture them with it. It was as if the Ministry of National Education was dead set on sowing the seeds of racism in the consciousness of every single one of the country's children. May God forgive you, Abu Tayyeb, may God forgive you:

> Death does not grab one of their souls
> unless there is a stick in his putrid hand.
> The slave is not fit to be the brother of one who is free
> even if he dons the clothes of a freeborn man.
> Do not buy a slave unless he comes with a stick
> for slaves are filthy, lacking any good fortune.

But Yazid never memorized the poem, nor did he remember more than one line. But, of course, he's no racist. The dung beetle is part of the universe, too. His only problem was with the smell.

"I can't take it, my friend. I can't stand it. It makes me nauseous."

What?! It makes you nauseous?! Who said that? The king of cleanliness in the cybercafe? Mr. Clean himself? The disgusting smell that comes from your sweaty feet, you prick, when you brazenly permit yourself to take off your dirty shoes to air them out . . . doesn't that offend you? Don't you notice that there are people who leave as soon as you take your shoes off because of the rotten smell of your socks?

But Rahhal had gotten used to keeping his conversations to himself. When it came to Yazid, he kept what he was thinking to himself. Just like that, in silence. And at night he'd set the record straight. He'd get up from where he was sitting to stand up in front of the son of Moulay Ahmed Malkha. He'd rip the computer up all at once, sending the machine flying over everyone's heads, slamming into the ceiling before shattering on the ground in pieces. He'd grab his cup of coffee and pour it over his head before grabbing the bastard's collar and punching him over and over again. He'd aim for his opponent's face as he bellowed after having lost control of his fist, which had started to hit its target like a machine without paying attention to the blood that was bubbling hot out of Yazid's mouth, nose, and head. Yazid would be howling like an injured dog. The girls would be screaming—Fadoua, Samira, Amelia, Flora, and even Asmae, the waitress from Café Milano (Rahhal didn't know when she joined the cybercafe's girls in the dream). She squeezed herself between them to start wailing and screaming in a melodious voice unbefitting of lionesses. The girls' screaming, specifically that of the Lioness, became even more intense in the decisive moment when Yazid dropped lifelessly to the floor of the cybercafe. Right then Yacabou appeared, his gaze moving between Yazid's corpse and the girls' lamentations. His look was not hateful this time. It was guilty and fearful. A frightened and suspicious look that seemed to say, "It was me. I did it." But the police didn't come to take him or Rahhal. Or perhaps the police did come and take him, but Rahhal wasn't there. Right then, Rahhal woke up. He got up gently from the bed so as not to disturb the Hedgehog. He went to the bathroom. He washed his hands. He scrubbed them with a loofah and soap and hot water to wash Yazid's blood from them—the dream's blood—after which he could then get a better sleep. When he went back to sleep he breathed deeply and didn't stir too much in bed.

In the morning, when he went back to the cybercafe, Yazid's stupid antics bothered him less. He started from scratch. "Hello? Helloooo?" A new telephone performance. A nasty insult after hanging up the phone. A sarcastic comment for a newcomer. A lame bit of ridiculous harassment for Fadoua. Then he moved right to broadcasting what was happening on the screen in front of him. But Rahhal had disengaged. Son of the People wasn't free to follow Yazid's antics. Hidhami has just posted something, and you, Rahhal, need to validate it immediately.

54

RAHHAL WAS IN THE MIDDLE OF THE DREAM when the phone
rang. It seemed that it had been ringing for ten minutes. But Rahhal, who had been absorbed with punching Yazid in the face, hadn't
heard it. Before the Lioness had entered the scene, or at least before
she started screaming, Rahhal noticed his cell phone ringing . . .

"Hello, good evening."

"Good morning, Rahhal. Go open up Hot Maroc right now.
Read Hidhami's directive and do what you need to do . . ."

"But I'm at home right now. I can't open the cybercafe so late at
night."

"What?! You can't?!"

"I'm really sorry, Mr. Hakim."

"But what do I have to do with the cybercafe? I don't care if you
open it or close it. You can close it day and night if you want. That's
not my concern. I just want you to log onto Hot Maroc so you can
get to work. Don't you have a computer at home?! Don't you have an
internet connection?!

"Unfortunately, Mr. Hakim, no, there is no . . ."

"What are you doing with your salary, you moron, if you
haven't used it even to buy the tools of your trade? I really don't
understand!"

"Actually, Mr. Hakim . . ."

"Don't explain a thing to me. I don't want to know. You need to
act within the hour. Log onto Hot Maroc and post more than one
comment. Son of the People, Abu Qatada, and the others, they all
need to comment. Your itinerary has been set by Hidhami. And you
need to align yourself with her to set a course tonight so that the
site's readers will find the way well-lit and clear when they wake

up. And if you don't do it within the hour, I can't guarantee what Commissioner Ayadi's reaction will be."

"But Mr. Hakim? What if . . . ?"

"I told you, hang up. You have an hour to act, you . . ."

The Hedgehog was all balled up, deep in sleep. Her contented snoring filled Rahhal with rage after this awful phone call demanding that he go to the cybercafe at this hour. Fuck, it was 3:30 in the morning. It wasn't even dawn. He thought about writing a word to assure Hassaniya, but then reconsidered. *I'll be back before she wakes up*, he said to himself. *I'll get the job done in five minutes and be back before the Hedgehog turns over onto her other side.*

It was a dark night. The garbage collectors hadn't yet passed through Dakhla Avenue. Their rickety truck never showed up before the dawn call to prayer. Generally, its rusty metal belly doesn't have enough room for all of this garbage. Lines of garbage piled up everywhere. The street vendors who have come to occupy the sidewalk right after the afternoon prayer and continue to descend on it from every which way after midnight leave their garbage on-site: cardboard and plastic bags and debris of all sorts. Even someone who was thinking about picking up the trash wouldn't be able to find a place to put it all. The municipal trash bins distributed along the length of the street fill up and overflow so fast that the building residents who take their trash out late have to pile it up next to the bins, then on the sidewalk, heaped up all over the place. Disgusting smells waft up from the garbage. You need to spray insect repellent on the sides of the shop now, Rahhal, to guard against morning fly and mosquito raids.

Besides the garbage, and a lone car whizzing past, the street appeared completely deserted, dark and empty. The Squirrel's heart was beating hard. Your heart will jump right out of its hiding place between your ribs, you coward. Rahhal began to rush toward the cybercafe when he noticed three specters reeling in the darkness. In the name of God, the Beneficent, the Merciful. Say, "I take refuge in the Lord of Creation. From the evil that He created. I take refuge in God from cursed Satan."

The Squirrel Enters the Blue Box | 257

Are these specters blocking your path human beings made of water and clay, or could they be devilish jinns, Squirrel? But the black phantoms looked somehow familiar. Very familiar. It was Amelia and Flora, Rahhal, with a third girl who was a bit taller, also Africano. Rahhal rushed toward the girls, as if seeking refuge with them from the pitch-black night. Amelia, Amelia . . . The girls noticed the Squirrel running toward them. Amelia and Flora came forward to meet him, whereas the third one jumped in fright. She took a step backward, terrified, and grabbed onto one of the columns of Café Milano. It seems that you've frightened her, Squirrel.

Amelia was staggering as if she were drunk. Both of the girls were drunk, Rahhal. And all heavily made up. Ah, how beautiful these two black goats are. How did you not notice before? Praise the Lord, you have seen in the dark what the light of day couldn't reveal to you.

Amelia's skirt was very short, and Flora's large breasts practically fell out of the top of her short soirée dress. Their tall, thin friend didn't pass under the Squirrel's radar either. She was wearing white pants that squeezed her tight bum and a red shirt that fit tightly around her waist and displayed her small breasts. And her long, hennaed hair hung down over her shoulders. It was longer than Amelia's and Flora's hair.

The two girls delighted the anxious Rahhal with slutty laughter and comments that they exchanged in their local dialect until he opened the door and went in, locking the door from inside. Then they went off reeling in the direction of the shy black gazelle. Rahhal turned on all the lights, including the one in the toilet. Thus, he regained a feeling of calm familiarity inside the empty café. No sooner did the lights flicker on all over the shop did he regain his equilibrium. He turned on a computer, opened the browser, and went right to Hot Maroc. Come on. Where are you, Hidhami? Where are you? I came to you believing in and trusting the news you have in your hands.

55

Exclusive

Top secret

THE SCOOP occupied the center of the news site's homepage: "Elite group made up of some of the country's most prominent politicians and national figures meet secretly with the goal of establishing a new party that will transform the Moroccan political scene. Hot Maroc alone reveals the names of the founders."

The news item was long this time, replete with details.

According to reliable sources, this group—made up of high-ranking politicians, union leaders, and important nationalist personages—had been meeting secretly twice a month for six months to define the major directions of a new political framework that would form an essential addition to the political landscape in our country, and that will deliver the country from its current state of stagnation.

The news was shocking and powerful. But the list of names left Rahhal dumbfounded and unable to comment. Who could have pictured that the retired, high-level official from the security apparatus Moha Sinhaji would walk hand in hand with two of the most notorious leftists—Said Bourkadi and Kamal Aufi—who had been sentenced to life imprisonment before receiving royal pardons at the beginning of the new king's reign? Two former ministers who left politics during the Hassan II days and devoted themselves full-time to moneymaking and business ventures returned to occupy the top of Hot Maroc's list: the Amazighi Berber militant Idir Nayt Bihi, director of the Tafoukt Center for Amazigh Culture, and Sallam Ould Khadij, the former leader of the Polisario Front, who came back to Moroccan soil in the mid-1990s following the former king's pronouncement that "the homeland is all-forgiving, all-compassionate." What? The learned jurist Sheikh Abu Ayyoub Mansouri? Good lord, what are you, oh venerable sheikh, doing next to Omar Nouri, the fierce defender of gay rights? There's also the famous singer Salima Ahmed. I can't picture her respecting the sanctity of your illustrious position during meetings, my good sheikh, she being so famous for her marble legs, short skirts, and flirtatious way of speaking. Former sports champion Hadi Alumayri graces the list, too. Bravo, bravo.

But it appears that the faucet of surprises refuses to close. You have this: Fatima Raoui, the Socialist leader who resigned from her party about six months ago and whose resignation created a great uproar and speculation in the national press, was front and center on the list. What are you doing, comrade, next to the professional electioneer Hammad Zougi and the rotten right-wing feudal lord Kamal Atouna? Did I say "rotten right-wing"? But it was *your* newspaper, dear comrade, that accustomed us to using these epithets for Atouna and his ilk.

Ah, Rahhal. It appears that you're late. Your comrades' comments are solid, my friend, and they're all plucking the same string. Welcoming the new electoral line number and cheering for it. Read what Ghitha from Errachidia wrote. Sahraoui's comment. A Girl from the North's interjection. As for your angry adversary, Abu Sharr Guevari, he has done away with his militant quarrelsomeness and famous anger, donning the cap of the wise this time:

"Readers of Hot Maroc all know my position on this country's political parties. For I am just one of Morocco's disappointed young people who have lost all faith in politics and politicians, who have collectively left the parties and their headquarters, and who have reluctantly, yet definitively and permanently, decided to leave in the wake of all of these electoral gains that have lost all legitimacy. Therefore, today I can only applaud any initiative that promises some hope and tries to extricate the Moroccan political scene from the state of paralysis and stasis it has fallen into.

"I lost confidence in the Socialists when they betrayed their principles by bearing responsibility for the Government of Song and Dance—sorry, I mean Government of Alternance—and became worse than the most arrogant liberals while they enthusiastically oversaw the unprecedented sale of people's property and the transfer of national companies to foreigners and elites. During the days of political activism, we banged our heads against the wall yelling out slogans preaching nationalization, decrying privatization, and warning the masses against foreign companies and the 'anti-nationalist' bourgeoisie and predatory liberals. But no sooner did they find themselves ruling next to Hassan II in 1998 than they turned into good students of the World Bank and stood behind the largest transfer of public sector companies contemporary Morocco had ever seen.

"I lost faith in the Communists after they all repented to God, and the Hajj pilgrimage to God's house became a basic requirement for the position of general secretary, until the title *Hajj* in their central committee became more common than 'comrade.' In fact, I heard that they demanded the Islamic Affairs portfolio during negotiations over the formation of the current government.

"And of course, the last ones you can bet on are the Islamists who, when you talk to them about development and its gambles, they talk to you about heaven and its bliss; when you ask them about corruption and tyranny, they remind you of hell and the misery of the covenant; when you debate them about democracy, they order you to obey your rulers. As soon as you disagree with them politically on an idea or position, they force you into a group of people they're angry with—the misguided strays, the heretic secularists—and they incite the mob against you. One of their sheikhs might even step forward and declare you an unbeliever, calling for your blood to be spilled if their political accounts require that. To them, democracy isn't in their creed other than as something they work pragmatically with, just something to ride to get them to power. And as soon as things start to go well for them, they wave the get-closer-to-God card in the faces of their opponents and allies and order them to adhere to Sharia law and raise their eternal slogan: 'No election, no constitution! The word of God and His messenger is enough.'

"You may have noticed that I've spoken about the Islamists, the Socialists, and the Communists, but I haven't said anything about the Makhzen parties that emerged from the womb of the Moroccan administration in the days of Hassan II. The legitimacy of these parties ended a long time ago, and no one asks them for anything anymore, good or bad. What would you expect from parties that, over their entire lifetimes, have never made a political decision that was made up of anything other than instructions and dictates? Parties that were always waiting for signs from above. When their leaders wrangle for positions and responsibilities, they seek refuge like defeated chickens in the rooster's coop—the office of Hassan II's Minister of the Interior—to complain to him and fight with one another, moaning and groaning and shedding tears before the grand vizier adjudicates between them according to his mood and fancy, outside of the organizational bases and legal curriculums that they had agreed upon in the formational conferences, of course.

"In the shadow of this miserable party situation, frankly I can only be gladdened with this new electoral party line, so let's give it the chance to present its positions to Moroccans and to propose its agenda and vision to them. We might agree or disagree. And I promise you that I will be the first to criticize this party on Hot Maroc if it turns out to be just another stupid party lining up with the others. But let's give it a chance first. Let's show our gratitude to this elite group that has taken the initiative to establish this party. At least it has tried to throw a stone into our stagnant political pond."

Oh, Abu Sharr, your contribution is exhaustive. All I can do is congratulate you, comrade. In the spirit of good sportsmanship, I tip my cap to you. You've said everything that needed to be said, and haven't left me anything to add. What can I add? I'll just repeat what you already said in your comment. I'll just say the same thing in my own way. In Son of the People's language that's relatable to a public that appreciates his verbal somersaults. Then I will have Abu Qatada bring forth testimony from the Holy Book and trustworthy prophetic Hadith for the newcomers. Why not, when it is the only party that managed to convince the sheikh, beloved by God, Abu Ayyoub Mansouri, to come out of his ascetic isolation to work with this blessed party to reform the country in a way that will satisfy the Lord of all His Servants? And the others will repeat the same thing, each in their own language, mood, and style. For that which is repeated is set. As they say, "Repetition teaches the donkey."

56

WHEN YACABOU and his two companions entered the cybercafe that afternoon, Rahhal was engrossed in reading the comments, dazzled by the direction they had taken. He didn't see the three Africanos come in, nor did he pay any attention to them. News of the new party was a great opportunity to pass judgment on the Moroccan parties. Everyone took the bait. The Islamists spared no effort in undermining the Socialists, Communists, and secularists. Progressive democrats had been on the lookout for Islamist slanders to accumulate evidence of their plan's corruption and their miserable exploitation of religion, to uncover their singular way of thinking and the double standards they stumble over. Analysts from the Far Left arrived right on cue, aiming their painful blows, sometimes below the belt, at the socialist parties that had become part of the governing Makhzen and that had betrayed their principles and the blood of the martyrs.

This is how Moroccans are. You know them well, Rahhal. You just have to set the tone for them to follow you, as if they were a blind orchestra. It took you back to your nightly commutes from the cybercafe to Mouassine in the crowded Djemaa Lfnaa shared taxis. The conversations were always along the same lines. It was enough for a passenger to utter a sentence, just like that, randomly, for the rest to dive in after him. If he said that "things have gone from bad to worse," the rest of the passengers would artfully provide evidence of how everything everywhere had crashed. If he said, "Our country is beautiful and may God glorify Morocco," the passengers would fall over one another to enumerate the country's praiseworthy attributes.

Taxi chatter is endless. Six passengers crowded in: two in the front seat next to the driver and four in the back. Still, they find enough comfort to chitchat and gossip. As soon as the taxi stops at a red light, finding itself out in front, the driver moves forward to gain a meter or two. That's how he gets in front of the stoplight. All the drivers who are out in front move forward. And since, unfortunately, the Lord hadn't given Moroccans eyes on their backs, it was up to the cars behind them to honk and alert them to the fact that the light has turned green. Sometimes, some of the ones who haven't been raised well lean too heavily on the horn. Beep, beep, BEEP! Rage strikes the driver and he begins to protest: "What's with these animals? They want to fly?" and the chorus joins in: "My friend, people have no patience anymore"; "God protect us . . . People have gone crazy, God lead us to safe harbor"; "You're only going to go where God takes you." All of them whistling the same tune. Repeating the same words. Everyone shows solidarity with the driver. All the passengers reassure him. All of them, what a surprise, are forbearing, patient, submissive, not in a rush.

But when the driver finds himself in back, he spontaneously hits the horn to warn the drivers out in front who aren't paying attention, and because they don't always react immediately, the driver protests: "D'ya see this animal has fallen asleep on us? He doesn't want to move." And so begin the comments: "I swear to God he's napping as if he owns the damn road"; "They don't know who's in a hurry and who has things he needs to take care of." Everyone disapproves and protests, as if that minute of hesitation the driver in front of them took was precious.

And now you see, Rahhal, how the morning comments on the news about the new party line did not steer away from what Hidhami and her gang had planned during the night. Bravo, Son of the People. Bravo, Abu Qatada.

He looked up from the screen. He rubbed his eyes and gave a satisfying glance out over the cybercafe. The Africanos had occupied their place next to Abdelmessih. He recalled Amelia's staggering last night. He felt that a wide smile had begun to form inside him without yet appearing on his face. Oh, Amelia. How lovely you are, you little black goat. But the two girls were engaged in a chat.

Only Yacabou turned and shot an ambiguous glance at Rahhal. It wasn't a piercing, hateful look that he would aim at Yazid from time to time. Nor was it a look of apprehension like in the dream. Rather, it was a vacant, indecisive look. A look of weakness and incoherence, and a bit of thirst. Something feminine. Shit, Rahhal. How did you not notice it yesterday? He is *her*! The timid black gazelle. The slim, long-necked gazelle. The frightened gazelle. How did you miss it, Squirrel?

The Animal Comedy

57

IT WAS AS IF the city was no longer the same city. As if a hidden hand had transformed the shop, the street, and all its landmarks without you having noticed, Rahhal. You opened your computer and wasted hours in its blue depths. From Facebook to Hot Maroc. From Hot Maroc to Facebook. And when you lifted your head up to take a look at the world around you this morning, you found that the shop was no longer the same shop, the street no longer the same street, and the city no longer the same city. As if you were one of the Seven Sleepers of the Cave, Rahhal. How long have you been in this virtual cave? Come out of your burrow, Squirrel, and take a look at the world around you.

But walking out the door isn't as easy as it once was. Do you remember the wide street that used to be here? Where is that street, Rahhal? It's as if someone folded it up, tucked it in his pocket, and left. Who took out the street and planted this market here? It's like Djemaa Lfnaa Square. Pandemonium dominates the area. Vendors shouting. Children yelling. Car horns honking. A group-hug party that's impossible to avoid. Waves intertwined. In front of the Atlas Cubs Cybercafe, pedestrians elbow their way through a narrow passageway because the large part of the sidewalk has been occupied by street vendors offering everything from used coats, V-neck T-shirts, jeans, sneakers, and socks, to different types of perfume, and even women's underwear. Behind the vendors, fruit sellers are lined up in spots meant for parking cars. Figs, oranges, peaches, grapes, watermelon, apples, or pomegranates, depending on the season. Then come the women selling bread, *beghrir*, and *msemmen*. Even though the street has more than one modern bakery, apparently the bread on the side of the road is tastier. There are also juice stalls, sausage sandwich carts, piles of boiled corn on the cob, and snails in herbed broth. Pedestrians get their shopping done in the midst of the congestion in spite of the suffocating street, while they drink juices and eat sandwiches seasoned with car exhaust. And because the car owners cannot waive their right to the spaces, they park their cars directly behind the stalls, right on the side of the street. Sometimes the front bumper of a car will make contact with the backside of a woman who is bargaining over a kilo of grapes or pomegranates and an argument will break out into which the vendor will usually insert himself to calm things down, asking the angry customer and the harassing car to curse Satan and pray to the Prophet. "Time passes, but everyone will get what they need. Just a bit of patience, that's all." And because layers upon layers of itinerant salesmen have driven their tent pegs into the street and even occupied the bus stops where buses used to let their customers off and allow others to get on, the drivers of the number twelve bus that goes up and down Dakhla Avenue have surrendered to God's judgment. It has gotten to the point where they suggested to those wanting to get off to do so at the top of the street. Then they started to drive at breakneck speeds down the jam-packed street so they wouldn't get trapped before their buses moved beyond Dakhla Avenue. But the passengers got wise to their ruse, and started to collectively block the way—like trained militias—to force them to stop. Then all traffic would stop, sometimes for ten minutes, while everyone waited for the passengers to get on.

Oh, Rahhal, this isn't the Dakhla Avenue you knew. Even Hassan II Avenue, which Dakhla Avenue branches off from, the street that you and Hassaniya used to drive daily in the Mouassine days, first on the moped then in Hassaniya's car, is no longer the same. When the French first broke ground on it in 1940, they named it Haouz Street. The street starts at Doukkala Gate, one of the largest gates of the Old City, where the bus station was established in the plaza next to the ancient gate. It intersects with Mohammed V Boulevard in front of the post office in Gueliz, and passes in front of the Haouz Office for Agricultural Development. It runs between the train station and the Royal Theater, cutting through Mohammed

VI Boulevard (formerly Boulevard de France). It continues its crawl toward Douar Laâskar, the old industrial quarter, then on to Massira and Douar Iziki.

In the 1940s, the French planted dozens of green trees along both sides of the street. Two rows of Ficus trees on each sidewalk. The trees were thick with leaves and intertwining branches. The city government took care of pruning them until they formed a long shady passageway, thick and luxuriant, that extended for miles. The idea was to provide a shady path for the hordes of workers from the Old City who would leave from Doukkala Gate and walk together to the olive and apricot processing plants in Douar Laâskar. The thick shade of the Ficus trees would protect them from the heat of the Marrakech sun as they walked to and from work. But the geniuses who took control of the city in recent years decided to get rid of the sidewalks and the trees that shaded them. They attacked the Ficus trees on Essaouira Avenue, the jacaranda trees on Casablanca Boulevard, and the oasis of palm trees that encircled the city. Even though the French colonial government had issued a law protecting the palm trees of Marrakech, making it illegal to uproot a palm tree without special permission, and that required the replanting of the uprooted palm tree in another location, the real estate mafia had a different style. They set about burning hundreds of thriving palm trees one night by pouring gasoline on their roots and lighting them on fire. It was attributed to anonymous perpetrators. After a few months, shabby buildings were planted in the oasis in place of the palm trees. "O Marrakech. A rose among palm trees," as the song goes. May God have mercy on your soul, Ismail Ahmed. Do you remember that song, Rahhal? It was one of the morning songs that used to fill you with pride when you heard it while making your way to Antaki Elementary when you were young. A song about Marrakech. About the city that hadn't yet become your city because, at that time, you still lived in Ain Itti, outside the city walls, before you moved to live with your uncle Ayad in Moukef. But today the city is lost to you and everyone else. Can a city be a city without trees?! Marrakech is implicated in the tree assassination.

The massacre continues and nobody protests. Bulldozers occupied Hassan II Boulevard and began to haphazardly uproot the massive Ficus trees. The idea was to widen the streets and open them up for the columns of cars, for the fresh breaths of the trees to clear the way for the smell of rubber. Hello, Marrakech. A city stripped of its sidewalks, trees, and shaded walkways to widen the road for more cars. For more horns. Honk, honk.

Even the cybercafe has changed, Rahhal. Ever since that morning when Hiyam came in, Emad behind her holding hands with someone you didn't know, you understood that something big was going to happen. Your knees started to tremble uncontrollably. You froze in your chair. Luckily for you, Hiyam, who is usually the one who worries about the details of protocol, didn't even look in your direction. As if you weren't there. Or as if you were a part of the shop's furnishings. But you braced for the worst. Were they going to kick you out of here? Had they brought someone in to replace you? Luckily, Yazid wasn't there. What if she had caught him haughtily picking fights with the customers, that dwarf, wearing his Marrakechi *deraiya*, smoking his cigarette, proud as a peacock, with his cup of coffee in front of him? He probably would have driven her nuts, turning the visit into a battle where you'd be the first victim, Squirrel. But God showed His mercy. Even the Africanos weren't there crowding three to a computer. Just Qamar Eddine, Salim, the Marrakech Star duo, and a group of students from Massira High School who were occupying the rest of the computers, with their classmates waiting their turn. The cybercafe was simmering, but the situation was under control. Emad turned toward Rahhal, quickly shook his hand, then turned back to his companion, who was busy with Hiyam measuring the place. That night, he told Hassaniya that they intended on expanding the Atlas Cubs Cybercafe.

"Expanding the cybercafe? But how? Will they also take over a part of the public road when they add to the shop?"

"I don't know. I heard Hiyam say that they were going to expand the shop, but I didn't ask for details."

The next day, the stranger came back with three workers. They asked Rahhal to stop work in the cybercafe starting that weekend for a period of ten days, and that he stay on-site with them. But after just six days they had finished building a wooden mezzanine that could fit an additional six computers. To ensure privacy, the workers made an effort to separate each station from the one next to it with a piece of nicely crafted wood. The upper floor was open to the ground floor, accessible by an internal wooden staircase. The cybercafe's space was transformed. It had become less spacious, more crowded. Yazid found the occasion just right for making fun of Rahhal:

"My friend, they need to double your pay now that you're running two shops instead of one."

Qamar Eddine likened the cybercafe in its new form to the double-decker tourist buses that drove through the streets of Marrakech, similar to the buses of London:

"I'm with you, Yazid. They need to double Rahhal's pay because now he's driving a double-decker bus. Like the English buses. And they need to pay him in pounds sterling!"

As for Fadoua and Samira, nothing was heard from them. They just winked at one another and went calmly up the stairs.

58

YAZID COULDN'T BELIEVE HIS EYES when he read the news. None other than Hot Maroc was humbling itself to write about Dakhla Avenue. He began to shout:

"Go! Go to Hot Maroc, you little shits. The Society section. They're writing about our street. Look at the title: 'Street Hawkers Occupy Dakhla Avenue and Close It to Cybertraffic'" (he means just traffic, of course).

Yazid's shouting disturbed Son of the People, who was occupied with commenting on a column by Naim Marzouk. But Qamar Eddine got involved, adding:

"These guys messed up the name of their website, mixing French and English. They need to make it Hot Morocco because *hot* is an English word, as in 'Hotmail.' In English, they want to say 'Hot Morocco,' not 'Hot Maroc!'"

"What's got you so hot under the collar that you want to teach us now? You're giving us lessons? Go fuck yourself and your broken English. These guys publish actual news, unlike those other disastrous sites. Those ones just scribble some nonsense then add the word *Press* to it: Dung Press. Fart Press. Shit Press. Hot Maroc has some real news. And not just news. Even their comments will satisfy your thirst. They have one son of a bitch named Son of the People. Awesome! That guy's dangerous. I always read him. An expert, my friends. An artist. He's got some incredible moves. He shoots just before the whistle blows, and goooooooooal!!! He nails it every time."

Yazid himself, Rahhal? Yazid? Is he, himself, admitting that he is among your readers, that he's fond of you? Would you have believed it had you not heard it yourself? But who said he was fond of you? He's fond of Son of the People. Of Son of the People's comments. Son of the People, the skillful commenter who stirs the murky waters of Hot Maroc. Not you, you dull squirrel.

The cybercafe's customers proudly read the Hot Maroc article about Dakhla Avenue. Finally, the venerable site had turned toward them, albeit with some unexpected reportage. Even though it was about the chaos that had come over the street, about the street hawkers, those itinerant street vendors who had stopped roaming about after having seized the sidewalks for themselves, every one of them having their own spot known to all with their wares all spread out; about the ruralization that Marrakech and its new neighborhoods were experiencing. But the mere mention of Dakhla Avenue on Hot Maroc was enough of a reason to be proud. Qamar Eddine suggested that the customers all comment on the reportage, and Yazid agreed:

"Yes, everyone should write, including this rat," he said pointing his finger at Rahhal while Qamar Eddine and the girls laughed. "If the comments continue to flow, it will make our neighborhood and Dakhla Avenue more well-known on the national level. And who knows? If the comments keep coming it could get Son of the People's attention and get him interested, maybe even surprising us with an epic comment about Dakhla Avenue."

The Squirrel ignored the customers' laughter. He buried his eyes in the computer screen and quickly came up with a silly, three-line comment that he signed "Rahhal of the Cybercafe." But, he secretly swore, deep down, not to make Yazid's wish to read a comment by Son of the People about Dakhla Avenue come true. Idiot. If he were more polite, he would have honored him with a comment he'd never forget.

The customers seemed to be engaged in composing comments that would appear one after the other on the screen, and they enthusiastically welcomed their postings. Everyone was plunged headlong into the game, intoxicated by it, except for Nesrine. As if it didn't concern her. In fact, it really didn't concern her. Because Nesrine didn't care about Dakhla Avenue or the Atlas Cubs or Son of the People. She was just passing through. She would show up like the full moon for two nights, then disappear for a month or more. She had a Yahoo account and a Facebook page, both of which she always made sure to glance at as soon as she entered the cyber-cafe before she started surfing science websites, most likely medical sites. Rahhal watched her closely enough to conclude that she was in medical school, and he guessed that she was an Amazighi from Agadir. Most likely she has relatives in Massira whom she visits from time to time. And during these visits, she would come in to the Atlas Cubs Cybercafe an average of two times a day.

All the young men in the cybercafe would yearn for Nesrine's visits. A short girl, but she walks tall and proud. She dresses a la mode, with a refined, youthful look. Her small body is beauti-ful. Elegant and well-proportioned. A bright, bronze-colored face. Shiny black hair that she always ties up high so that it looks like a bun, like a black crown that makes her look even more magnificent. Solid perky breasts like two pomegranates. Without a bra, her low-cut dress shows off their roundness. A thin waist, wide hips, and creamy tender thighs that Nesrine's short dresses allowed to spill out for all the predatory gazes. They drool over her, but she isn't even there. She's short like you, Rahhal, and like Yazid. But sensi-tivity to smallness doesn't eat away at her the way it does you. She doesn't try to make people forget her size by standing up straight so comically like your friend. She's an Amazighi from Agadir. At peace with herself, with her small body, and she doesn't want any-thing from the world. She smiles kindly at Rahhal when she walks in. And she politely says goodbye when she leaves. Aside from the pleasantries of coming and going, she rides her electronic waves and surfs far from the people of the cybercafe, and from Hot Maroc. All of Yazid's efforts to get her attention come to nothing. Even the exuberant way he dealt with the reportage in Hot Maroc about Dakhla Avenue was on account of her being there. He struggled in vain to get her attention. He did everything short of standing on his head and shaking his ass in the air like a clown. But Nesrine wasn't there. She didn't mean to ignore you all. Never. But she's uninterested in you and your noise that never seems to annoy her. She's completely disengaged. Her spirit floats around in the virtual realm. All that's with you is her enticing body, so take a bite with your starved eyes, you miserable pack of wolves.

But it seems that Yazid had other ideas. He walked out of the cybercafe and began to smoke in an agitated manner. He was rambling furiously, talking gibberish. And when Nesrine left the shop he took advantage of the throng and rubbed up against her. She didn't turn toward him. She thought the contact was unintentional, so she didn't turn. She was waiting for a chance to break through the crowd when he came at her again, violently, this time. She turned toward him in disbelief. She seemed shocked by his behavior. But Yazid hadn't had enough yet. In fact, he reached his hand out toward her bum and grabbed it. He lifted her skirt then hit her on her ass, yelling:

"Listen, missy. Pull your shit together, you slut!"

"What?" she asked in disbelief. "How dare you, you dog!"

"Your father's the dog. I told you, cover up your ass, your legs, and your tits."

"What did you say to me, you lunatic?"

"I'm saying that we don't want nasty-ass sluts like you in this neighborhood. No one here accepts your little whorish acts."

"But what are you talking about, you jerk? How dare you talk to me like that! And who gave you the right to touch me? How dare you lay a hand on me! Would you let someone lay a hand on your sister, you lowlife?"

"Lucky for me, I don't have a sister," chuckled Yazid nervously as his eyes darted around the crowd gathered in front of the cybercafe's door following the scene. He was satisfied that everyone was looking on complicitly. Their looks were empty, cowardly; they were curious and held a sense of expectation. But without condemnation.

"You don't have a sister? What a douchebag! What about your daughter? Your aunt? Your mother? Would you let a stranger squeeze your mother's ass out in the street?"

"What, you bitch? How dare you talk about my mother like that! This is about me and you. What does my mother have to do with it?"

It was difficult for him to imagine someone toying with Mrs. Lalla Betoul's ass in the street.

"Enough with my mother, you whore. Enough with my mother!"

He screamed hysterically before raising his hand up high and giving the girl a resounding slap. Nesrine couldn't absorb just how this happened. Her terrified eyes scanned the crowd that was following the scene with bated breath. She didn't hear a single word of condemnation. Not so much as a mumble. There was no one who said, "May God damn Satan." Her eyes remained wide open and the tears flowed from them, hot and silent. She remained stunned like that for a few seconds. Like a sleepwalker. Vainly, she tried to understand. To respond. But her strength had completely given out. She was unable to. Completely unable. They're all assholes: the one who slapped her, and those who stood silently by. Silently encouraging him. "You're all assholes!" She was shouting on the inside, without her voice coming to her aid. Then, she rushed off crying. And after that day, she never came back. Rahhal continued to expect a police raid on the shop, or a collective attack from her family in Massira, or a visit from one of her family members, even after some time had passed. But it seemed that the girl didn't complain to anyone. Neither to the police nor to anyone else. She bore down on her wounds and disappeared. As for Yazid, this move gained him more notoriety in the cybercafe, in Café Milano, and all up and down Dakhla Avenue. Even Mahjoub Didi, who avoided interacting with the customers of the cybercafe, got up from in front of his computer to warmly embrace him. He acknowledged his manliness and congratulated him for taking the initiative to change what was abominable with his own hand, and for his lack of fear of reproach from the reproacher for proclaiming what is right.

59

IT'S AS IF you don't know her anymore, Squirrel. It seems that Hiyam has started to gradually detach herself from you, just as she detached herself from Asmae. She has severed all ties between her and you, and everyone else. Today, Hiyam has no relationship to the waitress at Café Milano, nor to that young student she was that first day. Hiyam has become a star, Squirrel. And your fate is to tend to her stardom, whether you like it or not. It's enough that she has reached her Facebook limit of five thousand friends, not to mention the hundreds of people who interact with her page. And because more requests were flocking to Hiyam, you had to set aside a few hours each month to prune and clean her Facebook gardens and water basins. The most important of your tasks is to watch out for unimportant hangers-on, who silently lurk there without participating with likes or comments, and culling them one after the other to replace them with new profiles that you carefully pick from the waiting list, because Hiyam can't stand uninteresting snoopers. And there are dozens of requests waiting at the door. Whoever isn't interacting is thrown out of her happy Facebook kingdom without regrets.

Hiyam has started to disassociate herself from you, Squirrel. As much as you tend toward isolation and avoiding the spotlight, the girl seems intent on never wanting to be *out* of the spotlight. Her infatuation with likes is almost pathological. She counts them when she logs in and again when she logs out. In fact, she is prepared to bring whatever it takes to accumulate as many likes as possible, and then double them. She wasted a good part of Rahhal's precious time searching for pithy maxims, deep philosophical scraps, and beautiful poems. And from time to time she'd put intense conversation topics out there for her Facebook fans that contained strange views in order to provoke, to stoke the flames of discussion on her wall, and double the number of comments. Hiyam's people were chosen with care. They included writers, poets, artists, journalists, and well-known personalities in the political and economic realms. Even people like Emad Qatifa are categorized as commoners according to Hiyam's electronic standards within a defined quota system that she makes every effort to maintain in order to ensure diversity and democratic activity inside her happy kingdom.

In a moment of boredom, Hiyam thought about leaving Facebook. No, not really. But the desire to announce that she was leaving did occur to her. She was struggling with boredom. She was trying to escape this depression that had recently wrapped itself around her. So, quite suddenly, she posted a farewell note: "How happy your companionship had made me, my dears, in this electronic blue oasis of ours. I have shared many of my thoughts and musings with you, and you have overwhelmed me with your love and overflowing emotions. However, today I feel that the time has come to calmly leave. I have very private things that I prefer to keep to myself. But I didn't want to betray you by leaving without letting you know beforehand, and embracing each and every one of you. So please allow me to go, my loving friends, and I hope you live a happy virtual life, even if it is without your friend, Hiyam."

Rahhal wasn't imagining that his false announcement of Hiyam's departure would cause such a storm. Hiyam's people wailed on Facebook. They truly wailed. "No . . . Hiyam . . . No!" as if she were their mother and they would be orphans after she left. If there were a special place for demonstrations on Facebook, there would have been enormous demonstrations. They all commented. Even the lurkers. Even some of the corpses for whom Rahhal had been awaiting the right opportunity to throw them into the virtual dirt, without funeral prayers or burial rites; life pulsed through their veins once again and they posted, demanding that Hiyam reverse her decision. As if she were Gamal Abdel Nasser, the Egyptian leader who suffered such a painful defeat and wanted to step down, but was prevented from doing so by the people who filled the streets the following morning refusing to accept it, staging huge "spontaneous" demonstrations, sobbing in the streets and demanding that he stay. No, Hiyam. Your people need you. You are indispensable. They don't know how they'll swallow the bitter pill of defeat in your absence. No, Hiyam. No!

Hiyam had no other choice but to give in to what the people wanted and respond to their mass pleading: "When I decided to leave, I was in a state of depression and despair, and I was harboring feelings of uselessness. Truly. As I'm sure you noticed, I was gone for three consecutive days without opening Facebook. While it is true that my mental state has stabilized, and for that I thank God, the decision to leave remained a valid one to me. So, when I came back today to take a final look at the wall before putting my decision into effect and close it down, I was particularly surprised by your comments and messages. More than three thousand comments begging me to stay. Unbelievable. I didn't know you were concealing all of this love for me. So, let me say to you: Never, my dears. After today, I cannot leave you. You are my family, my people, my dear loved ones. Hiyam will always remain with you and could not bear being apart at all. So, thank you, thank you, thank you, you amazing people."

And because the surges of joy and glee celebrating Hiyam's decision not to leave continued for more than a week on his wall, Rahhal, busy at the time with Hot Maroc, couldn't find the time or the energy to keep up with this flood of emotions that Hiyam's people surprised him with. Nor could he find a way to respond to all these overflowing emotions and stirring comments. But, what about the pictures, Squirrel? Has your memory betrayed you? How could you forget about that? When Asmae came to the cybercafe for the first time, she had more than ten pictures with her. She sent five to the Italian email, and those were the same pictures you used to open this page with. But what about the other pictures?

Rahhal went back to the archive. Yes, yes. You have seven unposted pictures in your pouch, Squirrel. Asmae came with exactly twelve pictures that day. You posted the salon pictures, the most alluring and sexy ones. But there were other really beautiful pictures taken by the photographer in the hotel garden as well. Two of them show another face of Hiyam, more innocent and sincere. Her sexy body was relaxed so the photographer let it be and focused on the face, on its features and lines. Bewilderment, surprise, fear of the adventure, the vague fear inspired by Talios, and the shame of posing this way in front of a strange photographer had all gathered in her eyes, giving her a special, magical look. These pictures in particular will present another face of Hiyam and will light the fires in the ranks of her Facebook people. Perhaps she hadn't chosen the garden pictures then because they weren't alluring enough. But they're really beautiful, Rahhal, and they will be just right to serve as a surprise gift from Hiyam to her fans as they celebrate her decision not to leave. So Rahhal posted the garden pictures one after the other, and the wall lit up once again.

60

DON QUIXOTE? Did you say Don Quixote?

Don Quixote is tall, Qamar Eddine. True, he was thin, but he was slim and tall. Yazid is short and pudgy. How could he remind you of him? But Qamar Eddine wasn't thinking about height or girth. Rather, what he was thinking about was Sancho. Ever since a follower of Yazid's started to stick to him like a shadow, this nickname had stuck and he began to promote it in the cybercafe, when Yazid wasn't there, of course (even though Rabih, who was of medium build, didn't look like Sancho at all). He could be sure no one in the cybercafe had read Cervantes. But Fadoua, Samira, and Salim had watched the dubbed cartoon series *Don Quixote de la Mancha* and they knew what Qamar Eddine was talking about.

But where did the Don Quixote of Dakhla Avenue find this obedient follower who didn't mind waiting hours for Yazid outside the cybercafe door? A wait that wasn't without its uses. Because after less than a month, Yazid arranged a small job for him next door as a cigarette vendor and bicycle guardian. There, between a small line of randomly planted orange trees to the right of Café Milano, Yazid improvised a parking area for bicycles and mopeds. Rabih didn't work himself to death morning and evening. Rather, only when there was a soccer match. And because the soccer schedules had started to become more noticeably frequent, he had come to work guarding the bicycles more and more. Basically, whenever soccer fans filled the cafés. Especially lovers of the Spanish league. Everyone followed La Liga in the cafés of Dakhla Avenue. All the cafés started to show the matches live, and also made a rebroadcast available the morning after. Years ago, each café on Dakhla Avenue had customers of specific sorts. The Hanafi Café, for example, was for building contractors and their customers. The Taysir Café was specifically for used-car salesmen. Morning and evening, vehicles of different models were lined up out front. Some vendors practically entered the café by car so that dealers and potential customers could inspect them without leaving their chairs. The Hope Café was the official haunt for youth associations; young writers and playwrights who saw themselves as the neighborhood's vanguard. And since there was no youth club in Massira, their scholarly group met every day at the Hope Café. When they established their Masar theater troupe and a choir dedicated to politically engaged songs, the café became the de facto headquarters for these two new associations. It was natural, then, that this café in particular would face periodic police raids, resulting in its customers—who were steadfast artists—being taken down to the Massira police station on drug charges. The Farid Atrache Café, which is only three doors down from the Hope Café, was considered the permanent headquarters of the most famous drug dealer in the neighborhood, Omar Bouri. That's why this café received regular visits from police officers and detectives. Not to make raids and arrests, but rather, to get whatever the mood required from Omar Bouri, all at good prices. After midnight, some of the neighborhood boys would sneak to the upper level of the café, where they would always show porn flicks to a rapt audience. Café Milano was the favored space for teachers from Massira High School, as well as an elite group of employees who could be described as "honorable," but in recent years, when Talios made it his headquarters as his star was rising, so-called business and people wanting to emigrate in intricate ways crawled to him and transformed Café Milano into a nest of scum, as Asmae described it. But now, all the cafés of Dakhla Avenue had come to resemble one another after having been transformed into bleacher seats for soccer games. A huge stadium that extended the length of the street. The owner of Café Milano is a Real Madrid fan, so he forces the waiter who helps Asmae in the evenings to wear the Real jersey while he's working. Despite that, the majority of Café Milano's customers are Barcelona fans. There is a minimal level of democracy at Café Milano, and there's generally space for the two audiences to interact. The situation is more extreme in the Farid Atrache Café. Omar Bouri, who visited Barcelona in the mid-1980s and who claims that the love of his life was from Barcelona, absolutely forbids Real fans to enter the café. Omar Bouri is the café's mayor, the one who gets the final word there. Therefore, even the owner of the Farid Atrache Café has to embrace the Catalan creed, whether he likes it or not.

With odd regularity, Rabih would stand in front of Café Milano, ready to offer the right type of cigarette to whoever asked for it, then he'd go back to his post, fulfilling both of his tasks. One eye on the bicycles and the other on the café's clientele. Clouds of smoke float above the heads of those watching as they shout and yell insults. The customers smoke, provide commentary, and bad-mouth the players. They're all soccer experts. High-level specialists. They explained the strategies while smoking, coughing, and spitting. They all knew more than the coaches, they adjudicated the game better than the referees, and they criticized the players and told them—albeit too late—the shortest route to the goal and the best ways to exploit missed opportunities.

True, most of them don't play sports at all, neither soccer nor basketball, nor do they even walk much. But their sporting instincts are extremely well-honed. Some of them can give you a perfect report of the Spanish championships from the last five years that includes all the details on how the best and worst teams did. They compete with one another in memorizing the millions of euros that contracts are worth and that result in players moving around the league, all while they rifle through their empty pockets searching for enough change for a measly cup of coffee. Virtual athletes, following only on-screen and as spectators. But frankly, not to unfairly disparage the soccer fans, *all* Moroccans live their lives on-screen. The television screen or the computer screen. They know all countries through tourism and travel shows. All nationalities by way of Facebook. They're addicted to political television shows and they accept heated political debate on Facebook, yet they are withdrawn from the political party life of their country. The majority of them are covetous of their political purity, like wholesome, untouched virgins. Therefore, it's rare for them to cast their votes in elections.

Life is elsewhere. It's there. On-screen. Gooooooal! The match is intense and, as usual, the commentator makes you see what isn't there, deftly rhyming: "Fire, fire, fire, it's down to the wire . . . Messi is a sly one. The damage is done . . . Here's Messi, folks . . . the one with the diamond foot . . . with the header in goal . . . Finally, Messi makes joy erupt . . . and wins the cup!"

But Rabih wasn't interested in the cup or the championship. He's here to work. He left his Berber village of Tadarte, which sits on top of Mount Tichka, in search of work in Marrakech. He stayed with his relative, a doorman in the building where Moulay Ahmed Malkha lived, and that's where he met his son, Yazid, and began to work for him. He's happy with his new situation, and it doesn't bother him at all to play the role of Sancho.

61

IBRAHIM TANOUFI? No way. Something's not right here.

Rahhal went back over the title to make sure. The name Tanoufi was front and center, listing Tanoufi as the publication director of the *Future*. But this was inconceivable. How could the man be the object of all this abuse on the front page of his own newspaper? Rahhal didn't understand a thing. This column had been published in the *Future* first, before being posted on Hot Maroc the day after. And Hidhami hadn't alluded to it at all. That's why neither Son of the People nor Abu Qatada got involved. Same with Abu Sharr and those who stood with him. None of them commented. So, the field remained wide open for the epic avengers of riffraff, always ready to pick at the flesh of the first victim to fall in front of them. "When the cow falls, the pickers come in droves." Hot Maroc provides the army of butchers with knives. Although these knives cannot be compared to those high-quality Genovese knives, they are electronic knives that are always at the ready.

But Naim Marzouk's blows were those of a professional boxer. He strikes hard, but without drawing blood. He punished his boss without providing even the smallest bit of information on the subject, without revealing the secret. Hints, winks, doublespeak, and innuendos. The ambiguity of modern poetry seeped into Naim's article this morning. Only the rebuke was pure and injurious. What secret offense had Ibrahim Tanoufi committed to deserve such harsh treatment? And how would he react? No doubt he was immersed in his various projects and didn't look at the issue until after it was published. He certainly wouldn't remain silent.

Rahhal continued to wait for the response—the publication of the newspaper's next issue without his famous column; the publication of a release announcing the firing of Naim Marzouk from the *Future*.

Or at least a clarification from Tanoufi; or an apology from Naim Marzouk for his inappropriate column, so damaging to his boss.

None of that happened. For four long days, as Rahhal bought his copy of the *Future* in the early morning before the shop opened, there was no news or comment. As if it had never happened. And on the fifth day, Rahhal was surprised by a statement on the bottom left-hand corner of the page. A press release signed by Ibrahim Tanoufi. It was brief. It didn't explain or illuminate anything. It just offered a vague, incomprehensible apology. Ibrahim Tanoufi was apologizing to the state, the government, society, and faithful readers for an unknown, secret offense. And at the top of the page, Naim Marzouk was crouching on the paper's throne as usual. Naim opened his column with a discussion about how differences of opinion don't upset good relations, and he explained how apologizing for a wrongdoing is a virtue, meaning Tanoufi's published apology, of course. Naim didn't neglect to describe his boss as a decent person and that the democratic boss should be recognized for his open-mindedness. Then he praised the *Future*, its owners, and its editors, emphasizing that it was among the very few papers—not just in Morocco, but in the entire world—that allowed unfettered diversity of expression on its pages, even among members of the newspaper's family, in a fully responsible and democratic way. The end.

Do you understand, Rahhal? Do you understand anything at all?

Rahhal went back to Hot Maroc to go over Naim Marzouk's article in which he had crucified his boss. Perhaps, in the comments, he might find a reckless leak or a dim candle that could shed some light on the reasons that seemed completely opaque to him. But he was surprised to find that a secret hand had removed it entirely from Hot Maroc, along with its comments. As if it had never been published. As if it hadn't been written at all.

Do you understand?

When you don't understand something, Rahhal, you get hit with a wicked headache. As if a vulture is eating out of your head. It gnaws at it from the inside. Curiosity will kill you, Squirrel!

Rahhal closed Hot Maroc and limped over to Facebook. He was in a bad mood. That's why he decided to spoil the mood of the blue kingdom's people. No, Rahhal. Leave Hiyam and everything that has to do with her. Say goodbye to 24/7 Samir, because you have other things to take care of. Fortunately, Rahhal had another backup profile: Mounir Raji (twenty-five years old, a poet, a professor of history and geography). A reclusive young man whose Facebook activity was limited. Despite that, he managed to become friends with all sorts of people. But today, Mounir, you need to turn on them. No, not a war. Just some light incursions to ruin these creatures' moods, just as Tanoufi's cryptic apology had ruined Rahhal's mood this morning.

Gaza was being blockaded these days by the Israeli army. The number of martyrs doubled with each passing day. Most of the victims were civilians and children. Another reason for you to set *your* blockade, Squirrel. As Mahmoud Darwish said, "Besiege your besieger, it must be done. Strike your enemy, it must be done." Mounir opened up the welcome page. The beautiful actress Bahija Sourour had changed her profile picture. Bahija was strutting around in a short, extremely chic evening dress. The picture was beautiful, signed by a French photographer. Bahija's friends and fans flattered her with likes and comments celebrating her talents, her splendor, and how beautiful the picture was. Mounir slipped in among them and fired his poison arrow: "An innocent question, friends. All of you are members of a pure, conservative, Moroccan society, and thank God for that. So, would you allow your sisters to go out in the street dressed so shamelessly? Isn't the woman's body, which the Creator so generously bestowed, something that is sanctified, cheapened by clothes like these? I want a straight answer, not empty flattery and hypocrisy."

The well-known Moroccan intellectual Essam Louzi was participating in a major symposium hatched up in Beirut, and he had taken some pictures of himself with some Arab intellectuals on the sidelines. This is easy prey, Mounir. Don't let it get away from you. "Children are dying in Gaza while end-of-times intellectuals snap photos of themselves in five-star hotels, replaying their scratchy records in air-conditioned rooms in front of empty chairs before receiving their honorariums for their 'valuable' participation (in dollars, please). Shame on you, sir. If you were struck dumb, it would be better for you than irritating us with these symposiums that are of no use, and these photos that provide incontrovertible proof that you have painfully betrayed the community in this tense moment of our history. 'God is sufficient for us; an excellent Guardian is He.'"

But where is the love of your life, Rahhal? Where is your bosom buddy, your closest friend, Wafiq Daraai? It's as if he's disappeared these days. No, no, there he is. It's just that he's changed his profile picture. In the new picture, the poet appears wrapped in a Palestinian kaffiyeh as he raises the victory sign, with Palestinian flags fluttering behind him. The pictures were selected from a new album posted just two days ago on Wafiq's wall: Pictures from the Marrakech Demonstration in Solidarity with Gaza and Gaza's Children. Mounir wanted to leave Wafiq's electronic neighborhood to search for more fragile victims, but Rahhal made him linger for a bit.

Mounir, you can't pass by Wafiq Daraai's wall without shitting on it, or at least taking a piss.

But the man stands in solidarity with Gaza and the children of Gaza, so it will be hard to . . .

Solidarity? What solidarity are you talking about? Clear the way, you imbecile, and let me work:

"Houses are collapsing on the heads of those who live there in Gaza and you're organizing your show tours in the city's streets on Sunday mornings in the name of solidarity with its innocent victims? What hypocritical solidarity are you talking about? Haven't you had enough of your repeated slogans? Aren't you tired of participating in fake demonstrations that have no effect and resonate with no one? You're dying in a simple pleasant struggle. A struggle made up of slogans and victory signs in front of cameras. A struggle made up of photos. Look back through your album, poet, and you'll see how stupid you look as you peer so odiously into the camera! You smile hypocritically as you raise your fingers in a fake victory sign during these calamitous times. Children are dying in Gaza and you're taking stupid pictures and exchanging likes and flattering comments with one another. Aren't you ashamed of yourselves? As for me, my friend, I'm ashamed of your pictures and your hypocritical comments, which make me believe even less in this country's poets and militants."

Has your headache gone away, Rahhal? Have you forgotten all about Tanoufi and Naim Marzouk and their secrets? You seem to have had enough fun. But don't let Mounir leave before he has a chance to limp over to Hiyam's page, not to leave a comment on her latest post, nor to tell her how beautiful she is, but rather, to stir things up for her a bit. A sharp comment—couched in succinct, respectful language, not too abusive—that might make the Lioness' Facebook page more active and energetic. Hiyam will rise above responding, as usual, but her adoring fans and followers will jump all over you. But at least with Hiyam, Mounir, I guarantee you that she won't remove or block you from her list of friends like that bitch Bahija Sourour was so hasty to do.

62

YAZID DIDN'T IMAGINE his budding "enterprise" would face such a trial on the blessed Eid al-Adha holiday, but unfortunately, that's what happened. The idea came to him after a casual discussion with Rabih, from which Yazid understood that his follower was familiar with slaughtering sheep.

"Slaughtering?"

"Slaughtering, skinning, and butchering."

"And butchering, too?" Yazid thought out loud, astonished.

"Of course. You have to butcher it."

"Definitely, Rabih. Butchering it is the most important thing. Butchering the sheep is more important than slaughtering it. Otherwise, what's a family going to do with a dead sheep hanging in the middle of the apartment, in the house's central courtyard, or on the roof? The sheep needs to be cut up so the lady of the house can put the meat in the refrigerator."

"Yep, butchering it, too."

"Awesome, Rabih. Awesome. But how much time do you need to do the whole thing? Slaughtering the sheep, skinning it, then cutting it up?

"Slaughtering and skinning it takes less than an hour, whereas cutting it up takes some time because the sheep needs to dry first. It's best done the following day."

"Got it. How much time do you need to slaughter and skin it?"

"Less than an hour."

"So, half an hour, then?"

"No, not half an hour . . . Definitely more than that, but less than an hour."

Yazid's eyes shone. He leaned in close to Rabih and whispered in his ear:

"I don't understand, Rabih, why you'd travel home. You'll lose more than you'll gain by traveling to Tadarte. The cost of transportation, the cost of Eid al-Adha, and other unforeseen expenses. That's why I suggest you spend the holiday with us. You can stay in your relative's room in the building's basement. Send greetings and a blessed bit of money with him to your people and parents so you won't miss out on making them happy. As for your share of the sheep's meat, it's guaranteed. It's on your friend, Yazid. You'll celebrate Eid al-Adha with us, *inshallah*, God willing. Whatever we eat at home on the day of Eid al-Adha, you'll eat, too. But you need to stay here. We have a lot of work to do during the holidays."

And that was that.

Yazid posted a sign written in fancy script on the front window of the cybercafe that read:

> To the residents of Massira: Butcher with experience slaughtering, skinning, and cutting up sheep. The slaughtering will be done on the day of Eid al-Adha, according to required custom, and he will return the following day to cut it up. Make your reservations now. Note: Call the following number . . .

. . . and he wrote down his cell-phone number. He did the same thing on his Facebook wall.

The following day, Yazid's telephone didn't stop ringing. A number of residents from Massira I and II, and even III wanted to reserve right then. The calls kept coming in and the appointments piled up. Yazid gave priority to the residents of the buildings on Dakhla Avenue and around Massira High School. The closer ones first, then those further away. And in order to accommodate the largest number of requests, he decreased the slaughter time to just half an hour. That's how his calendar filled with so many appointments.

Before the Eid, Yazid bought a good amount of straw, barley, and green clover and erected a tent for Rabih in front of Massira High School. The students were on vacation now, so he could take advantage of the large open area in front of the high school without problems. That way, Yazid guaranteed that the residents of Massira had feed for the last days before the slaughter. The earnings were good, and things boded well.

But on the day of Eid al-Adha, starting with the very first slaughter appointment, Yazid realized that his day was not going to go well. First of all, they arrived a half hour late. This was on Yazid. The man wasn't used to waking up early and he wasn't in the habit of making morning appointments. But the worst part was that Rabih spent roughly an hour and a half slaughtering and skinning the first sheep. The poor guy was used to slaughtering goats in the mountains around Tadarte. Even the sheep there were lean to mid-sized; not like these gigantic sheep, which seemed more like calves than sheep. Also, Rabih had imagined that they would work together, he and Yazid, before discovering that his friend was sporting a shining white jellaba, traditional "Aladdin" trousers, and a pair of new yellow babouches. And if it weren't for the help of the people of the house, Rabih would have needed at least two hours for one sheep. Rabih was knee-deep in blood. He gasped for breath as he tried to bring the sheep to the ground. He huffed and puffed as he tried to tie the animal up to start skinning it. As for Yazid, he was like an employee working in the reception area of a large company. His phone didn't stop ringing, and he didn't stop taking calls. "Hello, yes." "Hello, *mabrouk* and congratulations to your loved ones." "Hello, we're coming, my friend. We're on our way." Nonstop calls. Jarring. Impatient. And Yazid would explain to them that he'd be there in ten minutes. He'd say to everyone: "Ten minutes." And everyone would wait. Yazid didn't know how to respond. And Rabih didn't know how he was going to finish up with his fourth sheep, what with his strength having been completely sapped. And there were other victims in their tiny apartments stuck dealing with their own sacrificial animals, with fat sheep taking up half the apartment and the damned butcher who had promised to come but didn't.

There was no solution.

And Yazid, being a dog that lacked loyalty, did not hesitate to turn off his cell before coming out sullenly after the fourth operation. Rabih dragged his feet behind him, dead tired. A stupid Don

Quixote choosing to fight sheep instead of windmills. And unlucky Sancho, following his lazy, egoistic master, who possessed no nobility or sense of cooperation.

Despite that, what Yazid made from the straw, barley, and clover, in addition to the six hundred dirhams he made from the four slaughters, prompted him to invest in another business venture, which came to him like a life preserver. This operation itself would make up for everything he had lost because of Rabih's failure to effectively deal with the sheep.

The idea was simple. There were beggars walking around the streets and alleyways of Massira claiming that they were widows and demanding their share of the Eid al-Adha sheep for their orphaned children. Yazid doesn't remember who told him once that buying the meat that piled up in the beggars' baskets and reselling it to poor bachelors and virtuous men would earn him a very pretty penny. Yazid began to follow the beggar women around and bargain with them, with Rabih in tow. He did really well buying pieces of meat that had piled up in their baskets for the lowest prices. He invested all the money he had collected in buying the meat, without considering how he was going to deal with it, and where he would store it. Not knowing what to do, he took out an old, chipped wooden table that had been left on the building's roof. He wrapped it in clean plastic and placed it directly in front of the closed cybercafe. He piled the pieces of meat haphazardly on the table and left Rabih there. He didn't forget to bring him some cold kebab in a piece of bread. Poor Rabih was planted on Dakhla Street, which was empty of pedestrians, selling meat from the sacrificial animals on Eid al-Adha. And he waited for the bachelors.

What bachelors, you idiot? What bachelors?

The ones engaging in this business are seasonal, for sure. But they're professionals. They know how to display their wares in the best possible way. They have large refrigerators good for storing meat for a few days until the bachelors come back from their distant cities and remote villages following the holiday. But what bachelor do you expect to come to you on Eid al-Adha?

In the evening, when Yazid returned home carrying bags of meat, he discovered that the house's refrigerator had no room for this much meat that, by now, had lost its color and freshness after being on display in the sun all day long. In fact, the smell of rot had started to seep into it.

Luckily, Lalla Betoul was an expert in making jerky. So, she stayed up late that night making jerky before it really started to stink. She mixed the spices in a big dish, then started to slice the meat into long strips that she'd throw into a red plastic bucket, and Yazid would help her pour salt and the spice mixture on the strips of meat. Gloomily, he helped his mother as he considered his ruined business. This time, he forgot to bring food down to Rabih. But Rabih didn't want a thing. No dinner or anything. He just wanted to sleep. He wasn't angry at Yazid. Quite the opposite, in fact. He felt as if he had let his friend down. He had let him down because he hadn't slaughtered more than four sheep of the list of twenty that Yazid, like an idiot, had overenthusiastically and overoptimistically prepared for that festive day. Who would wait for an Eid al-Adha butcher until the evening of the holiday feast? Rabih was also sad because he wasn't able to sell the meat to even a single customer. He was tired, sorry, and embarrassed. All he wanted to do was go to sleep and dream of Tadarte, of its Eid al-Adha—simple, warm, familial; there in the mountains where holidays are truly happy affairs.

63

RAHHAL'S EID AL-ADHA wasn't happy this year. As for Hassaniya,
no problems at all. The building's concierge is good at slaughtering.
He and his teenaged son take care of the slaughtering in this festive
atmosphere. The slaughtering takes place in the entranceway to the
building. Then after skinning it, the concierge's son takes the animal
up to its owner's apartment. Afterward, the concierge's wife takes
care of cutting up the animal. That's why the concierge anxiously
awaits Eid al-Adha, because of the income the occasion will gener-
ate. The building's residents considered themselves lucky because
they didn't have to run breathlessly through the alleys and streets
on Eid al-Adha like the residents of neighboring buildings looking
for an itinerant butcher. But Eid al-Adha wasn't entirely happy this
time, because of Abdeslam.

Rahhal had sent Ayad off with three thousand dirhams, the
amount he had given his family every Eid al-Adha since receiving his new secret salary. On the second day of Eid al-Adha, as he
always did, he took a sheep shoulder wrapped in white cloth and
went with Hassaniya to wish his family a happy Eid al-Adha in
Moukef. The sheep's head couscous was awaiting them there. Ever
since Oum Eid's death, Hassaniya would go with him to eat lunch
on the second day of Eid al-Adha, hosted by Halima the Pelican.
And you could be sure that the sheep's head couscous that Halima
always prepared on the second day of Eid al-Adha was second to
none.

"But where's dad, Mom?"

Halima turned her face toward the pot boiling on the flame, as
if she had just noticed the thick steam coming from the couscous-
sier on top. So Ayad stepped in to respond:

"Your dad went back to the village."

"He went home? What do you mean? For Eid al-Adha?"

"Yep, he went home," Halima repeated. "He said he missed the smell of the countryside and he left."

Rahhal didn't utter a word. But it was clear from the look of skepticism on his face that Halima's answer hadn't convinced him.

"Are we supposed to hold him here at gunpoint?" Halima continued sharply. "We're supposed to tie him up? Is he a cow we need to tie up?"

"And how long's he going to stay there?"

"He'll celebrate Eid al-Adha there, then come back. He said he was going to celebrate Eid al-Adha there, then come back," Halima answered angrily.

But Rahhal was worried about his father. Hassaniya sat motionless in the house's courtyard, watching the scene unfold with a neutral look on her face. Rahhal was standing in the doorway to the kitchen peppering the annoyed Pelican with questions. And his uncle remained just outside the kitchen like a mouse. He was smoking his nasty cigarette, the tobacco mixing its smoke with the steam from the couscous and the smell of the sheep's head.

No one said another word about it. Hassaniya, who for all of these years could never shake the feeling of being a guest in Halima's home, wanted to pass her one yearly visit without incident. And the conversation didn't go past the kitchen. Some Andalusian music was playing on the television. The couscous was delicious, as usual. Ayad's tea was sweeter than necessary. As soon as Ayad went to the mosque after the afternoon call to prayer, Hassaniya winked at her husband and he jumped to his feet.

In the car, she drove silently as she listened to the radio. Loved ones sending greetings to one another for Eid al-Adha, and a selection of songs from the East and from Morocco. As for Rahhal, his thoughts remained on Abdeslam.

"Did your uncle Ayad go back to work?"

The Hedgehog's sudden question snapped him out of his reveries.

"No, I don't think so."

"I thought he had gone back to work because the house seemed quite different to me."

"Yes, Hassaniya. It has changed a lot."

"In the last few years I've noticed the refrigerator, the tape player, the oven, and the washing machine. But this time, everything's new. The rugs are new. The furniture. The *zellij* tile on the floor is new. And the house has been repainted. I don't get it."

"Yes, for sure, Hassaniya."

"'For sure'? How can you say it so coldly? But how? From where? I told you, I don't get it."

"I think they sold some land back home in the countryside."

"'They sold some land'? You never told me about any land in the countryside."

"Because you never asked me. We never discussed it before. If you had asked me about it, I would have told you."

"Do I have to ask you for you to tell me?"

Rahhal didn't answer her. He remained silent for a few moments. He hesitated and tried to think of an answer. And when an explanation came to mind and he decided to continue the discussion, the Hedgehog cut him off angrily as soon as he began to mumble a response.

"Could you shut your mouth now? Can't you see that I'm driving?"

She turned the volume up on the radio in exasperation. The song was Andalusian. Abderrahim Souiri and Bajeddoub were singing a *muwashshah* together:

> Glad tidings for us, we have gotten what we wished for,
>> And being far from one another can't be.
> Accept joy and happiness,
>> Loved ones are together, you and me.

What's with you, Mantis? What did the Pelican do to you to make you run away from her to Abda on Eid al-Adha?

64

The email address was somewhat strange. As for the message's subject line, it came between two ellipses: . . . The Reminder . . .

And remind; the Reminder profits the believers. Just say, "Bismillah, in the name of God," and open the email, Abu Qatada.

His hand was trembling. He didn't know why or how. But it was trembling. And from the very first sentence, he understood that this was important:

"My good servant, Mahjoub Didi, son of Yamna, also known as Abu Qatada from Marrakech, may my greetings reach you and my eyes guide and protect you, and then . . .

"Don't find my message to you strange, and don't think too much about the fact that the Lord of power and might has sent this email to you and no one else. For I possess things that the other servants don't know. So seek my forgiveness and take shelter in me from Satan, the wicked one.

"My faithful servant, we have sealed messages with wise reminders that we preserved in a clear book, and with a faithful prophet, as a mercy sent out to those in the now and the hereafter. But man is the most argumentative creature. That is why I have chosen you, Mahjoub, from among a group of my good servants to raise my banner and remind them of my message, and to seek forgiveness, because I am All-forgiving."

Mahjoub's face turned pale. He started to shiver, as if suddenly stricken by fever. He was reminded of the chosen prophet, the best of mankind, and how terrified he must have been on the day he received the first revelation. But this isn't a revelation, Abu Qatada. You're not a prophet such that you'd receive a revelation. Nonetheless, your Lord has honored and chosen you from among

His creatures to receive this electronic message. But what more is there to do here? Leave this cave and go home. Pray to your Lord and ask for forgiveness, and wait for the order of the All-powerful Almighty.

Mahjoub was dazed. His mind had been snatched. His face was pale. But he held his head high as he moved slowly, like someone walking on clouds. He didn't look toward Rahhal, nor did he think about what he owed him. This was the first time Abu Qatada had left the shop without taking his card out of his pocket and meticulously going over how long he had spent in the cybercafe with Rahhal. Abu Qatada wasn't all there. He was walking with his head in the clouds.

65

RAHHAL DIDN'T BELIEVE that Yazid was so gifted in Arabic calligraphy until he saw it with his own eyes. And seeing is believing.

Yazid and Rabih came in that morning carrying a large roll of white cloth. In the morning, it's possible to go about normal life on Dakhla Avenue because the itinerant vendors and hordes of customers don't inundate the street and its sidewalks until after the evening call to prayer. But right then, the area was open enough for Yazid to easily hang up his pieces of cloth. The first piece was sixteen feet long: a respectable sign suitable for a decisive sit-in. Yazid hung the first sign up in the cybercafe's glass window and sat over it carefully and with focus as he wrote out a slogan he copied from a small piece of paper spread out in front of him. Rabih and another person with a thick moustache and stern features watched the process with interest. "The workers of the Sherouk Bakery are staging a protest against Hajj Bihi and demand their back pay and the annual vacation that is due to them."

On the second sign, also in broad, Maghrebi-style *naskh* script, Yazid wrote a generic slogan (in Moroccan *darija*) to the protesting workers of the bakery: "The workers are suffering, and the government is missing." The guy with the thick moustache seemed pleased with the second sign. Rahhal, who continued to watch what was going on from his desk with some surprise, guessed that he was one of these workers. He might even be the leader of the uprising against Hajj Bihi, the owner of the Sherouk Bakery. While the first banner clearly expressed the demands of the protesters, the second was much more powerful because it resonated further and wider, pitting the employees directly against the government. Hajj Bihi was a coward, and his blood-sugar levels would plummet as soon as the workers put up a sign against the government in front of the shop.

The guy with the thick moustache breathed a sigh of relief after Yazid told him that the second banner was a gift from him to the protesters on the condition that it be returned after the strike was done. The price was set at 150 dirhams per sign. One sign, really. But Yazid donated an additional sign to the workers of the Sherouk Bakery. And he didn't hesitate to support them in practical terms by participating in the work stoppage by taking responsibility for holding up the sign opposing the government, he and his sidekick, Rabih. Just as they would, with a militant generosity, participate in chanting slogans along with the demonstrators. The agreement with the guy with the thick moustache was to leave it to the striking workers to evaluate his participation and set the appropriate amount of remuneration for it accordingly, but not right now; that would wait until after the strike's success.

The difficult part of it for Rahhal was when Yazid stuffed the roll of cloth into the narrow opening that separated his office from the shop's glass window and put it there for safekeeping. He had found himself unwillingly transformed into a storage-locker guardian for the new secret business Yazid had established along with his partner, Rabih.

A week after the bakery worker strike, which included four days of intense negotiations with Hajj Bihi, life returned to normal, and Yazid went back to unroll his white cloth in front of the Atlas Cubs Cybercafe. This time he would make four signs. He was surrounded by the president of the neighborhood association and three of its members. As for the slogans, they were aimed against the head of the district, the city's mayor, the governor of Marrakech, and, of course, the prime minister—all of these parties held some responsibility for the degraded environmental situation in the neighborhood when the sanitation workers started to leave horribly smelling trash and garbage piling up on the sides of the streets and in the entranceways to buildings. As for the broken-down garbage bins, those had become a playground for stray dogs and cats. The French company the city had contracted with to take care of the city's garbage received its fair share of insults on Yazid's signs as well. A sign leveling an accusation of neocolonialism at this company and others like it was the most glaring example; another criticized the collusion of corrupt local officials for turning a blind eye to their financial scandals and questioning their reliability vis-á-vis their responsibilities. It wasn't enough for Yazid to write the slogans the stakeholders dictated to him; he made every effort to suggest new slogans. For example, he suggested two fiery slogans against the government, which were approved immediately by the president. The association's president was a cultured person and a philosophy teacher at Massira High School, and he knew more than anyone else about the dialectics of private and public enterprise. So, "the corruption of local officials comes from the corruption of their counterparts in the capital, and vice versa," as he explained to the illiterates who sat next to him on the committee.

The order was for five signs priced at two hundred dirhams each; this was the new pricing as suggested by Yazid. But it came with the promise of strong participation in the protest and the assurance of a good crowd of high school students, Atlas Cubs customers, and Sherouk Bakery workers, who brought lots of experience in agitating and shouting out slogans. It was this commitment in particular that made the head of the association turn a blind eye to Yazid's jacking up the price, and he gave him a four-hundred-dirham advance.

Rahhal was unable to attend the strike. But the cybercafe delegation that enthusiastically participated in it agreed that it was a success. And even though it was surrounded by police and auxiliary forces, there was no interaction between the two sides. The *Future* reporter in Marrakech covered the strike, and a part of it appeared in a video on the Daba Marrakech (Marrakech Now) website. According to everyone, Yazid made the cybercafe and its clientele look good and, truth be told, he exceeded expectations.

66

ABU QATADA was gone for three whole days. And when he came back, he didn't so much as look in Rahhal's direction or say hello to anyone. He hurried over to the first free computer he could find and anxiously opened his email. But as soon as he opened his mailbox, a look of disappointment came across his face. As if he hadn't found what he was waiting for. Rahhal watched him curiously. He didn't understand what was happening to Abu Qatada.

Mahjoub remained riveted to the screen for more than ten minutes. And he didn't try to move the mouse toward another electronic hole. He was frozen like a statue. All of a sudden, he broke into a smile, his face lit up, and he bleated, *"Allahu Akbar,* God is great!"

Amelia exchanged looks with Flora and Yacabou. Salim and his sister began to shoot suspicious glances at him, then at Rahhal, who was no less baffled than they were. As for Qamar Eddine, he was huddled behind his computer, completely absorbed in whatever he was doing. In fact, Qamar Eddine had shunned Mahjoub ever since he had denounced him to his father. He avoided him completely and didn't look in his direction, no matter how much he lauded and praised the Lord.

The message didn't come directly from the Mighty One this time. Rather, it came from an angel that didn't give its name. But according to its email, it was number 8723 in the troupe of the Merciful's angels: Angel8723@hotmail.com.

The angel's instructions were clear and precise: "You must go to the nearest carpenter, Abu Qatada. Get him to make you a wooden sword. Buy new white clothes: a jellaba, a turban, and a pair of babouches. Even the socks need to be white. Your underwear as well. Purify yourself with fasting and prayer. Begin fasting tomorrow and continue until *God might determine a matter that was done*. Pass by the cybercafe every three days to check your email. We will let you know what the next step is when the time comes. May God protect you, guide you, and show you the way. Amen."

Mahjoub kept up the fasting for more than a month. Every three days he'd visit the cybercafe, but to no avail. He no longer spent more than a few minutes there. Word spread throughout the cybercafe that the man had stopped going to work at the Regional Agency for Water and Electricity. Yazid verified that he had gone mad.

"He's completely lost it!" he cracked. "A coworker of his confirms it, swear to God."

As for Mahjoub, he cut himself off completely from this rabble. He devoted himself exclusively to fasting, praying, and reciting the Qur'an in preparation for the blessed email. And after a month, louder cries of *Allahu Akbar* were heard in the Atlas Cubs Cybercafe for a second time. Mahjoub was planted in front of the computer when the much-anticipated email came down to him. Angel #8723 finally honored him with his presence, and the instructions were much more precise this time.

"Praise be to God, none other than He will be praised even for something that is abhorrent. Go to Djemaa Lfnaa Square next Friday morning, Abu Qatada. Wear your new white clothes, have your wooden sword drawn, and carry your Qur'an underneath your arm. When you get to the middle of the square, O pure servant of God, take out your Qur'an, brandish your sword, and laud and praise the Lord's greatness. If you do this, a miracle will occur, with God's permission. Your wooden sword will be sharp enough to cut off ten heads, and the pages of your Qur'an will turn into wings of light that will carry you up and away, and by the glory of the All-hearing and All-knowing, they will soon form a winged horse from among the horses of Heaven. The blessed steed will fly you high above the square, and you'll gather up heads left and right. Your sword will only bring harm to *the unbelievers, the libertines*, the hypocrites, and the heedless. As for the righteous—praise be to those who are righteous—no harm will come to them by your hand, according to the will of the Lord of Heaven and Earth. This is your mission, O faithful servant, and your message and miracle. The time of jihad has come! Your appointed time is Friday morning."

"*Allahu Akbar*, God is great!" Mahjoub Didi yelled as he left the cybercafe. Yazid exploded into laughter, especially because he hadn't been in the cybercafe when Mahjoub had yelled this out the first time. He had only heard about it, and he was glad the scene had repeated itself in front of him today.

"By God, we have to shout out *Allahu Akbar*! This dude . . . the angels are calling out of his ass for him to come pray. Brothers, let's see what's happened to Mahjoub. He has seriously lost his mind."

67

NO ONE UNDERSTOOD how the protests descended on Massira like this. Every day there was a sit-in. The reasons were many, but the resulting protest was always the same. "Protests and sit-ins / to feed the struggle," as one of Yazid's signs read. Each protest had its own sign that laid out the protestors' demands. But there was also a wild-card sign that was fit for all types of protests. Signs against the government and its failed policies that have resulted in the country's decay. Another one against corruption and tyranny. Then there were some pictures that Yazid would add to his militant tool kit and protesting supplies: a picture of Che Guevara, another of Mehdi Ben Barka, a third of al-Aqsa Mosque in Jerusalem, and four pictures of King Mohammed VI in addition to some small Moroccan flags. The Moroccan flags and pictures of the king are very important in bread protests in particular.

The demonstrations and sit-ins came one after another in a way that surprised Yazid. The Atlas Cubs Cybercafe became a center for militant activities, where demonstrations would take off from and in front of which signs would be made. The business venture started to become unexpectedly successful. Yazid built up his kit bag with a high-quality bullhorn, and Rabih, who had a loud voice, mastered the most important slogans, which he would thunderously chant in the bullhorn wherever the demonstration or sit-in was happening. He had an Amazighi accent, no getting around it, but it didn't muddle the contents of the slogan or diminish the strength of his voice.

Massira High School parents staged a sit-in in front of the school in protest of the chronic absences of a number of teachers, and also of overcrowding, especially when some class sizes started to exceed fifty students. The teachers and administrators responded with a protest of their own inside the school against drug dealing around the high school and the students' complete lack of morals, along with the breakdown of discipline, where more than one instance of physical or verbal violence against the teachers was recorded.

Even Nour Mosque was stricken with sit-in fever, which, were it not for cooler heads, might not have ended well. It was a regular Friday sermon about spouses living well together during which the preacher, Si Belfqih, quoted verse 34 from the chapter on women: "And those you fear may be rebellious admonish; banish them to their couches, and beat them." "Trust in the Almighty God," some repeated under their breaths. But Si Belfqih, known for his sense of humor, smiled a bit, then directed his words to those praying in front of him: "What did the Lord of strength say?" Then he answered his own question as he moved two fingers on his right hand, the index and middle fingers together in a motion that evoked a stick. *"Beat them . . . beat them.* And today when some poor husbands want to exercise their legal right, feminist associations, human rights activists, or whatever, start to cry out loud. God's words are clear, my Muslim brothers: *Beat them."* A low murmur made its way around those praying when a sharp cry of protest rose up in the women's section. Si Belfqih noticed the uneasiness that had come over the mosque, so he reminded them of the noble Hadith: "Even he who tells his friend to listen while the imam is delivering the sermon on Friday speaks nonsense . . . And he who speaks nonsense, has no Friday at all." His sermon continued with no digressions this time.

It was Maria Taheri who raised her voice in the women's section. A professor of Arabic. A woman who is diligent about performing the prayers, but at the same time, a fierce militant feminist. Professor Maria convened a discussion circle in front of the mosque's door, making known her personal objection to allowing the imam's position of allowing violence against women to pass. And for those around her, she confirmed that this particular verse has been studied at length, and it was awful how the imam had abbreviated it so badly. The word used in the Qur'an, and as properly understood in Arabic, has no relationship whatsoever to its current meaning of *beating*. This particular word in the language of the ancient Arabs refers to separation, alienation, parting, and mutual disregard, not punching, slapping, hitting, or kicking. As in the Arabic dictionaries: "They beat a path through the wilderness," meaning "separating" and "alienating."

The problem was that Maria Taheri wasn't satisfied with just this linguistic clarification. Rather, she followed it up with her comrades at the local branch of the Moroccan Organization for Women's Rights. And because most of the branch's members did not pray regularly, they decided that the best time for holding a demonstration and making their voices heard would be the following Friday during the noonday prayer. Thus, Si Belfqih delivered a sermon to those gathered in prayer on the topic of "adorning oneself, beauty, and the importance of remaining mindful of how one dresses according to Islam," taking as a starting off point His exalted words: "Children of Adam! Take your adornment at every place of worship." The defenders of women's rights shouted out powerful slogans against exploiting the country's pulpits for the purpose of inciting violence against women. Yazid was responsible for making two signs for the women, charging two hundred dirhams per sign and renting them the bullhorn for the same price, but he didn't accompany them on their suicide mission. His instincts were correct, for immediately after the Imam said his second *salaam alaikum*, may peace be upon you, a rabid army of Salafi Muslims came out, praising God and yelling *Allahu Akbar*, hell-bent on teaching a lesson to "these brazen corrupt women who didn't pray and who dared to protest outside a house of God." Luckily, the police arrived before the end of the prayer and set about firmly dispersing the protesters. That's how the area was cleared just in time, and if it hadn't been, there would have been a slaughter in front of the mosque, the likes of which the neighborhood had never witnessed before.

68

YOU CAN DIVIDE the people of Massira into two types: "the neigh-borhood folks" and "the medina people." The medina people are the ones who come from the Old City, who had started to settle with their families on Massira's residential lots in the mid-1980s. These people have strong connections to their original neighborhoods in the Old City. Their families and childhood friends are still there, and it's natural that they remain in touch with them. As for the neighborhood folks, they're purely children of the neighborhood, born there in the late 1980s and 1990s, who came into the prime of their lives in this neighborhood that was known as Green Massira, a name given to it by Hassan II in 1975 in reference to the Green March to the Western Sahara. They know no other neighborhood. It's these ones in particular who might leave their neighborhood for Daoudiate, where the colleges of Cadi Ayyad University are located (as well as some of the graduate programs), or for Gueliz, where the cafés, restaurants, hotels, bars, and movie theaters are. But they always return to the warm embrace of Massira. However, their con-nection to the Old City and the Marrakech of the Almoravids, the Almohads, and the Saâdians is extremely limited. They aren't tour-ists who are crazy about going to Djemaa Lfnaa to snap pictures with the snakes and monkeys there. That's why, for example, the number of times Qamar Eddine, a son of Massira, has gone to Dje-maa Lfnaa Square could be counted on one hand.

But this time you have no choice, Qamar Eddine. You need to go. You need to be right there in order to watch the final episode of the series. You need to be there in the thick of it.

Qamar Eddine arrived before ten. He casually crosses Arset El Bilk. He looks up more than once, as if noticing for the first time how gigantic the trees there are. The horse-drawn carriages are lined up one behind the other next to the park. The horses are perfectly arranged. Standing still, barely moving. Perhaps they know that a hard day of roaming the streets of Marrakech awaits them, so they'd rather store up their energy and effort. As for the carriage owners, they are gathered in small groups around pots of tea and bowls of *bissara*, fava-bean soup with olive oil. Qamar Eddine cuts across the square, still empty of visitors and performers. He orders a glass from one of the juice carts scattered around the edges of the square. The orange juice refreshes him. He walks around a bit, then goes up to the rooftop deck of Café Argana. He orders a café au lait and sits there, watching the square from above.

White clothes aren't out of place on Fridays. That's why Qamar Eddine didn't notice Abu Qatada at first when he walked to the middle of the square. But as soon as the hysterical screams began and everyone gathered around this strange-looking character holding up a Qur'an and brandishing a wooden stick that looked like a sword as he yelled, *"Allahu Akbar,* God is great," and menacing the enemies of God and the hypocrites, Qamar Eddine jumped up as if bitten by a snake. He forgot to pay for his coffee. He ran quickly to get a close-up view of his hero. No, Qamar Eddine. This isn't the Mahjoub Didi you know. He had lost a lot of weight and his face looked drawn-out and pale, as if he hadn't slept for days. The man had truly gone crazy. He was foaming at the mouth. The front of his jellaba was wet, as if he had peed himself without realizing it. At first, he was praising God, then he started to rant and rave. All Qamar Eddine could make out were the names of the Mighty One, as well as Gabriel, Michael, and Angel #8723. He was pronouncing the angel's number in French, as if he were an electric meter. No, Qamar Eddine. The man has gone way off-script. Qamar Eddine was alarmed. He had wanted to use this plot to punish Mahjoub for ratting him out. A pull on the ear, no more, no less. But the man has gone mad, Qamar Eddine. The man has gone mad.

The police secured the area. They found it difficult to disperse the crowds. Djemaa Lfnaa's clientele love to watch spectacles, which is why they come to the square morning and night, fanning out among the different performance circles. But, this was an original show, no comparison to the dance and storytelling circles. A fresh show. As fresh as the orange juice served at the carts that surround the square. Journalists came as well and started to take pictures of the arrest of the crazy man who had terrified Djemaa Lfnaa this morning.

When Qamar Eddine passed in front of Nour Mosque on his way back to the cybercafe, he heard Si Belfqih giving his sermon. His thoughts were all muddled and he couldn't make out what the sermon was about. He thought about how all of them were there listening with authentic, or fake, piety: Professor Essuyuti; Moulay Ahmed Malkha; Hajj Bihi, who owned the bakery; Salim, who only prays on Fridays. But Mahjoub Didi wasn't with them. For the first time, Abu Qatada was missing the Friday prayer at the neighborhood mosque. Qamar Eddine's eyes teared up. He thought about going into the mosque and praying with them to ask his God for forgiveness, but he didn't. He continued on to the cybercafe. His face was pale and he looked tired. He tried to ignore everyone and buried himself in front of the first machine he found. But all the members of the gang were there, gathered around one machine. Even the three Africanos.

"Come here, come here, Qamar Eddine," Samira yelled to him, "Come check out the disaster."

They sat all around Rahhal, watching a video posted by Hot Maroc right then in its Breaking News section: "Crazy Salafi Muslim Attacks Djemaa Lfnaa Square and Terrifies the Tourists in Marrakech" (video of the arrest).

69

THE NEWS ITEM was first posted on Daba Marrakech. A woman had died during childbirth in the Massira Birth Center due to a shortage of blood in the hospital. Then Hot Maroc reposted the item on its Society page after having gotten statements from the grief-stricken husband, one of the midwives, and the regional representative of the Ministry of Health in Marrakech. The deceased was just about to give birth to her first child. A young woman, twenty-four years old. Her husband was a taxi driver and a member of the taxi drivers' union.

Salim passed by the cybercafe that morning when he ran into Yazid preparing signs for the strike that the victim's family, a number of the husband's colleagues at the taxi drivers' union, and a throng of professional neighborhood protesters would take part in. Salim's mother was a nurse at the birth center and the matter involved her, so Salim ran there to let her know about the sit-in.

It seems that Salim's mother did what she had to do, and within an hour, the birth center's general supervisor came to the cybercafe. He ordered two signs from Yazid with which they could face the protesters.

"But I won't write using *naskh* script. Rather, I'll use *rukah*," Yazid told the general supervisor.

"What's the difference?"

"No, it's just that I already made some for the protesters using *naskh* script. I don't want them to accuse me of betraying them."

"*Naskh* . . . blech. Who cares?! Please don't involve me with these details. What's important is that the slogan is legible enough to deliver the message."

The general supervisor had his conditions, too. That the bull-horn be theirs and only theirs during the protest.

The protesters' slogans accused the kingdom's hospitals of slipping into neglect and chaos. They insulted the minister of health and the prime minister. They repeated their slogans for more than half an hour. The director of the birth center gave the orders to lock the gates, made of thick bars that didn't prevent anyone from seeing in or communicating between the inside and the outside. After half an hour, the birth center's midwives and employees came out to the yard. They were carrying two signs written in *rukah* script. One of them expressed condolences for the deceased and announced that the hospital would be mourning her death. The second one asked a question that hadn't been on the minds of the demonstrators.

The painful question didn't remain solely on the sign because the director of the birth center decided to lay it out in detail for the hordes of demonstrators. She held a bullhorn and walked toward them calm and composed.

"All of us are in mourning, guys. All of us are suffering. And all of us were pained when that girl was snatched from us in the prime of her youth. But we aren't the only ones who are responsible. Excuse me, guys. This isn't a problem of our administration alone, or of the minister of health alone, or of the prime minister alone. This is *your* problem, too. We couldn't find any blood for this woman here or in the big hospital. By God, there was nothing we could do. We don't have labs where we can make blood, may God reward you all. You're the ones who need to give blood. By God, it's up to you, guys. Let me ask you frankly, who among you has ever donated blood? Whoever among you has their blood donor card, raise your hand right away . . . Just as I thought, no one. Yep, slogans are easy. Shouting is easy. Doing the right thing is what's hard. Just now the campaign has started today. Whoever really wants to do good for mothers and daughters, starting tomorrow can go to the blood center and give blood. *God will not leave to waste the wage* of one who does good deeds. Now, may God multiply what is best for you. Let us recite the Fatiha prayer together for the spirit of this girl we've all lost."

Yazid was surprised when he saw the guard open the gates wide. The director walked a few steps toward the demonstrators and the midwives followed her, then the employees and the general supervisor. Everyone raised their hands to the sky in supplication and began to recite the Fatiha. They had reached *the path of those whom Thou hast blessed* when Yazid and Rabih joined them.

Amen. Trust in the Almighty God. The director of the birth center walked toward the victim's husband. She embraced him as she cried. She expressed her condolences for his wife. The grieving husband felt true maternal warmth in her embrace. He hugged her as he sobbed and received her compassion with tear-filled eyes. As for Yazid, he rushed over to the general supervisor to get the bullhorn back and settle up with him.

70

RAHHAL DIDN'T EXPECT that the octopus that had started to move powerfully on the Moroccan political scene and on local and national websites, from Hot Maroc to Daba Marrakech, would dive so deeply into Massira, and that one of its long arms would find its way into the cybercafe. But that's exactly what happened. While it was true that elections were knocking at the door, and that the election campaign would begin very soon, the Squirrel did not imagine that the safe haven he occupied at the cybercafe would be violated to such a degree that it would become the center of activities. Even odder was that it was Yazid himself who brought him the news. With the gruff boorishness of a boss, he asked Rahhal to prepare himself for the intense election campaign that would launch from here. From the heart of the cybercafe.

But what does this have to do with that?

What did Yazid have to do with it?

That night, during their regular evening of sitting inert in front of the television, when the Channel One announcer was presenting the final news report, Hassaniya confirmed that the news was true, as she greedily and frighteningly buried her face deep into the pumpkin and lamb tajine that was for lunch the following day. Preparations were fully under way at the school. All the teachers had promised to support Emad Qatifa in the upcoming elections. In fact, they had started to call parents to gather their support as well.

"And the cybercafe?"

"About the cybercafe, I learned from Hiyam that one of the prominent neighborhood activists of the party, whose name is Moulay Yazid Malkha, is one of the customers of the Atlas Cubs. Therefore, the local party office put him in charge of Emad's campaign, which will launch from the cybercafe."

"Who?! Yazid?!!"

"You'll say you don't know him. Always. As usual. Like a deaf man at a party."

"No, Hassaniya. I know Yazid well. But you're saying he's a prominent activist in the Octopus Party. Uh, since when?"

"You're asking *me* since when?"

Hassaniya lifted her hand from the tajine and looked at Rahhal's face for the first time since they started talking about this. She was silent for a moment, then, that natural look of readiness to chide him vanished from her face and was replaced by the shadow of a mean smile. Then, turning her face away from him, she fixed her eyes once again on the television screen.

"Since the party was established. I mean, a long time ago."

The Squirrel smiled in turn. The announcement of the party's establishment had happened about two months prior, and here he was preparing for elections with an unprecedented enthusiasm, especially after caravans of wanderers—from notables and distinguished people to tribal sheikhs and election merchants—made their way to him from every party nook and cranny. From the Right, Left, and middle. Heck, even from deep underground. Party membership was growing at an alarming rate despite people being generally averse to politics there. The octopus possesses an amazing ability to reproduce from a distance, with no direct contact occurring between male and female. For that reason, this spontaneous group enrollment of party notables was considered proof that the new ballot-line number under its symbol had its share of support. Also, because the octopus' arms are covered with strong suction cups that allow it to easily hold on to its prey, from small fish to other marine life, the party was able to swallow a number of other small parties that, before, acted merely as election stores that would open their doors with every election market cycle before going back to their political slumber once again immediately following the elections. The octopus knows how to suck these parties up and transform them into additional blood, which courses through its veins so this predatory animal can grow ever more gigantic until it has grown to the size of those ridiculously large colossal sea monsters like the ones you see in the movies. A beast that sinks ships and frightens whales and scares travelers and everyone who allows himself to be seduced into crossing the vast ocean depths of the Moroccan political scene. The party leader, Moha Sinhaji, ecstatic from the victories his party had won since the beginning, and even before diving into any battle at all, verified in a detailed exclusive interview with the *Future* (republished by Hot Maroc) that the Octopus Party would spread its tentacles, God willing, over all parts of the kingdom. In fact, it would cover Morocco from Tangier to La Güera, to become the top party fielding the most candidates.

"But what about Emad Qatifa?"

"What about him?!" replied Hassaniya perplexed, as if the question had surprised her.

"I mean, what does he have to do with it?"

"Emad is the party's candidate for Parliament, representing Massira and the surrounding neighborhoods in the Marrakech-Menara District. Do you have any objections?"

"No, never," responded the Squirrel immediately in a confused way that made Hassaniya laugh. "Never, never. There's no way I would have any objections."

"No way? More like, not allowed. And then, who are you to object?"

The mocking look she gave him scarcely concealed her contempt. Rahhal lowered his eyes, which caused Hassaniya to shift her gaze toward the open window. He had decided to end the discussion when he heard Hassaniya break out quite on her own to summarize the whole story with a lucidity that surprised the Squirrel.

"Emad is a simple person with no connection to politics or parties. But the decision to appoint him as a candidate for the Octopus Party in this round was decided by the party's regional office without his consultation, but he couldn't refuse. His brother, Dr. Abdelmoula himself, assured him that he couldn't refuse, and that there was no way but to accept. That's how he found himself practicing politics in spite of himself. Abdelmoula and Hiyam and all his friends assured him that it would be crazy to refuse a gift like this. Prestige, status, a seat in Parliament—only a moron would refuse these things."

"Of course, of course," mumbled the Squirrel. But Hassaniya had ended their out-of-the-ordinary conversation and turned up the sound on the television to follow a report being broadcast on efforts the government was making to renew national fishing stocks of mollusks and the Ministry of Maritime Fishing's implementation of a national plan to establish octopus fishing.

Did it have to do with the new party?

Maybe it was just a coincidence. But really, Squirrel . . . It was Bachir Lamrabti, Moha Sinhaji's friend who couldn't have found someone more trustworthy than him to entrust the Octopus Party arm of Marrakech and environs to, agreeing to appoint Emad Qatifa. Biased people claim that the Octopus Party appoints its candidates according to detailed security reports prepared by the apparatuses and placed at the disposal of the (now retired) top state security official, Moha Sinhaji. After that, contact is made with these folks to draw them not just to the party, but to politics and the contours of the political battleground. Partisans of the Octopus Party found this method to be an innovative and untraditional way of renewing the political elites. But whatever the case may be, choosing Emad made sense. He had a good reputation, and he was mild-mannered and generous, despite your unjustified hatred of him, Squirrel. A third of Massira's residents would not have been able to so generously furnish their apartments without the favorable payment plan he had extended to them, and continues to do. So why wouldn't they vote for him tomorrow? All the everyday party faces who had been preparing themselves to be nominated in Massira were at a loss. Emad was a new, fresh face. His nomination baffled everyone, including those in the Camel Party, who issued a statement afterward warning the nobles of this country about the Octopus and its suckers and tentacles, which would wrap themselves around them and pull them down to the depths where corruption nests and shady spawning grounds flourish.

71

DO YOU REMEMBER the discussion circles of the National Student Union of Morocco, Rahhal? The party scene was well-defined in those days. Alignments were clear and party alliances were easy to guess. The Left was the Left, the Right was the Right; there was no middle ground in the Hassan II days. Militants in the discussion circles would discuss the ideological principles of the parties and completely demolish their electoral platforms, despite the fact that the majority of them didn't even vote. The Qaîdi Basista comrades and the brothers in the Justice and Charity movement had "no trust in the system or in Parliament," according to their well-known slogan. Do you remember, Rahhal, when a discussion about the name Organization for Popular Democratic Work took up an entire morning of the comrades' time? Why does *democratic* come first, relegating the relationship between the *organization* and *popular forces* to the background? What did that mean? And why did the Socialist Union of Popular Forces exclude the word *democracy* from its name? Debates not free of sophistry and drawing on tortured political arguments, but they were real debates, serious and adhering to principles that the politicians of today have lost.

Today, nobody is interested in right or left. Nobody is even interested in the party names that meticulously delineate their ideological and intellectual underpinnings. Everybody refers to the parties by their symbols. The Octopus. The Camel. The Horse. The Ant. The Heron. The Broom. The Airplane. The Hoe. The Candlestick. The Clasped Hands. The Stethoscope. The symbols were enough. Even the new one. Everyone in the newspapers and on the radio and television, even on Hot Maroc, referred to it as the Octopus. Just the Octopus. Simple, just like that. This is the national fortune the Atlantic Ocean generously gave to our country and is considered by

Moroccans to be an important source of hard currency, especially in our commercial dealings with the Japanese and the Spanish. This blessed resource was the symbol of the new party. The symbols are enough. "Because a sign is enough for the wise to understand," as Bachir Lamrabti repeated more than once during the party's first preparatory meeting for the electoral campaign that was held in the cybercafe. As for principles and ideologies, empty words. The platforms were empty words. "We're tired of words. The people want what's reasonable. That's why we don't say 'Socialism' or 'Liberalism' or anything else. We talk about 'what's reasonable.' The country wants what's serious and concrete. And we've chosen serious people for them. We don't care if they're important or simple people. All we care about is that they're 'serious' enough for Moroccans to trust them. As for the party's platform, we don't have any platform. Don't worry about it."

Yazid, floating in a rather large olive-colored suit that he no doubt borrowed from one of the neighbors at the last moment, was standing between Bachir and Emad on a small, improvised podium in the middle of the cybercafe. Rahhal and Rabih were helping Asmae deliver orders of coffee, tea, and soda to the attendees. Asmae gracefully and skillfully crossed Dakhla Avenue, which was jammed with cars and bicycles, a tray of orders in her hand as she moved with agility, especially since the Lioness had lost almost half her weight over the last few months. Larbi, the owner of Café Milano, sat in the back row and listened to the party regional secretary's speech as he watched Asmae's deft movements with satisfaction. The first row included prominent faces from the Octopus Party in Marrakech. Rahhal wouldn't have imagined for a moment that the Elephant would be in the vanguard. His professor, Bouchaib Makhloufi himself, was in the middle of the front row. Next to who, Rahhal? Next to who? Can you believe your eyes? Aziz the Greyhound, who, it seemed, had moved beyond the shock he had faced following his father's death that had cast him into the bosom of the Justice and Charity movement. Here he was, having come back to hunt once again for the Octopus this time. The sight of the Elephant and the Greyhound sitting next to one another in the first row was funny. But this isn't the time for laughter, Rahhal. The Squirrel was moving around his shop as if he were a stranger. No, not exactly. Let's say, like a servant. Like a humble servant. Neither the Elephant nor the Greyhound remembered him. Emad greeted him politely at the beginning then forgot he was there. Hiyam didn't see him. He was wiped from her field of vision. The teachers from the Atlas Cubs School didn't know him. Or it was as if they didn't know him. The Hedgehog remained in the corner, following the meeting in silence. Her narrow eyes only met his once the entire time. Even the tea she was drinking in her corner was ordered directly from Asmae. Yazid didn't let up showering him with commands, warranted or not, and with plenty of arrogance. Even Qamar Eddine took the opportunity to humiliate him. The drinks were free, it seemed, or they were on Emad Qatifa, so he first ordered a bottle of Coke and after finishing it off, he ordered an orange and pineapple juice. He was the only one there to order juice, and now here he was ordering again:

"A café crème, Rahhal my friend. A café crème, please."

Rahhal was tending to Qamar Eddine, getting his third order when Emad waved his hand. Larbi would have jumped up to take care of Emad's order, had Asmae not been in the right place, so she glided over to him:

"A tea, please, miss. And another tea for the gentleman."

Asmae removed the small, cold teapot from in front of Bachir and went to the café to freshen up the regional general secretary's tea, while Rahhal ran behind her to give her the new orders from Qamar Eddine and Moulay Ahmed Malkha.

Si Bachir cleared his throat and took two sips of tea from the glass in front of him, then continued his speech:

"Don't get me wrong when I say that we don't have a platform. This doesn't mean that we're a party without a vision or plan of action. Rather, our plan of action is clear. We have discovered that the best plan of action a trustworthy political party can build and defend in Morocco today is the plan of action set out by His Majesty, may God grant him victory. His Majesty has initiated huge works all over the kingdom, starting with the Green Plan for Morocco, which inaugurated a true agricultural revolution, and the Blue Plan, which has increased the number of tourists visiting our resorts and doubled the hotel capacity of our coastal tourist cities, and ending with the Mediterranean Port of Tangier Project, a huge complex that will change the face of the kingdom's north. We stand with these works and with the Economic Rehabilitation Project for the country. His Majesty has launched a genius initiative that has no peer in the entire Arab world—the National Initiative for Human Development—whose generous programs and projects have benefited more than nine million people from vulnerable groups. Naturally, we stand with this singular social rehabilitation project of His Majesty's. Even in our religious realm, if not for the genius of Moroccan sultans who unified us under the 'Ashari creed and the legal school of Imam Malik, we would be plunged into the same sectarian strife some of the Arab countries in the East are living through right now. That is why it is natural that we hold firm to the command of the faithful against any intruder who wants to destroy the spiritual peace of Moroccans, every extremist who seeks *fitna* infighting and calls for terrorism, and anyone who is tempted to sell off our noble religion and toss it into the fray of party struggles. This is why we prefer to gather around our king, the Commander of the Faithful, Defender of Religion and Faith, to ensure the stability of this secure country. This, in brief, is our vision, our platform, our project. And between you and me, without going on for too long, allow me to say this today with full political boldness: We are conscripted soldiers standing behind His Majesty, and whoever doesn't like it is an enemy to the nation, and can go jump in a lake."

The cybercafe shook with applause. Relief was clear on Emad's face. A relief filled with enormous pride. Bachir Lamrabti is one of the country's political stars. Ever since he was a child, Emad had watched him giving his speeches on television. A member of Parliament for more than thirty years. He was one of the founders of the Clasped Hands Party before switching over to the Heron Party. For the last elections he joined the Mill Party, and today he's one of the most important tentacles of the Octopus Party. If not for the strict guidance of the party that forced the national and regional leadership to go down to the people to support party candidates, Emad wouldn't have dreamed of being graced by Bachir Lamrabti's presence in the humble Atlas Cubs Cybercafe for this lavish affair.

The Dog and the Greyhound tried to shout out the party slogan, but Yazid messed up the first sentence, so Bachir pulled on the arm of the suit jacket he had borrowed from the neighbors, asking him to calm down. Everyone noticed. Yazid was a bit confused, but Bachir put his mind at ease with a compassionate, fatherly look, and finished up: "We are a new party. We still have time, Si Yazid. In subsequent meetings we will all have memorized the slogan, God willing, and we'll repeat it together with one voice. Right now, we've just begun. We've just started to build this blessed party entity that the journalists, may God excuse them, refer to as 'the new number.' We are not a number. We are *not* a number, please." He said it angrily the second time. "We are a party for Moroccans. Free Moroccans are not sticks. And they are not numbers. And by the way, speaking of slogans, there's a secret I want to share with you." He started to speak in a lowered voice, shaking with emotion, while total silence came over the cybercafe. "Did you know that our general secretary, Si Moha Sinhaji, may God protect him, has refused to come up with a slogan for our party from day one? We in the central office urged him to do so, but he absolutely refused. He told us, as his eyes filled with tears: 'We have one slogan, which is the slogan of all Moroccans—God, Nation, King. And we have one anthem, and that's the national anthem.' Si Moha, may God protect him, has summed up the party's entire identity in this statement. It is true that, later, we will decide on a slogan, which I will print out and distribute next time for you to learn. We've written it down only so enemies and lurking opportunists don't say that we want to privatize the country. Here is the party slogan right here in front of you, ladies and gentlemen. We're like the other parties in that regard. But keep in mind that Morocco is a country of consensus. Even rappers and hip-hop artists, who in other countries oppose their governments, here they all sing with one voice for Morocco. And their slogan, which you all know is '*Magharba tal mout*, Moroccans 'til death!' This is the Moroccan exception. And we know that whoever's heart is with this country will remain Moroccan 'til death, its first and last slogan being 'God, Nation, King.'"

Asmae was trying to move between the rows with the tray of new orders when the cybercafe shook with applause.

72

IT WAS LUCKY the *Future* opened up a refuge in front of Naim Marzouk where he could breathe different air and achieve his stardom
with a not-to-be-overlooked audience: the café people. Mint tea
and café au lait people. Frankly, Hot Maroc had started to suffocate
him. It was too constraining for him, and he for it. Ever since it had
fallen into the hands of one Anouar Mimi, its decline had gotten
on his nerves. A person who is only good at "behind the scenes,"
repugnant fake charm, and manufacturing a lack of restraint. Naim
knew for a fact that shuffling the cards had become part of Hot
Maroc's editorial line. But even cards, Mimi, need to be shuffled
artfully. Opening the news site's doors wide open to a complete and
utter lack of restraint in this manner was disappointing. Lack of
restraint with regard to language, news, headline selection, forming the material, everything. Naim remained a calm and composed
pen, theoretically, at least. He possessed a knowledge of Arabic, and
imagined that a minimal amount of respect for the language and
knowledge of its grammar was a requirement of this profession.
Naim was unable to suppress his anger. His opinion about his new
editor in chief gradually began to leak out. For Naim, even though
he usually kept his personal views to himself (considering what
he expressed in his daily column not to be free, personal views of
his), no longer refrained from showing his annoyance at the site's
decline during the Anouar Mimi era. He started to make fun of
him in front of his colleagues at Hot Maroc and also in front of the
journalists at the *Future*. And his provocations always found someone to deliver them hot to Mimi, who knew, deep down, that he
could exercise his authority as editor in chief over everyone, except
for Naim Marzouk. So, the only place he could find to vent was in
Casablanca's restaurants and cabarets during his daily soirées, and

as soon as drunkenness slurred his speech, he'd start to insult his adversary. For the benefit of everyone there who spoke positively about Naim Marzouk, thinking they were flattering Mimi with such praise, he would set out to explain that Naim wasn't the real author of the columns that carried his name. The articles actually arrived complete from other powerful places. He just adorns them with his own touches and linguistic somersaults and adds some of his special seasonings before signing off on them. That's how the Chameleon found himself in a secret struggle with the Mongoose.

I forgot to tell you that Mimi was a domesticated mongoose. Some might be misled by its soft fur and little feet, but its fingers are tipped with sharp claws. Generally, it isn't frightened by reptiles of any kind. Even alligators, majestic and mighty as they are, their eggs become its favorite lunch. As for the mongoose's skill in catching poisonous snakes, that's well-known. So, what do you think about the fact that, this time, his adversary was no more than a chameleon?

Things started to get increasingly tense when Tanoufi published an online version of his newspaper. That's how Naim Marzouk's column was published on the *Future*'s website at the same time that it appeared on Hot Maroc. Sometimes, Mimi would read it on the *Future*'s site before Hot Maroc had published it. It's true that those who steer from behind the scenes don't generally care about these details; to them Hot Maroc and the *Future* were the same thing. But you need to protect your pulpit, Mimi, to defend the number-one status that the online edition of the *Future* has started to challenge. He suffered more when he saw an investigation his newspaper's crew had spent more than a week working on handed over to Naim Marzouk, who did no more than rework it in his style that had become worn out, according to Mimi, then published on the *Future*'s site even before Hot Maroc. But who are you going to complain to, Mimi? Who? Therefore, it's okay to show some patience, and a bit of maneuvering. The mongoose, of course, is an expert maneuverer.

Mimi no longer made all the information he received available to Naim, even if this violated the directives. He held on to some of it to create a scoop on Hot Maroc's home page. That's how Naim Marzouk's columns came to be complemented by what was published by Hot Maroc in the middle of its home page in a way that saved face for the news site. Gradually, Mimi began to detract from the myth of Naim Marzouk, whose readers used to say that reading his column made the national newspapers, print or online, redundant. Naim sensed the trap, but he, too, couldn't complain. When information came from elsewhere, he knew it was complete, and all he needed to do was season it with his own spices and liberally add his wickedness, stings, and fabricated argumentative somersaults, which were conclusive nonetheless. But when it came from Mimi, Naim knew that he had to exert double the effort with the article and add more spice, pepper especially, to compensate for some of the essential details that Mimi had, no doubt, kept from him. It was the information that the Mongoose was skilled at playing around with in the title of his main article in Hot Maroc that made Naim look like he had been shut out . . . or at least, made him look like an analyst who lacked the essence of the cases and the issues involved.

The maneuvers were conducted in secret. No one but the two of them knew about it. Generally, Naim Marzouk was too arrogant to attend editorial staff meetings, either at Hot Maroc or the *Future*. Usually he'd work from home as long as the work arrived in his email inbox. But the few times he would go to Hot Maroc's offices, the Mongoose would embrace Naim warmly as if things between them were just peachy. He'd smile sweetly to his face and while they talked, he'd affectionately tap him on the shoulder from time to time, laying on the charm. He'd close his eyes effeminately, in a way that remained trite and repulsive, especially to an alpha male like Naim. But what could he do? This was the Mongoose's way of being welcoming, and seductive.

It was war, then. Each one lying in wait for the other. So, when he received that stray email from Mimi by mistake, Naim did not waste the opportunity. It was his chance to regain the upper hand.

Mehdi Aït Hajj—the billionaire and wild beast of real estate, known for his involvement in numerous financial scandals—had returned to the spotlight a few months ago. Two big cases before the court that were being followed according to current guidelines were enough to shake his real estate empire and put him behind bars. But it appeared that negotiations conducted between him and the Octopus Party, according to which Aït Hajj had pledged to finance part of the new party's local electoral campaign (as long as the party nominated him at the top of the list in his city), caused the two cases to be shelved, for now, until they could be put to rest for good. So, what was the news here? The email that Naim received by mistake from Mimi carried incriminating information that had never circulated in the press before; information that could destroy Aït Hajj's reputation in the eyes of public opinion and force the courts to immediately reopen his case to pursue his arrest this time. The email's subject line read "Explosive. Top Secret." Naim printed the email. As he sat there, stunned, having just started to read the horrible revelations, his cell phone rang. And just as he figured, it was Mimi on the line.

"Hello, my dear Naim. Good morning, love."

"Good morning," Naim said drily. He hated when a male flirted with him like this.

"Look, dear. You just got an email, right?"

Naim remained silent, and Mimi continued nervously.

"The important thing is that, if you received an email from me this morning, it was sent to you by mistake. That email means nothing. Useless. You might as well forget all about it, beautiful. It would be best if you deleted it. You've got nothing to do with it. Okay?"

Naim remained silent, so Mimi repeated his request:

"Okay, my dear? That email is useless, I swear. Just forget all about it."

Naim responded that he had just woken up, and hadn't had his coffee yet.

"Coffee first, Mimi. Coffee first. As soon I open my email and take a look at my messages so I can understand what you're talking about, I'll get in touch with you."

But Naim had already made his decision. He wouldn't let this opportunity slip through his fingers. That damn Mimi was toying with him, and he knew his maneuvers well. He had rushed and sent him the file, and now he wants to trick him and cover things up. What are you waiting for, Naim? To read the news item with its earth-shattering information on Hot Maroc's home page, after which you'll write your column as if it were a mere comment? So, you are no more than a simple commenter on Anouar Mimi's payroll then. One of the stupid Hot Maroc commenters like Son of the People and Abu Sharr Guevari.

Never. I won't miss this opportunity, you fraud.

Mimi got up from his desk and headed to the balcony. A cup of coffee in his right hand and a cigarette in his left. He drew deeply on the cigarette, then blew the smoke out. His office's balcony opened out onto Hassan II Mosque, which seemed to be floating on the ocean's surface, on the blue of the Atlantic, which was calm this morning, as if its waves were on vacation. The sky was clear. The sun was shining and it was a beautiful day. The morning was calm. *Perhaps it was the calm before the storm*, thought Mimi as he smiled wickedly. The stupid chameleon had swallowed the bait.

73

MBAREK, THE SAUSAGE VENDOR, rushed into the cybercafe and scurried straight to the toilet. He tried to open the door as he doubled over with cramps, but found it locked from the inside so he screamed out as he writhed, "Is that ass still in there?!"

Mbarek had come fifteen minutes before and found the toilet occupied, and here it was, still locked before his engorged bladder.

"Masmoudi's still inside," Qamar Eddine answered, concealing a mischievous smile while Rahhal buried his face in his personal computer, pretending not to see or hear anything.

Mbarek squirmed as he jabbered unintelligible insults. Mbarek has the cheapest sausage sandwiches in all of Massira. His competitors whisper to one another that he sells donkey meat. The meat he stuffs into those casings can't be calf or lamb. Even the cost of female sheep meat at the meat market wouldn't allow him to sell sausages at such a low price. But the sausages of this son of a bitch are tasty. Rahhal often resorted to eating his sandwiches. Not because he wanted to save money. Never! Rather, because they were really delicious. Mbarek's bladder was about to explode. It was clear that he was holding it in with some difficulty. He couldn't wait, so he began to bang on the door and yell:

"Hey, Masmoudi. Open the door, man. Are you giving birth? Should I go get you a midwife? The birth center is nearby. Right next door."

He turned around to see everyone in the cybercafe following the scene. He was a bit flummoxed, but he tried to overcome it with some rude levity:

"This son of a bitch is probably jerking off while I'm all stopped up and writhing in pain."

The three Africanos didn't understand a thing. Fadoua and Samira lowered their eyes out of embarrassment. Poor Rahhal, defeated, shrunk in his chair but kept craning his neck in order to follow what was going on, pale as a ghost. He tried to imagine the scene: Fat Masmoudi, the snail-broth vendor, masturbating in his toilet stall. Really, the man has been locked inside for half an hour. What could he possibly be doing?

Mbarek continued to bang on the door until the sound of throat clearing could be heard from inside:

"Calm down out there, Mbarek. Calm down. Just a minute, please."

Ever since the electoral meeting, about which a short article was published on Daba Marrakech that deemed it a closed party meeting for militants of the Massira branch of the Octopus Party, Rahhal had started to feel like a stranger in the cybercafe. Yazid had come to have the first and last word in the shop. And because every single member of the happy Atlas Cubs cyber family (except for the three Africanos) attended that meeting as members of the party—at least that's how Yazid introduced them to Si Bachir and Emad—they were all aware of Yazid's new status. Generally, Rahhal held no high aspirations. He remained in his place, guarding his virtual creatures as he carried out his daily tasks on Hot Maroc and coordinated Son of the People's and Abu Qatada's interventions according to Hidhami's guidance, as usual. Not to mention his routine job of keeping track of what time customers came and went and collecting what they owed. He had even gotten used to Yazid's vanity and haughtiness, but not this new situation. Rahhal's final defeat was the carte blanche Yazid the Dog had given to some of the lowly characters and itinerant vendors, who had ended up settling on Dakhla Avenue close to the cybercafe, to violate the sanctity of the shop and sully the most intimate of its spaces: the toilet.

Larbi, the owner of Café Milano, had decided months ago to close the door of the café's toilet to these folks. At first, he asked a seventy-year-old woman to watch over it. He entrusted her with cleaning the toilets and collecting a fee from whoever used them, whether they were customers of the café, itinerant vendors, or just people passing by. He considered what the old woman earned a charitable donation. But the itinerant vendors usually refused to pay the dirham the old woman asked for. And despite her apparent frailty, she knew how to show her strength by yelling, so the toilet, and the entire café, became a theater of daily arguments, nasty insults, and screaming. The old woman's yelling sounded like a wail and resembled a horse's loud whinnying when things got really bad. Larbi couldn't stand these daily battles, and he couldn't stand the woman's wailing in particular, so he had no choice but to let her go. He gave the key to Asmae and made sure she didn't give it to anyone other than café customers.

And now that Yazid was prematurely throwing himself into the electoral campaign, he started to attract shoplifters, hawkers, and itinerant vendors. He would write down their names and what they did, assuring them that the party would pay attention to them, and that he'd submit their names so they could benefit from the aid the state was offering to vulnerable groups as part of the National Initiative for Human Development. And to prove his good intentions to this riffraff and assure them that he was truly prepared to help them and shield them from injustice, Yazid suggested that they could temporarily use the cybercafe's toilet until Emad Qatifa won the elections and built them a public toilet in the small, neglected park next to the Dakhla Avenue overpass. That's how Rahhal found himself facing this serious mess.

The problem was that these rough characters were used to squat toilets, so the comfortable seat provided by the modern cybercafe toilet didn't help them too much. That's why evacuating their large intestines took more time than they were accustomed to. But what really made Rahhal mad was that most of them didn't flush the toilet so the water could carry their filthy excrement off to the sewer. They'd leave everything there and just walk out. It was enough for them to get rid of their excrement and then rush back out to inspect their pull carts and shabby items spread out on the sidewalk, Rahhal kept telling them. Qamar Eddine even entered the fray to impress upon them the necessity of cleaning the toilet after using it, but they didn't. That's how a new, disgusting responsibility was added to Rahhal's tasks. One that had never occurred to him before.

74

THE AFFAIR was like a volcano that Naim Marzouk's column caused to erupt. The article first appeared in the *Future*'s print edition, then on the website. Naim Marzouk's surprise volcano launched its flaming lava at the Right and the Left and caused fire to break out on more than one roof. A mysterious phone call received by Tanoufi on his cell phone caused him to agitatedly convene a closed meeting with the editors in chief of the *Future*'s print and online editions. He was as bewildered as a child who has lost his mother in a crowded market and no longer knew which way to turn. Tanoufi was well aware that the meeting wouldn't help him at all, since the directives given to the editors in chief were to make sure that Naim Marzouk's articles were published as is, with no changes or intervention. He read the column in the newspaper as soon as it was published, and his mouth hung open in surprise when he saw Naim mercilessly crucify Aït Hajj. But Tanoufi knew that Naim was inspired, and it wasn't within his rights to ask him to explain what he had written. And without Naim there, a meeting was meaningless really. But Tanoufi was lost and didn't know what to do, so he called the meeting. The central office of the Octopus Party held an urgent meeting, too. They were extremely surprised. They had thought that Aït Hajj's cases had been closed, and that reference to them just a few months prior had been a mere slap on the wrist. Otherwise, why would he have been given the green light to run in the elections, for them to bet on him as the most important electoral powerhouse this round? Ridiculous. Ridiculous! There was something strange going on here.

Anouar Mimi had it all figured out, of course. Lucky for him, Naim had delayed sending his column to Hot Maroc; he didn't do so until he was sure it had been published in the *Future*. This was enough for Mimi to make the decision not to publish it for moral and professional reasons until he had a chance to look over what was in it, or at least that's what he claimed. Also, Mimi had recorded his telephone conversation with Naim, the one where he begged him not to attach any importance to Aït Hajj. Thus, Anouar Mimi had protected himself, and now he was far from the eye of the storm.

The information Naim had provided was correct. It was fully ready for publication before it was revealed that secret negotiations with Aït Hajj had effectively put an end to his case in exchange for his providing the required support to the Octopus Party. That way he would kill two birds with one stone. He could wipe his slate clean and restore his political virginity with the new party (he who had slept in more than one party's bed over the last forty years). Aït Hajj didn't care about the octopus or the crayfish or any other mollusk. The only thing he cared about was getting out of a tight squeeze that had been planned for quite some time with his skin still intact, and without making waves. That's why he had to put up a credible struggle in the ranks of the Octopus Party and pay dearly until the party held the position it deserved on the national political scene. So how did they surprise him with this treacherous coup?

Naim Marzouk expected Mimi to ruin his morning mood with admonishing calls, so he put his phone on silent and took pleasure sipping his morning coffee in his apartment's salon. Fairouz's morning songs kept him company. The bookshelf in front of him was varied—novels, books on criticism and philosophy, and others on politics. There were newspapers piled up on the couch and underneath it, as well as on top of the desk. A beautiful chaos that Naim loved; he who preferred to wake up leisurely here in the salon of his luxury apartment on Anfa Boulevard, or sometimes in his spacious bedroom in the pleasant familiar darkness. He didn't usually open the shutters in the morning. He didn't do that until after taking his morning shower and eating his breakfast, right before he was about to leave. The clock pointed to 11:30. Hunger gnawed at Naim. There was butter, jam, cheese, eggs, and juice in the refrigerator. But he was hungry for lunch, not breakfast. He wanted something more substantial to eat. He remembered the housekeeper wasn't coming today. She had told him yesterday that her son was sick, so he gave her a hundred dirhams and let her take the day off. The calls were constant, but his phone was still on silent. Just as Naim guessed, more than ten attempted calls from Mimi, and more than twenty from Tanoufi. And numerous other calls from numbers he didn't have saved in his phone. He liked this game. It pleased him that everyone was trying to call him to condemn him or congratulate him while he didn't answer. Some months ago, a widely circulated French magazine wrote an article that stroked his ego quite a bit: "Naim Marzouk: Morocco's Number One Opinion Maker." In the article, they portrayed him as a unique media phenomenon. The article was published on a full page, accompanied by a picture of him. Generally, Naim doesn't like chatting on the phone and doesn't feel compelled to return calls; calls from admirers never stop. He is conscious that most callers—from well-known politicians and sometimes even ministers—simply want to flatter him. All he has to do is focus for just a moment on any one of them before they find themselves in some sort of trouble. That's why everyone feared Naim. People said he was fickle, turning like a weather vane in the wind. But in the end, he was just obeying orders. When asked to focus on Mr. X or Mr. Y, Naim has to do it. And as soon as he receives information, he kneads it into dough, no matter who the victim is. That's how Naim has become such a feared pen. Famous personalities wooed him and treated him as an extraordinary journalist, and it intoxicated him. Whose only worry before his glories at Hot Maroc was finding a newspaper that would accept him as an editor for its Culture section, and getting his novel manuscript (titled *The Mountain Crouching at the Spring*) published by the Moroccan Writers' Association; although the association declined to publish the novel because, as the reading committee's report made clear, its structure didn't hold together, its characters were weak, and its romance outdated. Its romance outdated?! Welcome, then, to Naim Marzouk's romantic world, you ingrates, you end-of-times intellectuals! That's why Naim devoted more than one column to flaying the Moroccan Writers' Association and making an example of every Moroccan writer who achieved something; who won a prize, for example, or whose work was translated into French or English. And when there wasn't a case serious enough for him to be ordered to work on it—say, an opponent or even a supporter who needed to have his hand slapped every once in a while to keep him in line— Naim was given a free hand, which allowed him to write what he wanted and enjoy the freedom of unfettered and unconditional slander that was available to him. He really enjoyed pillorying those stupid writers and making fun of their books that no one read. He belittled their miserable prizes and mocked the ensuing quarrels over the eligibility of this or that laureate, and he exposed the way they flocked to tours and festivals. People love what Naim writes. They love his inventive way of insulting people, of belittling them, slandering them, leveling false charges against them, and smearing shit on them without offending public taste. Free, proud people love these things. They have become addicted to them, addicted to Naim Marzouk's insults and false accusations.

In cafés, there was no tea or coffee unless they were accompanied by Marquise cigarettes and Naim Marzouk's columns. Naim became a true star, a popular hero, the one master of the café regulars. So that's why he was happy to cut himself off from the world this morning. He repeated the Mutanabbi verse to himself:

> I sleep soundly, heedless of the wonders I have just written,
>   while everyone, because of them, remains awake and
>   quarrels.

Naim made up his mind not to go out or to answer his phone that day. Hunger wasn't a problem, either. He called a pizza shop, tucked away at the end of an alley branching off of Anfa Boulevard not far from the building where he lived, and ordered a two-person seafood pizza. That's right, a two-person pizza. Because the chameleon's appetite is insatiable, and it grows while it eats.

But Naim didn't expect that his order would come so quickly. After just five minutes, the doorbell rang. It was odd, even though he knew that the pizzeria's owner and its employees were adoring fans of his. But of course they would devote themselves to serving him and rush his order.

The ringing continued, so Naim jokingly called from inside as he put on his tracksuit (he'd hate for the pizzeria employee to see him in his pajamas): "I'm coming, man. Usually I don't like my pizza so hot. If it cools down a bit, no problem. Just be patient, please." He went to the door. He opened it and reached his hand out to take the pizza. But as soon as he opened the door, three men in black suits and neckties sauntered in. Naim was stunned. He didn't know if this had to do with thieves or . . . so he screamed.

"Police. We're sorry to bother you. Please come with us," the youngest one said. A young man, less than thirty years old, elegant-looking with an attractive face, as if he were a movie actor. He said it politely, but sharply as well.

"With you? With who? Who *are* you? You must be kidding. Perhaps you don't know who you're dealing with."

"Mr. Naim, we know you very well, and we hold you in high regard. However, we ask that you come with us now. We'd rather you cooperate with us, because there's force down below that we hope we won't have to use, to preserve your dignity and your status."

The tone seemed harsher this time. So Naim figured it would be wise to go with them immediately. Luckily, he had changed out of his pajamas before opening the door. He stuffed his feet into some sneakers that were at the apartment's entrance. He made sure his two cell phones were in his pocket and went out. He was completely terrified, but he tried to keep his composure. Naim is very concerned about his image. Even in the darkest situations, he liked others to see him as completely put together. But a rumbling in his stomach reminded him that he was in an unenviable position. He tried to get as much of a grip on himself as he could, hoping that the place they were taking him to was close so that he'd get there before shitting his pants.

75

YAZID IS AN IDIOT. You wouldn't doubt it for a moment, Rahhal.
It's enough that the man would try to sell meat on Eid al-Adha.
Ever since Qamar Eddine told him about that incident, which they
made fun of for a long time in their building and in the neighboring buildings, too, Rahhal suppressed a mischievous laugh whenever he thought of it. Even the poor neighborhood kids and those
from the surrounding neighborhoods know how to emerge from
the holiday having made some decent money. The poorest and
least brilliant among them lie in wait for the sheepskins the house-
wives throw next to the garbage dumpsters or lean up next to the
buildings. They collect the animal skins and stack them in piles
that grow higher over the course of the Eid. In the evening, trucks
drive around the streets and alleys of the city. The truck owners
collect the sheepskins to sell afterward to the tanneries in the Old
City; one sheepskin for ten dirhams. Some collect fifty to a hundred sheepskins on Eid al-Adha. A small fortune. But Yazid always
thinks the wrong way about the wrong project, and always goes
about it wrong. So don't worry too much about him, Squirrel. You
won't be able to convince Yazid of anything. You won't convince
him, for example, that he's just wasting his time with Fadoua and
Samira. Marrakech Star might be able to vote in Mexico, Brazil, or
even Turkey, but not here in the national elections. The amount of
time the two girls spend in front of the screen following imported
series from these countries has connected them more to Guadala-
jara, Brasilia, and Istanbul than to Marrakech. So don't waste your
time with them, you moron. If God had given you some of that
gray matter that makes up the brains of human beings, you would
have turned your attention to the members of the association's
office that you supported while they were protesting against the

environmental degradation in Massira, or toward the workers at the Sherouk Bakery. Heck, even toward the owner of the bakery, Hajj Bihi. At least with these people there was room for give and take concerning these sorts of things. But Yazid is an ass, on top of the fact that he's a dog, and he'll never understand. He doesn't know that most of this rabble to whom he opened the cybercafe's door so they can stink the place up aren't even registered to vote, and thus, not part of the game. Even the ones who *are* registered won't vote until after receiving the price of their vote in hard cash, and the price was well-known: two hundred to three hundred dirhams per vote. Not to mention the fact that they would vote for other candidates in their villages and towns around Marrakech and not for Emad Qatifa, quite simply because they aren't from here. They don't live in Massira, you idiot.

But what does this have to do with you, Rahhal? First off, no one asked for your opinion. Not even Emad Qatifa imagined for a moment that you might be able to provide any helpful advice or that you could help out with his campaign. He knows you're here, just an apathetic squirrel, Hassaniya's husband, to whom they offered a small job out of respect to Oum Eid's daughter. The most you can do is to help Café Milano's waitress serve the party "militants" who are gathered in the cybercafe. And that'll be enough for you. As for Yazid, you can see how things are with him now. Even his coffee came to him as soon as he entered the cybercafe so he could dive right into his electronic organization of campaign issues that required emails, Facebook posts, and whatnot, with direct supervision from Qamar Eddine, who had been lured in to enthusiastically become Yazid's electronic right-hand man for a hundred dirhams a day. After less than ten minutes, His Grace arrives. Asmae rushes in carrying his café cortado. Rahhal didn't understand when Yazid had ordered his coffee or how. By telephone? SMS? Or was it just a favor granted to him by Larbi, who hardly ever got up from his chair at one of the front tables that took up all of the sidewalk, forcing pedestrians into the street? From there he watches everything that's happening on this section of Dakhla Avenue. Larbi, who had joined the Octopus Party, seemingly quite convinced, saw this gesture as a militant way of thanking Yazid, who had invited him to the meeting that day and given him exceptional earnings that evening. But the most important thing was that he had introduced him to Emad Qatifa and Dr. Bouchaib Makhloufi and got an amazing picture taken with Bachir Lamrabti. He would be sure to enlarge his picture with Si Bachir, frame it, and hang it in a prominent place in the café so it could be seen by anyone entering or leaving, and so Larbi could point it out to the members of the municipality's oversight committee who had become regulars at his place and at the neighboring cafés these days; so as to make them aware that they were unfairly occupying public property. Larbi had become accustomed to making generous payments to the committee, which were enough to satisfy its members when the visits had been infrequent, but now that the visits had started to come every month, he was unable to pay the fixed monthly bribe.

Perhaps Rahhal was a bit wounded because he didn't know how to convey his thoughts to Yazid concerning the riffraff the place had been opened up to, ruining the cybercafe's atmosphere with their rotten electoral stink. He might also have been hurt because Emad Qatifa hadn't thought of him, hadn't looked for a small role for him in this play. But who was Emad Qatifa in God's great dominion anyway? He was too insignificant to distribute roles to others. Wasn't he himself playing a role that had been imposed on him? An insignificant person who had failed to obtain his high school diploma. But because of the reports that were presented to the regional department of the Octopus Party that portrayed him as a spotless personality, beloved and popular, he was chosen. He didn't even have the right to refuse a role he hadn't chosen for himself. But now, Emad Qatifa was the candidate for the new party. They nominated him because they know better than you. Despite the fact that he had failed to obtain his high school diploma—something only you remember, Squirrel—they decided that Emad was right for this role.

Even Yazid, Rahhal. Don't make too big a deal of trying to diminish his qualifications. The man is not so simple. He is a powerful machine. His ability to move and connect with all sorts of people is nothing to sneeze at. You're sure that he's an idiot, but do you think that Bachir Lamrabti needs high-born people who can think? Not at all. The party is there to draw up plans and define what needs to be done. They just need a flock to put in the effort and work hard, to manufacture the necessary excitement and march in clamorous electoral marches, to dance in the streets naked if that's what needs to be done. Others are doing the thinking for them, so don't worry too much, Rahhal. Bachir Lamrabti is a smooth political operator. A sly fox. In Yazid, he sees the boldness and aspiration an Octopus Party militant needs, which is why he chose him and appointed him a member of the Massira branch of the party and put him in charge of Emad Qatifa's campaign. And now the people are working enthusiastically on what you refer to as a play. What play, you insignificant squirrel? Even if it *were* a play, could you handle even a small role with just a few minutes onstage, you coward? Would your knees come to your aid and stop shaking for even a moment in front of the audience? You're incapable of being in the spotlight, Squirrel. You're used to moving in the shadows. In secret. Behind the curtain. So you have no right to blame Emad for overlooking you. And besides, Qatifa is in no position to be handing out roles.

If the Squirrel received Emad's snubs and belittling with a sporting spirit that was devoid of hatred, the Lioness considered what happened on the day they met to be a horrible affront that could not be forgiven. Emad was eager to serve his guests, so he kept calling out to Asmae, "Come here, my girl, and see whether Si Bouchaib wants another drink. Another espresso for Si Aziz, if you could be so kind." He was speaking politely to her, in his condescending, repugnant way. And when she put on a baseball cap with the name of the café written on the front, Larbi asked her to stand next to him to greet everyone on behalf of the café in order to be sure everyone knew that Café Milano was always at their service, and at the service of the cybercafe, the party, and the nation. Right then, Emad slipped a hundred dirhams into her hand. A tip? Charity? Rahhal didn't understand.

You're giving charity to the Lioness, you bastard?

You've fucked yourself now, my little Qatifa.

76

NAIM SPENT TWO WHOLE DAYS in that room that wasn't really an office; in that office that might have been a prison cell. Detained inside a cell whose walls screamed silence. A sixty-year-old man wearing a worker's suit—the worn-out blue uniform that parking attendants also wear, not the recognizable makhzen suit—would come in every once in a while to bring him cheap sandwiches. *Kofta* with french fries and tomato sauce. And in the morning a cheese with jam sandwich and a glass of tea. All of his attempts to make a call using his cell phone failed. It was as if there was deliberate interference that prevented his two phones from catching their wireless breath.

On the third day, the trio that had seized Naim at home came to him. They were in the same suits and they looked the same. It seemed as if their days were all the same, and that they had been repeating the same mission over and over for some time. Thus, they had come to carry it out mechanically and extremely efficiently. He thought they were leaving. They would find a car to go somewhere else, somewhere more obscure. A bitterness in his throat and his beating heart prevented Naim from asking where they were taking him. He felt completely crushed. He almost broke down in tears before pulling himself together. But all it took was a little stroll through the hallways of that old building to find himself in a section that seemed more lively and clean. At least the walls here were whitewashed. And there was movement in the halls—citizens and police in their uniforms moving about between offices. They knocked on the door. They brought Naim in. They saluted the people inside and then left. The office was spacious and well-lit, simply yet tastefully and modernly furnished. There were five people in the room. The one who seemed the oldest, and the highest ranking, greeted him with respect. He was asked to take a seat. Naim sat down in a warm, comfortable, black chair. It seemed like the five people who were all around him now got up all at once. Tea or coffee? Tea, of course. Naim preferred tea over coffee. The tea arrived along with a small plate of Moroccan cookies: *ghorayba*, biscotti, and gazelle horns. The investigation began immediately.

The questions were precise. They went over in excruciating detail the information that had appeared in his last column, and the dangerous charges Naim had leveled at the billionaire Mehdi Aït Hajj. Naim was unable to answer. His intuition came to his aid and he declared that he would not answer any questions without his lawyer present, and that he would not reveal his sources. His responses were short and he kept repeating himself like a broken record. They didn't seem annoyed at all with his lack of response. With an air of neutrality, they wrote down everything he said. At the end of the meeting, the oldest one thanked Naim with the same tone of respect he had greeted him with. They all shook hands, then sent Naim, this time, to the civil prison. To a real cell. He was now officially detained in police custody.

New faces surrounded him now. He was on his way to an official cell. Naim was irritated that the guards accompanying him didn't recognize him. It wounded his pride somewhat, that they didn't know him, the big media star, but deep down he was okay with it because the situation was not honorable at all. It made him happier to have been given some space, specifically because of the anonymity it accorded him. In the police van there was a woman in her fifties and a teenaged girl. He was squeezed between them. They were asked to wait quietly and the door was shut. Just one guard remained waiting next to the van while the others went to bring more guests. The woman in her fifties sat silently, while the teenaged girl cried and vainly pulled at her short skirt in an attempt to cover up her exposed thighs. Naim guessed that they weren't together. When he first got in, he thought they were together, but it seemed that they were sitting there next to one another quite by accident, the same accident that had forced him next to them in this damned police van. Neither one of them turned toward him. He took the opportunity to remove one of his cell phones from the pocket of his dirty tracksuit jacket. The first one was completely dead in his pocket, while the second one still had a bit of charge. He'll call Jaouad now. Jaouad is the person Naim confers with on everything. A while ago Jaouad had gotten him the same way Officer Hakim had gotten Rahhal Laâouina the first time, practically the same scenario. Jaouad got Naim after his first year at Hot Maroc. And for all of these years, he has remained his number-one guide, his guardian angel, his reliable source, his connection to other agencies. All the other mysterious agencies. Shit! Jaouad wasn't answering. He tried a number of times, but to no avail. You need to do something, Naim, before the police come back to the van. You need to do something, Chameleon. That's why he finally decided to write a letter. He would write a letter of appeal and direct it to the chief through Jaouad. True, Jaouad had left him in the lurch right now. But surely he would look at the text message and he'd be obliged—knowing how professionally disciplined he was—to show it to the chief. Things were starting to take a turn you hadn't been considering, Naim, and you might not get the chance to compose another letter. So, you'll need to begin at the end. You need to apologize, to ask for forgiveness, to beg. For it to be a letter of appeal, the chief might direct it to whomever it concerned. A disjointed letter that would start with "Peace be upon you, in the presence of our supreme imam," and end with stock phrases like "admitting one's mistakes is a virtue" and "forgiveness is strength." Naim wouldn't let the opportunity pass to clarify that he had been the victim of a plot cooked up by Anouar Mimi and that he would know how to make things right; they just needed to trust him and give him another chance. He would apologize for every bad word he had directed at Mehdi Aït Hajj and he would make clear to his readers that a party hostile to the nation was the one who had involved him with this information that he, himself, had established was bad, only to discover, too late unfortunately, how fake it was. He would apologize to Aït Hajj in his own way. He would restore his reputation. They just had to trust him.

Before they threw him into his solitary cell, the guards stripped Naim of his phones. He didn't get a wink of sleep that night. The world darkened in front of him. His life flashed before his eyes, starting with his distant childhood days in that neglected village on the outskirts of Kenitra. His literary delusions. Then his glory days at Hot Maroc. At dawn, the cell's door was opened. Naim couldn't believe his eyes at first. He thought he was dreaming. It was Jaouad standing there in front of him with his striped beret that covered his baldness, and the spring jacket he always wore over a light shirt. He was wearing cologne, as usual. He always wore way too much cologne. Your first time smelling cologne, Naim, since being forced to leave your apartment on that unfortunate day. Oh, Jaouad . . . Tears poured from Naim's eyes. He looked like a lost child who had just found his mother in a crowd.

"What are you doing, you idiot?" Jaouad attacked him red-faced.

"I was a victim of my own ignorance. That jerk, Anouar Mimi, got me all caught up with information that had no basis in the truth."

"Why are you crying now? And why did you send me that stupid message?"

"Because Mimi, Jaouad, Mimi's the one who . . ."

"Forget about Mimi, man. Forget about Mimi now. You've become a hero, Naim. Heroes don't cry. And they don't write letters of appeal."

"What? But what hero are you talking about, Jaouad? Their investigation of me was harsh, and it looks like I'll go to trial soon."

"God give me strength. You're a hero now. Did anyone hurt you here? Was anyone rough with you during the investigation?"

"Frankly, no. They were respectful with me. But they took my phones. And look at me, Jaouad. My clothes are filthy, as you can see. I'm in a bad state."

He began to sob.

"But did you think you were in a five-star hotel?! Do you want a hot shower in the morning and perhaps a breakfast fit for a king in the garden? Get ahold of yourself. You're being detained. That's how it is, you who chose to be so damned reckless. You've shuffled the cards, Naim. You've shuffled them more than necessary. After I read your column, I called you five times that morning. I just wanted to understand. You didn't coordinate things with me before doing something so stupid, and you didn't answer. And when the chief called me to ask what was going on, I looked like an idiot, like a dummy. If you had shown your face in front of me right then, I would have torn you apart; I would have killed you without an investigation or a trial, I was so angry. But, whatever. That's old news at this point."

"And Aït Hajj, Jaouad?"

"You're still asking about Aït Hajj after what you did?! Enough, man. You've destroyed the man. But let's forget about all of that. That's why I came here. Things have taken another turn, Naim. Today we find ourselves in a new situation that we need to deal with intelligently."

"What do you mean, Jaouad?"

"The whole world is worried about your arrest. Also, the electoral campaign started two days ago, and your case is feeding the electoral debate, conspicuously weaving you into it. A situation we all need to profit from intelligently."

"But what about me, Jaouad? How can I benefit from this? It looks like I'm going to appear before the court."

"It goes without saying that you'll appear before the court. What did you think?! But we'll follow the whole thing, so don't worry. You just have to deal with things better. You're no longer Naim Marzouk, secluded in his apartment on Anfa Boulevard writing his daily columns and getting likes and adoring comments and that's it. Today you are rich material for the national and international press, and for the politicians' records in the electoral campaign. Everyone's preoccupied with your case. Inside the country and out, particularly outside. You are now the symbol of freedom of the press in Morocco, and you have to behave accordingly, but in a disciplined way this time. You can't make any more mistakes. They'll continue their investigation today or tomorrow morning at the latest. Don't change your statements. Refuse to answer until there is a lawyer present, and remain steadfast in not revealing your sources. Gird yourself with the honor of the profession, and so forth and so on. I imagine you'll be brought before the eyes of justice within three days. In court you'll find dozens of lawyers backing you. Deny all the charges being leveled against you and say that your trial is a trial for freedom of expression in Morocco, then raise up the victory sign in front of the cameras and be done with it. Your role is small and limited. You need to stick to the script down to the letter, but you need to play it expertly. The issue of showering will be arranged today, so don't worry. Also, you'll get clean clothes, just as you'll get newspapers starting tomorrow so you can get a clearer idea of how things are developing. You just have to stick to the script, understood?"

Naim didn't understand a thing. Anyway, there was no time to go back over his breathless conversation with Jaouad, to turn it over and examine it from every angle. What was important right now was that the matter of the shower was finally going to be arranged. He imagined himself rubbing his body with the loofah and soap underneath the stream of water. A hot shower, or a cold one, it didn't matter. He hated his skin, and he hated how much he stank now. So, the image of water flowing down over his body played over in his imagination. He was dreaming of water. Of the shower. For the first time since arriving here, Naim felt deeply content. He closed his eyes on the image of the showerhead and slept deeply, the first deep sleep he had had since his arrest. He didn't wake up until noon. Just after noon.

77

THE LIONESS lay in wait for her prey for more than a month until she caught a glimpse of him—after the official launch of the electoral campaign—coming out of his electronic hiding to like a video of a speech delivered by the head of the party that Qamar Eddine had posted on his Facebook wall. The like wasn't enough for Emad; he shared the video on his wall, too. This is your chance, Lioness. The time for revenge has come, Hiyam.

Hiyam liked the video on Emad's wall, but the like wasn't enough so she gave it additional strength with a small, silent comment.

☺

A small smiley face inserted underneath the video was enough to draw the victim out. Immediately, a private message arrived from Emad.

"Good morning, glorious day! Finally, your sun shines on my face, princess. On this morning fit for a king. You can't imagine how happy I am that Princess Hiyam has finally humbled herself and honored me by passing by. Poor me, who had nearly lost all hope."

"As long as there is life, there is hope. ☺ Hahaha."

"More than a year has passed without you responding to my messages, Hiyam. How can I not despair? But enough with despair, now. Today I'm happy."

"And I'm very annoyed."

"How come, Hiyam? What could there still be in God's great creation that could annoy Hiyam or put her in a bad mood?"

"You. You, Emad."

"Me?! God forbid. What? What have I done?"

"How could you not have told me that you're a famous politician? You left me to find that out on my own. I walked out of my house only to find a beautiful picture of you on the wall facing our building. I ran into you this morning, so I smiled at you. But you didn't return my smile."

"My dear, that's on me. Your smile is a crown I wear on my head. But frankly, Hiyam, you were mean to me. You didn't give me the slightest chance to speak with you so you could get to know me better."

"I've changed my mind now, and I'm ready to meet with you. But, too bad, you have no time for me. You're busy with your electoral campaign."

"Never, Hiyam. You're more important than any campaign. I have all the time in the world for you."

"Then, would it work for us to meet Friday evening on the rooftop terrace of La Renaissance Café?"

"Just say the word, Hiyam."

"Five o'clock?"

"Okay, my dear."

"Five on the dot. And by the way, I'm punctual. I don't like to be kept waiting. If you're even a minute late, you won't find me there."

"Oh, I'll be there. I'll be at the café from four o'clock on. I like to torture myself a bit by counting the minutes that will come between when I get there and when my princess arrives."

"Hahaha. You're too kind, Emad. But what will you be wearing for me?"

"What?"

"I mean, how will you meet me? What color will you be wearing?"

"I don't know, Hiyam. But give me a bit of guidance, my dear. Just tell me."

"I like light colors. Do you have a pink shirt, for example? I'd like to see you in pink. The color of love and hope."

"Unfortunately, I don't have a shirt that color. But I'll buy one, Hiyam. For your princess eyes, I'll buy one. Your wish is my command."

"No, never. I'm a simple woman. All I'm asking of you is to come to me in pink, like a rose."

"You're the rose, Hiyam. You're the rose of all of Marrakech. Oh, how tired I'll be for these two days. Waiting for us to meet is going to be torture."

"Okay, Habibi, until we meet, then. Friday. Ciao."

"What did you say? 'Habibi'? Pinch me, I'm dreaming. Tell me I'm not dreaming."

But the Lioness disappeared. Her mission was accomplished and she went back into her den, leaving the Squirrel to take care of the rest. Rahhal bought a SIM card. He used it to send more than one message to Hiyam, Emad Qatifa's wife. He presented himself as a do-gooder, a woman who felt sorry for her. Because she was, like her, a wounded wife who had experienced the treachery and deceit of husbands, she wanted to warn her that some whore was intending to snatch her husband away: "If you'd like to be sure for yourself, you just need to go to the rooftop terrace of La Renaissance Café, where they've had a regular rendezvous for over a year. Just go this Friday evening and you'll see for yourself. Note: your husband will be wearing a new, pink shirt that he will have bought especially for her because she loves pink."

Rahhal left his phone on silent and watched it. Hiyam tried to call ten times. As if the Wild Cow had gone crazy. That evening, he didn't go up to his apartment until he was sure to have destroyed the SIM card and tossed it in the dumpster next to the building.

Monday night, Hassaniya was eating her dinner in front of the television as usual—Rahhal's fish tajine prepared for the following day's lunch, which she was tasting as she usually did, or that's what she claimed before eating almost half of it. But this time she was just tasting it. She seemed distracted as she ate without appetite. After a moment, she let out a small sigh.

"What's wrong, Hassaniya? Is everything alright?" Rahhal dared to ask.

"Nothing's wrong. Why? Do I look like something's wrong?"

"No. You just look a bit different, and I was worried you were sick."

"Nothing's wrong with me. Don't worry. Just calm down." She said it sharply, before letting out another sigh. Then she added, as if deep down inside she was hoping he would ask, because she needed to pour her heart out:

"Poor Emad . . ."

"What's wrong with Emad?"

"That madwoman of a wife came to him raving mad, and right in the middle of the campaign. Without warning she took the kids, went to her parents' house, and asked for a divorce. She claimed that Emad was cheating on her with someone else, and that she had caught him in the act. Of course, no one believed her. A crazy woman."

Rahhal didn't say a word. And he didn't tell the dim-witted Hedgehog that he, completely contrary to how she felt about it, believed Hiyam.

78

JAOUAD KEPT HIS PROMISE. The prison shower was put at Naim's disposal, and they brought clean clothes straight from his dresser. They brought him another tracksuit, clean underwear, and three towels. There was also a black suit, a light sky-blue shirt, socks, and shoes; necessities for his imminent court appearance, Naim guessed. What else? Toothbrush and toothpaste. Naim couldn't believe it. They knew his habits well. He couldn't imagine himself living without clean teeth. Even when he was invited to an important dinner at a nice place, he would bring a small toothbrush and a mini tube of toothpaste so he could brush his teeth right after eating. He has a strange obsession with clean teeth. For sure, not being able to brush them had annoyed him ever since his arrest, but he almost went crazy when he smelled how bad his breath was. He put his hand up to his mouth and breathed out, and his breath made him dizzy. Also, he couldn't stand the little bits of filth that had gotten caught above and in between his teeth during this time. That's why he considered this gesture in particular a special nod from his guardian angel, Jaouad.

The next day, the newspapers arrived. Naim had just come back from a second interrogation session and found the papers on his bed, arranged in order of publication date. The first ones were papers talking about the Mehdi Aït Hajj scandal, followed by brief mention of the disappearance of Naim Marzouk and the possibility that he had been arrested. Parties hostile to the Octopus Party found in these reports the chance to gain ground on the new party and slander it. The Camel Party, in particular, didn't let the opportunity pass. It issued a strongly worded statement condemning corruption and the corrupt, denouncing the suspicious political entities that wanted to illegitimately impose themselves on the national political scene by bringing together opportunists and denizens of corruption to swell their ranks. The Camel Party also requested that an investigation be opened to determine how reliable the dangerous information was that the brave journalist Naim Marzouk had included in his column. Naim was dying to know the upshot of the story. He flipped the stack of newspapers over and began to search from the end for today's papers. He pulled out a copy of the *Future*, and from the very first page he understood everything.

Naim was shocked by his picture in the middle of the page, in the space where his column usually appeared. There was a caption in red above the picture: "We stand with Naim Marzouk against any restrictions on free expression in our country." Naim was flabbergasted. Tanoufi's paper was publishing a caption as strong as this?! He didn't understand a thing. Below his picture there were two statements sharing the lower half of the page. Naim went right to the first one on the right-hand side. It was a statement from the Octopus Party. The statement baffled him. The Octopus Party was announcing the suspension of Mehdi Aït Hajj's membership and stripping him of all party responsibilities, pending word from the independent judiciary. Also, bending to public opinion, the Octopus Party was pulling its endorsement of Aït Hajj, "Who is currently out on bail after the convulsive information brought against him by the journalist Naim Marzouk. Even though the accused is innocent until proven guilty, our young party, which aspires to reconcile Moroccans with politics and to establish the rules of modern, clean, and honest politics," the statement added, "categorically refuses to introduce suspect candidates to the Moroccan people." On the other hand, the Octopus Party gave its assurance that it was anxiously following the situation of the journalist Naim Marzouk. "Even though the party insists on respecting the institutions of the state and has great confidence in our fair judiciary system, it fears that what Naim Marzouk is being subject to might augur a restriction of freedoms, freedom of the press in particular, and *that*, the party categorically rejects. The free Morocco that we seek calls for giving space to the independent press so it can participate in building democratic structures for this nation." Finally, the Octopus Party announced its strong support for a free press that exposes corruption and the corrupt, and then underlined its unconditional support for the journalist Naim Marzouk during his ordeal.

Only now did Naim grasp what Jaouad had said and appreciate the seismic effect his column had had. Could you have pictured that the Octopus Party would have taken up Mehdi Aït Hajj's case so slyly, Chameleon? They've led the poor guy to slaughter and left him to fend for himself. The second statement shocked Naim. Shit! Who could have imagined that? An article by Anouar Mimi reprinted by the *Future* on its front page from Hot Maroc (with permission), also in solidarity with you, Naim. Can you believe it? Anouar Mimi criticized the arbitrary arrest of "our dear colleague, Naim Marzouk." He considered it a threat to the independent free press, and an abnormal and repressive practice unbefitting of a free Morocco. "Journalists are not above the law," Mimi made clear, "but they also won't come to form that low wall before the symbols of corruption. And those who still long for past days of tyranny need to understand that the country—king and people alike—has opted for democracy. And freedom of expression is the basis of every democracy." Mimi also praised the wide embrace of the solidarity committee that he was honored to preside over on the part of human rights establishments inside the nation and out, and also by all the international organizations defending freedom of the press. And he didn't miss the opportunity to emphasize that the amazing solidarity the readers and citizens flooded those organizations with remains the most beautiful tribute to Naim and to all of those defenders of freedom of the press in this country. The last paragraph was dedicated to paying tribute to Naim Marzouk's seriousness and professionalism, emphasizing that the trials he was facing right now were also being faced by the free national press, and his battles were battles for all honorable journalists in the country. Signed: Anouar Mimi, editor in chief of Hot Maroc and president of the National Committee in Solidarity with Naim Marzouk.

Were you expecting all this from the Mongoose, Chameleon? Deep down, you despised him, and you had started to denigrate him in the editorial rooms at the *Future* and Hot Maroc. And here he is today, proving to you that he's smarter and craftier than you. The bastard! He killed the man, and then went to his funeral. And he wasn't content just to follow the procession like everyone else. No, he walked up in front and received condolences in place of the deceased's family!

■   ■   ■

At 11:00 a.m., the guard opened the cell door and two clean-shaven police officers sauntered in, wearing their official uniforms. They respectfully asked Naim to prepare himself. The trial would take place that morning. In the police van, the police officers sat on either side of Naim. He sat in between them, although they didn't sit too close. His mind wandered as he tried to gather his thoughts, which were scattered like a flock of mountain sheep. One of the policemen whispered:

"It appears we're late."

"Yep. We're late."

"Yesterday they told me we had to be at the court by 10:00 a.m."

"Yeah, 10:00 would have been better. I don't know why the police chief was late this morning. I've been ready since 8:00."

"I came before 8:00. What time is it?"

"11:30. We'll get to the courthouse after noon."

"Yep. We're late. I can't imagine the pictures will appear in the afternoon newscast."

"No, I don't think so either. We're too late. But they'll put them on the evening news for sure."

"True. But the afternoon newscast is the most important. People watch that one more than the others."

"But even the evening news has a large audience."

"No, no one watches the evening news these days because it conflicts with the evening prayer time. People are at the mosque then."

"But still, it enjoys a good following. Not everyone goes to the mosque to pray."

"True, true. Not everyone prays."

Naim wasn't following the two policemen's conversation. He was trying in vain to organize his thoughts, imagining what the scene would be like when they got there. As if he were just listening to the two policemen talk about the afternoon and evening news. He didn't see how it had anything to do with him. But as soon as the van stopped in front of the courthouse and he saw the two of them smoothing their clothes and straightening one another's tie before getting out, he understood. The idiots, they wanted to appear on television at his expense.

There was more than one camera. And a large sit-in in front of the courthouse door. Journalists and human rights activists chanting slogans that grew more explosive as the van parked. More than one national and international channel was filming around the courthouse. As soon as Naim stepped out of the van, Ibrahim Tanoufi, surrounded by his two editors in chief, rushed toward him. Tanoufi threw himself at Naim and buried his head in his chest by way of a hug before lifting his head and yelling out loud in a quavering voice as he squeezed Naim's shoulders, "You are not alone, Naim. The *Future* is with you. The whole *Future* is with you."

Amazing. Tanoufi stands publicly with you, Naim. When did this coward drink from the cup of bravery?

Not far off, Anouar Mimi was giving a statement to a French television station. As soon as he finished, he turned his gaze toward the Chameleon. Naim stopped for a moment and shot a look at his adversary, but Mimi faced him with a neutral look. He was wearing an orange shirt with "We are all Naim Marzouk" printed on it in black. Mimi raised the victory sign in his face and stood frozen there like a soldier saluting.

You raise the victory sign in my face, you scoundrel? You want to provoke me?! You're raising the sign of your victory over me. Naim wished the plaza in front of the courthouse were empty. If they had been alone in that open space, he would have stuck out his long, chameleon tongue and shown the hateful mongoose what a chameleon could do with it. But the cameras are bearing down on you, Naim, and you have to remain calm. Don't let the Mongoose upset you.

Mimi insistently and furiously raised the victory sign in Naim's face, leveling a dry stare directly at him. Shit, Naim. He doesn't stand in solidarity with you! He's just reminding you of the instructions. Ah, Jaouad's instructions. Shit.

Naim raised the victory sign. He directed it toward the crowds of demonstrators, who were being kept from getting too close to the van by the quick reaction forces, then toward the cameras focused on him to take the historic picture. There was more than one camera, too. The two policemen stood on either side of Naim, smiling into the cameras. It was almost one o'clock. The poor guys had missed the afternoon newscast, so they sought the chance to set things right with this picture. At least they could expect their picture with Naim Marzouk to be in the papers tomorrow.

79

HE HAD GOTTEN SO CLOSE to that elusive shiver that made him fly, body and soul, so high for a few seconds in the heavens of the room when Hassaniya punched him. It wasn't the quill prick of a hedgehog, but rather a punch on his right side that took Rahhal's breath away. Somewhere between pleasure and pain.

"Why, Hassaniya? What did I do?" he would have asked her if only his breath would have let him.

Hassaniya pushed him off of her and turned away. Rahhal didn't know what he had done. He had closed his eyes in order to open them in his imagination to the killer eyes of the Wild Cow. He had pulled Hiyam by her great neck and threw her violently and wildly to the ground. He buried his face between her breasts and planted his sword inside her. He was just about to reach the peak of ecstasy when the damned Hedgehog winded him with a punch. Now she had turned her back on him and became still. As if she had gone to sleep. But what did you do, Rahhal? What offense did you commit to make her punch you like that? It was the first time she had done that. True, she would explode in your face from time to time. She might push you away in a fit of anger. But to punch you with her fist and take your breath away? This was the first time she had done that. He touched his penis and felt the sticky fluid. If only he could squeeze it to get more out, to empty it and relax, but he was afraid to anger the Hedgehog by moving, so he left his erect penis alone. He got up gently to turn out the light, then calmly went back to occupy his place on the edge of the bed. He was careful not to allow his body to come into contact with the Hedgehog's. That would be the safest way to go. He closed his eyes and tried to go to sleep.

But Hassaniya wasn't asleep. Hassaniya was silently sobbing. The bastard had wounded her. He said it without even knowing. He was just about to reach his moment of pleasure when he moaned, "Hiyam." Was he imagining that he was riding *her*? That disgusting rat! And it wasn't the first time. Hassaniya remembers a night when Rahhal's rude ramblings woke her up. He was mumbling, sweating, and he clearly called out her name: "Hiyam!" Then he went back to snoring. That whore. How did she bewitch them all?

Sleep fought with Hassaniya's eyes. She went way back into her memory. She was a teenager helping her mom at work on holidays and Sundays at Hajj Qatifa's house. Hassaniya was happy every chance she got to go to Hajj Qatifa's house only because she would meet her handsome knight there. Emad. She used to be in love with him. Still is. She never loved anyone else. And to this day she doesn't know how to cure herself of him and her love for him. He used to occupy her dreams. A casual smile from him was enough for her to walk around in a daze for a week. That's why she would go to their house whether or not there was any reason to. That's why she went with Oum Eid on that sweltering hot Sunday. Hajj Maâti Blayghi and his family had been invited for lunch at Hajj Qatifa's, so she went to help prepare the feast for the guests. Hassaniya was never any good at cooking; in fact, she hated to cook. But to run into Emad, she was ready to do anything. She stood next to her mother. She handed her whatever dishes she needed. She set the table with her and helped her wash the dishes afterward. That Sunday, her mom was sick. But she didn't tell her boss, the Hajja, how weak she was so as not to let her down, especially knowing how important Hajj Maâti Blayghi was to the Qatifa family. So, she went, and Hassaniya went with her.

Hajj Qatifa didn't treat Oum Eid like a servant. He was generous with her. He'd pay her before her sweat had even dried. He treated her as a neighbor. That's why Hassaniya and her mom ate lunch with them during these feasts and special occasions as if they were members of the family. Even though there was a special table set for the men in the salon that day, which Hajj Qatifa, Hajj Maâti, and Abdelmoula gathered around, Emad mischievously preferred to eat his food with the women. Because of her. Because of that arrogant Hiyam. He didn't take his eyes off of her, while she intentionally ignored him. Even when he laid on the charm or said something funny and the women would laugh, she wouldn't laugh. *I would laugh and be happy and love him even more, though. I would laugh to get his attention so he could see how happy I was with him. But he only wanted to make* her *laugh. And she tortured him. Everyone knew that he loved her and that she was torturing him, and no one would say a thing. Her family was proud of her academic excellence, and everyone knew that Emad's path in school was nothing to boast about.*

After lunch, Hiyam's mother asked the Hajja to let the girls accompany her to spend the night at her place for a change of scene, and she agreed. The girls left with Hiyam and her mom. Hajj Qatifa and Hajj Maâti went straight to the market. Abdelmoula went off to the college. And we stayed behind alone. Oum Eid was sick, so I told her to take a break and stay with the Hajja so they could drink tea together while I went up to the roof to wash the dishes in her place.

Was it really that hot? Was it because I had gotten my dress all wet that I left it to dry a bit while I finished up? Or was it because a teenaged girl intoxicated with love for a handsome boy wanted to free up her body. The important thing was that I had taken off my dress and was wearing just a see-through slip that showed my underpants, the only thing I was wearing underneath. My breasts were too small to require a bra. Was Emad watching me without my knowing it? I was bent over the dishes when I felt his hands wrap around me from behind. I turned to find him there. Emad. His face was flushed with desire. I couldn't believe it. I couldn't believe that it was him. The handsome prince of my dreams. As if I were in a dream. Breathing heavily, he pulled me toward him and started to kiss my neck. His breaths were hot. I completely melted. Like a small sugar cube dissolves in water. Emad pulled me to the little room on the roof. I followed him in a daze as my heart pounded. He laid me out on an old siddari bench that the women would crowd onto when they went up to the roof together to clean beans or split olives. There, he lifted my short, see-through clothes and removed my underpants. I didn't put up any resistance. But as soon as he lowered his pants and brandished his sword in my face, I fainted. When I came to, I found his penis between my legs. He was struggling to get it inside me. I wanted to embrace him. To take him in fully and lock him in there once and for all. I opened my legs so my beloved could penetrate me. I felt a bit of pain. But I found pleasure in it. I opened up more. I wanted him to go in further. To go deeper. I wanted Emad to go so far in that I would give birth to him again. So that he would be my child who knew only me. So that he would only look at me when we were at the table eating. Ah, Emad. Ah, my child. He was panting on top of me as I melted underneath him. I felt a bliss I had never felt before. I felt him turn into hot, sticky water. Seeping inside me, in my heart and my soul as I held onto him with a weak, shivering joy. The door to the rooftop room was open. It closed suddenly. No, it didn't close. It was just that the light was covered over. As if the sun had been blocked all of a sudden. No, not blocked. Just the two of them were there. They stood there, astonished. Oum Eid who was sick, was trembling, as if a cold wind had blown over her from somewhere, before the Hajja let out a tormented scream: "Oh my God! Oh my God! Oh my God!"

Bewildered, Emad got up off of me. As for me, I fainted.

Did Hajj Qatifa ever learn of the incident? Did the Hajja tell him that I had lost my virginity and that his son was the one who had eaten the apple? Emad stayed away from me after that. The Hajj also started to avoid me, and Oum Eid started to go over there on her own. She told me that the Hajj had stopped accepting the paltry rent money we used to pay him for the place in Douiria. Instead, he arranged to give my mother a fixed monthly stipend. And despite that, he continued to follow what was going on with me. I put on the hijab when I enrolled in the university. Doing what dignity required. Emad married Hiyam, the love of his life. And when Oum Eid told the Hajja that one of my colleagues at the college had proposed to me, Hajj Qatifa was very happy to hear it. He insisted that my hand be asked for directly through him. He said that all the costs were on him. Did he feel guilty? But what did he do? I'm the one who fell in love with Emad and wanted him to be my baby. My baby who was only three years younger than me. But it was Hiyam he loved. And it was her that he had chosen.

The many times I recalled what happened on the roof, I remembered Emad penetrating me in my semiconsciousness, saying her name. He was inside me, panting on top of me, and moaning, "Hiyam."

80

THE CAMPAIGN was in full swing when Emad suddenly walked
into the cybercafe that morning. Asmae was just putting a cup of
coffee down in front of Yazid. Emad greeted Rahhal with a fleet-
ing smile and headed straight over to Yazid. He was happy to see
Asmae. He asked her to get him an espresso right away; his head was
about to explode, as he put it to her. He sat and chatted with Yazid.
His face was gloomy. In the midst of the campaign, Qatifa looked
deflated, having lost his initial enthusiasm. He was unshaven and
his eyelids showed signs of sleeplessness. Rahhal didn't like to see
Emad like this. He felt sorry for him. The poor guy. The Wild Cow
and the Lioness had allied themselves against him while the elections were in full swing. Those two damned girls had pounced on
him and the spark that had once shone in his eyes had gone out.

Rahhal was scrunched up in his chair. His head was buried in
the screen. Still, he knew how and when to steal a glance of Yazid
and Emad to watch their exchange. He was surprised by the confidence with which Yazid talked about what was going on. He was
encouraged by the absent-minded way Emad listened, and went on
at length as if speaking at an event. Yazid was speaking enthusiastically and moving his hands all over the place while Emad humored
him with mechanical nods as his eyes darted around. No doubt
Yazid was bringing Emad up to speed on the new dimensions that
the Snail Affair had taken in Marrakech. He might have also been
telling him about the arrangements that were being made by members of the regional branch so that the electoral rally the party was
organizing at the Royal Theater of Marrakech that evening would
go well. And specifically that the regional secretariat of the Octopus
Party would rely heavily on the presence of the party leader, the
distinguished religious scholar Abu Ayoub Mansouri, to face the

Camel Party's adversaries with the final word about this invented affair, which the press had dubbed the Battle of the Snails. Suddenly, the telephone rang. It's your cell phone, Squirrel. At first, Rahhal didn't answer, confused and scared. But the phone started ringing again, insistently this time.

Emad cast him a look of annoyance, so Rahhal had to answer, if for no other reason than to stop it from ringing. It was Ayad.

"Hello, Uncle. I'm busy now. Call back later," Rahhal whispered, wanting to end the call quickly.

"No, my boy. Hold on, hold on, please. I want to tell you something. Your father, Abdeslam, may God forgive him and us."

"Amen, Uncle. Amen. May God forgive all of us. But as I said, I'm busy now. I just need to finish up with something and then I'll call you back. Okay? Bye. Say hi to him and my mother. Bye."

"Say hi to who, Rahhal? Are you really such a dumbass? I'm telling you your father passed away. God took him this morning. We're going to bury him after the noon prayer. And you tell me to say hi to him . . ."

The cell phone fell from his hand. Rahhal could hear Ayad on the other end repeating, "Hello? Hello?" But there was no hand to hold the phone, no voice to respond, and no strength to continue the conversation. He felt as fragile as a matchstick. Cold and heavy like a wet wool coat. His heart was pounding. A cold shiver came over him all of a sudden before the trembling wrapped itself around his body as if it were a blanket of ice. He felt weak, unable even to lift his head to look around. If only he could have broken into hot sobbing. But his voice betrayed him and the tears hardened in his eyes. He had never heard the expression "may God forgive him and us" that his uncle had surprised him with. He didn't understand at first that it was a formula announcing a death, and that Ayad was offering his condolences for his father.

Rahhal didn't know whether it was the shock that tied his tongue and paralyzed him and made him go stiff in his chair, or his natural cowardice? He continued to shiver as if invisible snowflakes were falling only on him. Suddenly, Emad rushed out when he saw that he was getting a call, then Yazid followed like a starving dog. Luckily, Qamar Eddine looked up as soon as they left, and appeared as a life preserver to Rahhal. Rahhal asked him to fill in for him as he would be out for the rest of the day. Qamar Eddine tried to make an excuse; because his obligations—obligations to the campaign—obliged him to be ready to move at any moment. But Rahhal begged him, which softened up Qamar Eddine and he agreed, taking the keys from him. Rahhal didn't explain a thing to him, just as he didn't think for even a moment about calling Hassaniya, as if it didn't concern her. In the shared taxi he was jammed in back with three other passengers. The passengers chatted with the driver. They were talking about the electoral struggle that had become quite intense between the Octopus and the Camel Parties, whereas Rahhal was thinking about the Mantis, who had suddenly departed.

You won't see the Mantis anymore, Rahhal. You won't see that man from Abda who lived his whole life defeated and isolated from the world and everyone in it. You'll never see him again. The tears finally pooled up in his eyes and flowed hot over his cheeks as if there was water boiling inside him because of the surprise call from Ayad this morning, and now it boiled over and gushed.

81

WHO WOULD HAVE IMAGINED that a fierce, heated battle would break out between the Camel and the Octopus Parties over some snails? But that's exactly what happened. It's true that Moroccans were used to ideological battles breaking out with every election season during the era of ideologies, when the parties still lined up in clear, ideological trenches. But things were quite different now. People didn't have the energy anymore for these abstract debates, especially for party principles and political plans. People wanted carnivalesque elections, complete with show and spectacle; song and dance; feasts and banquets; small, palpable gains they would win during the campaign. In the end, all candidates are the same. All of them will disappear to work for their own interests and become important people in the capital. You'll only see them on TV when live broadcasts of parliamentary sessions are shown—that is, if they are among the minority who bother to attend. Other than that, you won't see their bright, shining faces until the next elections six years later. That's why people don't care too much how things end up. What they are concerned with is the ritual of the electoral race itself. It attracts them like a show, the different wrangling acts that they follow with bated breath. They don't follow it as heavy, political discussion. That's why for the two strongest parties, the Snail Affair was a chance to give their electoral conflict a deep, intellectual dimension, but without neglecting two crucial elements: an element of proximity to the daily life of citizens (since snails are one of the most important popular foods in Marrakech, and squabbling about it remains at the heart of hot popular topics), and an element of provocation, which is essential for attracting more citizens to join and follow the political scene.

The scandal started when a number of new carts were distributed to the itinerant snail vendors during a large rally organized by the Octopus Party in November 6 Square in the heart of Gueliz. More than thirty carts were distributed to vendors from different parts of the city. Yazid, who attended the celebration as a representative for Massira and the surrounding areas, got four carts—one that he kept for himself for Rabih to use as soon as the campaign was over, and three other carts, which he distributed in the name of the party's candidate, Emad Qatifa, to Fat Masmoudi and two of his friends who were among the most well-known snail vendors on Dakhla Avenue. It wasn't clear whether the carts had been ready for a while to be distributed as part of the National Initiative for Human Development, and Bachir Lamrabti and his comrades had managed to grab them using their crooked means and delay their allocation in order to use them in the campaign after securing a monopoly over distribution. This would have been in collusion with members of the Marrakech municipal government who had joined the party right before the elections and had become dedicated to serving its foot soldiers, exploiting all the resources at the city's disposal. Or perhaps it was one of the wealthy members of the party who donated these carts to the Octopus Party, which means it had something to do with shameless electoral bribes that the other parties had every right to protest.

The Camel Party activists didn't let the opportunity slip away. They issued a strongly worded statement criticizing the operation, condemning it, claiming that this incident should be deemed electoral fraud, and calling for the Ministry of the Interior and the Ministry of Justice to get involved to put a stop to it. This was before they entered into a transparent and frank national discussion with the snail vendors, a discussion that wasn't at all fruitful. In fact, things did not go at all as expected, especially after this free, direct discussion with the snail vendors ended with two party activists in the emergency room of Ibn Tofail Hospital.

Saleh Regoug, regional secretary of the Camel Party, realized the extreme danger that the youth wing of the party posed. How can you convince a snail vendor, happy with his new cart, that he is involved in a case of electoral fraud, and that he must bear responsibility for it? What responsibility, for God's sake? A man standing on the street corner behind a cart with a big, steaming pot in the middle of it, surrounded by customers enjoying themselves as they sip the spicy, hot snail broth redolent with wild thyme, anise, lavender, caraway, nutmeg, and slices of lemon, taking pleasure in devouring the snails, which they extract from their shells with a small, sharp pin, and you come along and accuse him of corruption and fraud? Saleh Regoug's pragmatism forced him to admit that the two young party members ending up in Ibn Tofail Hospital was a logical result, and absolute proof of the inefficiency of this kind of communication. He decided to change tactics, to turn the heat up on the battle, to deliver the fatal blow without entering into direct contact with the citizens. So, he reached out to the party's council of religious scholars in the capital and asked them to issue a religious fatwa ruling against eating snails. And he got exactly what he wanted.

The fatwa was conclusive, airtight. The Camel Party's council of religious scholars cited a fatwa from the sheikh of Islam, Ibn Taymiyya, which asserts: "Eating impure things, snakes, and scorpions is absolutely forbidden according to the consensus of Muslims. He who eats them, thinking that it is permissible, must be called on to repent. Otherwise, he is to be killed." That was before they strengthened their argument with another, much clearer fatwa, which came from Imam Ibn Hazm, who said: "It is not permissible to eat snails or any insects, including geckos, beetles, ants, bees, flies, wasps, all types of worms, lice, fleas, ticks, and mosquitoes." Then, they concluded their fatwa with a straight Shafi'ite prohibition of this type of worm, with the justification that it was impure. God's words are clear in this regard, for he has clearly prohibited His servants from impure things.

The Camel Party's statement, which incorporated the entire text of the party's religious scholars' fatwa, also contained a curious paragraph that Saleh Regoug had added at the last minute, criticizing Octopus Party positions that cater to homosexuals and perverts by claiming to defend individual freedoms. It came as no surprise to him, then, that this dubious party would defend this lecherous worm, known in scientific circles for its homosexual tendencies. For one snail, the statement detailed, has two reproductive organs—one male and one female—and it secretes male and female gametes at the same time. Despite that, some people want us to eat these hermaphroditic creatures and to force them—wrongly and unjustly—into the category of all the good things that have been provided. *Ah, evil is that they judge!* Trust in Almighty God.

82

"THERE WAS NOTHING WRONG WITH HIM. We called him for breakfast, but he didn't want to come. When we insisted and called again, he came reluctantly. He drank a glass of tea, no more, then went back to his corner."

Halima was sobbing as she spoke. Her face was dim; her white mourning clothes made it even paler.

Ayad added, "Son, when we cleared the breakfast dishes, I went to him to see if he would go with me to the market, and I found him rigid. It was clear to me that he had died from the way he was all slumped over and the way the skin on his face looked, not to mention the fact that he wasn't breathing. I didn't say anything to Halima. I said, 'Let's make sure.' I went out and knocked on Si Ali's door. We know he's a believer. God-fearing and religious. He came back with me, may God reward him. As soon as he saw him he said, 'To God we belong, and to Him we shall return.'"

Si Ali coughed to demonstrate his humility in the face of Ayad's praise of him. He was younger than forty, despite looking older than that. Si Ali patted Rahhal's shoulder, and rubbed his thick beard as he continued, confirming what his uncle had said:

"It's God's judgment, my friend, and God's judgment is final. From the moment I laid eyes on him, I knew that he was dead. Praise God the Almighty. The dead cannot be concealed. From his sunken cheeks and the way the eyes were glazed over, I knew he was dead. The poor man died suddenly. Sudden death is a blessing and lifts the burdens of death; it is an act of forgiveness from the Lord when the deceased was virtuous, and it is vengeance and fury on the sinners, for the High Almighty rushes those ones to death before they can repent. He doesn't give them time to make up for their neglect and their shortcomings."

Rahhal was standing in the middle of the three of them in front of his old room, the room that his father had taken as a refuge in his final years. One of Si Ali's brothers in God was washing Abdeslam. He had volunteered to do it and brought the shroud and aromatic *hanout* ointment. Si Ali told them, "My friend, Musa, is a God-fearing man who fears death. He always keeps shrouds and *hanout* in his house, saying to everyone, 'If any one of you goes to meet the Almighty Creator before I do, I've got his shroud and *hanout*. So, I'll wash him myself, just as the Prophet Muhammad, son of Abdallah, the purest of blessings upon him, was washed; a washing according to tradition that will not contain a drop of irreligious innovation.' That's why I thought of him immediately this morning. Because Abdeslam, may God have mercy on him, is our brother, and is one of us."

The matter of washing and preparing Abdeslam's body was facilitated by God, who provided someone to take on that responsibility out of sincere faith and pursuit of God's pleasure. But what about the other arrangements, Ayad?

Luckily, Ayad had attended more than one electoral meeting of Taoufik Bahi, the representative of Moukef and Kechich in the municipality council, and a nominee for the Ant Party in the current elections. And because it was an occasion that Taoufik Bahi would not allow to go to waste while the campaign was in full swing, it was his chance to show the residents how dedicated he was in serving them, so he tasked one of his assistants who lived in the neighborhood—a fellow known by the name of Afshi—to do what needed to be done. Afshi brought the doctor from the Office of the Medical Examiner to prepare a declaration of death less than an hour after Abdeslam's death. He obtained the death certificate and burial permit, and took care of bringing the local council van that Taoufik Bahi put at their disposal to take the body to the cemetery.

The funeral wasn't anything remarkable. Abdeslam was an unknown figure in the neighborhood with no friends or acquaintances. So it was just Rahhal, Ayad, and four of their neighbors who participated, along with three of Taoufik Bahi's men, led by Afshi, and a few mosque attendees, in addition to Si Ali and Musa, who knew how much value God places on those who accompany the dead to their final resting place. The municipality van dedicated to funerals left with the dead body from in front of the mosque after the noon and funeral prayers. Ayad climbed in beside the driver and said to him, "To Bab El Khemis Cemetery, God willing."

But when the procession arrived at the cemetery, it was empty besides the graves. Even the beggars and rosewater vendors were gone that afternoon. There was no one there. Luckily, Rahhal noticed a cell phone number written in green paint at the entrance. He tried the number. He was still thinking about what to say when the voice on the other end surprised him:

"Is this about a death?"

"Yes, we have a dead person. We're here at Bab El Khemis Cemetery."

"Okay, I'm close by. I'll be there in five minutes. Look for Boumehdi, the gravedigger, and ask him to prepare his things for when I get there."

"There's nobody here. The cemetery is completely deserted."

"Okay. I know where he'll be, the son of a bitch. He'll be in front of the pumpkin patch, as usual. Not far from the cemetery. I'll pick him up and come. Don't worry. We won't be long."

The wait was heavy. Musa, the one who washed the body, took the opportunity to start in on his sermon as we waited for the cemetery guard and gravedigger to come. He talked about death: "The most generous Prophet urged us to remember death and to not ignore it. He said, 'Talk often about the one thing that ends all pleasures: death.' And he talked about the hour, the Day of Judgment that was approaching, and about how sudden death was one of the signs and portents of that hour. And one of the prayers of the Prophet of God, peace and blessings upon him, was: 'God, I take refuge in You from the end of Your grace, and the loss of good health, and the suddenness of Your vengeance, and all of Your fury.' Death that comes suddenly is one kind of sudden vengeance, and may God protect us all."

At that moment, Boumehdi rushed in with the guard following behind. The mute gravedigger rushed over to the trunk of the Mastic tree. He prepared his digging tools and asked the guard using sign language and facial expressions: "Where?"

"Really? Where? We have graves for two hundred dirhams and others for seven hundred dirhams in good spots where it's easy to get to for those visiting later, so which do you prefer?"

Afshi challenged him by responding in dramatic fashion:

"Give us a seven-hundred-dirham grave, man. Do you think the deceased is worth so little to us?" Afshi replied in a grandiloquent tone, flashing a false look of reproach and looking around the group to see what effect his intervention had had on the faces there.

The guard took the money, counted it, gave Afshi the grave number, then started to shuffle through the papers before shouting out in anguish:

"What's this, guys?! Here's your money back. No burial. This funeral isn't ours. You need to go to Bab Aghmat Cemetery. According to the deceased's national ID card, you're covered by Bab Aghmat, not us."

Ayad began to tremble with rage, then he yelled in the guard's face:

"What the hell are you talking about with your Bab Aghmat or Bab Rat's Ass? The dead man's cemetery is right here. He was here all the time, and today we have to bury him in his cemetery!"

"Excuse me? I don't get it! Do you mean to say that the deceased has prior experience with death and burials? That this isn't his first death?" the guard scoffed.

Ayad would have sprung forward to respond if Rahhal hadn't pulled him by his sleeve. What would you say to him, you obstinate rat? That he was a member of the army of Qur'an reciters who crowd around people visiting the graves of their loved ones and invade their privacy with their jarring recitations? He'll despise us even more and you'll humiliate us in front of everyone.

Musa and Ali took a few of steps back since they didn't understand much about administrative matters. But Afshi intervened to calm things down. He kissed the guard's head and pulled him away from the others. Their negotiations lasted a few minutes. Afshi put his hand into his pocket. It looked like he gave the guard some money to look the other way, and that's exactly what happened. Afshi came back all puffed up like a rooster. With a look of victory on his face, he shouted to the group:

"Let's go bury the deceased, men."

Boumehdi was shoveling dirt on the body while Afshi tried to plunge into an improvised prayer, all imbued with his victory, before being interrupted by Musa, who found it to be an opportune time to retake the lead. He chided him roughly and asked him to be quiet before addressing the group of mourners out loud:

"Beg forgiveness for your brother, and pray for his strength, for he is now being asked to answer for his deeds. But quietly, please."

That night, after the evening prayer, the house was full of large dishes of couscous the neighbors had prepared to feed all those coming to pay their respects. But no one came. Ali and Musa waited around for a little bit. Musa had prepared his sermon. But there was no audience for him there. He and his comrade finished off a plate of couscous with chicken, onion, raisins, and chickpeas, then left. The Pelican and the Rat were holed up in the kitchen. The sound of the Qur'an reciter 'Abd al-Basit 'Abd al-Samad brought some comfort to the house. Rahhal's tears flowed again. Then he remembered Hassaniya. He called her.

She had just returned home. She said that she wouldn't wait up for him. She'd eat dinner and go straight to bed, because she was completely exhausted.

Rahhal told her that he wasn't at the cybercafe.

"I'm in Moukef, Hassaniya. At my family's house in Moukef. My poor father, Abdeslam, may God have mercy on him. He died today."

Hassaniya was quiet for a bit. Rahhal remained listening, then he heard her sobbing. She sobbed a little bit at first, then began to weep. She was crying like she never had before.

83

SALEH REGOUG hadn't imagined that his party's last statement, especially its fatwa prohibiting snails, would cause such an uproar in the streets of Marrakech. But the snail fatwa became the talk of the town. Your camel, Saleh, has run off. Further than you were expecting. It has caused utter chaos among the people. Even women in the hammams discussed this calamity, and there was more than one case of fainting recorded in the women's hammams of the Old City after a fight broke out between some bathers from the two warring parties; women who couldn't bear the heat of debate *and* the heat of the hammam. Even Qamar Eddine found his father talking to him about it at the dinner table. Shihab Eddine Assuyuti, who sided with the Camel Party, seemed convinced of the fatwa prohibiting snails. As for Qamar Eddine, he found it difficult to go along with his father on this issue, not only because of his proximity to the Octopus Party and his work with Yazid in the party's electoral campaign, but really because he loved snail broth and insisted on having a bowl of it every evening when it was cold out.

The Octopus Party found itself in a difficult situation and had to find a solution as soon as possible. First off, it had to put a stop to the Camel Party before it caused any more damage. It wasn't right that the Camel Party resorted to its council of religious scholars to issue a fatwa for every social issue. This was a gross misuse of religion in a political battle that the party categorically rejected. Then there was Ibn Taymiyya's fatwa that the Camel Party brandished in the face of the Moroccan public known for its strong passion for snail soup and tasty snail meat. I mean, really, what does it mean that "He who eats them must be called on to repent. Otherwise, he is killed"? This clear call to murder is punishable under the law. Of course, since Ibn Taymiyya has been dead for centuries, he couldn't be tried today, but those who dared to resuscitate the fatwa, to wave it under society's nose, had to be prosecuted. And then, even if we decided to please Ibn Taymiyya, who would apply the death penalty? Members of the party? Who? And would we kill half of all Moroccans just because of snails? It would be a true *fitna*, chaos. And *fitna* is more serious than killing. So, the party needed to find a quick solution. It became clear that whichever party won the Battle of the Snails would win the elections in Marrakech, no question.

Only in hard times do we understand leaders' abilities. Some leaders of the Octopus Party, subservient to the progressive modernists who secretly made fun of this turbaned sheikh who attended meetings of the general secretariat with them and who left immediately after the work was done without accompanying them to the fancy restaurants where they would continue their militant soirées, finally admitted how visionary their leader, Moha Sinhaji, was. The way he linked a key religious authority such as the Malikite jurist Sheikh Abu Ayoub Mansouri with the party's general secretariat was brilliant. Only now did they appreciate it. In that regard, the party decided to hold an electoral rally, the theme of which would be the Snail Affair, and Sheikh Abu Ayoub Mansouri would be tasked with responding to the Camel Party's religious scholars and exposing their incoherence and the fraudulent nature of their fatwas.

Qamar Eddine was really sorry that the Squirrel, who had been gone since this morning, had him trapped in the cybercafe. He found himself tied to the shop, which meant he couldn't attend the speech that, in addition to members of the Octopus Party, was attended by numerous lovers of snail meat who were alarmed by Ibn Taymiyya's fatwa, as well as a number of Camel Party activists who went with the sole purpose of fighting and defending the fatwa issued by their religious scholars' council. Shihab Eddine Assuyuti went to attend the meeting, whereas Qamar Eddine was held hostage in the Squirrel's burrow.

Luckily, Daba Marrakech decided to stream the speech live online. That way, Qamar Eddine could follow the whole thing from his corner of the cybercafe. Yazid had parked three tourist buses in front of the cybercafe. Ridouane Aït Bey, one of the tycoons of tourist transport in Morocco, had put them at the party's disposal. Ridouane was a man who had remained far from politics before numerous problems with the tax authorities forced him to join the Octopus Party in the hopes that they might guarantee him some immunity. The Atlas Cubs occupied two buses: one for the school cubs and the other for the cyber cubs. Whereas a third bus was for Masmoudi and his snail-selling friends from Massira, Douar Iziki, Azli, Socoma, Douar Laâskar, Bahja, and Inara. Out of the required show of support under circumstances like these, they were accompanied by Larbi, the owner of Café Milano, Mbarek the sausage sandwich vendor, and Tamou the *beghrir* pancake seller.

The Royal Theater was jam-packed. Most people, of course, were from the Octopus Party, but there was a bloc of Camel Party youth on the far-right side of the open theater. Choosing this theater as the venue for this public meeting made sense, especially considering the fact that the theater was faulty and not suitable at all for theatrical performances according to technical reports prepared by Moroccan and international experts. Events of this sort of animal comedy might have been more fitting. All the national newspaper and website journalists were there. There were a lot of cameras around the podium, not to mention the Daba Marrakech camera, which made its mark by livestreaming this decisive electoral meeting.

Bachir Lamrabti ascended the podium first to the applause of the attendees and shouts from the party activists. He was followed by Bouchaib Makhloufi, who was wearing a designer jellaba. He stood before the gathering and tested the microphone. Then, he and Bachir turned to the podium and started to clap before Sheikh Abu Ayoub appeared, strutting toward them in a white jellaba, a gray burnoose, and a red fez on his head. His face gave off an air of magnanimity, and his beard was combed with care. The theater erupted with applause. The Elephant threw himself onto his hand and kissed it (it turned out that Sheikh Abu Ayoub had taught him in college during his Rabat years, and showing respect in this clear manner in front of everyone was one of the characteristics of the venerable elephant society). Bachir was happy to give a short welcome to the pious sons of Marrakech who had flocked to this blessed rally, and to welcome the venerable Sheikh Abu Ayoub Mansouri, "First and foremost a great scholar, then a distinguished leader in the general secretariat of our venerable party." Then he handed the microphone to Makhloufi, the meeting's moderator.

Makhloufi's scientific discourse was indeed remarkable. He emphasized the fact that snails were part of the animal kingdom, and that he considered their classification among insects to be a grave scientific error, which could be forgiven in Ibn Hazm's case, but not for the religious jurists of today. Makhloufi also rejected the notion that a weak land creature that feeds itself on cabbage and leaves could be impure, and reminded the audience of the nutritional value of snails, which contain minerals such as magnesium, phosphorus, and potassium, in addition to zinc, iron, and selenium, as well as many vitamins too numerous to name, including vitamins the Creator put specifically in *them* and not in other animals and plants. Likewise, he made sure to take issue with the Camel Party accusing this poor animal of sexual deviation. This is where Makhloufi got really angry, losing his self-control and flying into a rage, shouting into the microphone: "Isn't it enough for you to defame your political opponents and accuse them of depravity and debauchery? But do you have to then move from people to animals? Aren't you ashamed of leveling this charge of sexual deviation at an innocent creature of God? If you really had eyes, and looked at God's creation and took heed, you would notice that this innocent creature can teach us something about fasting. When we fast for one month a year, we grumble and complain of hunger and thirst, whereas this pure and virtuous creature fasts for three consecutive months without grumbling or complaining. So, fear God, O People of the Camel, of the end of time. Fear God in God's creation."

Professor Bouchaib Makhloufi's dazzling performance surprised everyone. The theater shook with applause and the sound of women trilling before Yazid poured more fuel on the fire by raising up a fiery slogan—inspired by the moment—that he and Rabih shouted out and began to repeat in a resounding voice: "No, no, and again, no! To the deadly camel, we say no!" A slogan that happened to resonate with many, for the people of the Octopus Party to repeat behind them with a hysterical enthusiasm that made the Camel partisans lose control. Thus, a violent fight broke out on the far right-hand side of the theater, resulting in casualties in the ranks of the Camel partisans, one of which was serious after one of the snail vendors bashed one of their heads with a metal rod he had hidden under his jellaba. Luckily, the paramedics came quickly. They promptly took the injured to the emergency room as the auxiliary forces intervened, decisively calming the situation.

As soon as Abu Ayoub took hold of the microphone, total silence came over the theater. After he praised God and asked that peace and blessings be bestowed on Muhammad, son of Abdallah, and his family, companions, and supporters, the sheikh cleared his throat and added in a strong, yet calm voice:

"Even though the noble Mr. Bachir Lamrabti has introduced me as one of the important men of this young party, I would like to address the sons of the virtuous Marrakech delegation as a man of knowledge rather than of party politics. I am a Malikite jurist first and foremost, and that is how I come to you this evening. My brothers, we in this country have chosen the 'Asharite creed, which does not deem even those who commit grave sins to be unbelievers. So what do we think of those who would like to provoke civil strife among us by issuing fatwas, may God provide protection, about killing people who eat snails? Is there a sedition greater than that? By God, this sedition is worse than murder!

"Then, by God," added Abu Ayoub in a voice that, while louder, had not lost its calm, "Aren't we Moroccans who live according to the legal school of Imam Malik? Is this not the legal school that those of us in authority have been satisfied with, and that has united us, thank God, for centuries? What goes through the minds of those trying to outdo us today with what the Shafi'ite and others say about this or that topic? We are Malikites, brothers, and our authority is Imam Malik and what this author of *The Muwatta'* said. Our imam's view is clear on this issue.

"Ibn Qasim, may God have mercy on his soul, said, 'Malik was asked about something in Morocco, something called *a snail* that lives in the desert, clinging to trees. Can they be eaten?' To which the imam, may God have mercy on him, responded, 'I consider them to be like locusts; they should be taken alive, then boiled or roasted. I don't see anything wrong with eating them.'

"That is all there is to say, and there is nothing to add to what the imam said."

The sound of trilling, applause, shouting, and chanting rose up. Sure, a political party could control its activists when things got out of control, but who could control the snail vendors and their comrades, the itinerant vendors, in a place like this? Their joy was rapturous. Some of them rushed the podium, threw themselves at Sheikh Abu Ayoub, and kissed his head and hands. One of them threw himself at his legs, kissing them, and knocking the sheikh down. If not for God's kindness and the intervention of the auxiliary forces, who beat the snail vendors off with their batons, the sheikh would have suffocated to death under them. For exactly this reason, the second half of the event was canceled and Bachir Lamrabti and Bouchaib Makhloufi snuck Sheikh Abu Ayoub out the back door. Meanwhile, the excited crowds left the Royal Theater and took the tumult out onto Mohammed VI Boulevard. They were hysterically repeating their new slogan: "No, no, and again, no! To the deadly camel, we say no!"

Saleh Regoug, who was in the party headquarters following the live broadcast on Daba Marrakech with his friends in the regional office, was dumbfounded, signs of distress showing on his face. He guessed that starting now, the Camel Party's fall in Marrakech would be a resounding one, and its echoes would resonate across the country.

84

AS SOON AS THE MOURNERS LEFT, Abdeslam's soul regained its tranquility. The grave was roomy enough despite how confined it was. Lying at rest under the moist earth was a thousand times more comfortable than living there in Ayad's hovel in Moukef.

Oh, Abdeslam, let God pour His mercy over you. How you suffered, and how much you withstood.

> My beloved son,
>
> I am writing this letter out of fear that I will depart without a chance to say goodbye to you.
>
> They will tell you, Rahhal, that Abdeslam died suddenly, but the grief goes way back, my son. Death is a grace from the Lord of the earth and the hereafter. I didn't die suddenly at all. My death was deserved and premeditated. I lived my final years wanting nothing but for this hour to come. Say, "If the Last Abode with God is yours exclusively, and not for other people, then long for death—if you speak truly." Trust Almighty God. I hoped for death, Rahhal. I hoped that it would be true, my son, and the All-merciful answered my prayers.

Ayad's eyes filled with tears as he read the letter he found by accident that night. He had decided to sleep in his brother's bed. In his little room where he had secluded himself during the last years of his life, and where his body was washed and shrouded. He wanted to confide in him. To at least smell him. He was rolling around in the bed when he heard a crinkling sound. He felt around with his fingers in search of the source of the noise and found the letter tucked underneath the pillow. He opened the yellow envelope. He removed the paper and began to make out the letters, he who had stopped reading in his Sidi Zouine school days. He had always concealed his jealousy for his brother, whose heart God had opened up and on it had imprinted the Qur'an in the *zaouiya* mosque. Abdeslam's handwriting wasn't completely legible, but Ayad managed to make it out. He read and reread it. And in the end, he decided that this piece of paper, scribbled on with a shaky hand, had to be buried with the one who wrote it. But because going back to the cemetery on that jet-black night wouldn't be easy, he headed for the toilet. He took out his lighter and lit the letter on fire. He poured water on the ashes and went back to bed. But Abdeslam's words never left him. It seemed that they had dug themselves deep into his memory, burrowed into his heart, and shaken his very being.

My beloved son,

When I married Halima that summer long ago, I was obeying the wishes of your Grandma Yamna. She's the one who chose Zanboub's daughter for me and asked for her hand herself. But they continued to condemn that marriage in the village. It was said that Ayad used to meet Halima often in the deep valley behind Zanboub's vineyards, and that he had her before leaving town and disappearing. They claimed that I married her just to cover up the scandal. But Halima became my wife. I protected her and provided for her in a way that satisfied God and I didn't care about people winking behind my back. Even when we took a long time to conceive and it was clear to everyone that there was no scandal there, they continued to fabricate lies. And when Ayad came home one Eid al-Adha, and Halima was pregnant a few months later, they said that he was the one who untied the knot that Abdeslam was unable to, and that he was the one who loaded the rifle with gunpowder, unbeknownst to its owner. I would secretly ask God for forgiveness for what I was hearing and I avoided them. For I am a bearer of God's book, my son, and I have no time for people's talk. While you grew up in front of them, they would deliberately hurt me with stinging insinuations: "It's just his uncle Ayad, praise Almighty God. He didn't take anything from you, Abdeslam. The eyes are just like Ayad's. Same face. Even the walk is the same. It's just his uncle Ayad, praise Almighty God." They would say this over and over in front of me with fake astonishment as they hid their wicked smiles. It tore me up inside and I begged God's forgiveness for myself and for them. You were blooming as an energetic child in front of me, always with a smile. All children are beautiful, my son. Children are always alive, cheerful. The world just needs to leave them be. As soon as I noticed that you were starting to close in on yourself and withdraw from people and avoid your peers, I decided to leave town. I understood that they were starting to do you harm, so I took you away from them and their unbelief, my son. I knew that if I let you grow up among them they wouldn't fear God's wrath, and that they would poison your life even more. That's why I brought you to Marrakech to seek refuge. It wasn't drought that hastened my departure; rather, it was a desire to protect you. I left my land and came to exchange God's word for a meager sum in the cemetery so I could raise you, so I could see you grow strong in front of me, far from those villagers and their wickedness.

When Ayad invited us to live with him, I praised his generosity. But as soon as you left, son, and moved to Oum Eid's house, then to Massira after that, my life turned into a living hell. I found myself living as a stranger with Ayad and Halima. They acted like husband and wife inside the house. They weren't happy just chitchatting morning and evening. They would talk. Confide in one another. Joke with one another. Laugh about something, or about nothing at all. I told myself that maybe I was the one who had encouraged them to act this way with my introverted nature and perpetual silence. I started to come out of my cocoon and tried to join them in conversation, but they would completely ignore me. Sometimes Halima would intervene just to snap at me and belittle what I had to say before going back to laughing with Ayad. It was like I was lost with them, not knowing how to escape, or to where. They slaughtered me more than once every day. My throat would rattle in silence with them and I was bleeding invisible blood that I hoped would clot inside me to hasten my appointed time to go.

That's why I cut myself off from you and the world, son, why I locked myself in your room, only coming out to go to the mosque or to eat. I would take just enough from their vile plate to keep me alive and go back to my terrarium before they finished eating. I couldn't stand sitting and talking with them anymore, and I implored the One Almighty to have mercy on me and take my soul to Him so I could find some respite from this injustice. And when I felt my time approaching, I came to see you in Massira. Your shop was crowded, so I didn't dare go in, not wanting to bother you. I stood at the door for a bit, and as a blessing for you I recited the Fatiha of the Qur'an, along with some verses from the Set Table, the Heights, and Repentance. I prayed to God to preserve you with what is preserved in the Qur'an, then I went to the village. I spent Eid al-Adha with the people there, taking advantage of the fact that the family was all present. Even the ones who lived far away came for the holidays. I made the rounds of my relatives, one by one, even those who had spoken badly of me in those days. I was sure I wouldn't see them again. That's why I hugged everyone and begged for God's mercy for me and for them. Then I came back and waited for my appointed time. *God's promise in truth.*

85

LIFE IS ELSEWHERE.

Rahhal knows that well and he accepts it. From the beginning, he chose to keep life at a distance. In fact, he preferred to leave it there. Elsewhere. Far from him and his daily routine. He didn't do that out of a dissatisfaction for life, or an aversion to it. Rather, he did so in order to cling to it, out of a desire for it. Specifically to preserve his life. His small, narrow, soft life. Scrunching up inside the Squirrel's hole was enough for him, and sleeping next to the Hedgehog at night did him no harm. That was his life and he was satisfied with it. Used to it. Clinging to it. Scared, in fact, of suddenly losing it.

Every day, Rahhal felt that his life was threatened. He was afraid of dying. That's why he always avoided travel. For example, flying on a plane was never something he dreamed of. He once tried the train, traveling round-trip between Marrakech and Rabat to take the entrance exam for the Teachers' College. He rode buses with Abdeslam and Halima when they used to take trips to Abda. Those falling apart buses used to terrify him. When he got older he stopped traveling to Abda or anywhere else. That's how he avoided the threat of dying in an awful traffic accident like the ones they report on the news. The ocean was also an untamed entity that scared Rahhal. Luckily, there's no ocean in Marrakech. The closest ocean to the Red City is over a hundred miles away, off the coast of Essaouira. And Rahhal had never visited Essaouira before. He had never seen the ocean with his own eyes. That's for the best. It would be terrifying to take one's last breaths while blindly battling the waves. He even refused to go to the Ourika mountain spring adjacent to Marrakech after the disastrous floods that killed dozens of vacationers and visitors in the summer of 1995, when the rushing water swept people, rocks, and cars away and destroyed the houses, shops, and cafés spread out along the banks of the river. Ever since the summer of '95, even though Rahhal had never visited Ourika before that year, he became even more reluctant to venture up there. Once, Hassaniya asked him to take a rare vacation day from the cybercafe so they could spend a Sunday in Ourika. It was a beautiful spring day, and she was in a good mood at that time. This was the first and last time she suggested doing something relaxing. On Sunday morning, Rahhal let her down. He said that he couldn't go with her. He couldn't go up the mountain. He would suffer from dizziness. He didn't admit to her that he didn't want to die. That he was scared of the mountain. Scared that their car would fall from way up high, or that the river would swell again and they'd be covered up by the flooding water. Rahhal even forbade himself from riding in elevators, even though it was rare that he found himself in a building with an elevator. He always took the stairs. Going up the stairs was safer than finding oneself suspended in the air, or dying of suffocation inside a hanging metal coffin.

Rahhal treasured his small life, clung to it. That's why he took every precaution. "Better safe than sorry," he would repeat to himself. He even stopped going to the hammam. He added it to his list of forbidden places and was satisfied with the shower after having heard some Massira High School teachers talking in the cybercafe about a colleague of theirs who went to the hammam next to Nour Mosque and fell asleep next to the water basin in the hot, interior room, and it was his last sleep. And after Daba Marrakech started to report on the asphyxiation of some building residents in Massira as a result of some Chinese gas heaters, Rahhal even did without hot water heaters. He started to take cold showers at home. And when it got really cold in December, he would heat up a bit of water on the stove. He would fill a pail with warm water and crouch down next to it to take a shower, quick as a cat.

But Abdeslam's death shuffled the cards. It terrified Rahhal and gave him a dreadful sense of insecurity. It's true that Oum Eid had also died unexpectedly. She hadn't been suffering from any illness. She had been fixed in front of the TV screen following her dubbed Mexican soap operas when her soul suddenly left her body. But Abdeslam's death shook Rahhal to his core. For months now, he had been living with a painful emptiness in his chest. Your heart has been emptied, Squirrel. The only person who you loved in the world has suddenly departed. Maybe you'll depart in the same, stupid way while you're at the cybercafe commenting on Hot Maroc articles, or in the kitchen preparing tomorrow's tajine for the Hedgehog, or while you're on top of her in bed on Saturday evening. Whenever Rahhal thought about these scenarios, his heart ached and tears filled his eyes. And when Qamar Eddine once noticed the falling tears, he made sure to console him. He embraced him warmly and prayed for mercy and forgiveness for his father. But Rahhal was crying for himself. He was crying for his life, which was threatened by a silly, expected death. An unfair, sudden death will snatch you from the cybercafe, Rahhal. You who stayed away from the ocean and travel and hot water just to remain alive.

But what sort of life is that?

Life is somewhere else, Rahhal. No, rather, it is everywhere. Everywhere else. It might be defective, but it is here. Life is walking close to you like a fat, lazy cat, here in this damn cybercafe, if you only knew. Look up from the computer for a bit. Lift your head. Try to look, for example, at the upper floor, where Fadoua and Samira crawl into the corner before they cut themselves off from the world below for hours. And as soon as Yazid goes up, they come down. Yazid had started to become interested in Marrakech Star. He swears to the seven holy saints of Marrakech that the two girls have gotten involved in stripping, displaying their charms, and even exchanging passionate kisses live on Skype in performances attended by special customers from the East, especially the Gulf. Silent performances they carry out without sound, or accompanied by whispered, intimate conversations. Payment was made through Western Union. A friend of Yazid's who works at the Western Union office on Dakhla Avenue confirmed that they had been coming in with suspicious regularity to the office over the past months to cash in the transfers that had arrived from here and there. And don't say you didn't notice, Rahhal. No one would believe you.

Qamar Eddine notified Rahhal right away that some cybercafes had started to set special prices for the upper floor. Just like the balcony at the movie theater. A ticket there costs more than on the main floor. Also, a customer couldn't go up without paying for a full hour in advance. At least an hour. That's how you block voyeurs. But he didn't do what Qamar Eddine suggested. Rahhal generally preferred not to get involved with anything that distracted him from his work at Hot Maroc. Even when Moroccans discovered Skype for the first time. Mothers lined up in front of the cybercafes on special occasions, holidays, and weekends to talk with their dear children who were scattered all around the world. The workers in these cafés considered this a chance to increase their income with the tips the illiterate women would leave in exchange for helping them connect and call back every time they were cut off. Rahhal remained uninterested. And today Yazid wanted to focus on Marrakech Star, even though it had absolutely nothing to do with him. Luckily, politics kept Yazid too busy to go upstairs to steal glances of those secret pleasures behind the lustful screen, as well as too busy to monitor Fadoua and Samira and sniff out what they were doing. Just as their quick responsiveness to his electoral performance and their sudden joining of the Octopus Party's ranks made him delay pursuing their case for the time being.

Qamar Eddine was enmeshed in an electronic love story of his own with a Danish woman who was about twenty years older than him. A divorcée with two children. But she had a beautiful athletic body and her face was attractive according to the consensus of the cybercafe's clientele who circulated pictures of her—especially those in which she appeared half-naked—and everyone blessed this relationship that had started to move toward marriage. Qamar Eddine surprised his friends at the Atlas Cubs with an exceptional act of noblesse after suggesting organizing regular visits to Mahjoub Didi, who had been committed to Amerchich Mental Hospital. Rahhal didn't even go once with him. Not only because it was impossible for the two of them to be away from the cybercafe at the same time but also because he was the only one who knew the secret of the devilish emails that had driven Mahjoub to madness.

Perhaps Mahjoub would have preferred death over a life without taste or color or smell there in Amerchich Hospital. Perhaps Abdeslam would have been happier had he known when his death would come. Abdeslam whose death was well-deserved. He died because he had to die. Sometimes death is more generous than a life with no meaning. Death might be more generous for you and for others, Rahhal. More generous than a stupid life on the margins, than the life of a miserable little tick, whose main purpose is to egregiously stick to a cow's tail.

. . .

Yazid might have been the only person who didn't offer his condolences to Rahhal for his father. The members of the Atlas Cubs family held a vigil for him in the cybercafe that everyone, including the three Africanos, attended. They recited the Fatiha prayer and honored the deceased before embracing the Squirrel one after the other. Qamar Eddine handed him an envelope in their name that contained five hundred dirhams. Even Salim, even though he was still a student, gave fifty dirhams, the suggested amount for each mourner. Rabih came by himself and paid his respects, without reaching into his pocket. The only one who neglected to even say anything was Yazid. As for Emad Qatifa, he completely surprised Rahhal. In the heat of the electoral campaign, despite his problems with Hiyam, who had left the marital home, and his preoccupations, which had increased now that he had to go to the school to take his wife's place, he insisted on duly paying his respects to Rahhal. Just two days after the death, Hassaniya came to the cybercafe and asked Rahhal to go home with her. They hurriedly arranged the guest room, quickly prepared a tray of tea, and just a few minutes later, the doorbell rang. Emad Qatifa was at the door with his parents, the Hajj and Hajja, and his sister Kenza, accompanied by the guard from the Atlas Cubs School. He was carrying a dozen cones of sugar in a canvas sack. Leopard-brand sugar to be specific.

This was the appropriate way of paying one's respects. Hajj Qatifa reprimanded Rahhal because the news didn't reach them in time for them to do what was necessary on the day of the burial and dinner afterward. The Qatifa family's visit was pleasant enough. After the tea, as they were standing in the foyer in front of the apartment's door, the Hajj placed some money into Rahhal's hand. Three thousand whole dirhams, which Hassaniya took as soon as the door was closed. She kept two thousand for herself and threw the rest onto the tea tray for Rahhal. But Rahhal asked her to hold onto the entire amount. She gave him an apprehensive look to make sure that he meant it and that he wasn't doing it out of malice, then she took the remaining thousand dirhams and buried them next to her breasts, which had suddenly become more noticeable (Rahhal wasn't sure why he was finding the Hedgehog more feminine and attractive these days). Anyway, he didn't tell her that Ayadi had called him personally to express how sorry he was—for she didn't know him either as a rat or as a commissioner—and that he had sent him twenty thousand dirhams to pay his condolences. Rahhal took half of that amount to Moukef and gave it to his mother in the presence of his uncle Ayad, while putting the rest in his secret national savings account at the post office in Massira, where he kept his small fortune that was growing month by month, without him being able to spend it.

Commissioner Ayadi's call wasn't just to express his condolences and to be nice; he also asked Rahhal to take a few weeks off. They would need him for some serious work, but after the elections. He should consider it an open-ended, paid vacation. After that, he would need to invent two, new characters like Son of the People and Abu Qatada for a new media platform.

"Officer Hakim will send you more details when the time comes. The important thing is for you to relax now. And again, may God provide recompense for the deceased. May God have mercy on him and be generous toward him, and may God grant you patience, Rahhal, my friend. And please give my condolences to your mother."

It was Moukhtar on the line. As if his former comrade was the one to end the call with him, and not Commissioner Ayadi. A familiar, sympathetic voice. A friendly, compassionate tone. Rahhal's eyes teared up out of emotion. Rahhal remembered Abdeslam's stories about Abda's caids a long time ago. If a person from Abda lost a relative, he'd leave the mourners in his house and go to present his condolences to the caid, because the caid was everyone's father, and he had the most right to receive condolences. Generally speaking, Moroccans don't go to offer condolences empty-handed. Perhaps it was a polite way for the caid to receive his share of the cones of sugar that came into the mourning household. May God have mercy on you, Abdeslam. Did you ever think that one day a high-ranking commissioner would pay his respects to you? Did you ever think you'd be so lucky, Mantis?

Although Asmae, the waitress at Café Milano, didn't offer her condolences to Rahhal—perhaps because she was not yet aware of the death—the Lioness took it upon herself to do so, and then some. On her wall, the deceased Abdeslam received an unimaginable number of compassionate notes for his pure soul. The Lioness received more than two thousand expressions of condolence in response to a message she had posted mourning the loss of her relative, the faqih acquainted with God, Abdeslam Laâouina from Abda. Rahhal's happiness with this number of people sending their condolences was equal only to the peace of mind he felt that he wouldn't have to feed them. Rahhal burst out crying when he saw the number of writers, journalists, celebrity artists, and politicians all sending their condolences to the Mantis and asking God to cover him with His abounding forgiveness and to give forbearance and consolation to his family. Among those were people who claimed— exaggerating flattery—that they had known the deceased, and they set out to enumerate his virtues. Who would have believed that such a grand pavilion of condolences on Facebook would have been opened for the unmemorable Abdeslam, in whose funeral just a few people walked? The Squirrel was greatly moved by the condolences posted on the Lioness' wall and he was filled with pride. He seemed comforted to the point where no one could ruin it, especially since his rival, Emad Qatifa, was far from this group of well-wishers after Hiyam had blocked him right after the Renaissance Café incident.

86

IN HIS CLEAN, white lab coat, Rabih looked like a doctor in a hospital. All he was missing was a stethoscope. Other than that, the handsomeness and cleanliness of this young, Amazighi man made him look like a medical specialist rather than a lowly snail seller. True, the cart was right up against the cybercafe door and blocked the customers' movement, but who would dare protest, knowing that it was Yazid's cart? The problem was that a young woman, about twenty-six years old and wearing white mourning clothes, had slipped onto the scene a few months prior during the electoral campaign unbeknownst to anyone. She was kneeling on the other side of the cybercafe's door with her hand out. A young woman with a pleasant face, beautiful eyes, full lips, and clear skin. Beautiful despite her hardened features. At first, she sat by herself at the cybercafe door. After that, she was accompanied by a child who looked to be about four years old. And in the past few days, her team was strengthened by a nursing child no older than two years old. Her good looks attracted the men who would hand her money. There were those who really felt sorry for her—a beauty in the bloom of her youth, widowed with two children. And then there were those who acted like benefactors while deep down inside, they were just attracted to her. The vitality of the cybercafe during the campaign had attracted the widow. Emad Qatifa, for example, rather than protest the fact that she had occupied the entrance to his shop, played with her two children before giving her some money. The young woman surmised that Emad was everything here, so she was reassured of this location and no longer imagined that someone would make her leave, especially since the man in charge of the place had shown such compassion and kindness to her two children. So, she didn't understand why this asshole who swaggered around with an inflated sense of self that didn't jibe with how short he was began to harass her. She guessed that the snail cart was his and that the young Amazighi man, whom she liked, worked for him. She felt sorry for Rabih, and her hatred for Yazid grew. Yazid was intoxicated with his party's victory in Marrakech, and with Emad Qatifa's election to Parliament. He continued to receive congratulations all along Dakhla Avenue for months after the elections. He considered all of it to be a personal victory. The only thing that bothered him was this beggar; he didn't know where she had come from and how she held such sway over him. The widow continued to avoid all contact with him. All of his innuendos and insults would come, but she would completely ignore them. As if she hadn't heard. They would fall on deaf ears. But this morning, it seemed clear that Yazid wanted to force her to react. He stood in front of her with fire in his eyes:

"Eh . . . eh . . . missy. Look at me. I'm talking to you."

She turned her body toward her two children and embraced them silently as she lowered her eyes to the ground.

"Poor you. As if you're really ashamed. But tell me, how much did you rent those kids for? I heard that you people rent kids for a hundred dirhams a head per day."

The pretty widow started to nod her head nervously, still looking down, and Yazid continued his vicious, performative barking at her, especially when people walking by started to form a circle around them and the cybercafe customers left their electronic safe harbors to crowd in front of the door to see what was going on.

"I didn't ask you about these white rags you're wearing. Clearly, they're a work uniform. You've been here five months now. If you were truly a widow and God had really taken your husband, then for sure the mourning period has ended." Then he began to look at the people around him, yelling: "Right? The mourning period is four months and ten days, right, Muslims? Am I lying? Five months have passed and she still doesn't want to change out of these white clothes."

Some of the people there nodded their heads in agreement with what Yazid was saying, while the widow's head continued to move nervously like an out-of-control clock pendulum that started to swing breathlessly back and forth. All of a sudden, Yazid kicked her and yelled frantically:

"Hey lady? I'm talking to you. Look at me, and cut the shit!"

No one could believe their eyes because what happened next left everyone speechless. That is, the pretty widow didn't just look him in the eyes. Rather, she erupted like a volcano and threw her strong body full force at Yazid. She shook him hard then threw him to the ground while twisting his neck. Yazid found himself at her mercy. She grabbed his throat then pressed down until his eyes bulged out. She said:

"Eh, I'm not taking off these white clothes. They're clothes for work. Like your friend, Rabih's white coat. And if you don't leave me alone, I'll dye these whites that you hate so much with your blood, you son of a bitch. D'ya hear me?"

He didn't hear a thing. His head and ears were ringing. Sitting there motionless with her knees on his chest, the widow looked like a mighty camel kneeling on top of an emaciated puppy. Yazid was underneath her, out of breath, helpless. He moved his lost, bulging eyes around the crowd that had gathered around him looking for someone to help . . . but, no, the audience was watching with bated breath. No one was coming to his defense. Even Rabih stood there dumbfounded like the rest of them, his mouth hanging wide open in astonishment. He wanted to do something for him but he couldn't. True, he owed Yazid a lot, but it would have been hard for him to intervene. It couldn't get out that he had assaulted a woman. If the beggar had been a man, the snail-soup vendor would have brought him to the ground with one kick. But, unfortunately, Yazid's assailant was a woman. Suddenly, the pretty widow got up off of Yazid. She kicked him and said:

"You can go this time. A temporary reprieve. But if you harass me again I'll shit on your mother's ass in front of all these men."

Then she kicked him again and spit on him as she snarled:

"Run along, you mutt."

Rahhal followed the scene, his eyes filled with tears of excessive joy. For some reason he thought of Nesrine, the Amazighi medical student. If only she were here today. He felt a compassionate hand on his shoulder. It felt delicate and warmly feminine. Was it Nesrine's hand? He turned around and saw Yacabou leaning on him from behind. That's who had put the hand on his shoulder. The Nigerian was craning his long neck, taken by surprise as he followed Yazid's ignominious retreat. Yazid dragged his tail between his legs, far from the cybercafe. The widow went back to her spot to console her crying children. As for Yacabou's hand, it didn't leave Rahhal's shoulder until everyone had gone back to where they had been sitting in the cybercafe. Oh Squirrel, if only your Hedgehog's hand were as gentle as Yacabou's, your marital life would have a completely different flavor.

87

TO THE CREDIT of the new coalition government that the Camel and Octopus Parties formed, they wouldn't dive headlong into their work until their leaders had toured the most important centers in the kingdom to spread news of their reconciliation and firmly establish trust and encourage the bases of the two parties to move beyond the scars and wounds of the electoral campaign. The new prime minister, Mr. Moha Sinhaji, immediately confirmed that the battle that had raged between the two parties was history as far as he was concerned, a thing of the past, and that the ideological differences and insipid political calculations were of no concern to him anymore. What most concerned him was rebuilding through self-sacrifice in the service of the beloved nation, starting from the idea of Tamaghribit—Moroccanity—true zeal for the unity of the community.

Thus, Moha Sinhaji and his brother, Salem Raïss—the general secretary of the Camel Party and the new minister of Foreign Affairs—presided over the packed rally held in the Royal Theater of Marrakech under the banner "Camel and Octopus: Hands Together, for Morocco Forever." A huge political wedding distinguished by Yazid's return to the fore after what had happened with the pretty widow. This time, Yazid came back at the head of a popular Marrakechi *daqqa* and *tkitikate* singing and percussion group that carried out his orders. It burst into flames on his signal. And as soon as the fire died down, someone stepped up to the podium and asked to say a few words. It was strange that Rabih wasn't in the group. Perhaps he preferred to remain at his new location on Dakhla Avenue next to the cybercafe. Something was tying him there. It certainly wasn't the smell of the snail soup. Rather, it was the confusing, seductive looks the widow would steal of him from time to time, and her mysterious, secret smile, which had started to shake his very being and cause a small muscle in his chest, which might have been his heart, to pulse. Marrakech Star wasn't at the rally either. There was a video posted by Daba Marrakech of two girls exchanging passionate kisses and lewd, sexual caresses in front of the camera as they jabbered away in a broken Gulf dialect. The video wasn't totally clear, even though the cybercafe community agreed that it had something to do with Fadoua and Samira. Rahhal breathed a sigh of relief when he could confirm that the video had been filmed in an apartment and not on the upper floor of the cybercafe, where the two girls would hole away for hours on end. The film quality was not very good, in any case, and Rahhal couldn't be sure that it was Marrakech Star. Nevertheless, Marrakech Star had been completely absent from Dakhla Avenue for more than a week, and they didn't show up at the Royal Theater rally that evening. But Emad Qatifa was there, in the middle of the first row with his fellow parliamentarians from the two allied parties. Hiyam had his arm under hers and a wide smile across her face. She looked proud of her role as the wife of the honorable representative. The clouds that the Lioness had released in her skies had finally cleared following his victory, and things went back to normal between Emad and Hiyam.

Sinhaji explained to the huge audience in the theater that politics isn't math or engineering, and that their two parties weren't parallel lines that could never meet. "Rather, despite the schemes of the schemers, we will join hands for the Morocco of tomorrow. We will join hands, brothers and sisters, because it is in the country's best interests. As for the poisoned pens in the hateful newspapers and websites that talk about a suspicious deal struck between myself and my brother, Raïss, or about the interest-driven logic that governs our alliance, I have this to say to them: The only interest that concerns us is that of the nation. We join hands for the nation. This is Moroccan ingenuity. This is the Moroccan exception that baffles the greatest international political analysts. We are an ingenious people that knows how to build consensus, and I assure you that your political elite, brothers and sisters, is mature enough to avoid loathsome selfishness and narrow party accounts, and that they put the nation's interests above all else." Sinhaji finished and turned toward Saleh Regoug and Bachir Lamrabti. He asked them to turn toward the front of the stage, where they theatrically embraced and patted one another on the back under a flood of applause, trilling, drumbeats from the Marrakechi *daqqa* group, and thunderous chanting, all while Sinhaji raised up Raïss's hand and the two of them waved their joined hands in the air.

But the atmosphere of reconciliation was not complete as long as some activists of both parties whose enthusiasm had gone too far during the electoral campaign remained sitting in prison. So Sinhaji moved quickly to issue a full pardon to all of the activists from the different parties who had been arrested during the campaign, and these were pursued for cases ranging from assault and battery to possession of a deadly weapon to attempted murder. That's how dozens of prisoners were let go for the blessed Eid al-Fitr holiday, even though most of their cases hadn't been adjudicated yet. The pardon was retroactive, and the name Mehdi Aït Hajj mysteriously slipped onto the list of beneficiaries without raising an eyebrow in the press, but at least the man hadn't planned on murdering anyone.

Naim Marzouk remained the undisputed star of those who were let go. Because on the day of his release from the civil prison in Casablanca, standing in front of the fans waiting for him at the prison gate, the Chameleon found no less than Moha Sinhaji and Salem Raïss. Both parties had taken up his case, and each one had tried to exploit it during the campaign in its own way. And today here they were embracing him like a national hero in front of the cameras of the foreign channels and organizations for defending freedom of the press and human rights. They had all adopted Naim's case in international meetings, and they had come today not only to celebrate his release but also their victory against the enemies of freedom of expression in Morocco. As for the release gift, it was a fancy headquarters in a glass building in Casablanca for a new independent newspaper which Moha Sinhaji had named the *Banner*. He and his ally, Salem Raïss, wanted it to be a newspaper for all Moroccans. And they wouldn't find anyone better to run it than the talented journalist and thunderous voice of the people, Naim Marzouk.

The *Banner*.

That's the exact name Rahhal had gotten from Officer Hakim in a text message, along with a short message that included a happy face emoji: "Your comrade, Moukhtar, says that the vacation is over." Rahhal opened up Hot Maroc, then the *Future*, and was surprised that the two news sites were welcoming the new platform and wishing Naim Marzouk success in his coming media adventures.

Can a professional team—let's say a soccer team, for example—dive right into a new season without doing some preseason training? Impossible, of course. So, you need to get some training in while you wait for the first issue of the *Banner* to be published, Rahhal. You are a professional player, and if Commissioner Ayadi says that the vacation is over, the vacation is over, even if your new newspaper is still just a news item. Rahhal found it difficult to settle on a name other than Son of the People and Abu Qatada. At first, he thought of Grouchy Smurf. But the new era might be the era of support and loyalty. It might be prudent to pursue a more sober course, to don the robe of the wise, and leave anger and fury behind. He thought about the Cute Camel. That way he could appear cloaked in a feminine voice for his readers this time, and from the heart of the desert. It would have been fun, especially since his Facebook guardianship of Hiyam gained him an expertise in the way women flirt, dodge, and maneuver in arguing and winning people over. But what if his guise as a female camel startled the Octopus Party allies? You still have some time to figure out the issue of names. You need to focus on your training, Rahhal. To occupy yourself with what's most important. To construct your new arguments.

The Squirrel went back to the Hot Maroc and *Future* articles in order to absorb more of the era's logic. He understood that what was being asked of him was to defend the government alliance and give it legitimacy, especially since some of the haters in the traditional leftist parties whose time had passed, and some journalists suspected of being linked to elements hostile to the noble kingdom, viciously attacked the alliance and talked about a betrayal of trust and the belittling of politics, leveled accusations that the popular will was fake, and expressed a general insult toward the intelligence of the citizens. Some of them were baffled at how a party with Islamist roots that considered fighting corruption a justification for its very existence could ally itself with a party that was formed under mysterious circumstances by even more mysterious elements—a gang of retired leftists, immoral feminists, and corrupt businessmen, a few elites, and the most famous election brokers in the country, while they attracted opportunists of all types in their corner, all with the one goal of keeping the Camel Party from governing. Especially since opposing the Islamists was considered the political platform of the Octopus Party. It was an alliance that went against all logic, against the logic of politics. Strong, stinging language that Anouar Mimi would definitely not be able to oppose. Only the mighty Chameleon could oppose these awful haters. The Chameleon and his two comrades, the Squirrel and the Skunk. (After following Abu Sharr Guevari's comments on Hot Maroc so much, Rahhal concluded that his colleague was an authentic skunk. He possessed many of the traits of this vicious, sharp-tempered nocturnal animal that would not hesitate to attack larger animals such as sheep or donkeys. Rahhal came to Abu Sharr's skunkiness by way of his style, the mood of his writing, and his way of maneuvering, even though he had never met him before and didn't even know his real name.) As for Anouar Mimi, his whole kit bag of cheap insults, petty incitements, and fake slanders wasn't enough. Also, Mimi's reputation was torpedoed after Mourad Chahboun, a young businessman registered with the Broom Party, exploded a bomb in the national press by disclosing how Mimi had targeted him personally with rumors and publishing false news about his successful company. When he called to find out the reason for this unexplained hatred, Mimi was "mollified" and promised to turn the page in exchange for advertising buys in his newspaper.

Unfortunately, Mourad Chahboun didn't record the call because he hadn't expected the attempted fleecing to be so direct. But public opinion tilted in his favor, especially after the tourism transportation magnate Ridouane Aït Bihi emerged from his silence and said he had also faced the same scenario before joining the Octopus Party, and that Anouar Mimi had used the same vile stratagem of blackmail.

Anouar Mimi was done, and Tanoufi and his reporters were not up to it. You, Rahhal, are among the men of the times. The Chameleon, the Skunk, and you, Squirrel.

Oh, how Rahhal was dying for the paper to be published. He started by sharpening his pencils to crushingly respond to the end-of-times leftists who still longed for the bygone ideological days, and the Islamists who deemed members of the established order unbelievers and pined for the return of the caliphate. He will drip hot wax on the mercenary journalists who abuse the atmosphere of freedom of expression that the country has granted them to reflect their vaunted interests for a fistful of dollars that enemies of the nation will bribe them with.

But when will the *Banner* come out?

88

RAHHAL WAS IN THE MIDDLE OF RESPONDING to one of the leftists' articles, as a way to warm up and sharpen his knives, when Ayad knocked on the cybercafe door. Rahhal glanced at the silver quartz watch he had bought after his father's death in a shop in Kennaria. It was 10:45 in the morning. Lunchtime was still far off. Rahhal asked Qamar Eddine to take his place and invited his uncle for a glass of tea at Asmae's. There at Café Milano.

Ayad told Rahhal that he wanted to discuss something important with him. He looked unusually out of sorts.

"Is everything okay?" asked Rahhal.

"Fine, God willing, my boy. It's just that Halima has taken off the white mourning clothes."

Did this rat have Alzheimer's or what?! Rahhal thought to himself.

"I know, Uncle, and I think I was there. I came over with Hassaniya the day she took them off, and we ate dinner with you—a free-range chicken you slaughtered yourself."

"I remember that well, my boy. It's just that you should know . . ."

Then Ayad looked down. It was the first time Rahhal had seen him so anxious.

"That I should know what, Uncle?"

"Halima is a widow, and now that she has taken off the mourning clothes, I mean . . ."

"What?"

"I mean, her being with me in the house might prompt some . . ."

"Some what?" snapped Rahhal before realizing what he was getting at. "Ah, I get it. I get it, Uncle."

They remained silent for a moment, as if they had both been struck dumb, before Rahhal picked up again:

"Give me some time. I'll talk it over with Hassaniya and we'll see what we can do. Hassaniya's not an easy one, but I don't think she'll refuse to take my mother in to live with us in the apartment. Our apartment is roomy, thank God, and I lived with her mother before, in a tiny house under more difficult conditions, until God chose that she dwell next to Him. So, I don't think that Hassaniya will . . ."

"No Rahhal. Don't get me wrong, my boy."

"How so?" asked Rahhal.

"I mean . . . I mean that . . ."

Rahhal remained silent as he waited for Ayad to continue. Right then, Asmae came with a bottle of water, which she set down in front of them and winked playfully at Ayad, then wiggled away. Rahhal noticed that the Lioness' behind had filled out recently, and that the girl had started to get back some of her previous perkiness. He swore there was someone in her life. A person interested in her, fucking her well, and making her feel that life was possible here, too, not just in that other Milano. The Milano that Talios had talked about before settling in "Canada."

"Tell me what you mean, Uncle. You're worrying me."

"What I mean is that I've come to ask for your mother's hand, Halima, the daughter of Wafi, according to the customs of God and His prophet. So, what do you say?"

That is the last scenario you would have imagined, Rahhal. A shocking scenario. Difficult even for a genie to have predicted. *Are you serious, Rat? Are you seriously asking that?* Rahhal was asking these questions to himself. He was asking them silently since his voice failed him.

"I didn't want to shock you, my boy. But, think about it. Halima is alone now. And I'm alone too. We've lived under the same roof for almost twenty years. Almost an entire lifetime. Why wouldn't I take care of her? Otherwise, who would we leave her to after your father's death? Who would we leave her to?"

Rahhal mumbled something that wasn't a response. Muddled words that Ayad couldn't make out. As if Rahhal preferred to keep them to himself. Or maybe he had hoped that the words wouldn't come out at all. Or perhaps he mumbled them that way without realizing it.

"What, Rahhal? What, nephew? What did you say?"

It appeared that Rahhal had snapped out of it. He had come back from somewhere far off.

"I said . . . I said . . ."

"What? What did you say?"

"I said I'll let you know later. I have to see what Hassaniya thinks."

"What?! Hassaniya?!"

"Of course, Uncle. I have to see what Hassaniya thinks."

"But what does Hassaniya have to do with it?" Ayad asked, baffled.

"Hassaniya is my wife. I have to see what she thinks," Rahhal answered him angrily.

At that moment, Ayad thought about punching this idiot in the face. But he got ahold of himself. He got up from where he was sitting, practically bursting with anger.

"Okay, Rahhal. Okay. God keep you, my boy. If your virtuous wife honors us with her assent, you know where I live."

. . .

That night, Hassaniya ate dinner quickly, then rushed to the bathroom. She came out red-eyed, wiping her mouth with her fingers and headed straight to bed. She had been in a bad mood lately. Nonetheless, you have no choice, Squirrel. You need to broach the topic with her. To do so, he scampered behind her. Her face looked worried and gloomy as she nervously changed her clothes. She gave Rahhal a dry look. The Squirrel was a bit troubled. He hesitated for a few moments before stammering:

"Hassaniya, please, I need to talk with you about something important."

"If you have something on your mind, it'll have to wait. I have something more important."

Without any introduction, she threw it in his face like a grenade, then turned out the light.

Rahhal felt his knees knocking from the frightful shock. All sorts of feelings swirled around inside his chest. He thought about changing his clothes, but he didn't have the energy. He laid out on the edge of the bed drained of strength. His heart was tight. He was filled with darkness.

In the dream, he saw a squirrel playing in an enormous field. A field with black trees, leaves rustling. A wide field, yellow as if it were sand. A desert field. All of a sudden, he was surrounded by rats. One was an old, skinny rat. The other one looked as if it had just come out of its mother; but rather than crawl along the ground and attach its mouth to its mother's teat to nurse, it lined up next to the old rat and they both bared their teeth at him. The eyes of the two rats were dark black. Their tails were long and they swung them around in the air like whips, then they started to whip the Squirrel. The rats' squeaking was loud and jarring. He tried to run away from them, but they surrounded him and continued to whip him with their burning tails, and their squeaking got louder and louder as he doubled over in pain.

The Squirrel let out a scream that tore at the room's silence. The Hedgehog turned on the light and found that he had fallen out of bed. He was balled up like a mouse. Like a true rat. He was panting and his forehead was drenched with sweat. He stole a glance at the Hedgehog's face, pleadingly, but she faced him with a neutral stare. He took a quick look at her belly and remembered the bomb she had exploded in his face before she had turned out the light, and he withdrew once again.

Yassin Adnan is a Moroccan writer, born in Safi in 1970, but has lived in Marrakech since he was a young child. He holds a BA in English literature from Cadi Ayyad University and earned a graduate degree in teaching English as a foreign language from the College of Education at Mohammed V University in Rabat. He published *Contemporary Voices* and *Poetry Raid*, two poetry journals that embodied the new poetic sensibility prevalent in Morocco in the early 1990s. Since 2006, he has researched and presented his weekly cultural television program *Masharef* (Thresholds) on Morocco's Channel One, and he currently hosts *Bayt Yassin* (Yassin's House) on Egypt's Al-Ghad TV. He is the author of five collections of poetry: *Mannequins* (2000), *Resurrection Pavement* (2003), *I Can Hardly See* (2007), *Rambler's Notebook* (2012), and *The Road to the Garden of Fire* (2017). He also has three short-story collections: *The Shadow's Apples* (2006), *Who Believes in Letters?* (2011), and *Girls' Joy with Light Rain* (2013). He cowrote *Marrakech: Open Secrets* (2008) with Saad Sarhane. He is the editor of *The Moroccan Scheherazade: Testimonies and Studies of Fatima Mernissi* (2016) and an anthology of short stories published by Akashic Books, *Marrakech Noir*. In 2017 *Hot Maroc* (2016) was longlisted for the International Prize for Arabic Fiction.

Alexander E. Elinson is head of the Arabic program at Hunter College of the City University of New York. He is the author of *Looking Back at al-Andalus: The Poetics of Loss and Nostalgia in Medieval Arabic and Hebrew Literature* (2009) as well as articles, reviews, and translations on the Arabic and Hebrew strophic poem (*zajal* and *muwashshah*), rhymed prose *maqama*, and modern Arabic poetry and narrative in peer-reviewed journals. He has also published numerous translations of Moroccan poetry and fiction into English that include works by Allal Bourqia, Adil Latefi, Ahmed Lemsyeh, Khadija Marouazi, Driss Mesnaoui, and two novels by Youssef Fadel: *A Beautiful White Cat Walks with Me* (2016) and *A Shimmering Red Fish Swims with Me* (2019), which was shortlisted for the 2020 Saif Banipal Translation Prize for Arabic literary translation.